THE TENTATIVE KNOCK

THE TENTATIVE KNOCK

KELLY CAPRIOTTI BURTON

Kell of a Story

Contents

First Printing, 2021

This is a work of fiction. Names, characters, organizations, places,
events, and incidents are either products of the author's imagination
or are used fictitiously.

Published by Kelly Capriotti Burton
Cover design by Kelly Capriotti Burton
Author photo by Rod Burton
ISBN: 978-1-7361174-0-8
ISBN EBook: 978-1-7361174-1-5
Kellofastory.com
Surfside Beach, South Carolina

For our David and Jesse,
who surprised us entirely,
changed the core of who I am,
and ended my 30s by making me brave.

And for Rod, my Holy Exhale.

Chapter One

I married an older man. He wasn't *so* much older, not scandalously so, and not even the oldest guy I'd ever dated, but eleven years older. And so, it was always a periodic topic of conversation... that he would probably die first, that I might be a relatively young widow, and whether (depended on the day) and how (with a gay bestie, my own Blanche and Rose, or any of several of the cast of *Lord of the Rings*) I would move on.

We met at a truck stop, Johnson City, Tennessee. Just kidding. Since we lived in the south suburbs of Chicago, and not inside a Travis Tritt song, we met at a pizza joint. I was there with my new sister-in-law Maggie, pretty much the only one of my friends from *before*—that is, before I got pregnant by a customer at the for-real truck stop diner where I'd been working, before I disappointed the "give-*it*-up-for-adoption" hopes of my parents and my older brother by deciding to keep my baby (Madonna song), and about 10 minutes before I decided that dating was never going to work out for me, as my boobs were about to leak and I was a little afraid my mom was at home trying to feed my baby boy marinara sauce on his pacifier (I think that's a Vic Damone song).

Maggie and I were in a booth, sharing a taco pizza and a renegade pitcher of Old Style Light that I was assured would not intoxicate my little Sam during his 2am feeding. Maggie had been married to my brother Tony for about six months at that point. She was currently on rant number three of the evening and clearly no longer on her honeymoon.

I listened to her talk about Tony's lack of communication on his shift days (he was a firefighter), his comments about her co-conut-oil-laden bathroom routine, and his insistence that their future baby would *not* be named after her dad, Leroy, who had passed away two weeks before their wedding. I remained mostly silent, because as much as I adored my friend from Literature of the Nations at Prairie State College, I never understood her and my brother as a couple. She was a sassy, independent black woman, and he was a very conventional, cut-and-dry white dude. Even in my inexperience, they seemed destined to have really pretty children and a lot of intense misunderstanding.

When Maggie stood to walk to the bathroom, a tall, barrel-chested man with dark hair, dark eyes, and a dark goatee walked directly to our table and stopped there. His smile was as broad as his chest and shoulders. I sat up straighter and instinctively looked down to make sure there were no telltale circular stains on my Nirvana t-shirt (God rest Kurt's soul).

"Can I help you?" I asked, eyebrows raised in hopes to convey disinterest. Because... he was interesting, in a Tom-Selleck-as-Magnum kind of way.

He responded by raising one eyebrow back at me, the smile

still in place. "I'm not sure. I was just over there admiring the way you eat your pizza, and I was curious what kind it is. Is that lettuce?"

I wasn't sure whether to feel offended or kindred. Taco pizza was a controversial choice just outside of Chi-town. It was not my go-to or my favorite, but when the mood struck, which it did for Maggie about every 28 days, it served its purpose very tastily.

Once I started talking to Magnum about the lettuce needing to be finely shredded, the appropriate amount of black olives, and the perfect spicy tang of the sauce, I got on a roll. The conversation turned to a few other specialty pizzas, the polenta fritti, and tentatively, the dirty martinis. I was barely 19 and my taste in liquor was about as sophisticated as spearmint Schnapp's in a plastic cup. Magnum was clearly a little bit older. Maggie raised her eyebrows and nodded toward his backside before scooting around him and back into her seat.

"Oh... this, this is my sister-in-law, Maggie," I said, fully cognizant that he didn't even know my name.

"Sister-in-law? Oh, my. Hi Maggie. I'm Randall Oakley. And you're, Mrs....?"

It took me a beat. "Mrs.?" I grimaced. "No, no. She's married to my brother. I am not a Mrs. I am a mom, though."

Maggie shook her head. Sam was 11 months old at that point, and I wore his existence like a badge. But really, what was the point talking anything other than menu items with the handsome stranger when he was just going to run away?

Except he didn't. He asked for my number. He came to my parents' house for our first date, armed with a taco pizza *and* one with sausage and peppers. He brought a stuffed Snoopy for Sam, and he fed him from a jar of Gerber chicken and rice while I ate heartily with two hands. He charmed my mom by clearing the table, impressed my dad with talk of his accounting job, and he stayed with me, with us, with the family we made, for the next 36 years.

So even if I should have been, I was not expecting *that* call.... the call wives get on my Generation-X version of soap operas, the hour-long dramas that skirt round the edge of smutty just enough to keep me somewhere between hooked on the story and sort of ashamed I am. It was a call from the hospital. It was a next of kin call.

It was a Monday in mid-March. It had been a normal day. Randall was "semi-retired," and to me all that meant was that he got paid two-thirds as much, worked almost as many hours (though he didn't go in on Fridays, which was nice), and didn't have to travel any more (amazing). He'd been auditing for a huge firm since his late 30s. Now he was consulting for the same company, talking to most of his clients or protégées or whatever over phone or video. He'd grown his hair a little longer and wore golf shirts instead of dress shirts and ties. But he still left the house at 8:45 most weekday mornings, after walking our Labrador, Cash, eating two eggs and two sausages, and kissing me goodbye.

I was running late and *gathering my affects*, as we always liked to say.... making sure Cash went outside, putting on some lip gloss and spraying on some "smell-good," deciding *not* to comment to the Facebook acquaintance who had, in the space of an hour, complained that women in bikinis who were over size 10 were too big *and* Starbucks drive-thru lanes were too small, and trying to decide whether I needed to bring my sizable planner *and* my MacBook to my meeting.

"Are you the wife of Randall Joseph Oakley?" the voice said, after I confirmed my own name.

"Yes."

"He's here at Water's Edge Hospital. Unfortunately, ma'am, he was in an accident."

An accident. Okay. Randall was sometimes a little reckless, like seeking a different station or just "glancing" at a score kind of reckless. He was okay. Of course he was.

"Is he okay?" I asked. Oh me of little faith.

"Ma'am, it's important that you get here as soon as possible."

That was all she told me. I don't remember her name. But I already knew my husband of 35 years was gone.

I was home alone, on my way to meet my writing partner Paul at our favorite satellite office, the creatively-titled Pier Diner, a mom-and-pop restaurant on the Surfside Beach Pier, for a short review of our current project, our swan-song. I called him and asked him to pick me up and drive me to the hospital instead.

He did, of course. And so it was Paul who walked with me when the receptionist led me to a private little cubicle. It was Paul who stood behind me and kept his hand on my shoulder while the doctor told me that Randall had had a massive heart attack and was dead before his Silverado crashed into a tree on a thankfully undeveloped and pedestrian-free road west of the beach. It was Paul who asked all the necessary questions that my own mouth could not utter.

After Paul called my oldest son, Sam, he also left a message for his own wife, Leah, to come to the hospital. Then he fetched me terribly bitter tea and carried my bag as we were corralled to another room. And when I finally began to digest the truth of my new reality, Paul held me while I cried.

And so I was there with him when his own phone rang with more news: Leah had died in an accident, too.

#

I watched the expression on Paul's face as he was catapulted from mourning his friend and comforting me to the shocking horror that his wife was gone, but I don't know what I said or did, because it felt like it was happening in front of some other woman, to some other man, somewhere else. I remember that all the crying gave me violent hiccups, and I thought I was going to vomit but never did. I remember that Paul had his hands in his lap and his head down, like he was closing in on himself. Once our kids filtered in, there were quiet tears and louder sobs. Some kind of time passed, but I don't know how much. My mouth was dry and images blurred in front of me, signature lines, tissues, paper coffee cups, my teenage grandson's hand, my youngest daughter's strawberry blonde hair, the wrinkled, gray sleeve of Sam's shirt as we walked together to a different room, a different place, and finally, my Randall, what used to be Randall, lying under a sheet.

I had seen my mom in the moments after she died. It had been striking and strange, how peaceful she looked, but also how unreal. She had always been there, and then she was not. This was the same and different. Randall had been there, and now he was not, but it felt like I was gone as well. Or at least, the person I was that morning, two hours ago, wasn't here anymore.

"He looks so... white," Sam murmured next to me.

"Too early for a tan," I said back. Was I trying to make my son smile, or trying to convince myself Randall didn't look like a shell, like a ghost?

I don't remember if he did smile. I didn't look at Sam. I only looked at Randall, but all I remember is how aware I was that he didn't look like Randall. He just looked gone.

We returned to the conference room and lingered long enough to piece events together, a feat accomplished by our collective brood trading bits of information and phone screens with each other and emergency personnel. It turned out that Randall and Leah had decided to surprise Paul and me at the diner and whisk us out for dinner to celebrate; Paul and I had sold our brand to its parent company and were moving on from curriculum writing. Randall picked Leah up on his way from the office, a simple matter of convenience. Apropos for her, she had carried only her phone in a small zippered carrier, which had been tossed from the car. Her ID had been much harder to confirm than Randall's. She was found in an embankment about 20 yards from the car, deceased from probable blunt force trauma.

Along with Paul's oldest daughter, Danielle, Sam took over the duty of details, gently guiding everyone to the strange and stoic conclusion that, close as our families were, freaky as the circumstances, we would arrange services separately and not burden ourselves with any joint activities or expectations.

I just kept alternating between nodding and shaking my head, trying to answer and assure whoever was around me, but also, as if to knock off the cloud of dust that shadowed my sense of the present.

#

Having a service for Randall posed an internal conflict for me, one I didn't share with anyone but Maggie. She only gave me a side-eye and pointed to my two daughters, who at that point were feverishly going through photos at our kitchen table without any prior discussion of a need to do so. Randall had always said he didn't want anything formal, and that always sounded perfectly reasonable and so *him,* until he was gone, and the thought of denying our four kids and two kids-in-law and three grandkids the chance to honor him and maybe gain some closure seemed selfish. And anyway, Randall wasn't here. What the hell say did he have and what could he do about it? Such thoughts seemed harsh and fair to me all at once.

We tried to do everything in his style, though, and kept it *in*formal, with Tennessee Vols paraphernalia scattered where flowers would be, a drop box for donations to Randall's favorite charity, Backpack Buddies, and plenty of fun anecdotes from our pastor and friend, Carter.

In the spirit of embracing "life abundantly," Carter reflected on Randall's tendency to spontaneously immerse himself in notions - going to the Hot Air Balloon Festival on a whim with Brittney and our now-20-year-old baby, David, winning a contest and co-hosting a cooking segment with Paula Deen at her local restaurant, or putting together a ridiculously intricate Halloween scavenger hunt for our church kids.

"And then there was his love for Jessie," Carter said, having just laughed and now needing to pause for composure. "It's sort of unconventional for a pastor, even here at the beach, to hang out at tattoo parlors, but when Randall decided to surprise his bride of 30 years with one he had designed and asked me to come along for the ride, I couldn't resist." The girls had curated the perfect photo montage, and the brand Randall designed for us, merging together the R, J, and O of our names, was displayed on the screen, memorialized in green ink on his muscular calf. It had certainly been a surprise, quite an uncharacteristic one, and it took me about three seconds to decide I needed one too, on the top of my foot and much tinier because that sonofabiscuit *hurt.*

I looked down at it now, plainly visible because I was wearing black flip flops... because I was Jessie Oakley and that was part of my uniform, even for funerals. Even for Randall's *funeral.* I tore my eyes away and looked at the screen while "Carry on My Wayward Son" added its fist-pumping feels to our hodge-podge memorial. David asked if we could end the service with "Rock and Roll All Night," and I acquiesced, making Carter throw in a few of our worship singers doing a little something-something in the middle so we wouldn't seem completely nuts and sacrilegious. There were only a few flowers, mainly from Randall's extended relatives back in the Midwest who couldn't grasp that we *really* didn't want any.

I shifted a little uncomfortably as Randall's brother Patrick gave his eulogy. It was fine, a little formal, filled with anecdotes of childhood that could have been lifted straight out of *The Goonies,* and perfectly peppered with God and Jesus and promises of Heaven. It was *fine.* It just felt like it was for someone else. Did Patrick know Randall anymore? Beach Randall? Our Randall? *My Randall?* Did he know that Randall wore toe socks to the gym? That he had a favorite hairspray, top three shampoos, and would only eat Peter Pan peanut butter? That he teared up every time he heard Tim McGraw's "My Little Girl" and had a teeny crush on Lady Gaga? That he always kissed me goodnight for a minimum of six seconds and still grabbed my ass every time he passed me while I was brushing my teeth or doing dishes?

Did anyone really know who we just lost?

I tried to listen to the noble and inspiring words. Of course I wanted everyone to believe in Heaven and make it there, but I also just wanted the whole thing to be over.

David and my oldest grandson, Travis, kept glancing at me. And my Mikayla, Randall's first born, just never stopped crying. I kept reaching behind me to clasp her hand. Her husband Altan kept his arm around her and whenever I reached back, his hand joined ours.

There was no graveside service. The kids and I all agreed on the cremation, and it was non-negotiable. We left the church and returned to our house. Maggie and Chrissy, Randall's sister, and a few of our church friends had arranged the meal, everything reminiscent of Randall's simple, sports bar-esque taste: buffalo wings, cheeseburger sliders, salt and vinegar chips, and chocolate cake.

After spending some time on the couch with Ms. Naomi, Randall's 90-year-old mother (medicinally tranquil because she had been absolutely inconsolable - and terrified of flying in from Chicago with Patrick and his family), I sat on the porch through most of the visiting, nursing a glass of tea with just a pinch of Bourbon and a plate of untouched cake. I smiled at everyone who came to sit with me, accepted their hugs and assured them

I would call for whatever I needed, be it a sushi night out, or someone to walk Cash, or help folding my laundry (I kind of thought that one was weird, but chalked it up to some helpful blog post somewhere meant for much younger mothers....)

Though it wasn't as if I knew what I *did* need.

It got easier when one of the last visitors greeted me. Danielle and my Mikayla were very close, so I was only mildly surprised to see her there. Leah's service would be Saturday. I looked at Danielle and thought of my beautiful friend, her shiny, chestnut hair, her flawless skin, and mostly, her generous, sometimes devious, smile. I didn't want to imagine her being anything other than fully alive.

Danielle and Mikayla flanked me on the porch swing. Mikayla rested her head on my shoulder, and I reached for Danielle's hand. There was such a solemnity in the moment, and sacredness too. I pictured the two of them the day of Mikayla's wedding, with Brittney, Sam's wife Abby, and more friends bustling around our hotel suite in Manhattan, make-up and champagne glasses and overflowing totes everywhere. Randall had stuck around long enough to be in some pictures and tease everyone and hug Mikayla until he managed to nearly ruin her eye makeup. He had left her with one of his signature hankies, blue and white plaid. I assumed it was the same one she'd been holding all day.

"Oh girls," I sighed, because even though they were very much grown, I still kind of saw Mikayla as a teenager, fresh from her braces, smiling more her sophomore year of high school than she had her whole life until then. "I have no idea what to say..."

"There's nothing to say, Ms. Jessie," Danielle answered. "We just have to get through this."

The simple truth was so devoid of any actual comfort, other than the "we." I always found comfort in company.

"It's just unbelievable..." I said lamely, for what seemed like the millionth time. "How's your dad?"

"Strong," she answered immediately. "But worn out. He was going to come over, you know, but Katy and Julie kind of insisted he go home and rest. Mama's sisters are cooking for him and the freezer. And he's not really sleeping."

"Oh, I totally understand," I said, like we were trying to schedule a game night to no avail. I didn't expect Paul to be around at all, and somehow, he'd made an appearance at the service. "You girls take good care of him."

"Of course," Danielle said. Then she smiled. "I think he's actually pretty sick of us already."

I forced a little giggle, as I sort of understood that, too, and I knew Paul was vastly outnumbered by females in his family. Meanwhile, Brittney, David, and Travis had slept over at the house all week, and while it was lovely and loving and thoughtful, I was starting to feel claustrophobic.

"I'm sure he's very appreciative," I told Danielle. "Please, please send my love. I'm so grateful he was there for me, and I am also just... so sorry..."

She leaned over and hugged me, reminding me so much of her daddy, open and warm. We exchanged the southern comfort known as "Love y'all," and she was on her way.

Mikayla and I were then joined by David, Brittney, and Sam. I couldn't remember the last time I was alone anywhere with just my four kids. We laughed as everyone smooshed and layered onto the porch swing together. Sam sat on the arm of one end, his own arm protectively around me.

"Mama, you know we are here for anything you need," he said, so seriously, like I would doubt him.

"I know, Sam," I said. "We're all here for each other. We're going to be okay."

"We know that, Mama," Brittney added, "But we just want to make sure you know *we are here*. We know how you like to do things on your own, your own way."

I smiled. One of the scariest and most incredible things about grown kids is how well they know you.

"I..." I sighed. I really didn't know how to explain it to them, or whether I should. I settled for, "I don't feel alone. I feel like... well, part of me is gone. The Randall part... And that feels... like words I don't have. But I don't feel *alone*. I have all of you." David and Mikayla were visibly crying, "And he is so apparent in each of you." I turned and met Sam's eyes. "You four are the greatest tribute to your dad that there could ever be."

David slumped into my side, and his brother reached over to muss his hair. I closed my eyes, grateful for the feel of all of them there, and almost afraid to look at them too much, because they were also a reminder of everything we lost when Randall died.

Chapter Two

The adage - and there are many for widows, I soon discovered - is that it's harder after the funeral and the fuss is over. In some ways, that was true. I spent two very long days being the sole receptacle for the grief of Ms. Naomi, Patrick, Chrissy, and their combined spouses and children. I was so grateful they came, and that they wanted to help in a vast array of ways.

Randall had been described over and over again with the same S words, depending on the age and vocabulary of the speaker: strong, solid, steady, stalwart. Also in the mix was "salt of the earth." He was a man's man, educated but not arrogant, loved sports and beef and his family. One never had to look far to see where he came from. His dad, who died before I met him, had been a general contractor and a church elder. Naomi had been a homemaker and a Sunday School teacher. Why they ever accepted their eldest son falling for a teen mom was one of life's great mysteries, as my own mother reminded me frequently. But Junie (short for Richard Jr.) and Naomi were those people... not just church pillars, but grace personified.

It feels disloyal, still, after years of absence, to compare them, but they were so different from my own family, who excelled at fulfilling obligations and made everything seem like one.

So the Oakleys were hanging around just being themselves. One nephew cut our tiny patch of grass and power washed the siding. His wife bathed Cash, put herself on dog poop detail, and made constant food runs. Chrissy's husband Joel had my car detailed. Chrissy and her daughter did all my laundry, even the sheets, and made the futile offer to help me go through Randall's clothes (way too soon), and Patrick helped Sam get started on all the estate and legal stuff. This left me to "rest," or rather, sit with Ms. Naomi and drink tea and reminisce during the long mornings, and participate in more of the same with all of them plus our kids into the night. The only "break" I took from all of it was for Leah's funeral on Saturday, but Brittney, Mikayla, and David were my faithful chaperones for that. The only break I wanted was for Maggie to come have happy hour with me on my porch.

I was a bewildering mix of relieved and grief-stricken all over again as I said goodbye to the Oakleys at the airport that Sunday morning. My own parents had been gone for almost half my life, my own brother hadn't shown up for almost as long, so it felt like the only link I really had to a foundational family was being severed. We talked about meeting up in the mountains (Chrissy and family lived in Knoxville, also products of Big Orange Nation) and there was a family reunion in Michigan scheduled for the following summer. Maybe I would go. I invited them to spend "Christmas at the beach." But deep inside, I knew I probably wouldn't, and they probably wouldn't either. Our lives were our lives.

I drove home from the airport and put myself back to bed

with plans to sleep *until*. I felt absolutely alien being alone in my house. For so long, it wasn't a thing at all.

Randall travelled, and we had four kids. When David was born, Sam was 17 and doing his own thing - and contrary to popular belief, requiring as much mental and emotional parenting energy as a newborn required physical assistance, hands down. The girls were eight and nine and homeschooled and, at the cusp of puberty and fresh from a family tragedy, needy. They were needy of *me*. I could have spent weekends tossing them to Randall, saying, "You're it," but I wanted to be with him, too. So the notion of Time Alone in My House was akin to magically learning Russian or waking up a size two. Utter, unattainable fantasy.

This day, I was alone, not quite in the way I had dreamed I'd be back in those mamahood trenches, when my whole body and soul would melt like wax into Randall upon his return. I was so much better as part of a team, and he was my holy exhale. I called him that so many times that it probably should have been his tattoo.

Now that he was gone, it felt strange to be craving solitude almost as much as I did back then. So I reveled in it, staying in bed until dinnertime, when I woke to walk Cash on the beach, and felt a little bit of renewal in my sandy sanctuary. I assumed I'd be returning to an empty house for the second time that day, until I saw Travis lying on the couch face down. I thought he was sleeping, and then I heard a sob.

Teenagers, to quote the funniest book read in my pre-adolescence, *Freaky Friday*, would "rather die than cry." It was a morbid thought for the time, but Travis was 17, and it held true. He cared about surfing, college football, and red-haired Cali who worked with him at Chick-Fil-A. But here he was, heartbroken over his Grampy, and crying like no one could hear.

"T?" I said softly. "I'm home."

In those moments, it's impossible to even know what you *want* to happen. There was only one other time in my life that I felt as sad and stricken as I did now, and there were kids to comfort then, too. Part of me, a selfish corner of my id, wanted Travis to ignore me, not to need comfort, so I could slip back into my bedroom and feel whatever was coming. But that didn't happen, so when he sat up, his chin trembling, his face wet, and expectation in his eyes, the rest of me, the part that always won, sat next to him and hugged him, cried with him and rocked his 5'10 frame akin to the way I had almost daily for his first two-and-a-half years.

Ten minutes later, we were dried and put back together. Twenty minutes later, Abby arrived with his younger siblings. Thirty minutes later, Sam arrived with pizza and wings. (I could hear Randall making a good-natured but sardonic comment about one household bringing three cars over). And as though they could smell it from wherever they'd been, Brittney and David were there right behind him.

The next week looked much the same, except for the inevitable return of everyone to full-time work and school. Mikayla and Altan took over dinner and keep-the-fridge-stocked duties, as it was their slow time of year anyway. I did make all of them stay away on Tuesday, so I could have tacos with the grandkids like always (we let Uncle David join whenever he was home from college). There were more episodes like the one with Travis on my couch. I cried sincerely and companionably each time, I comforted whoever needed it. I let them comfort me, too, but it all felt like an out-of-body experience.

#

Two weeks off were all I could stand. David returned to his campus apartment, and I kindly but pointedly told Mikayla and Altan that I wasn't eating again, ever. Sam cut his calls and texts back slightly. I put everyone else on notice that I wanted - and *needed* - to get some stuff done, that I wanted and needed to figure out a new normal (I had always hated that trendy/made-up/bloggy term, and now I hated it more because it was perfectly fitting). I would resume Sunday dinners and Taco Tuesdays as soon as I met my deadline, which would be just a week or two if I could work in peace.

I tried not to bother Paul, but I wasn't used to working without him. We had been working together at least a few days a week, at the diner or in his garage office, for 15 years. And really, the whole arrangement had all been Randall's idea.

The summer David turned five, not long after Sam and Abby had graduated, gotten their grown-up jobs, and enrolled Travis in daycare, Randall whisked me away for a whole weekend, and over a barbecue chicken picnic next to Lake Michigan he brushed my hair from my face and insisted that David, Brittney, and Mikayla start attending public school that fall.

"You've lost yourself, babe," he said earnestly. "The kids are fine. The house is fine. We are fine. But we need to get the sparkle back in your eyes. There is more to you than intricate lesson plans and seasonal crafts and raising poster children for the Fruits of the Spirit." He gently went on to suggest "shuffling the deck" and doing life differently for a while.

I wanted to argue with him, that our children were our treasures and we should be their primary influence, remind him of
dumb relationships in my adolescent years that led to my being
a teenage mother, point out Mikayla's propensity for anxiety or
Brittney's abilities in art and ineptitude for math. But basking
in the sun, with no one interrupting our conversation, in a sundress that was not black nor stained, and sipping wine at one in
the afternoon, I felt a little too free to deny how bound I *had*
been feeling.

So we shuffled. It did take Mikayla some time - and overflowing, hormonal tears - to adjust to eighth grade, while our social butterflies Brittney and David took to school immediately.
And after a few months of spending at least a few hours a day
alone in my house, doing crazy things like reading books straight
through and learning yoga from cable On-Demand, I also spent
some time having ideas, organizing my thoughts, and writing
about the things that had worked well for me as a homeschooling mom. I published a series of blog posts about it on Live Jour-
nal and Myspace.

And then one day right after New Year's, Randall came home
and told me about his co-worker's friend, someone in search of
a "creative partner" who, ideally, could copyedit and do some
graphic design and write a little. He was a former headmaster
of a private school and was contracted by a publishing company
to create new Christian-based humanities curriculum, starting
with a then-innovative interactive website.

It sounded like the world's most perfect job had been sent to
me gift-wrapped. A few days later, I met Paul for an interview
at IHOP. We both ordered pancakes (mine were blueberry; his

were pecan) and took our coffee light. We also agreed that flavored syrups were an abomination, but Paul nearly fell out of his chair chuckling when I pulled a small Mason jar of real maple syrup out of my bag and set it on the table. (Why mess around with fake stuff? Don't even get me started, IHOP...)

In the first six-months, we wrote and rewrote feverishly and launched the website, and it took another year to complete our first printed, commercially available project: a history/language arts set for intermediate grades. We celebrated those milestones by having a touristy, seafood buffet with both of our families. Shortly after, Paul and Leah started coming to our church. Through the years, we became linked like lifelong friends do. Now half of us were gone, and I hadn't seen Paul since Leah's funeral, and maybe I no longer knew up from down.

So intending to regulate myself, I gratefully embraced my first days back to work. Our editor Rachel had extended a deadline for us. Ken the Website Coder had gone as far as he could go without us. We were essentially adapting everything we had ever published in book form to be digital: not necessarily all the grunt work, but updating articles and creating, finding, or in some cases, commissioning more web-friendly graphics. For the supposed pièce de résistance, I was writing a new series of essays on transitions: from homeschool to conventional school or vice versa, from traditional texts to online study, and even from community co-op groups to online communities, an idea I actually abhorred but that was becoming important in rural areas or households with single parents who were dedicated to homeschooling.

In the midst of my own transition, the one before this big

one, none of it interested me. The moment David walked the stage with his high school diploma, my passion for education had seemingly oozed out of me like butter from chicken Kiev. I tried to shake it off, but Paul had noticed. I was scared to death at first, thinking I was tanking the work that had become his professional legacy. But he laughed. He laughed like he had at that Mason jar of maple syrup when we first met.

"I'm more than ready for something new," he'd said. "I've just been along for the ride. You've been steering this for a while."

It was a flattering endorsement from an ABD lifetime educator, and in spite of myself, I knew he was right. The changing times of social media, content creation, and increasingly innovative schools had never captured him. He just wanted kids to have fun learning, to know their history, to tell their stories. The method didn't interest him so much, and it seemed my waning enthusiasm only matched his.

Paul sealed our "retirement plan" by playing "Another Brick in the Wall" and pouring us each a big glass of sweet tea. It had been a happy day.

#

But readying our catalog for its spin-off was a huge job, and, tragedy or not, we were down to the wire. Paul had plenty of other income to rely on with his and Leah's assortment of rental properties. Randall's insurance was going to take care of everything big for me, but the payoff I'd be earning as a result of my completed contract had already been earmarked for my retirement, even before the accident, and I wasn't going to let go easily.

Buoyed by the needed solitude and the pressing goal, I took

the personal parts of my narrative as far as I could, working through the weekend and a pot of Italian wedding soup. I was assisted only by a few brief texts back and forth with Paul when it came to reference points in education.

His responses alternated between terse and apologetic. I hadn't seen him since Leah's funeral, at which he managed to be the picture of a graceful gentleman, even with an uncharacteristically tense posture and bags under his eyes. When I stopped in front of the casket and gave him the perfunctory funeral hug, we held on just a moment longer than what seemed perfunctory, but we couldn't speak. I was worried about him, of course. But what was there to say after the preposterously life-altering hours we had spent together at the hospital?

Our work demanded words, though, and by the Monday after my catch-up efforts, my brain was drowning in terms, and I had plateaued in my ability to organize (every article required three cross-references within our library of curriculum and commentary). I needed the fresh eyes of the project's adviser, so I began attempting to reach Paul late in the morning. Hours passed, and by dinnertime, no responses came. I finally scanned all my initial choices one more time, cringing at those that seemed like too much of a stretch, and emailed the link to Rachel. Then I ate a spinach and mushroom omelet while standing up and stretching at the kitchen counter.

The tentative knock on my door was barely audible over the strains of my "Eclectically Moody" playlist, featuring Alanis Morissette, Adele, Miranda Lambert, and the King of Moods and my clear favorite, Johnny Cash.

I dried my hands on the dishtowel and walked to the door,

only to see Paul standing there, looking mostly blank but also a little perplexed, like he forgot where he was or why he was there. I certainly felt the latter. His lack of response and unannounced visit were unprecedented.

I held the door open and managed a "Hey."

"Hi," he said, stepping through and standing just over the threshold.

He hadn't ever just *stopped by*. He'd never been there without at least part of his family. And mine.

"I..." He paused, ran his hand through his closely-tousled hair, and sighed. "What's going on?"

I probably didn't do a great job of controlling my facial expression. I wanted to feel tender and empathetic toward him, but I felt irritated and edgy and kind of abandoned.

I shrugged. "Um, I'm just making some tea. I was going to head down for a walk."

"Oh."

Oh?

"I just sent the drafts to Rachel. I... she extended the deadline twice. I couldn't wait any more."

He nodded. He knew.

"I left my phone in the Jeep most of the day." I wasn't used to him mumbling. I waited for further explanation, but none came.

"Oh," I answered back. One would never have guessed the two of us published actual multisyllabic words.

"I have sweet tea in the fridge," I started, trying to be charitable. "We can sit on the porch, if you want?"

"You don't have to change plans for me," he said, leaning against the doorframe.

"Plans" was stretching it. I studied Paul. His black shirt was wrinkled and hanging loosely around his shoulders. Leave it to a man to lose weight in his grief. I had looked at a blueberry muffin the night before and gained 2.5 pounds by morning. Meanwhile, there were circles around his eyes and a very atypical five o'clock shadow on his face. He sported the Myrtle Beach early-spring uniform of jeans and flip-flops. He was jangling his keys in his right hand, and his left hand still bore a wedding band, as did mine.

At Randall's memorial service, Paul had snuck in the back with his twin daughters Katy and Julie, and stayed long enough to love on each of my kids. I hadn't seen him or heard his voice since Leah's funeral. Today, the energy that usually crackled in his eyes was gone. It hurt to look at him.

"Are you getting any rest?" I said, but, of course, it wasn't really a question.

He just sighed again, with a barely noticeable shaking of his head, and walked to the couch, arranging himself neatly there. I turned back toward the kitchen and set about getting our drinks. Hot tea with a bit of honey and whiskey was my evening beverage of choice, but Paul wasn't a drinker. I wished my iced tea was decaf. His hands looked twitchy to me.

A few minutes later, I handed him a glass garnished with lemon wedges and mint leaves, held on to my own sturdy, steaming mug, and looked over at him.

"Want to sit outside?" I asked, feigning some cheerfulness, trying to feel hopeful.

He looked down. He was more an outdoor person than I was, a recreational softball player, an avid gardener and golfer, born and raised in Surfside Beach, just south of Myrtle. That's where Randall and I had moved a few years after getting married, and we had fallen in love all over again, with the salty air and the more casual living than we'd had all our lives in suburban Chicago. I learned to love the coastal lifestyle, walking the dog barefoot and taking nightcaps on the front porch, but I didn't consider myself an outdoor person so much as a beach person. There were no flowers outside my house save for the perennials that were planted before we bought it, including several gorgeous rose bushes and a magnificent magnolia tree. Paul and Leah's house, meanwhile, looked like a botanical garden.

He shrugged. "Whatever you want."

Now I sighed.

"This is the hardest time of day, I think," I said, settling on the opposite end of the couch, where Randall used to sit. I thought I was suggesting conversation, but since he remained silent, I asked outright, "How about for you?"

"Now, you mean? I guess." Another shrug. "Dinner... is weird. I don't feel like going anywhere where people want to... talk to me about it."

"No wonder you look 10 pounds lighter," I said. He forced a smile. "I ordered a smart TV today. For the bedroom. Can you believe that?

He didn't get it, even though we'd talked about it a hundred times in the past, how Randall was adamant that in our post-small-kids, "adult time" life, in which we could watch all of any kind of programming we wanted in our own living room and didn't have to retreat to watch shows about zombies or sex scandals or medieval versions of both at eleven at night, we would not have a TV or other screened devices in our bedroom.

"But now," I mused, "time seems to stand still around 8 o'clock. I feel like a rebel. I let Cash sleep on the bed, and I keep my tablet with me. I read really intellectual stuff like EW-dot-com until I pass out. And I have big plans to have Sam mount that TV right above the tallboy. It's all Maggie's fault." Suddenly single so many years ago, she was gently cheering me on, reminding me that no matter what might seem like an affront to Randall's memory, he would want me to be comfortable and even happy without him. I doubted 40 inches of hi-definition '90s dramedies would equate to happiness, but I welcomed the help easing to sleep each night.

When he still said nothing, I got more direct.

"Paul..."

When he looked up at me, his eyes had changed, and I was no stranger to the look in them. They were somewhat... pleading. I'd seen that look a few times in our past. Once when his mother, with whom he'd had a mostly-contentious relationship, had passed away. Once when Katy, then 18, took off for California, in his convertible. A few other less-descript times when big life stress set him on a precarious edge. Leah was not an overt nurturer, and I was CCO – Chief Coddling Officer, pretty much anywhere I went.

I didn't know how to do that this time.

"We can just sit," I said, mostly to myself. My own walls were built much higher than usual. It wasn't that I didn't want Paul there, just that my presence and every word I could say would bring him an automatic reference to grief and loss. *They died. They died together, loving us.*

I didn't see a way we could possibly be good company for each other at that point.

I clutched my own mug and drank, staring at a collage of momentous family events on the wall: Sam and Abby's simple wedding on the beach. Mikayla and Altan's grand wedding in Central Park. Brittney's graduation from University of Tennessee. One of David's surfing championships. All three of the grandkids. And then us... our own wedding a million years ago. Our vow renewal right down the shore from our home. Our Ruby Wedding, which I insisted on titling our 35th Anniversary party, even though half of our friends hadn't seen *Bridget Jones' Diary* and were a bit fuzzy on what they were being invited to. All the photos were strategically placed to allow for more weddings, more grandkids, more happy milestones.

I looked away only when I heard the shatter. My mug had slipped from my hands and crashed on the floor.

A startled Paul immediately started picking up the larger ceramic pieces. I wordlessly and foggily headed to fetch the broom. We cleaned up the mess in companionable silence. The quiet should have been awkward. Normally, all we did was talk. Normal had left us exactly 23 days prior.

He didn't bother to get up from the floor then. When I walked back to him after discarding the mess, he was leaning against the couch and looking at me again.

I sat down beside him. I allowed myself to take his hand. It wasn't shaking as much as mine was, and it was familiar. He exhaled deeply at the touch. "I don't know how to do this," I offered. His response was, "Neither do I."

He took back his hand.

I waited for a moment, wondering what to say next or whether giving up and going for my walk was a better option than words. But then I heard a heaving, almost choking sound from beside me and saw Paul's face in his hands, his shoulders shaking. That familiar, quasi-maternal wave of compassion swept over me, but I didn't try to hold him. The moment almost felt too private to intrude upon. After a moment, I leaned over and rubbed his back, like I used to when the kids were actively vomiting.

When he straightened his posture, deftly removing my touch again, it had felt like hours, but probably only been a minute or two. He hastily swiped at his cheeks, as though I hadn't seen tears fall down that face before.

But it was different. I knew that, and I let him have his dignified and necessary space.

"You want to go for that walk now?" he asked quietly, avoiding my stare.

I did.

#

When Randall, Sam, and I had moved to the beach, I'd had a pretty Midwestern view of what The Beach actually was. Though I'd visited the ocean before, the beaches I grew up with were boat-populated lakes with white, gravelly sand that we'd visit over Fourth of July weekend. The idea of Living at the Beach was as romantic a notion as moving to Italy for me. And it proved mostly true. It took about a minute for me to giggle gleefully at our outdoor shower and grow blind to trails of sand through the house and random seashells left on the counter. Sam learned to swim in the ocean, and the babies that followed learned to walk on its shores.

The long-standing locals whom we got to know, Paul and Leah included, told us that we'd eventually get over it. The beach is crowded in the summertime. The sun gets you wrinkled. The salt gets in your hair. The sand eventually stops being endearing when it's in your food or clogging up your washing machine. But we never got over it. We settled in "east of 17," though still about a mile walk to the actual ocean. And when Sam and the girls were out of the house, we tipped our hats to the traditional yard and plentiful trees (and HOA) that had graced most of our child-rearing years and told David he was going to have to "settle" for beach front property. The three of us downsized into a one-level stilt house with a huge master suite and two much smaller guest bedrooms, as well as a glorified dumbwaiter that would serve as our elevator when we got too old for the stairs. It was on the second row, basically across the street from the water, but the front porch, living room, and our bedroom offered the view and sound of the ocean. I wanted waterfront, but we weren't millionaires, and Randall had insisted upon keeping an extra bedroom for office space, grandkid sleepovers, and the ever-looming possibility that a grown child could return home at any point.

Once we moved Right There, I woke up most every day and hit the sand. I hated gyms and wasn't a huge fan of cardio (evident from the 20 extra pounds I gained after having Brittney and never lost), but I could stroll on the beach for hours and not feel like I was making an effort.

Paul trailed slightly behind me now. He had left his shoes on, which always felt like an abomination to me. The sun was already setting and though it was April and very spring-like during the day, there was a chill in the air. After a few minutes, I stopped and turned to him.

"How are you *actually* doing?"

It was stupid, and we both knew it, but what else was there to start a real conversation?

He stopped too, then looked out at water and shrugged. "Fine. Tired. I don't know."

"Yeah," I started. "I... I wish I could help."

"Jess..." Now he looked at me to acknowledge the absurdity. "I'm sorry about not getting back to you today. But I'm not asking you for anything. You can't even help yourself right now."

Um... I resented that. I was sad, and I was confounded, but I was doing okay. It occurred to me then that part of the reason I was so tense around him is because I was prepared for him to blame Randall. *This could be it,* I told myself. *The* conversation and maybe the last one we would ever have. I also told myself I was ready.

"Um, Paul, I couldn't care less about unanswered text messages. Your wife died. My husband was driving. And we are almost done anyway. There are plenty of good reasons why you didn't answer me."

"You think I ignored your messages because Randall had a heart attack? *Jesus*, Jessie. Do you even come up for air?"

I almost scolded him not to swear at me, but I refrained. Everything started to feel murky.

"It wouldn't be... a *stretch*, Paul... for you to be mad. I'm mad! This could have gone a million different ways." My half-Italian hand gestures were unleashed. "Why didn't Randall see his doctor more regularly? Why did they need to surprise us on a Monday night? Why couldn't they wait for a weekend like normal people? At least Randall would have been at the office or at home instead of the car. Or he would have been by himself and Leah wouldn't have been there. Or..."

"Or you would have been in the car and died instead, and your kids would have lost both of you. Or maybe for fun, we all could have been in the car!"

"Futile," I sighed. I had exhausted each of those options and others several times over. I should have told him about the one where Randall had decided to pick Travis up from baseball practice. My rumination only got grittier to make reality seem less horrid.

"You should be taking less blame, and more time," he said.

"It's not blame, it's just... analysis."

"Then less analysis," he repeated, shaking his head at me. "You can't figure this out. There's no rhyme or reason. It couldn't have happened any other way because it didn't happen any other way. All you can do is move forward with what's left." He shrugged. "But you don't even have to do that today."

"Except I did," I said, trying to keep blame out of my voice. Being honest and raw, however, felt kind of amazing. "I want that bonus. But even more than that, I want the job to be done.

I want that part to be over too, so I can just... figure out what's next."

The waves were roaring a little louder, so we were almost yelling to be heard. "When it's over, we won't see much of each other."

I had thought of that, too. It didn't thrill me. It would be another loss of my everyday, cherished normal.

"I don't... I have no idea what life will look like. I mean, this was it. Randall was going to leave the firm, for real. We were going to sleep a little later and hang out with the grands more. You know, dust off the ice cream maker and maybe finally learn to shag. We had a bucket list! Ten places to visit we'd never been to before. We were finally going to try parasailing! And now I have no idea what I'll do with *myself* when it's all done."

He shook his head, and I watched him choose his words carefully.

"Anything you want. You have to know that."

Now I looked out at the ocean, which had been my constant companion and sometimes my best friend for the last 30-something years. I didn't see what Paul was seeing.

"I know that just yesterday I was forty-ish and shuffling four kids all over town and cleaning my kitchen 18 times a day and never going to the bathroom alone and breastfeeding a hangry toddler until he was three. And today I am like crusty old Alfred, putzing around the bat cave with no Batman to wait for."

"Crusty!" He offered a small laugh and a long pause. "Maybe..." His voice lowered to almost inaudible as he shrugged. "At least until we're done, I could be Batman. I can do better."

That was odd. I stepped closer to him. The breeze was picking up, and I folded my arms across myself. "You're fine," I said, feeling bad for expressing one ounce of annoyance toward him. "Maybe I'll be my own Batman."

"I believe you will," he said, looking away. "But I will miss being imaginary superheroes with you."

"Imaginary superheroes," I echoed. "Imaginary superheroes who save the world, or at least some Christian school kids, from boring geography."

He smiled. "And unrelatable literature."

"Sentence diagrams," I groaned.

"Verb conjugation."

Awkward tittles. In all those years, the occasions on which I'd felt awkward around Paul were minimal.

"Paul..."

"Too bad we can't write the book on this," he sighed. "Well, too bad someone else hasn't."

"I'm sure someone has. Wasn't it an episode of *Friends*? Didn't Monica do the catering?"

Another giggle.

I was known for coming back from even the briefest beach visits soaked to the knees. The salt water always pulled me in with an irresistible thrall. At that moment, I let the water lap my feet and the silence wash over me. My father had been gone most of my adult life. My brother had decided not to be a part of it. Randall, my sons, and then Paul, were the most important men in my life. The fathomless heartbreak of Randall's absence would only be intensified with Paul's.

"Can't we still be friends?" I asked softly.

There was a soft laugh again, but it was tinnier and less sincere. I watched what I could see of the side of his face as he stared into the water, grateful, as I always was, that Daylight Saving Time had begun.

"I'm sorry you have to ask," he finally said.

He sounded so sad, and even that thought was ludicrous. *Sad* was what we feel when they kill Sybil *and* Matthew off of *Downton Abbey*, or when Chipotle is out of guacamole. There really was no word for these mystic depths of grief.

"Paul..." I felt a surge of energy, wanting to make something better for him, impossible as it seemed. I forced my signature fake, exaggerated grin. "I don't seem to have any of the right words. I'm just so sorry."

When his eyes snapped back to me, there was something different. It looked like anger, but surely, I must have been mistaken.

"*Why* are you apologizing to *me*? Why are you trying to comfort *me*? Jessie! This happened to you, too, not just to me."

"Okay..." I stammered.

"I didn't come here for you to console me!" he added hotly.

"Then what do you want? And why did you come?" My fire rose to match his. What had I done to make *him* angry? Or even aggravated? "It wasn't to help me get *our job* done, so *why?*"

Just like that, he went from indignant to taken aback.

"I don't know..." he started. "I guess I hoped... I'm sorry."

He tilted his head in a signature Paul move, normally to show he was contemplating every word he was hearing and saying. He didn't say anything else, though. And I felt my defenses melt.

I stepped toward him and wrapped my arms around his neck.

"I'm so sorry," I said, the words vibrating off his already-salty skin.

His embrace was familiar and strong. This time, I was crying, and he was not. I let my face press into his shoulder. I let my weight rest on him. I let myself breathe his clean, sagey smell. Then he tightened his hold on me and let out a deep, lingering breath.

Was it a holy exhale?

For a moment it felt too intimate, but I wasn't cheating on anyone because no one could claim me anymore. And it wasn't lust I felt, just safety and solace and understanding... and so I didn't want to let go.

But we did. Once we began sinking a little in the sand, it all felt weird. We both shifted, but his arm stayed tentatively around me. Like so many tiny and friendly gestures between us, this was not completely foreign. Yet I found myself wondering about the fluff around my hips and whether there was the look or smell of overzealously-sprayed olive oil on my jacket.

The sun was almost completely gone. I shivered.

"You're shaking," he murmured, and took all pretense away from me as he again pulled me closer. "We can go back."

"No, we can't," I answered sardonically and almost with a giggle.

"So, let's not," he said. He didn't move.

That's when the other atmosphere shifted. Not the breeze, but the whole feeling of the world. It got smaller. It got heavier. It got scarier. A very particular subtext became barely-hidden and fully-loaded, so no matter what happened from that point on, everything would be different.

If I was being honest, I had wanted him to pull me closer. Not just to warm me, but because I wanted to be close to him. To Paul. I wanted to feel *Paul's* steadfast frame, I wanted to hear *Paul's* voice closer to my ear. I wanted to make him smile... and then bask in his smile.

And he had not only pulled me closer, but his face was resting in my hair, his lips brushing my hairline, his breathing just a little unsteady.

What the hell is happening?

I didn't want to be the one to call out anything. I didn't know *how* I wanted this moment or this uncharacteristic visit to end. It was startling simply not to want it to end. I wanted him just to stay, but...

"It's warmer if we keep walking," I suggested.

Somewhat to my dismay, he removed his arm and we started walking again, destination unknown.

Chapter Three

Walking on eggshells did not go well for us. Two hours later, I was sitting in the hospital with Paul yet again, waiting for someone to come give us any bit of attention. The combination of sand, flip-flops, and darkness has not been kind to him.

We had walked quietly and companionably until the sun went almost completely down, and then Paul stumbled in a huge hole in the sand (damn tourists) on our way back up shore, ending our time at the beach on a very sour and dramatic note. His manfully-suppressed cries of pain and inability to stand sent us struggling to make it across the road and landed him in a curtained-off triage bed with a half-melted ice pack on his still-sandy right foot.

"This is stupid," he grumbled. "I've done this lots of times. I have ice at home. Let's just go, Jessie..."

I shook my head for the umpteenth time. "That is the ugliest ankle I have ever seen, and I was basketball team mom for six years. You're not leaving without an X-ray."

I was pretty sure he was mad at me, but he was also a little pale and certainly not in any condition to storm off. Thankfully, a few minutes later, an equally surly nurse named Ned came to collect him and wheeled him off to radiology.

"What are we doing?" I asked aloud.

Were those vague notions of romantic tension on the beach? Was it simply heightened atmosphere because of our sadness and our almost-fight? Whatever it was, it had been knocked out by a clumsy, intense injury and a not-quite-in-CrossFit-shape almost-60-year-old basically trying to piggy-back-ride a humiliated grown man to the car. Paul didn't say a word unless I counted his grunts in response to my questions. It was the very opposite of our normal prattling on and even talking over each other.

Normal. Normally, Paul would not be walking on the beach on an early April evening. His and Leah's house was about 3 miles inland, which isn't a lot, but it's also far enough to require getting in the car and paying to park somewhere, and they didn't care enough about it to bother. Normally, he and I didn't see each other after four in the afternoon unless we were having a double dinner date with our spouses.

... like we would have had *that* night. *Okay. Get a grip, Jessie. This is family. This is* Paul *and me. Just like it was Leah and Randall in the car. It doesn't mean anything.*

But nothing was normal that night. Nothing had been normal since the last night we'd been at Water's Edge Hospital, which wasn't on the ocean's edge at all. And I wasn't sure what the next normal, the stupid, proverbial *new normal,* was supposed to be.

#

Paul was silent and slightly paler when he returned. I fetched him some water and tried to share some Peanut M&Ms. He shook his head with a hint of a smile. I preferred plain ones and he knew it; I had shifted all too easily into caretaker role.

"So, you need the name of an ortho?" the young, Pantene-commercial looking doctor said as he came in. He looked like he sashayed straight out of *Grey's Anatomy*, and I wanted to ask him whether the sniper attack or the plane crash had been a more terrifying experience.

Paul sighed. "I have one."

"I thought you might," he continued sunnily, nodding to me. *Geez*, he was pretty. "No signs of a fracture, but from what I see, this was probably not your first rodeo..."

Paul rolled his eyes at me, and I listened carefully as Dr. McDreamy gingerly prodded my miserable friend and rattled off terms like "instability" and "RICE," and ended with an emphatic, "no weight-bearing until..." When he finished and left the room, I grimaced in sympathy at Paul, who was now sporting a look that was equal parts mortified and nauseated.

"You can go," he said quietly. "I'm sure Matt can come get me."

I glanced at the clock, even though I knew exactly what time it was. "You're not getting their whole household rattled at 11 o'clock at night. I can take you home. I can find your crutches. I can even tuck you in," I added dryly.

"They'll get me crutches here. I used to do this all the time," he said. "I can manage."

"You used to do *this* all the time?" I was trying really hard not to laugh at the absurdity of our evening, since he was clearly not ready to yet.

In fact, he was all business. "One break. Mostly sprains. All the time. Softball. Water skiing. Walking. It's just been years since I did it this bad. I'll be fine."

"Okay." Now I felt embarrassed and like maybe I had read more into the whole evening than what was actually happening. "Okay. I'm going to wait out there while you get finished. I can call Danielle if you want. I don't have Matt's number."

"No. You were right," he mumbled. "Let's not wake them. You can drop me off. And thank you."

I nodded carefully and left the room. A gal of semantics, I could spend the next segment of waiting considering his use of "let's" and "drop off."

#

I pulled up to the door, to fetch Paul, who'd been right about the crutches. He was slow and careful and had a prescription for anti-inflammatories sticking out of his shirt pocket. I turned the radio up and hummed softly to "Wanted Dead or Alive," pretending I was alone or at least that Paul was actually Richie Sambora.

His house and yard were pitch dark when I pulled up. I used my phone to light his path behind me and worked on unlocking the door. I was more irked than worried that he wouldn't accept any sympathy. If he fell down again, I was prepared to point and laugh and start belting out "Free Fallin'."

He made it, though there was a thin sheen of sweat on his forehead as he followed me. I turned on every light I could find to guide him. "Where are we going?" I asked quietly. Our office was in his converted garage, and I had never, ever been in this house without Leah in it. We did most of the hanging out we did at restaurants. I couldn't necessarily recall in which direction the master bedroom was.

"Just the couch," he muttered. There was no longer any posturing. He bit his lip as he first sat and then carefully pulled his legs onto the couch.

I excused myself and scavenged for everything I could think of... a bag of frozen corn, a bottle of water, and four ibuprofen. He swallowed them while I positioned a throw pillow under his foot and gingerly placed the frozen bag, wrapped in a kitchen towel, over it. I set the crutches next to him on the floor and skimmed his discharge instructions.

"You're supposed to ice once an hour for 20 minutes," I said. "How are you going to manage that?"

His eyes closed, he shrugged. "I probably won't." And before I could respond, he added, "Jessie. I promise you I have this. The Advil will kick in, I'll sleep, I'll get to my own doctor tomorrow."

"Okay," I said. It wasn't really my place not to believe him, and from the looks of the swelling going on, a little bag of corn wasn't going to help much anyway. "Well, I'll get your prescription filled first thing and either drop it off or send it over. We'll get your car back at some point. Are you going to call Danielle?"

"The baby has a wellness visit in the morning," he said quietly. "But I'll call Julie. I think she's off tomorrow."

"Please let me know if she's not..." I felt so out of place. I was not part of these aspects of his life, his family's schedules, his medicine cabinet, his bare feet on the couch. It was time to go. "Good night, Paul."

"'Night..." he echoed. There wasn't another sound as I pulled the door closed behind me.

Chapter Four

I couldn't sleep well. This was nothing new, and there were some huge thoughts taking up too much space in my brain to allow for rest. *Was Paul okay? Should I have left him? How could I have possibly stayed with him/that would be so inappropriate? Why is it inappropriate; we are good friends? Yeah, except what happened on the beach? Why did you move closer to him? Why did he smell your hair? Why did he come over in the first place? Why are you thinking more about him tonight than you are Randall?*

The first hint of dawn was a relief. Cash and I were on the beach by 6am. I was careful of holes and saw none. I focused on Randall thoughts, how he would send me here every time I got close to a supernova, how he only came if it promised to be a short visit or Jacob or Summer asked him. He could have lived anywhere. His family had resettled in the mountains, which he loved. He moved us to the beach for me. He set up my whole happy life.

I was drying my eyes as I walked back in the door a half hour later, very surprised to hear my phone, which I hadn't bothered to bring, chiming the sound of text after text. As Jess and Marie told Harry and Sally, "No one I know would call at this hour."

Every message was from Paul.

6:04 a.m. *You up?*

6:04 a.m. *I'm not up but I'm awake.*

6:05 a.m. *From the feel of it, I won't be up for awhile.*

6:07 a.m. *You there?*

6:09 a.m. *I can't believe you're sleeping through this.*

6:10 a.m. *Golf carts going in reverse wake you up, but not me in my time of need.*

6:11 a.m. *Beeeeeeeeeeeeeeeeeep*

6:11 a.m. *Animated GIF of a golf cart*

6:13 a.m. *K. I was trying to be cool last night, but this sucks.*

6:18 a.m. *We should have left a bucket by the couch before you left.*

I paused to mentally picture him struggling to the bathroom. Oops.

6:18 a.m. *Anyway. K. Call when you can.*

6:21 a.m. *: whining emoji: whining emoji: :whining emoji:*

6:21 a.m. *Animated GIF of a cat on crutches*

6:23 a.m. *:sad face emoji:*

6:26 a.m. *:many sad face emojis:*

"Oh my God," I said aloud, immediately summoning images of Randall with the head cold that landed him in bed for three days once or twice a year. Meanwhile, four days after I'd had my C-section with David, I was cooking dinner with one hand and breastfeeding an infant with the other. The dichotomy was a Mars and Venus given. But I knew virtually nothing about Paul as an up-close patient other than the all-out awkward replay of the previous night. I flipped on my coffee maker and dialed his number.

#

By 6:00 P.M., after I'd substituted my Taco Tuesday dinner date with the grands to a milkshakes-after-school date, Paul was resting and elevating on the recliner end of *my* couch. Turned out Julie was not only off work but had gone out of town, Katy lived an hour away and taught music lessons most evenings, Danielle and Matt had a four-year-old and a baby, and Paul wasn't up to dealing with any of it. When I got to him with his filled prescription that morning, he was sleep-deprived, in pain, and, therefore, understandably grouchy. By the time the amped up meds kicked in, an appointment with his orthopedist was made, and a chicken biscuit was in his stomach, he'd decided that the day or so of convalescence he'd need might as well be "near the beach." We both ignored the fact that it would require him utilizing my rickety elevator, and he couldn't care less about the beach. As long as we pretended everything was normal, the energy between us stayed that way, too.

It was fortunate he managed to get an appointment, and I had a feeling his historical relationship and trademark charm had something to do with it. He was swiftly diagnosed and put in a walking boot for at least two weeks. I had stayed behind in the waiting room, but apparently the doctor, who knew him well, had mentioned potential surgery if he didn't give himself a chance to heal. This led me to my own diagnosis of the patient: he did not like being fussed over, he would second guess everything anyone said if it included extra time off his feet, and he was in hard-core denial over being 63 rather than 30.

Now he was on the phone with one of his daughters, denouncing the need for operations, rest, therapy, and if I heard him correctly, ligaments in general. Once he'd ended the call and our tostadas were in the oven, I sat on the couch beside him. "I didn't realize you were moonlighting in sports medicine all these years."

He managed to glare and smile at me at the same time. Then he launched into pretty much the same tirade. I indulged him for about 10 seconds and then held up my hand.

"So just do what you want," I said. "Ignore the doctor. Power through. Oh... is she the same one who operated on you last year?"

This glare was pure. Paul had a torn bicep repaired the previous fall, and he'd put it off so many times, he'd ended up with extended time in a sling and away from the golf course.

"Shut up," he said, grinning from behind his glass of tea.

I handed him the remote and went back to fuss in the kitchen. I put a decorative swirl of sour cream on his plate and garnished it with cilantro. I put two more pills in a little terra cotta bowl and a scoop of salsa in another. I put all the guacamole on my plate because I knew he only ate it with chips, not meals, which made no sense to me. And then I looked at him, stretched out with his foot propped on my "Alice in Wonderland" throw pillow and Cash resting next to his arm. He seemed like a mystery to me in so many ways, yet my dog was cuddling him, and I could serve him a meal without asking a single question about his preferences.

It was strange territory. His overnight bag was sitting in the guest room, but none of our kids knew he was there. I don't know what he told his, but I wasn't sure if I could ask him about it.

When dinner was plated, I brought everything to him on a tray. I stood next to him trying not to be awkward while he assessed the simple meal. Without looking up, he asked breezily, "Are you eating?"

"Of course," I answered, trying to be casual, and went to grab my own plate.

We ate in silence for a few minutes before he asked, "Do you normally eat at your table?"

"Mmm," I answered, wiping my mouth, a fan of my own cooking. "*Normally* normally, or in-the-last-few-weeks-normally?"

"Now. New normal," he said with a smirk, knowing my thoughts on the phrase.

Since David had been away at college, Randall and I had actually taken to eating dinner in the living room – like newlyweds, we joked, because that's exactly what we did when I was still practically a child-bride and we wanted to watch mindless TV after putting Sam to bed. In our empty nest, we had breakfast together in the kitchen during the weekends, and neither of us was home a lot for lunch. Since he'd died, I was gulping green shakes in the morning and the odd sandwich over the kitchen counter. In the evenings, I'd have an omelet or some chips and salsa, sitting at the table and flipping through magazines or mail with some music on. I reported that to Paul.

"Why do you ask?"

He shrugged. "Just wondering. We ate dinner out most of the time. Dinner time has just kind of been the weirdest. When I don't feel like going out, it's a lot of chili from a can or Bojangles."

"Eek. Not together, I hope. Anyway, I bet Danielle would love to have you around more at dinner time," I said. "You can entertain the babies, and she can use both of her hands." Danielle's son was four, and her baby girl was somewhere around three months. Thinking about little Vivian made me think of Leah and remember the sadness of a new mama not having her own mama around.

Paul might have been thinking something in the same vicinity. "I've been there a few times, but she has a pretty tight routine. I tend to get Christian all wound up, and Vivi only wants Danielle anyway. I'll get over there soon."

Shrugging, I said, "You don't have to justify it to me. I was just wondering. I know I could hang out at Sam and Abby's more, too, but I kind of like making *my* own routine." I paused. "It just hasn't been that long."

Paul set his plate on the table next to him. It was half eaten, but I could tell that he was done. He cleared his throat, a characteristic sign of subject change and seriousness, and gave me that green-eyed stare that usually came with it.

"It's okay for us to do this."

I nodded. "To eat gringo-Mexican and watch *M*A*S*H*? To stay in rather than risk further injury?"

He did not find me humorous. I tried again, my voice small. "Right. I mean, we aren't actually doing anything, right?"

"I think it's safe to say this is something."

He might have meant that to sound casual, but his voice was all gravely. It sent butterflies raging in my stomach and a neon sign flashing in my psyche, "Warning! Point of No Return!" I had not felt this *something* with a man in *decades*. With Randall, it had occurred on our third date, the third one of just the two of us, because Sam had joined several before we got to that point. By that time, I knew Randall wanted to move away from Illinois. I knew he wanted lots of kids. I knew that he was older and had had one serious relationship that had ended the previous year, and he was not only unafraid of a woman with a kid, but totally ready to settle down. So when he took my face in his hands and said, "I already know I love you. But I will wait until you get there," it wasn't just the atmosphere that changed, but the rotation of my whole world. The only thing that gave me pause was my fear that he was too good to be true.

And maybe that was part of the fear this time, but there was a brand-new feeling as well, like I was going to snap a tether that no longer existed, a phantom chain to a pillar that had crumbled. This was not anything like a third date. I was not anything like a 19-year-old who'd been stupid and burned. And the person sitting close to me (*so close...* I thought a little excitedly), was not a stranger to me, but was new in enough ways to set my nerves on fire.

I shouldn't be nervous. I shouldn't be... anticipating. But I didn't know why he was there either, really, or why he had come over the night before instead of just calling me.

"Why did you come yesterday?" I asked. "You never answered me about that. I mean, you never just stop by, and 80% of our work is over text."

"It wasn't a work thing," he responded immediately.

"Then..."

I could barely handle the way he was looking at me. I felt my face flush as he continued. "I am trying to stop thinking in terms of *always* and *never* and *normally*. Everything is different. Life changed completely in an instant."

"And that *just* happened."

He nodded. "A month ago, I most likely would not have come over last night. But yesterday, I had no reason not to."

"So, you did, because...?"

"Because it was a rough day, Jessie. I was at all these appointments: lawyer, insurance agent, bank. Then I had to update the girls on everything. All I did was talk all day about what life is going to be like *now*, without Leah, and..." He took a deliberate breath. "I kept finding myself just wanting to talk to *you*."

My cheeks burned.

"You're not getting me. You're trying to put me in some context that doesn't exist anymore." He reached over and put his hand over mine. I wondered what else had changed, since not 24 hours earlier, he had pulled the same hand away from me. "You are one of the people who has known me best for so many years now, and I just wanted to be understood without having to explain everything, just for minute. I just wanted to see my friend. I wanted to just... exhale."

I almost shivered at the word. I looked at our hands. His nails were always clipped super short. Mine were still manicured and painted slate from a morning out with Ms. Naomi and Chrissy. Widow nails. I hardly ever got manicures *before*. They just didn't last. His thumb was caressing my wrist, as though it were the most natural occurrence in the world.

Trying to be steady, I answered, "Well, I'm not going anywhere, Paul. You're... you're family to me. And like you said, this happened to *us*. I mean, we can go through as much of this together as we need to."

"Not just 'this,'" he answered. And before I could register anything with clarity, he was pulling me toward him. It was extremely awkward, me leaning over the pillows he was using for an arm rest, with my butt kind of in the air, but then I let my forehead rest against his face, and I heard him inhale with a not-hidden hint of longing. Re-centering myself, I put my hand on his chest, feeling his heart, and held the back of his neck with my other hand. He exhaled and caressed my arm.

"What else?"

"Can we just see?" he asked. "I don't know for sure, but this seems good to me."

"Yeah..." I answered. I wondered if I sounded as unsure as I felt.

#

In my head, I made a list. Had there been no dramatic baggage between us, it was simple enough. He was good, to his core: trustworthy, charming, funny, loyal. He was steady: a hard-worker, educated, solvent. Random injuries notwithstanding, he was in great shape, had a movie star smile, and charmingly carried that penetrating, attentive look in his eyes. We lived in a small town, and he was relatively well known. The single gals of a certain age would be making their plays soon enough, whether I thought the timing was appropriate or not.

And I... was fiftysomething. Widowed. Single? Single.

But there was another list, comprised of all my emotions. I *liked* how it felt to be the object of his attention. I reveled in the steadiness of his embraces. I appreciated how, for these 24 hours, he hadn't been in a rush to get through our conversations – quite different than how it was when we were blazing through projects together.

But there was so much wrong with the whole picture. A million or more things kept popping into my head like adware on a celebrity gossip site. We were both newly widowed. We were both newly widowed under very freak circumstances. We were both newly widowed under very freak circumstances *and* we loved each other's spouses and kids, and our families were already linked in a completely different context. And where would this go? What if we were not compatible as more than friends? How would it end? Did it have to end? What if it did? What would happen to all the other context?

#

"I can hear everything you're thinking," he said, looking remorseful as I scooted myself, with nary a modicum of grace, back to my side of the pillows.

I giggled. "That I have to pee?"

He laughed. "So do I."

"I'll get the bed pan," I called as I headed down the hallway.

When I returned from the master bathroom, Paul was sitting at the kitchen table, foot dutifully elevated on a chair. He'd apparently managed to visit the powder room, carry his plate to the sink, and pour himself what had to be his twenty-third glass of sweet tea that day. I had no idea how he didn't weigh 400 pounds of pure cane sugar.

"Don't push it, gimpy," I said, sliding into the next chair.

"Don't mother hen me." Then he added, "Please."

"Mother hen is not a verb to me. It's a lifestyle. You should know that by now... you know everything about me."

"I bet I don't," he said.

Was it a dare? Should we engage in Paul and Jessie Trivia or maybe get out the Taboo game? Was this a date? Did I need to come up with something to impress him?

My thoughts were interrupted by his laugh. "Chill, Jessie. I just meant... there are still many layers and themes to explore."

"Spoken like a true professor," I said, still in a fog. "Paul, we have talked all day long to only each other for a whole lot of days. And then, we were together for the worst moment of our lives. There can't be that many surprises."

He stiffened for a moment. I hadn't meant to bring up That Day so casually, but the shock of it had worn off. The shock that was left was how shockingly it had woven into the fabric of life. I was Randall's wife. I had a big family and steady support system nearby. And my husband had a heart attack and died in the ensuing car wreck with one of our friends. That was my life.

And now that friend's husband was sitting in my kitchen at 8 P.M., waiting for me to say something, what? Surprising? Flirtatious? Amazing?

"Well, let's try," he finally said, a little less playfully. He drained and set down his glass. "Tell me one thing about yourself that I don't know."

"Oh geez," I answered. Maybe we could just email each other some "20 Things About Me" lists and be done with it. Coke or Pepsi? Football or baseball? Sad widows or inappropriate harlots?

"Okay. Ummmm... I had my appendix out when I was 13. And my gallbladder when I was 31."

"Cliché," he retorted. "And I knew that."

"Fine. I... have... never been camping..."

He rolled his eyes. "You're not even trying."

"Then *you* go!" I said. "Wait. Okay. Back in 1999, Maggie and I went to a talk show taping, and we had passes to meet the host... a particular handsome bald one, beforehand. And well, to this day, Maggie says they had an AOL instant messenger affair. Like, he legit got divorced the next year, but she refused to move with the girls to New York, so, they moved on." Yeah, I heard myself. He'd probably already heard that story, too. It was kind of infamous in our circle.

"That is *ridiculous*," Paul laughed. "And I said something about *you!*"

"Whatever!" I snapped again, getting up from the table and starting to put stuff away. It was my signature deflective move. "You are one of the only people who shared ample non-momming time with me in the past decade-and-a-half. I'm telling you, you already know it all."

He started to reply, and I cut him off. "Seriously," I said. "What fascinating tidbits do you want to know? That I only use white bath towels because my sixth-grade teacher said that was the best way to check for spiders? That I wore a size seven shoe until I had Brittney, and now I wear a size nine? That I rewatch the show *Brothers & Sisters* over and over again on Hulu, even though it's now probably not even relevant and certainly not groundbreaking, but I love that there's a big family and all the kids love their mom, and even though she's not always a great problem solver, she's *always* throws gourmet dinners? But now it feels weird because the dad died, and my kids' dad died, and when did we stop being the people in the primes of our lives and become the *older* people whose husbands and wives are dead?

"Am I supposed to enjoy that show now? I mean, Nora Walker... she dates. She *dates*! Is that accurate? Is that what we're trying to do? Because I don't even know what dating means in the 21st century, much less for us. I mean, my grandson is 17. *He* dates! I hang out with you and eat Chex Mix and try to decide which picture of the Great Pyramid would look best on a timeline. I don't know how to date. Are you really trying to say that's what you want to do?"

At this point, my counter was pristine, and I'd wrung out my silicone sponge so much that it was practically dry. I dropped it in the sink and looked at Paul. He was smiling his unapologetically twinkly smile at me. I was sufficiently unnerved.

"That's my girl," he said.

"Are we trying to date?" I asked with a sigh.

"It sounds like we're going to try watching some Hulu, mostly so I know what the hell you're talking about," he said. "But if you want me to take you to dinner first, I will."

"We just had dinner."

"Then I'll take you for ice cream and make it respectable," he chided. "Or we can go to the store for some Chex Mix."

"You're supposed to take it easy for *two weeks*." I reminded him and walked back to his side. He took both my hands this time.

"You're doing it again," he murmured.

I let myself return every ounce of that stare. I drank in those intense eyes, familiar, sad, hopeful, hurting, tired, excited. Everything was there. I loved knowing him. I could even freely say I loved *him*. But it couldn't possibly be that simple.

"I don't know how to date," I said. "So you're going to have to let me take care of you."

Chapter Five

We really *didn't* know how to date, as proved by us waking up together, shortly after dawn, on the couch. Paul was fully stretched out on his back, both feet on my hip, as I was curled against the other end and would probably need a chiropractor to get fully uncurled.

We spent the first few moments of the day in startled silence, and then some sheepish quipping ensued. I went through my mental hostessing checklist to keep total awkwardness from setting in, but once Paul consumed eggs-over-medium, ham, toast, Advil, and one-half of a third cup of coffee, he sought the inevitable:

A shower. He's survived the previous day with only a Whore Bath™ (thank you, Maggie, for my most often-used inappropriate slang term of all time). We take a lot of those down south, using wet wipes and deodorant. Otherwise, our water bill would skyrocket, and we'd smell even worse every July. Even Paul had to admit he needed some help with the real thing.

He tolerated a series of questions from me about how he'd managed this in the past, his pain level, and his degree of modesty. With four or five kids of a wide age range running around the house for so many years, degrees of nudity were kind of a casual given to me, but I'd not gotten that vibe from him, nor from the Jameson household in the past, and if I stopped to think about it for too long, this was pretty different than the time Sam had broken a rib three days before his wedding.

Even so, a few minutes later, with my eyebrows silently raised, my heart racing, offering no eye contact whatsoever, and Paul clad in his T-shirt and a towel around his waist, I had gotten down the removable shower massager and set it on the built in bench, duct-taped a grocery bag around his boot, and exited to wait outside the partially-opened door, on my bed with a magazine. I heard Paul huff and puff a little as he got settled and then giggled as he started singing, "Amarillo by Morning," editing a line to be "broke my leg in Surfside Beach." He was usually decent in a rewrite-the-lyrics contest. This was not his best effort.

I got lost in a *Southern Living* article about freezer cooking for two. Before I knew it, Paul emerged in loose, gray linen pants, a fresh black shirt, and no plastic bag. His hair was damp, and he smelled like my pineapple shower gel and *Paul*. He gave me a small but fully charming smile.

"I did it."

"Yaaaay!" I teased back, clapping. "Amazing what good coffee and a ginormous, geriatric shower can do!"

"Yeah, well..." He sat on the chair facing the bed. "I hate to keep asking you for things, but you can probably take me home. I really think I've got this walking thing mastered."

"Oh." I was glad he was feeling better, if he really was and wasn't just faking it, but I knew he packed clothes for at least two days. Maybe it was my smell in the morning. Morning smells were also new territory for us.

"Sure," I said, all fake nonchalance. "Just let me change and—"

"It doesn't have to be right now, Jess," he interrupted. "I just thought Maggie was coming over today anyway."

"Oh," I repeated. We hadn't really talked about whether he was going to go somewhere else while Maggie was there, helping me to start sorting Randall's clothes, but the assumption made sense. Meanwhile, the whole situation was having a terrible effect on my ability to make words. "Yeah."

"Maybe we could have dinner later?" he said. I tried not to read the sunniness in his voice as condescension, like he could tell I was disappointed and wanted to patronize me. This was ridiculous. I was newly shattered over the loss of *my husband,* and here I was entertaining the lovely angst of a potential crush.

"Paul..." I carefully folded the corner of my page – recipes for Shepherd's Pie and Cranberry Pork Roast – trying to think of what to say. He helped me.

"We probably have some work to catch up on too, right? Any feedback from Rachel yet?"

"All she sent me was a quick email that she'd have notes in a few days and the end was in sight."

"Thank God for that," he sighed. "I promise I'll read everything before you come back over. And then maybe I can make *you* dinner."

I rolled my eyes. "I think you shouldn't push it. Just because you managed to bathe doesn't mean you need to be hoofing around all day. Is that why you want to go home, to mow the lawn? Retile the bathroom?"

He rolled his eyes, too. "This makes me nuts. No. No chores. Well, I do have stuff to get done. Setting up my God-bless-ed PT appointments is one. Reading over your articles is another. Not that you need me for this, at all."

"What? Yeah, I do! You should be writing it anyway, not me. I'm not even a real teacher."

When Randall and I had gotten settled in South Carolina, and long before the girls were born, I had finished my English education degree at Coastal, a class or two at a time while I worked the odd tutoring jobs and occasionally wrote for some local magazines. However, when it was time to set up my student teaching - the dreaded 15 weeks of legal free labor required for certification - I discovered I was pregnant with Mikayla. It had taken us years to conceive, and it took me all of 30 seconds to tearfully tell Randall that I didn't want to put a baby in day care full time, and I definitely didn't want to have such an important and challenging professional experience while I was *growing the miracle of life!* He shook his head and as always, told me he trusted my instincts. So, I was trained as a teacher in every way but the practical; hence my job experience in after-school centers and the Oakley Homeschool Table.

Paul had two Master's degrees: one in Social Science Education and one in Administration, and enough extra credits to equate to an educational doctorate. He had skipped the dissertation when he got twitchy in the eighteenth year in the career. But still, to me he was Principal Paul, and through the years, well before he was sleeping on my couch, I felt like an insecure partner, making it up as I went along.

"Maybe when we're finally finished, you can be done making

nonsensical statements like that," he said pointedly. "Anyway, you're the writer, and this transitions thing is *your* story, Jess. It's Jessie-in-a-box. You really don't need me for it at all."

I felt myself blushing a bit. "Thanks... but I do. Your ideas always bring everything together."

He carefully stood then, one hand on my desk. He studied me for a minute, and then limped three steps to the bed and sat right down next to me.

My heart was pounding, and my stomach was swirling. I tried not to breathe him in, but the scent of him next to me, clean and an inch away, stirred me, threatening to draw me nearer, and so I scooted a bit away from him, tilted my head away, even closed my eyes.

And then I felt his hand on my face.

"Look at me, Jessie."

I couldn't. I actually shook my head in protest. He was moving again, methodically arranging his feet onto the bed, one shod in black Brooks, one stabilized in his bulky boot. It was all really the opposite of sexy, me with my hair in a top knot, gray running shorts, and a Bike Week 2011 tank top. Maybe the silliness of it all would override the intensity. I opened my eyes at that thought, but it was a mistake. He'd closed the gap between his face and mine. I could feel his pepperminty breath. I saw his hand move back toward my face, and this time, I rested my cheek against it, closing my eyes again.

"*Look at me*, Jess..."

I did, knowing he was right there, knowing there was absolutely no return from this moment, and I was, at the moment, okay with that. I invited the feel of his lips brushing mine, gently at first, and then with more pressure, more longing. My lips parted to invite him further, and his tongue traced them before darting into my mouth, lingering. Yeah, we were lingering. I managed deep breaths at every pause, wanting to inhale the scent of him like a vapor and let it intoxicate me.

"Paul..." This time, my hands went to his face. I held it close to mine, pressing my lips more firmly against his. One, or maybe both of us, moaned.

"Jessie." His voice sounded much more grounded than how I felt.

It was too much.

I forced myself to break away from him and collapsed backwards onto the pillows.

"I don't know..." I said, as though he asked me a question. His response was a low "Mmmmmm..."

After a moment, he began to shift and scoot again until he was lying down next to me. My arms were resting parallel to my sides. Randall always found it amusing when I lay that way, like a corpse, another thought that just felt inappropriate anymore. Paul picked up my left hand and held it tightly.

"You don't have to know anything," he said. He kissed my hand and then my lips again. Then he laid his head right by mine. "Let's just rest a minute."

#

"JESSIEEEEE!" The voice sounded closer than a dream. *Oh shit.* "Jess? Oh! Um... hey."

Maggie was standing in the doorway. Somehow, it was 11ish in the morning. Paul and I had fallen back asleep like two toddlers taking our pre-school nap, and there was absolutely no hiding it from her.

Fluidly, Paul removed the arm he had draped across my waist, rolled over, sat himself straight up, and breezily ran his hands through his hair. "Hey Maggie," he said. God. I always knew he was charming, but I found the Hugh Jackman-level of it all astounding. New light.

"Heeeeey..." she said, looking at me.

"Um, Paul's hurt and needed some help, and his girls were all pretty busy with things..." I started.

She just nodded, her look of bewilderment turning rapidly to amusement. "Anything I can do?" she asked, matching Paul's nonchalance rather than my veiled panic. "You okay, Jess?"

"Me? Oh yeah." I had already sprung to a stand, grabbed my hoodie from the desk chair, and crammed my feet into a pair of Tom's, because having shoes on always made me feel more in control. "Paul, you need help getting, um, up?"

By the time I got the words out, he was taking Maggie's hand and rising slowly to greet her with a hug, the big damn teddy bear. I rolled my eyes and felt my stomach roll as well. I never thought I'd be turning back to junior high levels of romantic inclination in my 57th year.

"Jessie was just going to bring me home," he started explaining. "I have at least two weeks of hobbling and Uber-ing ahead of me."

"Well, I can take you," Maggie replied cheerfully. "Or Jessie can get herself together while we visit, and she and I can drop you off on the way."

I looked at her murderously. "Are we going somewhere? I thought we were—"

She shushed me with a hand wave. "Just a few little stops. Get dressed. I'll entertain the patient for you."

Paul was barely suppressing laughter, and Maggie had already started walking him to the kitchen. I turned to the bathroom and could hear her pouring more coffee and telling Paul all about the benefits of cypress oil. Just a random Wednesday morning. Nothing to see here...

It took ten minutes for me to apply some foundation, eyeliner, mascara, illuminator (for crying out *loud)* and pull on my uniform of jeans and a sleeveless shirt. I chose blue instead of black so we wouldn't look dressed alike, for God's sake, shoved my sunglasses on my head, and grabbed my purse for what would surely be the most awkward outing thus far of my new life as (an apparently dating) widow.

#

Throughout two consignment stores, lunch at the tea room, and the start of Project Reorganize My Closets before Maggie drilled me: Why in the world had Paul spent the night, and how in the world did we end up in my (marriage) bed that morning?

It was simple enough, if slightly scary, to fill her in on some details, starting with the beach and ending at her arrival. She didn't buy my faux calm for one second, and she wasn't wasting a day off on my non-answers to her pointed questions.

"It just doesn't make sense that he wouldn't go stay at Danielle's if all he needed was some nursing," she said, adding two old scarves to my Goodwill pile. "I mean, what's he going to do tonight? They don't put you in those God-awful boots unless you did a number on yourself, even at our age."

I scrunched my nose at the age phrase and shrugged at her question. "Apparently he's a pro at this. And you know as well as I do what this time is like. I mean, Tony didn't die, but you certainly didn't want Moni and Nora in your business during the divorce..."

"I don't see the grounds for comparison here. Do you want this hat?"

I took the black newsboy cap from her hands, saw it was wool, almost had a hot flash just thinking about it, and threw it on the pile. "I just mean... he still has mourning and processing to do, and he doesn't want to do that with his daughters all up in his grill, grown or not."

"But he can mourn and process with you, while you're mourning and processing? And his hair was wet, Jessie. How'd he mourn and process in your shower if he can't walk unassisted?"

"We worked that out," I mumbled, and dumped three more hats on the pile. "Why do I buy hats? I don't wear them, like ever. Don't let me buy any more."

She picked up a straw beach hat from the top and tried it on. "If I'm going to stop you from doing anything, it ain't got nothing to do with hats..."

"What does that mean?"

"Three *weeks*, sister. I mean, you're a grown-ass woman, but this is *fast*."

"We didn't sleep together. Well, we obviously *fell* asleep together, but nothing is happening. Nothing unusual. We've seen each other almost every day forever. We're just continuing and... and, expanding. Maybe? I don't know!"

The next hat I took out of my closet was Randall's, a Vols baseball cap. The bright orange of University of Tennessee was one of my least favorite colors in the world, yet it had been a staple in our home forever. He loved that team. I loved him. What was I doing?

"I'm not over him," I said softly, more to myself, and maybe to Paul, than to Maggie.

"I know that, Jessie" she said. "Paul is like, the greatest guy. Spend all the time together you want. All I'm saying is, be careful. There are emotions flying all over the place right now, both of yours, all the kids'. You don't know how you're going to feel in a week, or three months, much less forever. Just... proceed with caution."

I nodded, glancing at my bed. Twenty-five days ago, it had been *our bed*, mine and Randall's, and we'd unashamedly loved it. He would brag on it whenever he returned from a trip. I would collapse gratefully into it at the end of long days of parenting. And now, its teal and red and white quilt was still wrinkled from the spot where Paul had slept that morning, and I wondered how I could be missing them both so much at that exact moment.

Chapter Six

There wasn't much time for more of anything, cautious or not, in the next few days. Maggie and I worked on the closets into the evening, and Paul didn't text until around 8 P.M., apologizing that he slept through dinner. It worked out; Rachel had indeed sent her first round of edits, enough for two solid days' worth of work for me, and I wasn't done at the end of them.

Paul spent those same two days in an NSAID stupor *and* under the watchful eye of Julie, who had cut her trip to Savannah short to help her dad. But when her working schedule resumed (she was an OB nurse), his physical therapy was scheduled to begin. After a nearly exhaustive text exchange (the kind when you know you should have cut it out and actually called the other person about a dozen messages ago), we agreed that he would take an Uber to the clinic for his first appointment, but I would pick him up and we'd work that Friday afternoon.

I got out of the car to make sure he could get in okay, and though he did kiss my cheek, he was quiet. I remembered how grueling the first days of PT were after Sam, my accident prone one, had torn his ACL in high school. Paul grunted when I asked how he was doing, and he had dozed off by the time I reached the Sonic Drive-Thru. I ordered a limeade and a sweet tea and headed to his house.

Whatever that crazy thing is that wakes us when we're home, it worked. Paul opened his eyes in the driveway, and he also completely melted me with his groggy smile. We headed to the office, where he settled himself in the recliner and I sat at the iMac. For three hours, we talked through the all suggestions from Rachel and the fixes still to be made, and where we were going to spend our evening.

#

We ended up spending it 30 feet away, in the living room. Paul was hurting and worn out. To ease the blow to his man card and my lack of readiness for questioning public eyes, I insisted I didn't feel like going out either. So after we ate BLT sandwiches for dinner, I brought him an ice pack and gingerly placed his feet on my lap, pretending to admire his impressive bruise. He rolled his eyes at the "coddling," but his grateful smile superseded the gesture.

We were catching up on that week's *The Walking Dead*, and I felt completely out of bounds in Leah's living room. Everything about it was colored with her touch, from the placement of the white and yellow throw pillows on the white sofa to the whimsical elephant coffee table (which Paul had always and relentlessly made fun of). For whatever reason, even though Randall's memory was never far from me, I felt much more comfortable with Paul at my house. I wondered if it was the same for him, but when I looked at him, he was intently watching the latest mass-zombie-killing and angsty aftermath.

The show ended without me having any real idea of what had happened to Rick Grimes, et al, and I gently rose from the couch.

"Where are you going?" he asked.

"Home. You need to rest."

He grimaced. "That hour and a half the other morning was the best sleep I've had in a month. Of Sundays."

I ignored his cheesy reference, surprised that it *had* been almost a month. And that hour and a half *with him on my bed* was somehow almost all I had thought of for the past two days. "I don't... I mean, is there anything I can do to make you more comfortable?"

Paul closed his eyes and scrunched up his nose, mimicking my signature think-it-over response. Then he looked at me, in the pleading way that was my undoing.

"Let me come back there with you?"

"I thought... I mean, you *can...*" Yep. Articulation abilities lost again.

His eyes were open just enough to peer at me. "You're practically asleep now." I said.

"I guarantee you I am not. If you pack a bag for me, we can scoot out quicker."

I sighed. "I think you should be still for tonight. Maybe tomorrow..." My nonchalant tone of voice sounded ridiculous even to me, because I wanted him to come, but I didn't want to say it.

"Jessie." A different tone in his voice alarmed me, and he reached for my hand. "Does the concept of waiting for tomorrow not scare you, at all?"

"Paul..." I realized the tone was fear, and I blinked away what threatened to fill my eyes.

He was right. It was far too easy to be distracted with work and the house, his injury and my plans for Sunday dinner with the kids. I was not pausing for the kind of reflection that he was clearly having. I was not letting how our lives had just changed influence how they *would* change.

Wordlessly, I went to his (and Leah's room). His duffel bag was sitting on the floor by the closet. I found his essentials as quickly as I could. I looked at their bed, draped in white and cream with touches of midnight blue. It was pristinely made, and I wondered if he had slept in it at all that week. I also wondered what exactly I thought I was doing, not only planning another slumber party with another man (*Paul, it's* Paul, my heart insisted), but knowing full well it would involve not the couch, but my marital bed.

Randall was gone, but was he actually gone? How gone from a life can someone be after 35 years of sharing everything together? And how would Leah feel, knowing her husband was looking at me the way he was, sleeping next to me, kissing me?

I swiped at the stray tears that had escaped. Paul wasn't at all gone. He was here, close, and I couldn't be with Randall, and Paul couldn't be with Leah, but maybe it was okay for us to be together.

\#

It was after 10 when we got home (*my home. Jeez)*, and I had him get comfortable on (in?) the bed while I showered. I directed him to what used to be "my side" of the bed. I could sleep anywhere, but Randall always had to have the left, facing outward. I decided to take that half over. It seemed a reasonable compromise for someone else lying next to me, even though it meant sacrificing the ocean side.

Why are you sacrificing anything for something that doesn't exist anymore?

I ignored that voice. It seemed so callous and rude.

But sleeping next to a new man isn't?

I didn't like that voice any better.

So I shaved my legs, and I slathered on my expensive Moroccan lotion. I wore yoga pants instead of my usual shorts and a sports bra layered beneath my tank top. I was a bit worried that a hot flash might make me spontaneously combust, but then again, that would solve several issues. All the thinking served to delay my exodus back into the bedroom.

"Hey," he said softly when I finally came to him. The bedding was pulled back, but he lay uncovered in dark green athletic shorts and a white undershirt.

"Hey," I answered, setting my tea mug on the nightstand. "This is weird, Paul."

He laughed tentatively. "You're overthinking, Jess."

"Really? You have no sense of unease about this?"

"I have a sense that we are going to have this conversation over and over again until *you* don't have unease about it."

"Touché," I replied. "Just... what about Leah?"

I expected a more dramatic reaction to her name, but his steady voice remained so. "I love Leah. We had a full, challenging, wonderful marriage. And now it's over."

"You're still married," I said, nodding toward the ring on his left hand. He looked at it too.

"In some ways," he murmured. Then he switched his very

steady gaze to me. "But we said until death do us part. And Jessie, they're... dead."

He let it hang there for a pause, like I needed to process it all again. Maybe I did.

I met his eyes, signaling he could continue. "It's an ugly word and a terrible time, but how can you be disloyal to a memory? We can't change what happened, and we're... left..."

"Left," I echoed. I felt like I was watching someone else slide into bed next to him and pull the covers over us.

"You always sleep with the balcony door open?" he asked with a smile.

"Randall drew the line at 59 degrees, I drew mine at 79." That made me smile. It was a constant debate for hot-natured me and my husband.

"He was so..." Paul trailed off. "So funny. He so loved you. Jesus, Jess, I get it. All of it. All the things you aren't saying. It's just that... we are still *here*. And I... also... love you."

My insides were absolutely quavering. I didn't know how I would ever manage to go to sleep. I only knew that Paul beckoned me closer and I rested my head on his chest and listened. He was ready to talk, about sorrow and chaos and the circle of life and new dreams and how I looked with my hair pulled away from my face. And I was ready to let him.

#

My initial observation in the morning was that nighttime, bizarre as it was, had been easier. Things were quiet and of course dark, and we were both free from the expectations of the outside world and our sizable families. Paul seemed to sleep well, but I was pretty restless, and when 6:30 rolled around, it was almost a relief for me to get the coffee started, take Cash for a short walk on the shore, and come back to check on Paul's status.

He was sitting up in the bed, looking adorably rumpled and scrolling through his phone. He grinned at me and said, "Beach?"

"Of course." I kicked my shoes back off and handed him a mug.

"I could get used to this," he said, taking a sip and making that coffee-noise addicts often utter upon the first taste.

"Yeah, well... I feel like we're in the twilight zone, or a pretend vacation. You have stuff to do today?"

"Hmmm. Well, I don't have to go back to the Annihilator until Monday afternoon. My participation in the Ironman Golf Tournament is obviously cancelled. I said no to Danielle's offer to rent a scooter so I could hold the baby and hang with them at the farmer's market, and I will probably be able to walk on the beach with you again just in time for the tourists to take it over like fleas on dung, *next* summer. So... not much. Maybe I'll lie here all day and watch Discovery Crime and you can bring me snacks."

His good humor was addictive like always. I found myself settling back in against the pillows. "That's a good plan. I'm in," I said, relieved he was going to take it easy. "I actually planned a quick run to the farmer's market myself. Want me to bring you back something? Or invite Danielle and Matt and the kids over here?"

Paul scoffed. "It's so pointless this time of year. Won't be anything there but hipster moms and elderberry syrup. And please, no. We definitely have some time before we get *there*."

The mere thought of getting our kids involved in... whatever this was... made my stomach feel sour.

"I'm getting eggs," I said. "Quiche for Sunday supper tomorrow."

"Sounds great," he said. His eyes went back to the screen for a second. Then he admitted, "I guess I wish we actually were in the twilight zone. And you could have supper with me tomorrow, and it could just be us for a minute..."

"It's definitely easier," I murmured. He put down his phone and I automatically scooted closer to him, this time letting him rest his head on my shoulder.

"We probably need to just get it done. Like a Band-Aid," I added. "Unless you want to wait and sneak around."

"Not even a little bit," he answered. "I want you to have tomorrow with your family, and I'm sure I'll be with mine. But Monday, we have work to do, and then maybe you can drive me back to PT and cook us dinner, and we can fall asleep right here again. And somewhere in there we will figure out a way to tell them."

I was quiet. I liked the plan. I liked his certainty. I liked that he was ready to let me take care of him a little without negotiation. But seriously, "And what to tell them?" I asked, stroking his back and deciding supermarket eggs would be just fine.

He nestled his chin against me. "That life gave us a tornado four weeks ago, and this is where it threw us."

Chapter Seven

After a day balanced between welcome, communal rest and unavoidable errands, and History Channel versus the Food Network, I was near-mournful as I dropped Paul back off at his house late that night. He held me against him for an extra-long moment in the driveway, and I was startled at the pang of regret I felt watching him make his way inside.

We'd decided that with Sunday being church and family time, it would be too complicated for both of us to spend the night together. We also decided that we'd warm up everyone by mentioning the extra time we'd been spending together and leave it at that. It was practical, since he couldn't drive, and we were working. And, I told myself, it was also not *that* surprising and therefore shouldn't be traumatic for anyone. The rest of the reveal could wait; at that point, it barely felt real to me.

I was comfortably in my element the next day, setting out two pans of strata as soon as I got home from church and going to work on cranberry orange scones and dark chocolate brownies. Everyone would start rolling in around one, and I preferred to have most of the work done before they arrived, so I could enjoy them.

Brittney was there first, setting a 6-pack of some kind of cane sugar soda on the counter and attempting to hug me as Cash jumped on her. "How's it going, Mama?" she said in my ear. I pulled away to look at my strawberry blonde girl and smiled with all the newfound excitement that was in my heart.

"I'm actually pretty good, Brit," I answered.

If she thought that was odd, she didn't let on. She poured us each some ginger ale over ice and filled me in on her week, one of her first in a new position at the tourism bureau. She was hired to write copy and handle all their social media, and she found it fulfilling and amusing to answer comments and inquiries about show discounts, ocean bacteria, motorcycle helmet laws, and bed bug reports. I was so glad she liked it. It sounded horrifying to me.

She was in a middle of a story about a health inspection gone array at a seafood buffet when David crashed in. He'd gotten into town Saturday but stayed at his friend's, and now he had a laundry bag slung over one shoulder and his hideous orange Crocs in his other hand.

"Ew, David," Brittney screeched as he kissed both of our cheeks. "You need to stop driving barefoot! And stop wearing those fugly shoes!"

He grunted and grabbed a scone out of the basket on the table. "Why? You don't share my gas pedal."

"It is kind of dangerous," I said. And then I thought, *why?* I mean, it seemed like a perfectly maternal thing to say, but I had no idea whether driving without shoes was even a thing.

"It's legal in all 50 states, Mom," he assured me. *Amazing he knows that but forgets that Thanksgiving is the fourth Thursday in November.* Then he noticed his favorite person in the world wasn't in the room. "Where's Sam?"

"I assume on the way," I answered, setting two kinds of hot sauce on the counter. At that moment, Sam's nine-year-old daughter Summer came slipping through the door. She went right to her Aunt Brittney for a bear hug and then presented me with a bouquet of freshly-picked magenta azaleas.

"They're going to die in a few hours, Mimi," she said matter-of-factly. "But we should put them in water anyway. A Mason jar is good." She grabbed a blue canning jar from my stash without waiting for my response and prepared the bright centerpiece for the table.

They all filed in in the next few minutes. Sam and Abby, bearing a huge garden salad, were followed by Travis and his six-year-old brother Jacob. And Mikayla and Altan were last, setting their bottles of champagne and orange juice down before wrapping up the greetings.

I received all their embraces and started mixing and passing mimosas, marveling at the already near-empty basket of scones (*double that one next time*) and at the volume, the most normal it had been *since*. I smiled as Sam stood next to me and slung an arm around my shoulders.

"You doing okay, Mama?" he asked quietly.

I looked at my firstborn and wondered if maybe he would understand what I was soon going to bestow on them, even if the rest of them didn't. After all, he understood better than any of them what it meant to choose your family. Many years ago, given the opportunity to connect with his biological father, he'd said the ancestry websites told him all he needed to know, and Randall was all the dad he needed to have.

I wasn't totally delusional though. This was so different, so I stopped even attempting to fool myself. I just answered Sam as I had Brittney: "I'm doing really well," I said, but he wouldn't let it end there. He started peppering me with questions about the hospital bills for Randall, the status of the car insurance payout, whether the landscape guy was coming by to trim the palm trees that week, and how my last project with Paul was coming along.

Abby and Mikayla walked over to the counter to join us. I dutifully answered his questions in chronological succession, thoughtful when I got to the last one.

"Everything is coming along," I said. "We had some catching up to do this past week, of course, but now it's mostly me writing and Paul...consulting... which is good."

"Oh yeah, Julie said he broke his leg or something. Jeez," David said, rummaging in the fridge.

"It's almost ready, son," I said, curiosity peaked. Since when did he randomly talk to Julie?

"Yeah, Danielle posted a picture on Facebook from church this morning," Abby added. "Christian was trying to use Paul's crutch."

Oh yeah. No one needs to actually *talk*. I snickered. Paul might just hate that being out there as much as he probably hated using the crutch. He was basically Facebookless (I ran his "page," but there wasn't much on it) and damn proud of it. I had gone to the earlier church service and missed them.

"He's fine," I said. "Just a bad sprain that has him out of commission for a few weeks," I added. "He can't drive just yet, so I'll be taxiing him some while we try to get this deadline met." There. That was honest and innocent enough. Hopefully no one asked how it happened.

"What happened?" Mikayla asked. "Freak golf accident?"

That would have been a great cover story, but Paul and I had agreed not to lie. "Actually, we were over here, on the beach the other day. Some idiots didn't fill in their really big hole. He just missed a step. So yeah, a freak accident." The oven dinged. "It's ready!" No one came back to the subject, thankfully.

We'd gotten Sunday supper down to a pretty scientific level of chaos. I had given up bringing food to our big farmhouse table, seating for 12, and always left everything on the kitchen counter. Everyone made their own plates and settled themselves. As we tucked in, Jake told us how excited he was about his new baseball team and Summer chimed in about Travis' prom plans with Cali. Travis, after swatting her on the shoulder, gave us the obligatory update that school was fine, golf team was fine, serving up Heaven's chicken was fine. Altan and Mikayla talked about their kitchen remodel, and I panicked for a minute when Brittney suggested they eat dinner at my house every night until it was done.

"Look at Mom's face," David chided. "She is so done having us in the house all the time."

"I am not..." I protested, somewhat weakly.

But he kept going. "My spring break is in a week, Mama. Do you need me to camp out at Sam's instead?"

Sam looked a little panicky at that, while Abby shrugged. I

knew the feeling. One more person when you're in the trenches already doesn't make much of a difference.

"Don't be ridiculous," I said. "Mikayla, Altan, y'all can come here whenever you want." My son-in-law smiled at "y'all," as he always did. "Just... tell me first. I'm a little less regimented these days. No more Meatful Mondays." Randall had been a staunch carnivore who laughed his ass off when I suggested some budget and eco-friendlier meatless dinners. He coined a new term and took over planning something beef-based to start every work week. It still made me shake my head and giggle.

But the table went silent for a moment, as though we all had to pay homage to Randall at the mere thought of him. David was sitting in his chair, looking just like him. Mikayla and Travis looked close to tears, and Summer wordlessly got up and moved to my lap.

"Hey..." I said, giving her a squeeze. "It's okay, you guys. I miss Grampy, too. I didn't mean to make you sad."

"We're sad anyway," Mikayla said. "It *just* happened."

I felt a stab in my chest as I played with Summer's hair. "I just mean... it's okay to think of him and not be *sadder*. It's okay to think about when he was here and how he was and how he made us feel. And all I was trying to say is, for now, I'm not cooking a real dinner most nights. But you all are welcome here, whenever. Always. Okay?"

"Thank you," Altan said, holding Mikayla's hand. "We're getting by pretty well on Which Wich and Chipotle. Doesn't require the kitchen at all."

"You must really miss New York sometimes," Brittney murmured.

Mikayla smiled then and started in first on when they were planning to visit "the City," where she and Altan had *met cute* at Central Park, and continuing with a story of Randall once ordering "all the steak" for his Chipotle burrito bowl. The remember-whens took me out of myself and my thoughts of Paul to a different time, one that existed both one month and one whole lifetime ago.

#

It was after five when everyone left. After supper, we had walked to the beach, letting whosoever wanted play with the soccer ball and frisbees and Cash, and whoever else just sit and chat. I'd taken a lovely pier-to-pier walk with Abby, Brittney, and Mikayla, and we made plans for a girls' night out later in the week. I was looking forward to tapas and live music, but I also felt a little pang over not spending Thursday evening with Paul.

Sam hugged me for an extra-long time when the day was over, and I looked through his sunglasses into teary eyes.

"Oh, Bud..." I said softly.

He shrugged. "It's just never going to be the same."

"No..." I agreed lamely.

"It feels like I'm 16, and he's away on a trip, and we're just waiting for him. I feel like... I'm holding my breath for something that is never going to come."

Oh, how I understood.

"I guess I just thought we had a lot more time," he added, with finality.

"Of course you did. We all do that," I said, grabbing his hand. "So we miss him, but we... we live through the grief, and we learn from it, too... and... and... Sam, we just *live*. And try not to take time and togetherness for granted." I learned that when Mom had died. I wanted it to serve me well now.

"You're doing really great, Mom. We're all proud of you."

I felt another sharp pang - was it guilt? - at his words. But why? Why should I be ashamed of *how* I was moving forward? Were there rules for this? Who made them?

"Thanks, Honey. Your dad... he gave me everything I needed for this life right now. I have very few worries about the house or finances, for sure. But more so, he gave me confidence that I can do anything. Even get through this! So I'm going to keep living a full life, enjoying the beach and my work and my friends, and especially all of you, and, maybe... finding an adventure. That's what Dad wanted for all of us. Happy, brave, and free, right?"

Sam smiled at the shout-out to an old, somewhat tongue-in-cheek family motto, and swiped away the single tear that had escaped. I hugged my son hard and said a little prayer. I was shaking on the inside from my speech. Randall and I *had* created an amazing life, an amazing family. Paul had said we were strong enough to withstand a tornado, even if it had thrown us all around, and I just wanted to convince myself it was true.

#

Paul and I talked on the phone, with voices and not text messages, for over two hours that night, reliving the day spent with our respective families and sharing whatever else popped into our heads (including but not limited to freezer cooking for two, towel curls, the latest *X-Files* reboot, our office space, and what he would do with himself Thursday night). I *abhorred* phone conversations, but I missed him in an absolute, teenage-crush level sort of way. We both agreed about halfway through our conversation that it would have made much more sense for me to just come over for the evening, but somehow not being able to go a whole day apart seemed embarrassing. So instead, we decided to start our Monday in the morning rather than the afternoon, but he insisted on taking an Uber over to my house.

At 8 a.m., I was waiting for him in the little alcove where our elevator dumps onto the front balcony. He smiled almost shyly at me as I took a step and wrapped my arms tightly around his neck. He sighed softly and rested his head against mine. I finally had the word for how it felt to be near him. It was *peace*, and at that moment, I knew there was no turning back from it.

Chapter Eight

Thirty days after Randall died, I dreamed of him for the first time. I'm not even sure it was a real dream. It was more like an awareness, or maybe a memory. It was him, lying next to me in the bed. There was a pillow tossed between us, but his heat (I sometimes called him The Radiator) and his scent were there. I reached over with my foot to touch his leg. I reached over to thread my fingers through his. And at that moment, instead of the bare arms and broad torso I was used to feeling, there was a soft cotton shirt on a slighter frame. I jumped.

"Hmm? Hey! You okay?" Paul's voice broke through the quiet and my reverie. I was sitting up, my heart palpitating in my ears.

"Yeah. Yes. Just a dream. I'm sorry." I reached over consciously this time and smoothed his hair back. "Sorry I woke you."

"Come on. Still time to sleep," he mumbled, burrowing further into the covers. He'd been sleeping like a log, right there next to me, for the past few nights. But he'd already picked up on the fact that I was restless and rising early. I glanced at the clock. It was 5:36 a.m. I would try.

The thing was, it was Thursday. And tonight, we both had

plans to start breaking our families into the idea of us being together. Or spending time together. Or just being more than co-workers and friends.

No wonder I was dreaming of Randall.

Randall adored Paul, just like I did. They'd met at one of those free luncheons that companies hold to get new clients, and Randall, under some sort of quota for how many he had to attend in a year, actually liked them. They usually meant he was home for the whole week. Also, he loved seafood, and seafood buffets were the chosen cuisine of many coastal business luncheons.

Paul had just left education on some early-retirement situation (later he told us his views had become too liberal for the Christian school he was heading, but he was so beloved by most of the parents that the board used a cover story and asked him to resign quietly). He and Leah were managing vacation properties all around the beach, and while he was casually considering hiring a financial adviser from Randall's company to help them with investments, he was also looking into creating curriculum. They instantly bonded over crab legs and Gamecocks football before Randall decided I was a perfect fit for Paul's new endeavor.

Through the years, they traveled to football and basketball games together, sometimes with Sam and David or another combination of kids towing along. They bought boats the same summer, and promptly sold them two years later due to a low ROI (Leah hated theirs; our family was always running in six different directions and rarely used ours). They took a road trip together in September 2011, when Randall had a job out in New Mexico and our girls freaked out about him flying on the tenth anniversary of 9/11. They weren't best friends, per se, I guess, but doesn't that mean different things for men? If one of them needed something, the other was there. They'd argue over something political or NFL-related and then be laughing and ganging up on one of us 10 minutes later.

I asked myself for the thousandth time what Randall would think. Would he be happy that I wasn't alone? Would he be relieved that someone who already knew and cared about our family might be the one who would maybe be around them in the future? Would he think it was too fast, or inappropriate, or disrespectful? In my head, the assumptive answer to the latter was that *of course* he would; *everyone* would.

"Would an arbitrary time frame make it better somehow?" Paul had asked the night before at dinner. "Would it help if I was some strange guy you met online?"

"No. I don't know. Probably..." And that was the truth I arrived at all thousand times. "Are you telling me you have no reservations about how Leah would feel?"

And then he sighed, poured more sweet tea, and launched into a dissertation about how, "A," it was a completely moot point since Leah was feeling nothing, except for, according to our faith, peace and bliss and stuff, and "B," Leah had always teased that if Paul died first, she would be "shopping" at his funeral. Lord knows Randall had said pretty much the same thing on many occasions, and when I had young kids to care for, I kind of felt that way, too.

"I'm just having a hard time figuring out how to justify the why, the why *now*? It's not like I need to be taken care of," I had said. He looked at me with a disarming mixture of amusement and offense in his eyes. Were we already *needing* each other? I suppose we were. "I just mean, Paul," I said, with more patience and hopefully a softer bent to my tone, "It's not like I'm a young mama with kids to feed or even an old mom with a house payment. Everything is set. Technically, I probably don't even *need* to work anymore..."

"Except you do," he answered, eyes flashing a bit. "You need to work because it suits you. It gives you a creative outlet, a voice in something that matters to you and has mattered to your family, and it does put food in someone's mouth – yours. And all the people you still take care of, whether it's by feeding them an elaborate Sunday supper or taking them your flippin' freezer meals when they're sick or sending a contribution to every other Go Fund Me page you see. Those things are necessary because they *matter* to *you*."

It saddened me that he trailed off. Was I in the driver's seat here? Did I have the ability to give or withhold feelings of security to *him*? It was such a strange place to be sitting, years after I had dated anyone, years after choosing the last man I'd hope to date, who had rarely needed affirmation from me.

And *Paul* had rarely needed it either. Under stressful circumstances, he did appreciate being understood, and being shown compassion, but for the most part, he was confident of the people and relationships around him. His mother and Katy had been the only ones ever to undo him, far as I knew.

I didn't want to be in that company. If we were going to risk family drama and public scrutiny, I wanted everything about us being together to make him happy. Here are some tulips. Let us tiptoe through them.

"Yes. Thank you for framing it for me," I said, and thankfully, his eyes regained some of their twinkle. That phrase was my tried-and-true way of either saying "You're right," or simply, "Got it," whenever he helped me over a hurdle in one of our projects. One of his talents was being able to envision something – similes versus metaphors, documentaries versus historical fiction, The Civil War versus The War of Northern Aggression (bless his southern heart) – in a way that made perfect sense to the world, but typically, also made something in me respond, *Hallelujah.*

"I guess that's one of the reasons I need *you*," I continued, nervously pouring from my cup to one I still wasn't sure I had permission to fill. "Because I absolutely depend on and appreciate your perspective."

"And I love *you*," I whispered, there in the bed, 5:42 a.m. He didn't stir, but I hoped he'd heard me.

#

I dozed on and off for another hour or so, then Paul finally gave up and started the day with me. He made breakfast while I walked Cash, and it was sweet to return to blueberry pancakes and cinnamon coffee and the still-sleepy smile on his face. During those past few days, we seemed to be developing something like a routine. It was completely different from mornings with Randall, in which we did a semi-chaotic dance of readiness, even after all the kids were gone. We had different tastes in breakfast. We usually had online stories we were following (ahem, Fox News for him, social media for me), or seemingly urgent messages to answer. He liked listening to talk radio, and I preferred my carefully cultivated iTunes playlists.

Paul and I kept the background completely quiet. For the most part, our phones were put away. God knew I should have been hammering away at work every chance we had (best I could tell, I had eight topics left to cover), and Paul constantly had an issue or two happening with one of his rentals), but those first mornings we spent together were deliberately unhurried. It still took him extra care to get showered, and he was very methodical in getting his exercise and rest in every day, his goal having evolved from being macho to avoiding surgery at any rate.

"Thanks for making breakfast," I said, starting to clear the table.

"I haven't made pancakes since the twins were in middle school," he said. "It's kind of nice to be around a woman who isn't going to pee on a ketone stick while I load the dishwasher."

"Hmmm. I'm not really sure how to take that." Leah and all their daughters were positively skinny. But Leah was always watching something: carbs, sugar, all white starches, dairy, meat, all the above. I couldn't do it. I liked to cook, and I liked to eat, and having sweet cream in my coffee and a plate of nachos when I felt like it was worth the extra padding around my waist and hips to me. I walked several miles most days, I went to yoga at least twice a week; I was healthy and plenty strong. But all I could picture now was what Maggie made fun of me for calling my "fluff" - I was perfectly average everywhere, and perfectly round in the middle. I'd cop to having curvy legs and clear, youthful skin, my long, brown hair was still full and highlighted by the sun (and some burgeoning silver), and perhaps my breasts weren't nearly as saggy as they should have been (I thanked genetics and all the burpee contests I'd had with David and Travis during their inseparable elementary school years). But I tended to think of myself as a little sloppy (*boho* if I was trying to be cool). Yes, I always wore a little make-up. No, I was not the type who went to the store in jammie pants or skipped even a day of showering or went more than a few without shaving. But Leah always looked like she scooped an outfit off of Pinterest and buffed herself to a shine before leaving the house. She had a signature shoe style (opened-toed wedges for nine months of the year; pointed, two-inch booties for the winter) and nail color (rose gold, even before it was cool). I was not that and never would be.

"C'mon," Paul answered. "I'm not... I'm not comparing. You know, Julia Child said people who love to eat are the best people."

I scrunched up my nose. I loved that quote. Why did Paul even know it?

"That's quite a quote for a non-foodie," I said, scraping at the griddle.

"Are you mad?"

Damn him. Why did he always know everything? "I'm not," I answered, shaking my head in contrived protest.

"Then what are you?"

"I don't know." And I didn't.

"We talk about Leah and Randall plenty. Why are you bothered now?" He walked to the counter and refilled my coffee cup.

"I don't... know..." I sighed. "I'm just not anything like her."

He nodded, slowly, a very Mars vs. Venus look on his face. I almost felt bad. I was definitely uncomfortable, but I didn't want to make him feel like he needed to walk on eggshells. Plus, he hadn't actually said anything about my looks or Leah's.

"Well, there are some ways you two are alike." He was still speaking carefully. I put down my sponge and turned to him, now inches away from me at the counter.

I tilted my head to indicate my full attention, just a little worried about what was coming.

"You both love coffee slightly less than your children." Haha. "You are discerning critics of television, movies, and award shows. You both like funky earrings and a great pair of jeans. You both *usually* know when to stop."

"... a skill someone should share with you," I said, eyebrows raised, hand on his.

"Done with this?" he asked.

"Really am." I answered. "And I'm sorry. You... Leah was beautiful. And she was thin. And I am a woman who has never been thin and loves pancakes. So, I was just having a moment. You don't have to indulge me in moments like that."

He leaned forward and kissed my neck. Actually, he kissed my neck repeatedly and then sort of burrowed his face there. I sighed, putting my arms around him and pulling the rest of him as close.

"I don't mind indulging you," he said, the words vibrating off my skin.

I brought his lips to mine, with plans to linger. I suppose I didn't really mind either.

Chapter Nine

Number of the eight articles I completed on Thursday: Approximately one-third.

Number of naps Paul and I took: Two (one on hammock, one on couch).

Number of times he talked me out of cancelling my night out, plans to have The Conversation, and my phone service: Lost track.

#

Abby picked me up. She and Sam actually lived the closest, sort of. Everything outside of coastal Surfside Beach was basically 20 minutes away, whether it was because of old through roads or too much traffic. They were in the next coastal town south of us, Murrells Inlet, which wasn't on the coast of the ocean so much as it was on... an inlet... that was once Captain Murrell's, even though the locale name has no apostrophe. And technically, there was a town in between, Garden City, except it's not a *real* town. Technically, neither is Murrells Inlet. Don't even get me started.

Anyway, The Inlet was close enough that Sam's family could

feasibly drop by whenever they wanted, and vice versa. On and off for years, and during the first two weeks after Randall died, we took advantage of that often. Lately, not so much, and I was selfishly grateful.

Abby and I were meeting Mikayla and Brittney at an upscale southern comfort place where Randall would never eat, and Paul would eat (if we were actually dining in public) but complain about the price of things like deviled eggs topped with candied bacon and grits with goat cheese and pine nuts. This was the kind of outing that usually made me love having daughters. But I thought of Mikayla's tears at the dinner table just a few days before and couldn't imagine that my news wouldn't damper the thrill of a muscadine and Fireball brined pork chop.

On the way, Abby kept the conversation easy, telling me tidbits about Travis' planned "promposal" to Cali, Jacob graduating from T-ball to little league, and Summer's upcoming dance recital, where she was playing Belle from *Beauty and the Beast* and would get to wear a version of *that yellow dress!*

She asked how I was, in that somber, *it's okay to admit you're awful* kind of way. I stuck to my strategy from Sunday. "I'll be better when I get through with all these articles," I said. "The irony of writing about transitions is clever and all, but I'm kind of tired of talking about schooling. Kids, go. Parents, make them finish their crap. Isn't it that simple?"

"Good thing you're transitioning out of this medium," Abby snorted. "Though I'd love to have you write a How to Get Your Kids Through Standardized Testing Weeks. If I get one more call from the district reminding me that my children need food and sleep..."

We both laughed now, and then I answered her initial question because I knew she would ask again. "I really am doing fine, but I admit I wouldn't mind a little break from... just kind of everything."

"You do seem tired," she said. "Is there no way to put some of this off for a while?"

"Not really. We have just this and one simple, little companion book left on our contract. I think we both just want to get it done, move on."

Abby brushed a strand of dark brown hair behind her ear. "How's Paul doing?"

"Um..." Words, please don't fail me again, now. This should be an easy question. "He's doing okay, too. Itching to be driving again, working through a lot of legalities with his and Leah's properties and stuff."

"Sam thought he saw the two of you in your car last night," she said. Was that a breezy tone? I couldn't see her eyes, but was I imagining some prodding? "Did you guys go to Bible study?"

"Nooo..." I said, also aiming for breezy. "I picked Paul up from his therapy appointment, and we decided to grab some dinner. Just a quick burger. You know, they never eat at home..." *They. He. We. Oy.*

"It's nice you guys can do that," she said. "I guess some people would be uncomfortable or whatever, but you're pretty used to each other anyway."

"Mmm-hmm," I declared boldly, looking out the window. After all these years, I still couldn't decide whether I liked the pine or the palm trees better.

The rest of the ride, which wasn't long, was pretty silent. This confirmed to me that Abby was either feeling awkward about the Paul conversation, or she thought I felt awkward about it, and either way, that I was just insanely paranoid.

We walked into the restaurant and were told our party was already seated. I was pleasantly surprised to find a peach tea already in my place, and not only Mikayla and Brittney, but Maggie awaiting us.

Hugs, hugs, hugs, and "How did they get you here?" I exclaimed.

"I ran into Brit at the gym," Maggie answered, giving me a very knowing look. "And basically invited myself."

"You don't *need* an invite, ever, Aunt Mags," Mikayla added.

Maggie flashed a smile as we all got settled. I had told her exactly what I had planned for the evening, and her show of support was beyond welcomed. It was also good for her; since Nora and Moni lived in Charlotte, enjoying bigger city life, and she missed the energy our table was about to exude.

Small talk, small talk, small talk, and then we ordered our first round of appetizers. Excuse me, small plates. I rolled my eyes toward Maggie at the term. I seriously think every generation figures out new ways to make things a bigger deal than what they are by renaming them something punny or grandiose.

Kind of like you at this very moment, I thought. I would wait until the *physically small plates filled with appetizers* arrived and then get into it. I had rehearsed it and was afraid I'd lose my words, again, if I didn't hurry.

And so it was after we'd heard from Maggie about the 20-something female trainer that had flirted with her at the gym, from Brittney about the local banker who got fired for sexual harassment and came to the Chamber looking for job leads, and from Mikayla about the honeymooners who were caught, um, canoodling on a jet ski, when the fried pickles-okra-and-gator platter and the She Crab soup, appeared, I took first a big bite and then a big breath.

"So..." I started. "I kind of wanted to talk to you about something."

Maggie shoved a gator bite in her mouth and sat up straight. Abby folded her hands as if to focus more sharply, Brittney looked nonplussed, and Mikayla looked worried.

"Well, you know, Paul and I have, well, obviously had a very intense few weeks. The... aftermath, and then this deadline for us, and then Paul needing some extra help after his injury..."

I took a sip of tea. No one's expressions had changed. It wasn't obvious to them at all.

"I just... I don't really know how to say this, but, you know, Paul and I have been very good friends for a long time. We know each other very well, and we're blessed to have a comfort level that takes years to cultivate." I was in presentation mode, talking with my hands, wishing I had Keynote slides so the focus would be off my face. "And so, we've chosen to go with the flow that circumstances have swept us into."

Abby was nodding, still concentrating. Brittney was showing signs of a smirk, possibly because I ended a sentence with a preposition. Mikayla dropped her fork.

Maggie tilted her head and helped. "How would you characterize that flow, Jessie?"

I managed to look carefully at each of them but rested my

eyes on Mikayla. "We are... together. Spending time together. Just... being together."

"Like... what, Mama? You mean sleeping together?"

My eyes snapped back to Brittney. "Brit, there are multiple levels of togetherness. My generation, even before we were the old people, didn't jump straight into bed."

Mikayla full out started choking. Abby pounded her on the back and stared a bit incredulously at me. Maggie took a sip of her wine and silently shook with laughter a sister could shrug off, but a despondent niece would not appreciate.

"Anyway, it's not your business, Brit," I continued, trying to be serious and soothing and retain some sort of dignity. "And no, it's not like that." Yet. "I guess you could say, well, the word seems silly and we aren't exactly out on the town much right now, but I guess I'd describe us as dating."

"What?!" Mikayla dropped any pretense of holding it together. "Mama, I... how... I mean, how can you? Daddy..."

Abby and Maggie were now looking on sympathetically, as though trying to decide whether to diffuse the reaction. It was Brittney who surprised me. She put a hand on Mikayla's arm and leaned in.

"It feels fast, Mama, but... Paul?! Paul's great! Are you happy?"

Mikayla looked like she tasted sour milk but was trying to pretend it was a chocolate malt. I sighed.

"Oh Brit... Mikayla, honey. It's so complicated. I miss Daddy. That isn't even close to being accurate. I can't even describe how I feel. I imagine maybe like losing a limb. Daddy is a part of me and always will be, and I will always feel like there is part of me missing."

No one threw anything or yelled, so I continued. "Spending time with Paul does not change any of that."

"I just don't understand... What about Leah?" Mikayla exclaimed.

"Leah is gone," Maggie answered for me, softly, but directly.

"It feels disrespectful," Mikayla said. "Y'all were friends. They died in the same accident, doing something nice for you." Like I didn't know. "And it's been a month, Mama. One *month!*" Her hands were flying now, too. My girl. "I just can't believe you're telling us this like you're telling us you bought a new toaster. This is a very big deal!"

"Of course it's a big deal." I looked at Maggie. I wasn't sure I should actually ask for help, but I was kind of running out of things to say.

"Mikayla, your mom is showing nothing but respect by taking the time to share her heart with you."

"You have our support," Brittney said. It was quiet but swift. Mikayla gaped at her.

Abby hadn't said a word. I looked at her while my daughters engaged in their own silent sidebar.

"You do," she told me, with a subtle shrug. "You're always trying to make sure everyone else is happy, and Sam and I want *you* to be happy. You have a lot of life ahead of you. Live it. Dad would want you to."

I smiled at her with all the gratefulness I felt. She reached over and squeezed my hand. And then she tucked into her soup as though we had indeed just discussed toasters.

"Mom," Mikayla said, her voice no longer quavering. "This is so hard. Of course I want you to be happy. I just don't really understand. I mean, Brittney is right. We support you... we just... Paul isn't a replacement for Daddy."

I stared at my daughter, reaching deep inside to the part of me that used to know everything about her, the mood she would wake in, the clothes she would choose, how to order her meals, how to absolutely soothe every fear. All I could do was try.

"No one replaces your dad. Not in any way. Not for a second." I took a sip of my drink and nodded my affirmation. "But we are all free to add to our lives, at any time. I was not looking for this to happen. The fact that it is... it just feels like a gift."

It was Maggie who came in for the kill with a post-Frosé Jesus Juke. "No one should be alone if she doesn't want to be." We had to respect this wisdom from a woman who'd been jilted twenty-five years ago, stayed single, rocked her life, and basically only ever confessed a *little* bitterness to me, and maybe twice. "We all know God gives good gifts to His children. Your mama would be ungrateful and probably a little bit stupid to let this one pass her by."

Mikayla's tears spilled over at that point, as did mine. Maybe it would have been simpler, at one point in my life, to put aside what felt good to me for the sake of my children's feelings. I just didn't think I could do it this time.

The conversation certainly wasn't over, but I was done making statements. I flashed the "I love you" sign around the table and picked up my menu. "Now, what goes best with all the biscuits?"

#

The truth will set you free. At the very least, it will set your daughter-in-law at ease when the two of you are alone again. The drive back to my house with Abby was much more easygoing. Until we pulled in the driveway and I saw Sam's truck there.

"What did you do, Abby?" I said. I didn't think telling my sons would be as complicated as telling my daughters, but I was already tapped out on trying to express myself for the night.

"I promise, it's all good," she said. I had a feeling that the idea of Paul and me had been discussed between Abby and Sam prior to it being discussed around the table that night.

We got out of the car and before I could reach the top of the stairs, Sam was outside the door and heading toward me. For a moment, he looked like the trembling 20-year-old who had affirmed his life's direction to me 17 years before, but he wasn't. He was a grown man, and I had no idea what he was going to say.

"Mama," he said, wrapping me in his 6'1, barrel-chested frame. People were always taken aback that he wasn't biologically Randall's. Sam shared the same mountainous build, providing a place of refuge with every hug.

What a lucky woman I was.

There were no more words exchanged that evening between my first-born and me. He'd just given me his blessing, and I just realized how much I'd been needing it.

Chapter Ten

After Sam and Abby left, I called Paul, but got no answer. I decided to take a risk and drive to his house. Based on his inability to drive, he said I should have a key "just in case."

Dear Jesus. When I thought of that, it really did seem like we were moving at breakneck speed.

The house was dark when I pulled up, and I hesitated. It was possible he was out; he did have a life and didn't share every plan with me. It was also possible he was asleep, and I would scare the fire out of him letting myself in this late.

I tried to text one more time, and then, completely selfishly, I walked to the door and inside, where he was passed out on the couch.

Sigh. The TV was on and his phone was inches away from him on the coffee table, so I knew he must have been knocked out. I envied his ability to be unconscious in the midst of turmoil, but then, he didn't seem to be nearly as knackered by the potential misgivings of our families as I was.

I told myself he shouldn't stay on the couch and needed to be woken anyway.

"Paul..." I placed my hand on top of his, rubbing vigorously. "Paul. C'mon. Go to bed."

After a moment, his hand flicked upward, and he smiled, eyes still closed.

"Hmmmm..."

"You need to get off the couch," I said. "But I'll tuck you in bed if you want."

He opened his eyes narrowly and studied me. "You can take me home with you."

I looked away as things became clearer. It seemed more and more likely that he didn't sleep in the master bedroom at all.

I decided not to be sheepish this time. "You can always come home with me."

Now I had his full attention. "Dinner must have gone well?"

He struggled a little to sit up and grinned at me all through my recap of the evening, finally laughing a bit when I described Sam waiting for me at home. My eyes were brimming with tears. Though not all the way there, I felt somewhat unburdened.

"So what did you do tonight?" I asked, moving from the floor to a familiar position next to him, his feet in my lap.

"Well..." He cleared his throat. "Katy is in town, so I had dinner with the girls. Vivi included, thank God."

"Uh-oh... Is Katy upstairs?"

He rolled his eyes. "She's at Julie's. And it was fine. Not much different from your kids' reaction. Danielle was stalwart and mature and very cautiously pleasant. Katy basically said, *Duh*. I think she's secretly just relieved that she might not have to be the one changing my diapers someday." I winced at that. "But Julie... did not take it well at all."

"Didn't take it well, or had a meltdown?" I had a feeling.

"She thinks I'm being insulting to her mama, that you and I are obviously using each other for, and I quote, *cheap comfort masquerading as something better than booze or pills*. So, there's that. I guess you could trade me in for a few extra cups of your special tea every night and none the difference."

There was an air of nonchalance in his voice, but the undertones of hurt were not completely masked, not to me.

"I guess that sort of response is to be expected, somewhat," I said.

"I don't think I ever *expect* my offspring to be disrespectful to me." His hand shuffled his hair, his agitation increasingly visible. "And make no mistake: I don't believe we need their approval. These conversations are out of respect *for* them."

"That's exactly what Maggie said to Mikayla," I murmured. "But Paul, let's not kid ourselves. This is fast. For us to declare ourselves *in a relationship* a month later... that means there was some build up... that means it started even *sooner* after the accident. That's incomprehensible to *me* most of the time, and I'm in it. So I can have some empathy for Julie, and Mikayla, and anyone else who doesn't quite get it."

"Hmm." He shook his head but softened his tone. "Anyone else? I don't care. I mean, I *really* do not care. Our kids... fine. They can feel their feelings, and I'll respect that. But they still don't get a say. This is *us*. Our path. They have their whole lives ahead of them to make their own decisions, whether anyone agrees with them or not.

"And as for build up," he added. "There wasn't any, Jessie. Please try to get out of this mindset that we are doing something wrong. I *did* come to you. I wanted to see you and talk to you and be comfortable with *you*. I'm not going to try to put arbitrary manacles on something that just *happened*."

Now I sighed aloud. Intellectually, I agreed with him to the letter. Yet here I sat, feeling like an intruder in *Leah's* home, and from the looks of it, he wasn't comfortable there himself. But I didn't know how to ask him about that, so I just nodded, let my hands caress his, and sat for a few more minutes before we inevitably returned to my house.

#

David was coming home for spring break the next evening, and I decided to wait until then before attempting a discussion with him. Conversation was typically over text, or if on the actual phone, extremely brief. For this reason, I wasn't worried that any of his siblings would have told him first.

However, I was about to learn my first lesson in a blended family: one must consider *all* the siblings involved.

After feeding him slow-roasted lamb chops and garlic mashed potatoes, and while watching him primp (put on shoes and a shirt with a collar...) for a night on the town, David not only told me that he already knew, but that he was *dating* his information source.

"Julie? *What?* She's...she's 27 years old, David." Inside I was panicking... *panicking*! But he didn't need to know that.

"Seriously, Mom?" I absolutely hated when he sounded just like me. "Dad is... Dad was ten years older than you. And Paul's older too, right?"

"It doesn't matter once you're over 40," I muttered. He'd made his point.

"I love her," he said. His earnestness, God help me, reminded me not only of Randall's, but of Paul's. "So I kind of need to know where this is headed with you guys..."

I pounded my cup on the counter a bit harder than I meant to. Luckily, this one didn't break. "Good grief, David, I don't know. Right now, we have replaced working lunches with social dinners. That's about all I got!"

"Mama." My sweet son was now pouring me more coffee. "From what I hear, you guys have dinner together six days a week and maybe breakfast too."

Well, crap. Apparently, many blanks had already been filled by our mixed brood. "Is spring break over yet?" I snapped. "Or, I mean, don't you have a thesis to type?"

"A term paper," he chided. "But I ran out of correction ribbon for my Commodore 64."

"That was a computer, not a typewriter, smartass." I took a sip of the perfect cup he'd given me. I stared at his shaggy, tawny head and thought of how Randall and I used to secretly smile at each over it, in awe of this last child of ours, who was always happy and chatty and seemed a little magical. The subject was ripe for teasing. David was doted on. David got away with stuff his older siblings did not. David was charming and cherubic and funny and... well, maybe on the verge of a hot mess sometimes. He was too old to use his charisma as a safety net. He needed to get a little serious, and he and Julie made no sense.

"First of all David," I started. "This is the second night *in a row* we aren't having dinner together." I looked at the blue eyes that inexplicably matched his dad's brown ones and put a hand to his cheek. "I don't know. I really don't. Paul is the best. You know that. Just... neither one of us knows what we're doing. We just... I mean, we just lost our spouses. *I hate that generic word.* And we do... love... each other, but we don't want to hurt each other out of this being some ridiculous, teenagery-coping thing. So, every step is cautious."

He raised an eyebrow at me, another signature Randall gesture. "But it's a big enough deal that you told all of us? Over meals? And you made me cookies. And you already started my laundry..."

"Sometime," I said, "You should ask your brother about me. You didn't have the pleasure of knowing me in my youth. When it comes down to big decisions, I'm pretty much an all-or-nothing girl. Also, Sam kinda got screwed on the meal part."

"You'll make it up to him, I'm sure," he said, passing me a cookie. "So, um, are you and Paul trying to make a big decision?"

I took a bite and nibbled thoughtfully. "Yes," I answered. "But I don't know what it is."

#

"I don't believe this," Paul was saying, for the tenth time. "She works all the time. How the hell did she have time to start dating a college kid who lives three hours away?"

I shook my head, stifling a giggle. "Love finds a way, Paul."

He rolled his eyes at me.

"They've known each other a long time," I added, somewhat lamely. "They have social media to keep in touch. They both just lost parents. Maybe there's just something there they normally wouldn't have seen." I mean, *I* still couldn't put my finger on what a 27-year-old nurse who sees the miracle of life and sometimes the saddest of deaths every day had in common with a

20-year-old analytics major who surfs in all his spare time. But clearly, I knew nothing.

"I bet it started at the hospital," Paul murmured, looking somewhere I couldn't see.

Within an hour of Randall passing and Paul's phone call about Leah, all seven of our combined offspring, plus in-laws and Travis and Maggie and Pastor Carter and his wife Morgan, were at the hospital, somewhere. David had spent an extra day in town after a weekend at home, so even he was there. Most of it was an absolute blur to me. I remember Paul's face and voice in the most distorted way, as he struggled to tell me about Leah. I don't remember what he finally said or how I interpreted it into the actual news, but I do remember the all-out horror I felt in the moment, that the world seemed much too small for everything that was happening, and that even though he had just held me in the worst moment of my life, there was not a thing I could do for him in his. I was paralyzed. We sat next to each other in mauve office chairs at a long meeting table. I was staring at the wall, a painting of the ocean with an octopus sand sculpture on the shore, still crying. I don't know if Paul was. We didn't touch or directly speak again that night.

It wasn't long before Sam and Abby were there, Abby sitting at my other side, and Sam talking quietly with Paul until Danielle got there. I always think of that conference room as the *triage* room. Paul and I had not once, in the dozens of conversations since then, talked about those hours. For me, placing him in it from this side made the memory a thousand times even more painful.

But he was putting himself there.

"Julie and David went to get coffee for everyone. And because they are twenty-somethings, they couldn't get it there at the hospital. They had to drive to Starbucks for some of it and Dunkin' Donuts for the rest. Because when your mama just died and your whole extended family is in turmoil, the perfect blend is of utmost importance."

Ouch. I wasn't sure whether to be a good listener or lend some perspective.

"I don't relish any thoughts of that day," I said carefully. "And I can't recall many of the details. But I do remember my son bringing me an absolutely perfect cup of coffee."

Paul snorted, but he also reached over and took my hand. We were sitting on the porch, where we could see and hear the ocean, and it had become our favorite spot to talk. "Then it's your fault," he chided. "You legitimize their superfluous coffee habits."

"I suppose it is, because I do." I took my hand back. That memory had already cast a shadow over me, and I wasn't sure I could share it with him.

I was especially grateful for the sound of the waves as the silence between us gained heaviness. He kept shifting in his seat; I was zipping and unzipping my jacket. I hated when words failed us. They were our foundation.

"We can't judge them," I finally said. "So they found their way to each other through unconventional means; so did we. And we want everyone to go with our flow..."

Paul shook his head. The heaviness had moved to his voice. "It's not the same, Jessie. Don't do that to us."

"What?" My genuine confusion came out like frustration. "Do *what* to us?"

"You are constantly, in some way or another, apologizing for this. For us. For what? For us spending time together? I don't understand it."

"I'm not apologizing..." I said, but it sounded unconvincing even to me.

"All our kids know," he continued. "With whatever hesitations some or all of them have, they're dealing. Are you? Can we?"

I turned my head to meet his gaze. Even in the dim glow of the porch light, his eyes were still as penetrating as always. I looked away quickly, because I knew I didn't have the answer he was looking for.

"I honestly don't know," I said simply. "I like sitting here with you. I don't like how it feels to try to plan my next move anymore."

It would have been easier to say I was scared, but Paul and I had always been quite successful in interpreting each other's half thoughts, so I left that hanging, confident he knew exactly what I meant.

He got up and scuffed into the house. He'd graduated from walking boot to brace that day, which was a moral victory for him, but he was still limping profoundly, which probably didn't help his mood.

When he returned to the porch, he handed me one of the oatmeal cookies I'd baked for David. He finished his before saying, "I'm trying to understand your fear, Jessie."

Was I obvious or was it just his all-seeing knowledge of me?

"I'm trying to understand your lack of fear!" I answered, a little defensively.

"What is there to be afraid of? You keep saying we've lost everything..."

Did I say that? "Paul, I never said we lost *everything*. I mean, what we did lose... We lost the future... the ones we were banking on."

I couldn't express myself clearly. It felt ungrateful to say we lost everything when we both still had our kids and our homes and our faculties. But it felt small to say losing my husband had meant less than everything. I stared at him, hoping he knew not to press me for the words.

"So, are you afraid to re-bank? Are you afraid of planning anything? Can I still take you out tomorrow tonight?"

His smile covered his whole face.

"Oh my God."

"We never argued when we weren't dating," he said, and when I looked at him this time, there was a single cookie crumb on his upper lip, and he was stifling a laugh.

He was like a microwave, and I was a damn plop of butter. Randall and I would have incredible, hours-long debates or gut-wrenching arguments without me even dreaming of giving in. One doting look from Paul and I had no desire to fight, much less be the victor.

The stakes were so different. I had to keep telling myself that.

Nothing had been resolved, but I didn't feel like it ever could be anyway, so I rose and kissed his waiting lips. "You better take me some place good."

Chapter Eleven

"I really, really, *really* appreciate this, Jessie."

"Yeah, Mama, thank you!"

My adventures in surreality continued. Mikayla and Danielle were heading out to an early movie, and baby Vivi, Paul's grandbaby, was staying with me.

"Matt has to replace our garbage disposal, and it's such a load off for him just to have Christian to deal with for a few hours, and Mikayla reminded me that you are the baby whisperer..."

"I also told her you might still be a wet nurse," Mikayla cracked.

I raised my eyebrows at my own daughter, then smiled at Paul's. "I was never actually a wet nurse. Not officially, anyway. But I pumped and donated so long after David weaned that Randall was scared I would lactate forever." Mikayla was shaking her head, somewhere between impressed and embarrassed, but Danielle was ever-gracious, like her own mama.

"I think that's amazing. I have a hard-enough time keeping Vivi fed. I can't imagine carrying on with the pump when she's done."

"Girl, please. Lots of babies need it, but lots of mamas need not to lose their ever-loving minds, too." I smiled at both of them, remembering a much younger and frenzied version of myself, who felt responsible for everything. *Hmm.* "I wish someone would have told me that taking care of my own kids was the most important thing I could ever do. And also, to relax."

Now both of them looked wistful, and I knew exactly why. Danielle's mournfulness was easy. She missed Leah, poor darling. And Mikayla – my heart ached for her. She had miscarried right after Christmas, right at the end of her first trimester, when she should have been getting glowy and elated. She and Altan had started trying again right away, but nothing so far.

Randall and I had lost a son when I was 19 weeks along. It had been a surprise pregnancy, and the aftermath led us to our sweet, easygoing David being born just 12 months later. I could not imagine life without our *#lastbaby!*, whom we had raised with the pure joy and confidence of parents who knew struggle, loss, how quickly time flies, and which battles to pick. But I still thought of Jamie every single day, and even wished, somehow, that we could have had them both.

I was determined to remain hopeful for Mikayla, who would never again know the wonder of pregnancy without the fear of such a loss. She was already so prone to melancholy that I prayed a successful nine months might turn her whole life's perspective around.

But for the moment, I just wanted her and Danielle to have a good time.

"Vivi will be great," I said, kissing the sweet head nestled on my shoulder. It was so long since Jacob had been a baby, and little newborn noggins were absolutely irresistible to me. "Go have fun."

I spent a few perfunctory minutes playing with Vivi on the couch, speaking in the silly rhythms of babydom, tickling her feet, trying to keep her from noticing her mama was gone. When she started to cry, I quickly changed her diaper, strapped on my old baby carrier, and grabbed one of the bottles of liquid gold Danielle had sent along. Vivi was going to get some salt-air therapy.

It was the perfect late afternoon to walk with her. The sun was warm, but clouds blew across it in quick succession, keeping us from sweating on each other. We enjoyed a podcast Rachel had sent me earlier in the week, from a blogger whose home-school convention she thought would love to feature me. I hadn't told her yet that if I was going to travel any time soon, it was not going to be to Decatur to talk about using the Bible in literature curriculum.

Vivi seemed to like hearing about scripture copy work and how to transfer the love of God on to our children's hearts with grace-filled routine. I smiled. It was exactly the sort of thought I subscribed to when I was raising little kids. Now it sounded, not wrong, but so complicated.

"Just love them," I said to Vivi. "They'll be all right."

I let the audio fade and started singing with one of my playlists instead. Tom Petty was getting to his point and con-templating another joint, and Miss Vivian finally passed out. I turned around at the pier and walked her back to the home base I had waiting, which consisted of a small tote bag holding her bottle, my water bottle, and a blanket. I sat on the sand and wrapped the blanket around her.

I lost the rest of the lyrics and fumbled with my phone to find a more acceptable playlist for nap time on the beach. It was a special sadness regarding the mothers of babies, that so few of them would actually take the time to sit here like this, without all the accoutrements we are told (or tell ourselves) are necessary to outings with children. Even though I had inevitably stressed myself out after David was born, his infancy was not what did it. No, by then, I'd learned enough to know that I could nap when he did (if the girls would let me, and with the proper snack-and-a-movie bribe, they usually did), that it was okay for him to get dirty or wet or sandy, because everything was washable, and that sacrificing a balanced home-cooked dinner for PB&J was a perfect tradeoff for 30 extra sun-soaked minutes by the ocean.

Vivi was probably not going to require much from me at dinnertime, and I hadn't talked to her Poppy since that morning. "Sleep away, darling girl," I murmured, nestling my chin on her and closing my own eyes.

"How did I know you'd be here?"

Paul's voice startled me so much I jumped. Vivi did too, but thankfully squirmed herself right back to sleep. I looked up to see his sunglasses shimmering down at me and looked down to see his familiar Brooks and something I thought I'd never see.

"Don't say a word," he warned.

"I said nothing. And shhhhh. Don't wake her."

Paul dropped his cane and arranged himself next to me in the sand. "I forgot you were watching her today. And here I was going to surprise *you*."

"She's a pretty great surprise," I agreed, smiling fully at him. "As are you. I'd pass her to you, but I don't think I can get her out of this thing without waking her."

"It's okay," he said. "I like watching you with her."

"Been watching long?"

"Just while I was walking toward you from the street," he answered, "Which took about three and a half hours."

"Haha." I paused. "I really didn't think I'd get you at the beach any time soon."

He grunted. "I figured since I had this damn thing, I might as well get something out of it."

Julie had brought Paul the cane the same weekend he'd stopped wearing his boot. I honestly thought it was a sweet gesture, but he was fuming, and she ended up matching his indignation. When he told her she only sees him as an old man, she shot back with various versions of, "I thought you could use it when you're walking on the beach with your *girlfriend*." At least, that was his rendition of it.

"I'm glad you came," I said. "And I'm glad I didn't know, or I would have been worried about you anyway."

"I'm fine," he murmured, running a hand along Vivi's back, overlapping where my hand rested on her. She made a sweet baby noise and shifted her head. We both sighed, then looked at each other and laughed.

"She's magical," I said. "The secret revealed when you become a grandparent."

"Sweet elixir of life," Paul agreed. "I bet you can't wait until Mikayla has hers."

"Yeah. Jacob starts *first grade* in the fall. It's been so long since there was a baby in the family," I said absently. "Hopefully..." And then I stopped, because Paul's comment suddenly rang back in my ears as more pointed than casual.

"Wait until *who* has *what*, now?"

He focused his eyes on Vivi, rubbing her a little more vigorously, and failing in his attempt not to smile.

"She's pregnant?" I whispered, as though Vivi would tattle on us.

He kept rubbing and nodded ever so slightly.

"How do you know?" I asked. "Danielle?"

Another nod.

"Why hasn't she told me?"

He stopped rubbing and looked very solemnly at me. "She's eleven weeks along. She's known... awhile..."

I felt a fresh stab in my chest. Mikayla was charting her temperature every morning. She would have known practically the moment that she got pregnant.

"She knew when he died?" He nodded at me, but it wasn't really a question.

"Oh, my God... Oh, that's so... awful. And so stressful," I said. "I wish she would have told me. I hate for her to be afraid or worried about this. It should be such good news..."

"She told Danielle at the hospital. That night. Um, Sam and Abby and Brittney know, too." He cleared his throat and let his hand rest on mine. "I think she's just waiting now another week or so. She didn't want *you* to worry. They just told me, a few days ago."

"They?"

"Mikayla and Altan were there when I had dinner at Danielle's on Tuesday." He was working hard to meet my eyes.

"I see." I didn't see. I didn't totally get it. "So Mikayla told *you?*"

"Not really. Matt almost slipped, I guess, and then they kept talking around it. So, I said something like, *Congratulations, Mikayla. Can you pass the rice?* She freaked out and begged me not to tell you, so here I am certain that by the end of this day both of you will be mad at me instead of each other. Three decades of marriage. Three daughters. This is hardly a new position for me."

His face held its usual calm demeanor, and the glint in his eyes beckoned me as it always did. My hand still on Vivi's back, I scooted as close to him as I could and leaned on his shoulder. My heart rate reflected that vague, unsettled feeling that was closing over me. Perhaps he and the baby together could bring me back to peace.

#

A few hours later, Paul and Danielle escorted each other out, carrying between them the balance of Vivi's diapers, the balance of the meal train lasagna I'd rescued from the freezer and heated up for Paul and me, and sweet Vivi herself. I noticed Paul resumed use of his beach-cane when Danielle arrived and kept my mouth shut like a good girl. I was personally glad he was being careful.

When I came in from the porch, Mikayla was standing at the counter drinking a glass of water and holding up one perfect and tiny pink sock.

"To this day," she said brightly, "no child exits your house without leaving a piece behind."

"Nope," I said, reaching out to fondle the teeny piece of cotton, recalling years of our revolving lost-and-found of dolls, books, bathing suits, singular shoes, lunch boxes, and occasionally, a little cash. "Hopefully she'll come back for it. What a doll, huh?"

"She's ridiculous," Mikayla agreed. "I love that you got to watch her. Danielle wasn't sure. No one but Leah has stayed with Vivi before."

Wow. "That's... Well, I'm honored, babe. How sweet of her to trust me. I know it must be hard," I said. My own mom had relocated from Illinois to South Carolina three months after my dad died. She spent time with the girls, who were both still in diapers, every single day. And then, three months later, she passed away in her sleep. After she was gone, for the longest time, I rarely let anyone stay with Mikayla and Brittney.

"We... I mean, Danielle and I, at least, we feel like you and Paul are... well, you're partners. I mean, you have been partners for a long time anyway, and all the new... stuff... is... Oh Mom. I just mean Danielle trusts you, and I trust Paul, not that you're replacing her mom or Daddy. We just..."

"Mikayla," I cut in, trying to save her. "I understand. I'm glad Danielle asked. I hope she knows I will be there for her however I can be. And we won't draw up any adoption papers yet, but of course Paul would be there for you, too. All y'all," I added, with my exaggerated southern accent.

"I know," she said, looking at her hands. *Please,* I thought. *The door is open, Mikayla. Just tell me.*

"He was at Danielle's the other night when Altan and I went for dinner." *Yes! This had to be it.* "He didn't really act any different from any other time, just... it was different like everything is different now. He was without Leah but still him. And tonight, seeing you two in the same room. I don't know. I guess it's just nice, Mama. You're... very comfortable together."

That obviously was not where I expected her to go, but I found myself exhaling deeply. I had been a little concerned when Danielle's SUV pulled up while her Daddy was still on my couch. Paul had calmly sat up from resting his head in my lap, scooped Vivi from his chest to my hands, smoothed his hair, and waited to greet our daughters at the door. Cool as a cucumber. My heart was racing like tropical storm wind, but apparently, I'd hidden that well enough.

"I am very comfortable with him," I agreed. "So it's hard to distinguish what is the bond that was already there, what is two friends going through the aftermath of tragedy, and what's brand new territory." That was deeper than I'd planned to go with her. "I guess I am just trying to enjoy him. He's a very pleasant person." I smiled into my own glass. My stomach felt a little fluttery.

"Yeah..." she said. "He's easy to talk to, right?" I nodded, trying to remain casual. "When he was at Danielle's the other night, he sort of, um, picked up on a little something we had been talking about."

"I'm not surprised. He's super intuitive. It's annoying sometimes."

She nodded, taking a deep breath. "So anyway, I want to tell you before, well, I'm sure he doesn't want to keep anything from you about your own kids. The thing is, Mom, I'm pregnant. Almost 12 weeks."

I looked at my daughter, her layered brown hair falling perfectly at her shoulders. Her apple cheeks were a little flushed, and her big brown eyes were looking at me with so much expectation I wanted to cry. At any age, the power motherhood gives us is astounding sometimes, and I grasped for the perfect words to say.

First, I reached out and hugged her. I caressed her back much as Paul had caressed Vivi's. Then I said, "I think this is the most wonderful news I can imagine hearing."

She pulled away to look at me. "You're not mad... that I didn't tell you first? I just... I didn't want to worry you when you're already going through so much."

"Baby, it's okay." I brushed a stray hair from her brow. "That was a very selfless thing to do. When did you know?"

Her chin quivered ever-so-slightly. "The night before..."

"Oh, Kayla." I hugged her again. "What a rough start. This kid is undoubtedly going to be a rock star!"

She giggled. "That's what Altan says. He's already convinced it's a boy!"

I pictured her in a hospital bed, Altan's arm around her as she cradled a little blue bundle with Altan's olive skin and her own cocoa eyes. I pictured me, too, snapping a photo and straightening up. And someone else there in the extra chair. The Grandpa. The Poppy? *Paul.*

This isn't about you, I told myself. But everything was about Paul if I didn't stop myself. My mornings were listening to his news commentaries and counts of how many cups of coffee I consumed. My afternoons were emailing him notes as I rewrote snippets and feeling schoolgirlish when he added sweet little emojis to his responses. My evenings were either impressing him with a great meal or rushing through one so we could reunite on the front porch or cozy up on my couch.

And night times, almost every one of them, were falling asleep with my hand in his, in a bed that had been mine and Randall's, *until*.

And there were the other times, which could be any time of day, when I was nearly consumed by guilt for how much I was consumed *by* my feelings for Paul, and more guilt for the unanswered question of whether I was using those feelings to bury my grief over Randall.

How could I love anyone but Randall?

"Whatcha thinkin', Mama?"

I flipped the switch and smiled brightly at Mikayla. "Just about the future," I said, with more boldness than I felt. "I can't wait to hold your baby!"

Chapter Twelve

Maggie's new midweek day off at the bank had quickly become our favorite thing. We had taken to planning our playdates out weeks at a time, and she excitedly picked me up when I was ready to resume them. Even though Mikayla wanted to keep the baby news low key until after her first sonogram, Maggie and I allowed ourselves a clandestine shopping spree.

I had always planned to keep some baby stuff around, but when Randall and I had downsized, it didn't make sense to hold on to a high chair and a portable crib that would be out of style and maybe just plain too old for the next grandchild.

Maggie swung back and forth between keeping me sane ("Don't get a cradle yet. What will you do with it if the unthinkable happens? No one is ever going to put that baby down anyway. Take it easy...") and losing her own mind a little ("Oooooooooh dear Lord! Would you look at that little Gamecocks dress?! And the matching sockies. Auntie Mags needs to buy this!").

Our last stop was at Kohl's, where I just happened to spot golf shorts on sale as we were passing the men's department. Maggie snickered when I stopped and then looked just a shade outside of appalled when I took a pair of teal ones and another tan off the rack.

"You take up golf?" she asked lightly. "Because I don't think those will fit the baby..."

"Shut up," I answered and continued walking. "Paul needs some. He asked me to look for him."

"Thirty-four waist," she said, shaking her head. "If you're going to be all domesticated, might I suggest you fatten him up a bit?"

"I already put butter in everything." I stopped at a rack of candles and started sniffing.

"Jess, can I ask you something?"

"Sure." I put the lid back on an Ocean Breeze. I'm convinced there hasn't been a single candlemaker in the world who has ever actually been to the ocean.

"Are you and Paul as serious as it seems you are?"

I peered at her over a Raspberry Sorbet. "How serious does it seem?"

"On a scale of one to 10, it seems like a Tim and Faith duet. With a black and white video."

I snorted. "We are spending a lot of time together..." I was done with the candles.

"That's not really an answer. I mean, *we* spend a lot of time together, but you don't cook me dinner or buy my drawers. Though if you're offering that service, I might take you up on it."

"I didn't buy his *underwear*," I whispered. "Give me a break." I led her to a checkout line and glanced around to see if anyone we knew was nearby.

"Jess, don't sound so scandalized. I just mean, are you spending time together because it's what you really want, or is it, you know, convenient, maybe...?"

"I can see where that question might seem valid..." I said airily. "But honestly, there's nothing convenient about it. I feel like I am constantly dodging questions or adjusting my tone of voice or just flat out keeping secrets. It feels a little like I'm a soc sneaking out of the house at night to see a greaser. Nope. Definitely not convenient."

Maggie peered at me with a confounded expression. "Ok, Cherry Valance. Why in the world should it feel like that? You're two grown people and all the kids know. Sneaking for whose benefit? And is he Ponyboy or Sodapop?"

"Oh, he's Darryl. All the way." I was always convinced Patrick Swayze's eyes could melt butter, too. He'd been deeply mourned when he died of pancreatic cancer, almost 20 years after the same disease killed my dad.

After a requisite moment for Daniel Romano, Patrick, and Randall, I looked around and hissed, "And Maggie... *he spends the night!*"

"What? Oh, for fu...uuugh's sake." She flashed a wide smile to the cashier as she collected herself, handing over a skillet and three bras.

Once she'd listened to the speech about Kohl's Cash expiration policies, Maggie turned to me and said, "Of course he is. What are you talking about?"

"Just wait," I said, piling my purchases on the counter. Twenty-percent off, O-M-G-Kohl's-Cash, yes, I'm using my card, here is my blood type and great grandma's maiden name. "Have a nice day," I finished.

"Why can't we just buy our crap?" I muttered on the way to the car. "I don't need step-by-step guidance to purchase baby jammies and placemats. If they want me to fill out a questionnaire, they should be paying *me*."

Maggie rolled her eyes. "*Anyway*. Next time just say you're already on the list. Now what? What is causing you to sneak? Or feel like you're sneaking?"

I slid into the driver's seat and turned the AC on high. "I *am* sneaking, Maggie. Of course I am. You think his kids or mine would understand why he's staying over every night? He's been walking on his own for two weeks now. We don't really have any other excuses."

"Walking? Excuses? What?" She was shaking her head emphatically. "Are you saying he started off spending the night *solely* so you could help him shower?"

"No. Just... no."

"Are you sleeping together?" she asked impatiently.

"Well, yes. I mean, he spends the night almost every night. Not on the weekends usually because we have church and family stuff going on, but most of the other time, yes."

"*Sleeping* together. Okay, Jessica! Are. You. Having. The Sex?"

I slumped into my seat, grateful I hadn't started driving yet. "Oh my God, Maggie. No. No, we are not having sex. We are *sleeping together*. Literally. No sex."

She looked confused again. Even though I knew Maggie had a fairly consistent roster of lovers since my brother had left, Famous Talk Show Host notwithstanding, it still annoyed me that she'd made the assumption about *me*. Paul and me. Is that what everyone was thinking?

"Oh," she said simply. "Okay. Just... why does he spend the night then?"

I dramatically turned my face upwards and looked at the heavens. "I don't know, Maggie. Maybe because he suddenly craves the sound of the ocean at night. Maybe because we watch all the same TV shows, and we're saving some electricity. Maybe because we are both newly widowed after years and years and years of marriage and we have no idea how to date or transition or form new relationships."

Maggie reached over and flipped a piece of my hair affectionately. "You worried he can't perform?"

She said it so casually that I almost missed it, but a millisecond later I was guffawing so hard I doubled over.

"Fifty-*six*," I breathed. "I'm having this conversation at 56-years-old. Pinch me."

"I won't," she said defiantly. "I've been having these conversations for almost twenty years, and I'm older than you. Things don't always work out how we planned. Most of the time they don't. So get used to it, Princess Buttercup. You don't have a husband any more. But you have a very charming, incredibly handsome, little on the lean side, boyfriend who looks at you like you invented the back nine. So cuddle all you want. Just know that no one is going to hand you a prize for stopping there. True Love Waits was for youth group (you flunked it, by the way), and in case you didn't notice, that was a long time ago."

Sigh. "I know that, Mags. But I am a product of the eighties, not this new millennium. I realize that makes me sound ancient.

But in spite of the fact that I was branded a teenage whore, *we* did not automatically hop into bed with everyone we dated. It was... sex was still a *thing* for us. And it still is for me. I'm actually kind of mortified that it might be an assumption that Paul and I are... intimate. Do you think *he* assumes we should be?"

"Oh honey, I honestly have no idea. He's a classy guy. He's in his sixties. It's all new and blah blah blah. But he is a man, and I assume things are still in good working order for him. So even if he's too polite to assume you *should* be, I'd be willing to bet he wouldn't turn you down."

"I haven't had a bikini wax in 21 years," I said. "My nipples have hairs. I wear homemade deodorant and I swear sometimes I smell like a goat. I can't imagine—"

"He wants to," Maggie said, more emphatically this time. "Now, first of all, go buy some clinical strength Dove, for the love of Moses! Everyone's gotta die some time, even if it's from aluminum filled tumors. Then let's get you an appointment at my salon. They do decent white girl hair. Because whatever you have going on in your nethers, your actual hair roots are looking rather desperate."

"June Carter Cash—"

"Yes, I know," she said. "You've got the June Carter Cash look rocking hard," Maggie assured me. "But darling, she died first. If Johnny had beat her to the punch, I guarantee you one of those daughters or a well-meaning, gorgeous friend of hers, probably Dolly or Loretta Lynn, would have insisted she get some toner on those roots."

"I'm sure you're right." I started driving. "Ho ahead and call."

She giggled at my pun and started scrolling through her contacts. Paul had a golf game that morning but was supposed to be over later for dinner and whatever. Now I was questioning a whole new type of everything.

#

Lexie worked me in around lunch time, and two-and-a-half hours later, my long, wavy locks were two inches shorter and my sun-bleached brunette was now a sun-kissed, metallic bronze ombre or something. I had to admit, the color looked amazing, so feeling emboldened in spite of the rest of my hair situation, I suggested we stop at Paul's to drop off his shorts. (And if I was honest, to check on him, since that morning had been his first post-sprain golf outing).

When we pulled up, Kate's little red pickup was in the driveway. Before I could utter a word of hesitation, Maggie spoke. "So what?" she said. "You're at his office all the friggen time. Sack up, girl. Katy is breezy anyway. What does she care? She probably has some golden Adonis with her using the pool."

Everything Maggie said was spot on. Katy was, in fact, the most mellow and pleasant person I had possibly every met. She had none of Leah's formality, all of her generosity, and twice the amount of Paul's easy charm. In fact, a few days after Paul's announcement dinner with his daughters, she sent me a little Facebook message just to say she was glad her dad had someone "so awesome" to spend time with. I could do this. Katy was an ally.

Except Katy didn't answer the door. Julie did.

The definition of night and day, those twins were. Katy was the transcendent unicorn found in every family (except for ours; thanks to Brit and David, we had two). She was also the hellcat who hightailed her blonde head all the way to California when she was 18 years old. She was practically a Dixie Chicks song, running off in her Daddy's red Mustang with nothing but her guitar case (stuffed with jeans and make-up), her guitar (riding shotgun), and the contents of the savings account that had been meant for her first year of college. Randall had actually accompanied Paul out west on his first attempt to bring her home. That had gone over much like the Dixie Chicks country radio career: a bunch of fireworks and then a quick, horrifying fall. Katy stayed out there for something like four or five months before she returned home broke, shaved practically bald, and with nothing in that guitar case or the passenger seat. Paul promptly traded in his Mustang for a Jeep.

Julie's response to all of that was to be more of whom she had been her whole life: perfect, or at least, perfectly controlled. She was an honor roll student all through high school. She decided early in her teen years to be a nurse and finished her four-year degree in three years. She volunteered at a pregnancy clinic in her spare time and, I knew from conversations with Leah, had broken up with two different doctors whom she'd deemed shallow and juvenile. I had no earthly idea why she was dating my son, who seemed enough like Katy to automatically earn Julie's disdain. All I did know was that Julie was not happy her dad was spending so much time with me, and here I was, holding his new clothing in my hand.

"Hey Julie!" Maggie said brightly. "Great to see you!"

Julie smiled at her and let it fade as she turned to me. "Um, Dad's not here. I thought y'all were off this afternoon. Katy and I are just cleaning up a bit and—" She broke off, clearly wondering why she was giving me so much information. In the meantime, Katy bounded up to the door.

"Aunt Jessie! Ms. Mags! Yes! Hey!" She pulled the door open wider, and Julie was basically forced to step aside and let us in. "Come on. We're cleaning out Dad's disgusting refrigerator and then we're going for a swim. Julie just made sangria. You're *just in time!*"

Maggie actually answered with a "Whoop-whoop!" and only beamed back when I glared at her. This was a recipe for *disaster*. Absolute disaster. But before I could think of a subtle way to exit, Katy was handing each of us a melamine goblet filled with fruit chunks and sweet wine.

"Lord, have mercy, this is delicious," Maggie exclaimed. "Julie, is this your own recipe?"

Julie's back was to us as she sponged off a shelf in the refrigerator. "My mama's," she answered, more than a bit hotly.

Maggie cocked an eyebrow at me and took another swallow. I sipped my drink too, wondering how to gracefully exit.

"Thank you, children, for not having lessons today!" Katy said. "I was overdue for some day drinkin'." She took a swallow that only left a drop in the bottom of her glass. I couldn't help but raise my own maternal eyebrow. "Spring break has destroyed everyone. It's one of those weeks when I just need to observe Friday Eve as a hallowed day. God bless Mikayla, but no one's pregnant here!"

Julie only grunted from her station at the fridge. Maggie was laughing right along with the ramble, and I murmured in agreement, wondering how many people knew Mikayla's *secret* news. And Katy did have a point; there were plenty of seasons in life when day drinking was frowned upon or impossible. I was not in one of them.

"I'm going to use the washroom," I said. Katy and Maggie were chattering away, and Julie didn't acknowledge my voice. I carried the package for Paul discreetly with me and used the powder room just outside the master bedroom. When I was done, I stepped in quickly and laid the bag on the foot of the bed.

"Unbelievable." Indeed. Julie's voice rang out curtly behind me. I braced myself and turned around.

"Hey Julie. I was just leaving this for your da—"

"I'm sure he appreciates it," she said. "He's probably going to be home soon. You could have just given it to him. I mean, trouncing on in here with us home seems like a bit much, don't you think?"

"I..." Sigh. "I wasn't planning to stay and wait for him. I don't want to crowd you or make things uncomfortable."

"So you snuck into my mother's room instead?"

There was that word again. "I wasn't sneaking," I said lamely. "I don't want to argue. I'm sorry. We'll go." I walked past her back to the kitchen. Maggie and Katy were carrying on like two sitcom roommates. I grabbed my purse unceremoniously from the counter.

"Are we leaving?" Maggie said, finally coming to attention.

I widened my eyes and nodded emphatically. Katy didn't miss it. "What? No. Jessie, stay. Julie, what did you say?"

"Don't start, Katy," she answered. "Can you please put the drink down and help me with this? Daddy will be home soon, and I don't want him walking into a mess. If he can even walk after his stupid golf game." She shot a pointed look at me, which everyone noticed as well.

"Wait, what?" Katy said.

Maggie echoed her drinking bud. "Did you stick pebbles in his shoes or something?" she asked me, feigning confusion.

Julie didn't laugh and neither did I. "I don't think he would play if he didn't think he was up to it, Julie," I said. "But we will get out of the way so you can finish."

"Of course he would play. He's been gallivanting all over town with you. Walking on the stupid beach. Did you know his doctor recommended surgery? If he doesn't take care of himself, he'll be laid up for months. But yeah. I'm sure it's no problem getting in a golf game when he needs a cane to go to the bathroom."

"That is not even true," Katy said, and I had to admit, I was fuming. Paul was definitely a bit heroic about his injury, but he was not an idiot. "Dad sprained his ankle, like a month ago. What do you want, to shoot him, like a horse? He's not *lame*."

"He rushed his recovery," Julie said adamantly. "Ligament trauma is worse than a fracture. He probably *shouldn't* be walking yet. With everything he's been through lately, he should be resting, and he's never even home." She shot another look in my direction.

"Okaaaaaaay," Maggie started, but I held up my hand. *Aunt Jessie* was about to show a different side of herself.

"Why don't we take our sangria by the pool?" Maggie suggested. Katy just shrugged and followed her out of the room.

"Julie, if you have some things to say to me, it's fine. I understand. But please don't second-guess your dad. He's a grown man, and he's worked really hard in PT..."

She shook her head. "He doesn't tell you everything."

"Nor does he have to," I said. I already sounded angrier than I'd planned to. I was not going to argue about this with her. It was Paul's business.

"Do *you* have something else to say to *me?*" Julie asked, starting to place bottles and jars back on the door. "Or did you just want to stand in my mother's kitchen and tell me how well you know her husband?"

Ouch. She definitely had Paul's gift for words.

"I adored and cherished your mom, Julie," I started. "Nothing about my... relationship with your dad is meant to be disrespectful to her at all."

"And yet..."

"And yet," I agreed. "I don't expect you to understand. To be honest with you, I don't quite understand myself. But here we are, and we'd love if everyone could help us make the best of it."

"David told me that all of your family is just over the moon," she said. "I mean, that's nice. I'm not going to argue with him about that. My dad is a great guy. But he's mine. He's ours. It's very fast for me to lose my mom and then have to share him with all these other people."

"No one is laying claim to him, and he is not *replacing* Randall," I said firmly. "Any more than I am—"

"Please," she said. "Please don't even say it."

For a moment, her veneer gave way and she just looked young and sad. I watched her arrange the condiments in perfect alignment on the refrigerator door and then place a pitcher of sweet tea on the top shelf. There was hardly any food in the fridge. Paul was rarely home to eat these days.

How would I feel if I were her, trying to make sure my dad was okay and having him give so much attention to a new woman?

"I had two babies and a little boy when my dad died, and my mom died six months later," I said quietly. "I never had to deal with one of them moving on."

"It hasn't even been close to six months," she retorted.

"You're right," I said. "Julie, there is likely nothing I can say that will matter to you or change your view of things. So allow me to please say this: I adore your dad. I—"

"I thought you adored my *mom*? Aren't you a writer? Because I'm not understanding your semantics here. Don't you have other words?"

"Okay. Well, let me explain something, please." She closed the door and leaned against it, looking at me with a *little* less contempt. "The older you get, the less... singular... your relationships become. Maybe less defined is a better way of saying it."

She clearly had no idea where I was going, but at least she'd stopped snarling at me. "When you're younger, at least when I was, there were categories for everything. Romantic love. Family love. Extended family love. Then friends. Work friends. Church friends. Mommy friends. Friends-friends. Friends who are family. And on and on.

"And then life shifts, and suddenly, raising those kids takes up so much space that you basically have room for two categories: who's in, who's out. Maybe it's *family* and *everyone else*. And your dad, and your mom... they have been family to me. For *years*. I adore *them*. I cherish *them*. Together and individually." She started to respond, but I held up a firm hand.

"I promise I'm almost done. Family means a lot of different things, and this is no exception. Through the years, with your dad, I have served the role of mama hen, of doting little sister, of defensive big sister, of teasing brother, of humble protégé, and always, always, of adoring friend. None of that was hidden from Leah. None of that has changed.

"Maybe this doesn't matter, but Paul is family to me. He always will be. I would not do anything to hurt your dad. Anything."

"What if you are hurting him?" she asked quietly. "What if this *relationship* is hurting his family?"

I nodded slowly. It was a fair question. "Julie, all we are doing is spending time together. We are enjoying that. And I trust Paul. I trust that he is wise and informed and knows himself and his daughters. For me, he is the voice of authority on himself. On *his* family."

Now she nodded. There might have been the glisten of tears in her eyes, but she wouldn't look at me long enough for me to tell.

"We'll go," I concluded. "Again, I am sorry for making you uncomfortable. I hope... I hope time allows for better."

I headed out the front door. I would text Maggie from the car. Much as I could have used another glass of what really was amazing sangria, it was definitely time to leave.

Chapter Thirteen

I wasn't sure how Paul would react to the afternoon's events, but I hoped it would be better than I was doing. After Maggie and I parted ways, I spent 30 minutes lost down a social media rabbit hole, having realized Julie, while dating my son and telling me what an ass I was, had unfriended me. So of course, I had to look through every post she had that was visible to me and every comment or "like" she gave to one of our mutual friends' posts. I scrolled relentlessly as a non-friend. As her late mother's friend, her dad's current, well, best friend, really. And as her boyfriend's mom. But her *unfriend*. Okay, Julie. Have a nice pout.

Okay Jessie, I told myself. *You do the same.*

I texted Paul to meet at dinnertime at Dead Dog Saloon, one of my favorite restaurants. It was nestled on the inlet and boasted a quintessential low-country view. It was probably not the kind of venue where we could pass our dinner off as a business one, and it was definitely too loud for the conversation we might be having, but I needed the background noise to drown out the tension I felt.

He was already seated when I walked to our table, an empty glass and a full sweet tea sitting in front of him.

"You finally take up drinking?" I asked, sitting across from him. Immediately, I could see the weariness and the edge in his eyes.

"What do you think goes best with sweet tea?"

"Oh, tequila, vodka, gin, rum, all the above..."

He didn't respond. I glanced at the happy hour menu, though there were only about five minutes left. "Must have been some game."

He looked at me somberly. "The game was fine. You want to talk about your conversation with my daughter?"

"Hmm. Probably not until after some *all the above.*"

Paul shook his head. "Don't be too mad," I said, trying to alleviate some of the strain from the onset. "She's concerned for you."

"I am a grown-ass man," he snapped. I winced, though I'd said the exact thing to Maggie the moment we were back in the car. "She had no right to get into my business like that. None."

"How did you even know? Did she tell you?" The waitress returned to us at that point. I decided to stick with Moscato and ordered a bottle.

"Katy told me," he said, practically spitting indignation. "She told me what she knew, anyway, and then I made Julie spill the rest. But please, feel free to fill in the gaps. I'm sure she left out anything that makes you sound like less of a fire-breathing dragon sent to destroy remains of her family."

"Oh geez." He was totally charged up and not even meeting

my eyes. "Why don't you tell me about your return to the PGA first?"

He rolled his eyes. "It was stupid. I couldn't get my stance right with this stupid brace. I took four mulligans on the first nine. Then I pretty much just gave up and hit for the practice."

Randall didn't play golf. Whatever Paul has said made my eyes glaze over. "Well, at least you had fun."

"Eh. A bad golf game isn't all that fun to me," he said, draining his glass. "I felt fine, considering I should be in a wheelchair, according to the family nurse."

Clearly, we were not going to get anywhere until he was done being mad. I smiled gratefully as the waitress set down my glass and poured. "And you might want to bring him a pitcher," I added, as she took Paul's empties away. He forced a smile.

"Be mad," I said. "I would be. I kind of am. But we both know it's not going to do any good. It's not going to change her mind."

"I don't care," he said.

"Yes, you do," I argued. "Or you wouldn't be sitting here with fumes rising around you. Calm down."

"I *hate* when people tell me to calm down."

"Okay. Should I just go? You seem more suited to anger than company tonight."

He didn't answer, and I couldn't think of anything else to add. The waitress had set down a basket of hot hush puppies and neither of us moved. There was nothing companionable about our silence, and I wondered if he'd notice if I did leave.

My head was pounding as I searched for something to say. I distracted myself with the thrall of honey butter and finally dipped in a hush puppy, trying to smile at Paul as I popped it in my mouth. He just grunted.

"Okay, seriously," I said. "Would you rather we just do this some other night? I have a headache anyway."

He grunted again. How had I not noticed that annoying habit before? "Probably from all the wine."

Did he know about Julie's sangria? Was he judging me? "Are you kidding me right now?" I asked.

"Nah. Not at all. Maybe you should have some more," he said, lifting the bottle to top off my almost-full glass.

I put my hand on top of it. "Maybe *you* should!"

He raised his eyebrows. "I probably should!" And then he laughed.

I watched him for a second like I was watching an insane man. But lo and behold, he was just Paul, who typically didn't stay mad very long. His laughter was hearty and genuine, and it took about two more seconds for me to join in.

"There you are..." I murmured.

He looked at me very seriously then. "It's all me, Jess. I get a little stormy sometimes. Are you going to want to run away?"

I stared at him. Of course, I had seen him get stormy a few times before then. I thought back to the day he got the call that his mother had died. I was with him in the office, and before he finished the conversation, I'd figured out what happened. His posture went rigid and he closed his eyes. He stood behind his chair nodding and probably grunting, in response to whoever was on the other end of the line before summarizing what he thought he would do (*Call Charlie. Be there tomorrow*). When the call was over, he let the corded phone hang at his side, just for a minute. Then he turned back toward his desk, slammed it down, and stood there, unmoving, facing the wall. He was frozen, and I remember thinking it was like watching someone hold a painfully heavy bag, about to drop it, but afraid of breaking everything inside.

At that point, Paul and I had been working together around three years. We were friendly, but still mostly semi-formal and work-related with each other. I knew some of his stories, and he knew some of mine, but nothing compared to what twelve more years would bring. Leah wasn't home, or I would have gone to get her. Instead, I walked to his side and just said, "Paul." Not as a question or even a sentence starter. Just his name.

I only know the bird's-eye view of his background, and therefore knew that "Paul" wasn't the name his mother had given him. She had named him Walter, after his father, but from the moment he started school, he told everyone to call him by his middle name. When he was 18, he legally changed it, becoming simply Paul Jameson. Walter Jameson was not a name Paul wanted to hear, much less be identified with. (I never asked about the specific nature of Paul's abhorrence, but he was such a restrained person, his employ of the vague term "abusive" was enough on its own). When his older brother Charlie was 16, he left, taking Paul with him. They lived briefly on the run – friends' houses and parked cars – before child services put Charlie in a group home and returned Paul to his parents. Paul left again a few years later, when he was 16 himself. He had never told me where he lived, how he made it through college, or what happened to Charlie, Walter, or his mom. I only knew she called from time to time; Paul was always sullen and silent afterwards.

He didn't respond, so I put a tentative hand on his shoulder and tried again. "Paul. Paul, please turn around."

It took him a few seconds, but he did. He didn't look at me at first. The storm showed itself by way of shadowed eyes brimming with tears. "My mom died," he said.

"Oh, I'm *so* sorry." I knew there was nothing like that feeling, but I couldn't relate to what else he was experiencing. "Do you know what you need? You want me to call Leah?"

He shook his head no. Then muttered, "Yeah."

"Okay." I turned to grab my phone, but his hand reached for mine. I looked back at him, startled, and the storm swelled. Though he was clearly trying to keep everything at bay, his head fell, his eyes poured, and his shoulders shook. For this, I only had one very simple solution in my arsenal. I wrapped my arms around him and held him as tightly as I could, and I said his name over and over again, much like I would with one of my kids. He leaned on me and cried, soaking my shirt and breaking my heart, while time seemed to stand still.

When he did collect himself, he called Leah, and I stayed until she got home. He left town for a few days to "take care of things." We didn't talk much about it beyond that, but after that day, we were better friends, close friends, and I made it a point to use his name more often.

Now I looked at Paul Jameson, completely open to me in ways I'd never dreamed he'd be, and I wanted to reassure him at least a hundred times more than I had on that afternoon, because now, he felt like *mine*.

"Paul. I can't... Sometimes I will want to run away from *me*. From *my* storms. But not from you. I'm here for you. I just hate to see you... well, anything less than absolutely joyous. Giddy, even."

"Ha!" He wasn't laughing though, and for me, what I said was true. Since that moment, that phone call, I had always felt protective of him in an absolute fall-on-my-sword kind of way.

"It's gonna happen sometimes," he said. "And today was one of those days. Along with Julie's hostility toward you, I found out she's gotten Leah's sisters all riled up. They're acting as if you and I are hightailing to a Vegas chapel. So I spent the afternoon talking down all three of them, plus Julie, plus Katy was threatening to burn down the house if they didn't leave me alone. It was... yeah. It was a good time."

I sighed deeply and looked upward. Heaven had to help, because I was at an absolute loss. I hadn't even stopped to think much about the extended families: Leah's sisters, Randall's family, not to mention neighbors, church people, the rest of Facebook. Was everyone going to want to weigh in individually? Should we host a town hall meeting or maybe just start a group text?

"Vegas... actually... sounds... good..." I said, shrugging and reaching for my glass.

Paul nodded, a kind of far off look in his eyes. "Let's keep it on the list of options. And let's eat these puppies before they go cold."

Storm weathered. For now.

#

"I can't believe you're out here... at night," I said, a few hours later, well after dark, pulling my tattered beach quilt over our legs.

I could hear the eye roll in Paul's voice. "Why do you think I was in such a hurry to rehab? I knew I'd eventually have to follow you here in order to see you. Besides, I'm pretty sure this brace is made out of steel. I'm like Iron Man."

I tapped his encased ankle lightly with my foot and nodded in agreement. "I thought you were Bat Man," I reminded him. "In any case, thanks for working so hard *for me*. I'm sorry the sand and waves and salty breeze and ability to walk are all such a burden to bear..."

He chuckled. "You know, I really have never cared much about the ocean. But even... before... I've enjoyed seeing it through your eyes. You love it like you love all your people. Big and all-encompassing."

"Well, that's sweet," I said, leaning my head on his shoulder for a moment. "Ever feel like our... coming together... has turned you into a big, syrupy sap? I mean, you kind of make my ego swell."

His arm was around me and he pulled me a little tighter. "Yes," he answered immediately. "Except today. Not a lot of syrup coming from me."

Well, no. He was correct. Once we got through the initial tense rundown of the afternoon, it still took most of dinner for Paul to relax and me to stop walking on eggshells. Taking into account that he was really mad at Julie, achy from his first golf game in several weeks, and smarting from his encounter with Leah's sisters, whom he genuinely loved and respected, I really didn't want to upset him any further.

Except I was upset, too. I didn't think a total lack of understanding and grace toward Julie was going to help much. And I hated that he felt guilty and conflicted over the sisters.

"I know we don't talk about your extended family much," I said carefully, "but I know they mean a lot to you. I don't want... I don't want you to lose them, or feel alienated from them, or feel like you have to keep the pieces of your life separate." Though I knew men were generally good at that. I envied that quality.

"Thanks," he answered. "But maybe it's okay if they're separate. I mean, the sisters are spread out anyway. Leah's parents are up in Raleigh. It's not like they were a part of *my* everyday life, and the more grandkids got born, the more they were only part of Leah's life by phone."

"Yeah. I get it. I just wish it didn't have to be that way."

"It doesn't *have* to be," he said, pausing to take a few slurps of his soup. "Heidi and Claire were pretty understanding about everything. Sharron was *opinionated*. A little preachy, a whole lot of *just sayin'*. And between her and Julie, they just about got the other two going. But when Katy started going after them, Sharron backed off pretty quickly. I mean really, what skin do they have in this game?"

"I'm guessing their sister's honor." It was a little depressing. My own brother didn't show a bit of interest in my life in the wake of new widowhood, although Maggie, who felt like the truest sibling I had, was my biggest supporter. How could I be mad at Leah's sisters for trying to ensure her memory and her family were protected? "Also, this is damn confusing," I added.

Paul had nodded in agreement, but then put his spoon down and gotten quite solemn again. "I get it. I get all of it. All the feelings and loyalties and questions. But the fact remains: I am doing *nothing* to hurt my kids or the family or Leah. A part of my life ended when she died. That part isn't getting erased or rewritten. It's being remembered. It's treasured. But should that mean I don't get to have a life anymore? How is that okay to all these people who supposedly care about me? How could they know Leah and think she wouldn't want happiness for me?"

I took a long swallow from my wine glass, a bit embarrassed at how well I was doing with that bottle. Paul raised a question I hadn't been able to verbalize yet, but now seemed as good a time as any.

"You think she would?" I asked quietly. "*Would* she be happy? Not just that you were moving on, but that you were moving on with *me*?"

"Leah loved you," he answered swiftly.

"Of course," I shot back. "As a fun gal who worked with her husband. As a fellow mom. As her girlfriend. But as a successor to her? A few weeks after she died?"

"If you want to know how Leah would feel about this, think for a second how Randall would feel..."

I narrowed my eyes, brows raised.

"Right. You already have. A million times. And you don't know, because you can't ask him. And I can't ask her. And any hypothetical conversations either of us had over the course of two very long and fine marriages have ceased to matter, right? Because you can't ever really know how it's going to feel, how things will go down. But I *can* and *did* and *will* say this: If Leah were the one here, if she was the one left behind and alone, and someone was there that made her feel the way I feel when I'm with you, when I even think about being with you, then I would haunt anyone who tried to get in her way or make her feel bad about it. I would want her to be happy because I love her. And because I have no doubt she loved me, I know well enough how she'd feel about *us*."

I leaned my head back in my chair, suddenly zapped.

"Paul. Seriously. *How* do you do that?"

And he seemingly came to life, his real smile back across his face for the first time all night. "Do what?"

"You know what. Putting everything in this amazing perspective. Taking all the crazy, flying thoughts and feelings swirling around us and putting them in a neat package that somehow makes sense. If there was an award for summaries of complicated shit, you'd be thanking me in your acceptance speech."

He shook his head. "I just know what I know. And I knew Leah. And you knew Randall. Better than anyone else who wants to have a say in this. For me, I have to be able to definitively explain where I am coming from... *once*. Because I am not going to let my daughter or anyone else try to tell me how *my* wife would feel and what *I* should do."

"Okay." The more well-spoken he was, the less I knew what to say... the less I felt I needed to say.

And on the beach, I felt more sure of myself and what I wanted him to know, and I was okay with words not being required. I put my arm around his waist, nuzzling into him and stroking his hair.

"Mmmm. Thank you," he sighed. I returned the gratitude with a kiss to his neck.

Without all the opinions and cautions and analysis, loving him was just so easy.

Chapter Fourteen

Suddenly it was May first, what would have been Randall's 69th birthday.

We had talked a few times about what we would do. It didn't take a huge occasion for me to suggest the mountains or Randall to suggest a cruise. But we thought we'd celebrate the end of his 60s doing something with more of a bang. Vegas it would be. *Vegas, baby!*

The last time we'd gone was around my 50th birthday. We spent three days there alone, and then Sam and Abby met us for two more. We saw the Cirque du Soleil adult show, *Zumanity*, which had me giggling and Randall cringing throughout. We rode rides on top of the Stratosphere. We toured the Coca-Cola and M&M stores. And the only thing we did more than eat and drink and gamble was walk. I wanted to see everything on that trip, probably because by then David was 11 and all the kids had stayed with Maggie, and I really had nothing to worry about. It was the time of our lives.

We hadn't gotten around to actually booking anything for this one, which was par for the course. We were planning to stay at The Venetian and see the Cirque du Soleil Beatles show this time. Randall wanted to eat steak every day. I was going to book him a massage.

Instead, I woke up alone that morning. I walked Cash on the beach for an extra-long time, thinking all my thoughts and releasing plenty of tears. When I got home, I had messages from Sam, Abby, Brittney, Mikayla, Altan, Travis, and Maggie. I smiled. Per our agreement the day before, I didn't text Paul. I'd insisted that I needed that day to focus on Randall.

So I went to the store to get a few things I was lacking in order to make Randall's favorite lemon pound cake. We were going out to our favorite Mexican restaurant and then coming back to the house. I needed some ginger ale and walked to the soda aisle.

I could remember like yesterday the first grocery store trip Randall and I made as South Carolina residents. I could not find the *pop* aisle anywhere. And even though I was very aware of the regional differences in terminology over carcinogen-enhanced fizzy drinks, I was appalled when the precious little stock boy answered my "Can you please tell me where the pop is?" with an empty look. I changed to *soda*. That and aisle 11 were my answers.

Now Randall's soda of choice stared at me. Cherry 7up, sometimes diet. I would sing the "Cherry 7up, can't get enough" '80s anthem *every single time* I brought it home.

I stared at the small display of it there at the Food Lion. Should I buy some for the kids? Drink a 12-pack myself? Get some to keep in the house? Toast to Randall tonight?

And at that moment, I missed my husband so much that I could have dropped to my knees right there in the store. I left my cart and speed-walked to my car, where I dialed Randall's number just to hear his voice mail, on the line I still hadn't cancelled. "Where are you?" I sobbed, feeling hopeless and like a fool all at once. "I don't know how to do this without you!" I hung up and lay my head on the steering wheel. I wanted to find Randall and feel him. I wanted time to turn back to when we were together and the rest of everything made sense. I didn't understand how he could be gone.

#

The night before, just as we were reaching the perfunctory and increasingly absurd "Should I stay or should I go now?" part of Paul's evening visit, I pointedly cleared my throat. Using whatever secret magic he employed, Paul answered that small utterance with, "How do you want to handle tomorrow?"

"I don't want to handle it at all. I would like to stay in bed and let it be the next day before I get out again."

"You could, you know." He rose from his chair on the front porch and took a step in order to be standing directly in front and just a few inches from me. "You can handle it however feels best to you."

"Oh, I know..." I felt my defenses reinforce a bit. "I just, you know, the kids want to..."

He leaned over and kissed my cheek. His response to my defensiveness appeared to be acquiescence. "You're an amazing mom, Jess. And the strongest woman I know." And then he turned toward the stairs.

"You're going." It wasn't a question.

"I don't think there is room for any more than Randall's

birthday tomorrow," he said. "I'll say a prayer for everyone, and I will give thanks for my friend and the life he lived."

I wanted to pause and marvel, again, at how Paul had the perfect words all the time. Instead, I felt the now-too-familiar stab of guilt knifing me in the throat. The last few weeks had been more comfortable between us, but I also felt myself growing more distant from everyone else as I tried to reconcile what was happening. And now, I was just convinced I could not, should not have Paul helping me through this milestone, nor could I console one of my husband's closest friends in his own grief. I had to get through it by myself. Randall deserved that.

"Thanks..." I said lamely.

There was no embrace and no goodbye, and I felt a very anxious chill go through me. Something about the moment made me wonder if I was about to lose Paul too.

#

But when I returned from the store, his Jeep was in my driveway. A lump in my throat, I climbed the stairs and found him waiting right where he had left me not so many hours before.He looked determined when I first glanced at him, but when he saw my face – a red and blotchy, mascara-tracked mess, I watched him melt.

"Oh Jess. I'm so sorry..."

"Why?" I said, almost exasperated. "You don't have to be sorry. You miss him, too. And you are going through the same, damn, horrible thing. You don't have to feel bad for me. You don't have to help me. I want *you* to be ok..." The tears had started again. I was most likely uncorked for the day.

"That doesn't make sense, Jess," he said. I could almost hear him counting to 10, patient Paul. "So because you're not the only one grieving, you have to grieve like some kind of hero? No one who cares about you can just be sad *for you*? Sweetheart... you know better than this. You *do* better than this, for all of us. Everyone around you. Why can't you have the same grace for yourself?"

"Because I left him!" I yelled. And when I did, I felt as if all the oxygen left me. I was doubled over, sobbing, maybe wailing. The sounds of me were foreign; I had not cried that hard for Randall since seeing his lifeless body at the hospital.

Part of me had been on autopilot since then.

The rest of me had been falling in love with Paul. And trying to deny it.

And that was why I was turning myself inside out, raw and wounded and desperate for some kind of resolution.

I opened my eyes to Paul. He had kneeled in front of me, hands clasping me at the hips. His eyes were like steel and his voice was low.

"Jessica Romano Oakley. Listen to me. I love you. *I love you.* I understand this pain. I share this. I want to help you. I want *you* to help *me*. But I am not going to just let you punish yourself. You didn't leave anybody. Randall *died*. He was the best, and you had an amazing life together, and then he died. *They* died! And being alone or pushing me away or torturing yourself with these lies about leaving him or disappointing your grown children is not going to bring him back."

"But I would if I could," I whimpered. It felt true, but it also felt so selfish. The reasonable part of me was trying to raise its voice above the crazy and say, *Don't hurt him. Don't you dare.*

I looked at him, but there was no telling whether those particular words made him feel any worse than he already did. He returned my gaze, unblinking and expressionless, waiting. I never wanted him to look at me that way again. I closed my eyes to block it out. He didn't reach for me, but I felt both his desire to do just that and the restraint he was employing in order to leave this up to me.

Randall loved me. My amazing Randall. My life without him would never be the same. I missed him today more than I had a month ago.

And I loved Paul with a purity and passion that I couldn't deny in spite of the timing and the constant, nagging confusion.

"I don't even understand how any of *this* is possible," I said softly, and he just nodded.

In a movie, I would have sunk to my knees next to him and bridged the gap. As it was, my knees didn't bend that fluidly, and I wasn't totally sure how he planned to get up from kneeling the way he was, so I opened my eyes and held my hands out to him. He braced himself and stood with me. There, with our hands clasped, his expression changed and so did my mind.

"I'm so sorry," I said, with fresh tears. "I don't know what I'm doing."

He laughed, and then I saw the tears brimming in his eyes. "I think we do know, Jess. It's so simple."

There he went again...

"Let's just follow this path," he continued. "I love you. Let me. Let yourself love me back. And when you're sad, be sad. And when you're happy, don't apologize. And if you feel like staying in bed, by yourself or, even better, with me, then do it. You are allowed to figure this out along the way. You don't have to write the book on *this*. You are living it. And I'm *with you*."

I drank in every word he said. I wanted to tell him that it almost sounded like a marriage vow, but I couldn't speak just yet. I just crossed the rest of the space between us, collapsing into his waiting embrace, holding him as tightly as I could and wishing it could be tighter. Cake and memories would have their place later. Right now would be the simplicity of sadness, alongside the gift of one who understood.

#

So Paul spent the day with me. We didn't say much. He fetched the ginger ale for me. He read on the porch while I baked the cake. He made me a peanut butter and jelly sandwich at lunchtime. We cuddled on the couch like two bunnies, and he handed me tissues as needed. I texted all the kids and told them I decided the restaurant was the perfect place to celebrate and we wouldn't come back to the house tonight after all. If anyone protested or thought it was strange, no one said anything to me.

At Los Cabos, we toasted Randall with Coronas, everyone ate steak fajitas or steak burritos, and Summer and Jake blew out a candle on their Grampy's cake. It was precious and sad and strange, and my heart stirred as I looked at what Randall and I had created together.

But then I went home, where we'd decided Paul would be waiting for me. We didn't say a lot. He made my tea the way I liked it. He lit a marshmallow-scented candle in the bathroom and took Cash for a walk while I showered. When I climbed into bed next to him, he chastely kissed my temple and turned off the lamp next to him, just like the other nights he stayed. As usual,

I was watching *Friends* on Netflix, and before one episode was over, he was asleep, breathing rhythmically next to me, one hand on my leg and our feet touching. Two more episodes flashed by – Monica and Rachel took their apartment back, and it was now after midnight. Randall's birthday was passed, I was wrung dry, and for the first time in almost two months, I knew exactly what I wanted to happen next.

I switched the TV over to a music station. Country. '90s. The Dixie Chicks were singing about cowboys and stars and new love. That felt lifetimes from where I was. I didn't need Paul to sweep me off my feet or ride me into the sunset or even take care of me. '80s country was better. Ann Murray, God bless her, was singing something much more befitting, filled with dried tears and finding our way home.

The feel of Paul next to me stirred everything in me. I just wanted him. I wanted his sunny laughter and his gentle eyes and his astute observations, his warm embraces and sweet whispers, his scars and his dreams, the way he knew me and the way he touched me, the way he challenged me and the way he saw the best in me. I wanted it all.

I nestled over next to him and kissed his ear. He didn't stir, so I tried again and moved to his neck. "Mmmm," he said sleepily, and then his hand went to the side of my face. The next moment, he was kissing my mouth, more deeply than he ever had, and somewhere in my head I heard Maggie saying, "He wants to..."

I moved my body closer to him, pressing against him, and he suddenly stopped kissing me back.

"Jess?" he said, a little breathlessly. "Is it time?"

I couldn't help it. I giggled. "Sorry. Reminds me of waiting for a baby."

"Good God, no," he answered, peppering his words with kisses. "But a life change. If you want one."

"I do. I want *you*," I said, and felt tears prick my eyes, proving I hadn't cried them all. They were different this time, though.

Ann Murray said it best. I needed him. And he was there.

"I adore you," I added, kissing the smoothness of his neck. "Without any *arbitrary manacles*. I want us together. I don't want to keep waiting and--" God, he smelled good. "I don't want to waste any more time. I love you."

He inhaled deeply. I was already wriggling out of my shorts, but before he moved again, he took my face in both his hands.

"I love you, Jess. Not... not the way I've always loved you. More. Completely. With everything I have left. I'm... I'm not going anywhere. I'm here and—" I cut him off with a kiss. He kissed back and said, "I'm here, and I love you."

My response was to ease closer to him, meeting his eyes and drinking in that amazing way he looked into me.

If apart we were lost, maybe together we were home.

Chapter Fifteen

It was a perfect spring Sunday. May at the beach was only surpassed in gloriousness by October, and only because May brought some craziness with our two annual bike weeks (motorcycles, not Huffys). But we were not there yet, and so the only din that could be heard from my house was that of the waves and of course, the occasional golf cart in reverse.

The beeps really did grate on my last nerve.

I'd impressed the hell out of the kids, and a little out of myself, with an offering of Greek salad, tzatziki, and with a flourish, spanakopita, complete with homemade phyllo dough, which took 12 eternities. My productivity was a result of an insomniac Food Network marathon, Paul spending Saturday on his properties, and Maggie coming over to assist me, though she rather randomly refused to come over the next day to enjoy it.

Altan, who had been born to Turkish parents living in Greece, swelled my head with his compliments. I had been a little nervous cooking this one for him. He'd left Greece for New York when he was 19, and he met Mikayla while driving her and her cousin Nora on a pedicab tour of Central Park. He and

Mikayla spent a lot of time Skyping and riding Spirit Airlines back and forth before they got engaged (on Bow Bridge, because, of course!). They got married there, lived in NYC for about a year, and then moved back when Altan decided he wanted to try his hand at tourism somewhere warmer. He and Mikayla worked their butts off in whatever jobs they could find until they saved enough to start their own company: a small marina renting jet skis on the inlet. It was a tough business, especially during our short but impactful winters (cold water is *cold* water!), but they both took side jobs and made investments – Mikayla was working on her yoga instructor certification – and they impressed us for making the kind of life they wanted.

I never really understood why Altan had agreed to leave the much more diverse and exotic sights, smells, and tastes of NYC for our small town in the southeast, but they were happy. He kissed my cheek sweetly as he stood from the table and said he would clean up. Mikayla caught my eye and smiled.

"If we keep him well fed, he'll never miss New York," I joked.

"He might not, but I do," she said wistfully.

"No place to raise a baby," Brittney retorted. "Unless you're Kelly Ripa, and I'm here to tell you, you are not. Although, your bronze husband is just as cute as hers."

"Thank you? I think?" Mikayla said. "Anyway, New York is a fine place to raise babies. Just think, you don't even need a car seat because: no car!"

"Yes, but you'd have to take that 200 dollars, multiply it by five, and buy one of those amazing buggies."

"Prams, I think, is what you have to call those," Abby chimed in. "The CityWalk! And I think it would be exhilarating. A lot to get used to in comparison, but think about the fact that you can walk to the market, the doctor's office, the zoo! And, when you're up all night nursing, you can have cheesecake *or* a nice curry *or* eggs and pancakes delivered."

"Spoken like a mama who knows what is truly essential," I said. When I looked at Abby, it was always with the marvel of how she'd gone from a green, barely-20 and always anxious mama to Travis, to the "pick your favorite cereal for dinner," Zen-mama that Summer and Jacob were enjoying. I totally got it, and I was totally happy for her that she grasped the *breezy* earlier in life than I had.

"Just remember," I said, injecting a tone of foreboding, "You might be able to walk to everything, but you will be walking in the bitter cold and the nasty, nasty snow. None of you lived in the Midwest for years on end, much less the north. Winter is not a fairy tale. It is a nightmare. *Game of Thrones*, only sans dragons."

"Snow is *pretty*," Mikayla, of the one year in NYC, insisted.

"So is the sand," I said knowingly. "Snow is much less enchanting when you're knee deep in it. Plus, it's *cold!*"

"Mama?" Sam's voice called from the living room sofa. "Can you come here for a minute?"

"Yep." I left the table, leaving the women to their next topic, which was what stroller Meghan the Duchess of Sussex had chosen (much research ensued).

"What's up, Hun?"

He had his business face on and his tablet in his lap. "Just wanted a chance to talk to you about some of Dad's... stuff." He could never just say "will" or "bequests" or "estate."

"Okay, Love. Go ahead."

He cleared his throat, looking downward. "Well, the main insurance policies are cut and dry, as you know. The check has been sent to pay off the house. The funds for the four of us are being put into accounts at BoA, and Abby and I have already set up 529 accounts for the three kids, per Dad's wishes."

"Perfect," I said. Play the odds. Somehow, Randall and I had ended up with four kids finishing college, or at least close.

"We just uncovered two policies that didn't have your name on them."

"Hmm. Really? What's the story?"

Sam looked up at me, finally. Tears glistened in his eyes, and he handed me the iPad. I read the vital information... each sizable payouts, each sole, unrelated beneficiaries. My Randall. I couldn't imagine a more noble tribute from him. In fact, the words I read even gave his untimely death some sudden meaning.

I said nothing, just nodded, smiled, and hugged my son.

And it was at precisely that moment that Paul knocked on the door.

Hmm. We had talked for a millisecond about him stopping by later in the day. We didn't say when, or if he would check with me first. So here he was. As well as most of my offspring. *Hmm.*

"Hey!" he called out brightly. The door opened into the living room, so he could immediately see that it was a crowd and not just me there to greet him.

I stood up like I had been cattle-prodded. "Hey!" I said back, too loudly, too sunnily. Paul looked at me like I was nuts and accepted my very demure, Pentecostal side-hug.

"Hi Paul," Sam called over my shoulder. He had stood up from the couch and was now giving Paul a gruff, back-slapping man-hug. This was not unusual, of course. He was pretty much "Uncle" Paul. It was just *weird*. *Dad is gone and Mom is sleeping with Uncle Paul and everyone in this room knows it.* (Well, maybe not Jacob and Summer, though they were pretty intuitive for their ages).

I listened to their banter in a panicked stupor. Only seconds went by before a contingent came over from the kitchen table, and even Travis emerged from his gaming in David's bedroom. I had nothing to do with the group of males who headed downstairs to throw something around at the beach. Paul casually glimpsed at me as he turned around, but that was all.

The contingent left behind, namely Abby, Summer, and Mikayla, looked at me pleasantly when I turned around. There was a hint of a laugh in Abby's eyes as she helped Summer spread Memory cards across the table.

"Mama, maybe I don't want to play," Summer said.

"You just got it out, Summer."

"I know, but the boys went to the beach. I wanna go!"

Abby looked at me as though for permission, and I just shrugged. "You want to, Kayla?" I asked, believing that I sounded casual.

"Gotta potty first," she announced, causing Summer to giggle as she began returning cards back to their red rack.

#

Three hours later, it was dusk, and my house was returned to its state of quiet. Paul sat silently at the counter watching me scrape and scour the stovetop. When we had returned from the beach, I'd decided to make a "quick" Mexican hot fudge sauce for sundaes, and Summer helped me... make a huge mess of it.

When I stepped back to admire the shine my special/all-natural cleaning paste had helped me achieve, I saw him giggle and shake his head from the corner of my eye.

"What?"

He kept shaking it. "You. You're straight out of an HGTV episode. Or ripe for a lifestyle blog. Or that crazy Pioneer Woman's long-lost sister."

"I wish. I *love* her."

"It amazes me that this relaxes you," he observed. "This many people would drive Leah up a wall. She would have to plan for days before and recover for days after."

I laughed, recalling conversations Leah and I would have about entertaining. She just wasn't into it. When I mentioned that it could be as simple as putting on some coffee and serving sandwiches, she looked at me like I was insane and said, "No, it can't!" Her southern sensibilities ran deep and ran formal, even if it was just her kids coming, and she found my "throw it together" philosophy alien. Dinner every Sunday for the Jamesons was a choice between their favorite Italian place and their favorite barbecue place.

"Well, Leah enjoyed stuff that I never did," I remarked. "Gardening. Clothing. Decorating. If we all could do it all, we wouldn't even need *you* guys."

"You don't have to tell me," he said. "But this does? Still? It relaxes you?"

I dried my hands and turned to fully face him. "I mean, *relax* is not the word I would ever associate with hosting, even when it's just all the kids. It's just... natural, I guess? I plan, I cook, I chat, I multi-task, I eat. It plays to all my strengths." I shrugged. "It's what I do, so it doesn't stress me out or anything."

He was looking at me a little funny, and my chest tightened a little.

"Does it... does it stress you out?" I asked, carefully. "Because... I don't... I mean, this part, Sundays, I don't see it changing any time soon..."

"Aw Jess. That isn't what I was trying to say." He paused, considering. "This is the first time I crashed. It was fun. Your family is great; they were very welcoming. Altan even asked me to come to the marina and have lunch with him this week. You just seemed a little... I don't know... I honestly can't think of a word. It wasn't stressed. Maybe it was... stretched."

Now I paused to consider. It wasn't the cooking. I really did love finding new things to create and revisiting favorites. I liked making things for the kids, especially for Abby and Mikayla, that they wouldn't have time to cook themselves during the week. And to be honest, since Randall was no longer with us, there was a wider range to choose from. He would have never enjoyed something like spanakopita or the orange chicken and pineapple fried rice I made the week before. (Although, bless his heart, he would have happily enjoyed a few microwaved chili dogs while everyone else ate what they wanted. He just didn't care about it that much.)

"Hmmm..." I exhaled, smiling at him a bit nervously. I was not afraid of his judgment. Rather the opposite, I was scared of my own. "I guess... oh, man. I don't know how you manage to see these things in me. I love them all. I love them all wanting to be here. I love the food and the vibe. But if I am being totally, totally honest... small crowds seem to suit me better these days. I just... it doesn't matter, though, right? By default, we are not a small crowd. We are only going to get bigger with time."

Paul's caring eyes were just the balm I needed in the moment of difficult confession. "I think," he said, rising from his stool and crossing to me, "that Abby and Mikayla would be happy to rotate these dinners. And Brittney would be happy to call and reserve a table for everyone at Creek Ratz or Wahoo's or anywhere else. And if you give those wonderful humans you raised the chance, they will prove to you that they can adapt to change, including their mother's need for some space."

Damn him. Really. "I know you're right," I said. "About them adjusting," I added hastily. "But isn't this what's supposed to happen? I decrease. They increase. I mean, in a few months, I won't have a job. What's the big deal if I spend one day a week cooking for a crowd? They're my *family*."

"First of all, John the Baptist, it's not time for you to decrease. Your kids are just not kids anymore. And just from watching them with you for one afternoon, I'm convinced they love being around you because you're *you*. You don't have to *mom* them. They just want to hang with you."

"Second of all?"

He wrinkled up his nose. "I don't really have one. I just wanted to use the John the Baptist comment with some indignation."

"Didn't Obi Wan Kenobi say that, too?"

"Maybe, but John was first."

"True."

"Paul..." I didn't think he necessarily wanted a response from me, but my default with him was to talk things out, and he opened a compartment I'd had sealed shut for some time. "I have been the same version of me for a long time now. I thought... Well, I thought with Randall gone, I would just keep being me and things would go on as best and as closely as they could."

He didn't respond, but was watching me intently, giving me the space to analyze.

"It won't work, though," I finally said. "I'm not the same. And I can't make things the same as they were."

He nodded and took one more step toward me. I readily accepted his embrace, suddenly completely done.

"This is *hard*," I said.

"I know," he answered, just as soberly, and I believed him.

#

The next morning, I pulled up to our church, file folder tucked into my bag. Pastor Carter's assistant, Evie, greeted me outside his office. We hugged, she did the head tilt, and then she went right in to how much they had missed me the past few Sundays.

I smiled somewhat stiffly. I was a Jesus girl at heart, through-and-through, but my thoughts on churchgoing had been morphing since David became a competitive surfer in his pre-teen years. Many competitions took place on Sundays, and so whenever we had to miss church, I was adamant about "making it up," as though that precept was laid out with "Love your neighbor" or something. By the time he was in his sophomore year and also playing basketball and baseball at school, I threw up my hands a little. We went to church most of the time, but we didn't volunteer to be ushers or nursery workers, so we could miss when we wanted to miss. We visited sick neighbors and I organized or participated in twenty thousand meal trains and we generally felt, as my family made fun of me for saying for years, like we "had the Jesus thing covered."

So Evie knew I was not a church-every-Sunday person, and yet this observation was among the first she'd made. It didn't bode well.

I looked in her eyes and said gravely, "Sometimes I just don't want to leave the house." It was true, after all.

"Oh, Jessie!" She stepped forward with another ginormous hug. There was a sniffle, too. I felt my simmering sense of guilt bubble up. She was a perfectly nice person and maybe she did actually miss seeing me. *Calm down, Defensive Tackle*, I told myself.

"Pastor and Morgan are waiting for you," she said sincerely. "We are all happy you're here."

I offered a slightly more generous smile and let myself in. Carter and Morgan were sitting opposite each other around the coffee table and both jumped to their feet to greet me. Their embraces were solid and welcome; they had been in our lives for nearly the entire time we lived at the beach. They'd been with us when we lost Jamie. They dedicated David when he was born. We supported them through Morgan's breast cancer some years back. They were trusted friends, whom I had allowed to slip outside my circle in the past few months.

"Sit down," Carter said, and I settled in on the love seat next to Morgan, who passed me a coffee cup and grasped her own. We made small talk for a few minutes. How were the kids? Had I heard their youngest proposed to his girlfriend? Would I like to come for dinner once my schedule got easier?

All of those were perfectly pleasant topics, but the butterflies were going to tear up my stomach until I got through the business at hand.

"So, um, one of the things I've been busy with, of course, closing... transitioning..." *(that damn word again)* "I guess, dealing with, Randall's estate."

They nodded.

"I thought it was cut and dry enough, but he had a few specific requests, and two insurance policies I didn't know about at all. One will fund a one-time scholarship in Jamie's memory." My heart surged every time I thought of it. "And the other, well..." I leaned forward and handed a document from the folder in my lap to Carter. "Salt Life Church is the sole beneficiary of this one."

Carter looked down at the paper in his hand. It was breathtaking to me when I had found it, but the expression on his face might have surpassed my own feelings. Perhaps because by then several other nuggets of incredibly considerate forethought on Randall's part had been uncovered. That he left our home church of nearly three decades a million-dollar bequest didn't surprise me more than a little. But Carter looked shaken.

"Randall..." he said, still staring at the document. Then he looked up at me. "Jessie, I don't know what to say. I... he..." He shifted a heavy glance to Morgan. "This will pay off the mortgage, handily, and fund Lunchbox Buddies for... years..."

Tears pricked my eyes. Lunchbox Buddies was Randall and Carter's project together. They'd taken over from another local organization a few years back. Every weekend, kids at local schools were sent home with enough food to feed them for two days, and every summer, the program was expanded for weekday meals. Randall's dream had been to include less processed sugar and more whole foods, more protein. It was a tall order, and his untimely demise was going to help see it through.

"I'm so proud of him," I said, shaking my head. "And I am so grateful he'll be part of this legacy. It's so worthy."

"It will be *his* legacy," Carter said. "Along with yours, and your family's."

I smiled, tipping back my coffee.

"Jessie," Morgan said gently, "We were so happy you were coming in today. And I think I speak for Carter as well that this was not what we expected. It's truly amazing."

"Yeah... I was... excited?... to give it to you." I smiled knowingly and shook my head. "I don't seem to have the right words for any of this. I feel like there should be an asterisk next to every adjective I use. I'm not excited that Randall died; I'm excited that the church and hungry kids will benefit from it. I'm not happy for the reason I'm here, but I'm happy to see you both."

They returned the sentiments, having dealt with all manner of human emotions and complications during their tenure. It was relieving not to have to over-explain everything I said, and so we went on, discussing general life things. It felt normal. For awhile.

"It's really, really good to see you, Jessie," Morgan said again, but this time, she eyed Carter, which seemed to signal a shift. He sat up straighter in his chair as his gaze moved to me.

"We tried to stop by last Wednesday on the way home from Bible study," she said, with forced breeziness.

I didn't have to think very hard about where I was or what I was doing the previous Wednesday. It had been the night after Randall's birthday, and Paul had stayed over nearly every night since then, usually driving himself over.

I should have let them off the hook. They were old friends. Dedicated pastors. They had never, ever done an untoward thing to me. But I couldn't. In the moment, I didn't feel like anyone should be less uncomfortable than I was. So I answered, "Oh? Why didn't you?"

Carter shifted, clearly *the* most uncomfortable one in the room. When I looked at him just then, I didn't see my pastor, but Randall's friend. It melted my defensiveness for a moment.

"We saw Paul's Jeep in the driveway," Morgan began. "I understand you've been working hard through the acquisition of your company, it's just... the front lights weren't on, and we had heard that maybe..."

My hand covered my mouth. I was gaping at her. She was fine until the "we heard," and suddenly, *I* heard the voice of a dozen church ladies, back when I was 18 and pregnant with Sam, needing faith and support more than ever before in my life and instead getting judgment and gracelessness. They were voices that drove my parents straight out of the church they'd raised me in, possibly even the voices that drove my brother from church altogether. Those voices never had anything helpful to say. One of those voices had even donned me a "Jess-ebel." Thank God there wasn't social media back then; I might have even gotten meme'd.

But I was no longer a teen in trouble; at 56, I was plenty supported, plenty full of faith. I might have doubted my own decisions, but I did not doubt my own *intentions*.

"Morgan." I turned completely around in my seat, facing her

fully, ignoring that Carter was even in the room, and leaving no room for interpretation. "I'm certain you've heard something. Maybe a lot of things. Because I've been hiding *nothing*. Paul has been our dear friend for years. He remains dear to me. So please, ask me your questions right here, right now."

She looked at Carter and then back. I struggled to suppress my remorse. This was not the conversation I wanted to have today.

"Well... are you and Paul pursuing a relationship, beyond friendship?"

I raised my eyebrows, universal sign of indignance. "Yes."

"And your families know? It's *not* a secret?"

"It's not a secret, Morgan, no." I sighed. "I mean, I haven't changed my Facebook status. In fact, it still says I am married to Randall Oakley."

"Okay. Okay... Jessie, I just need to ask you something else. You have every right to be angry at the question, but as your friend, and as your pastor, I need to ask. Okay?"

I gestured for her to go on.

"Did... did this just start?"

Oh, Morgan.

I knew, *I knew*, someone was going to ask this. I just wish it hadn't been her.

"I was not cheating on Randall with Paul." My voice was tittering on the edge.

"And..." she sighed. "Randall and Leah?"

This time, I did snap my head back to glare at Carter. "Jesus God! Are you kidding me right now?"

His head dropped. She sighed again. I was unleashed.

"Morgan, do you remember, back after one of your surgeries, when I rode up to the hospital with Carter?"

"I... I guess...?"

"Did you ever think we were having an affair?"

"Jessie! Of course not."

"Yet a car ride is the summary of evidence that has catapulted you to ask me this question about Randall and Leah, who had probably never been in a car alone together, and just happened to get killed the first time they were. It's ridiculous. You hear me? You agree, right? The circumstances, all of it. It's ridiculous. And if I could turn back time, and make them be here again, I would. I'm certain Paul would. Because I madly love all three of those people—and this? This *sucks!*"

Carter got up then, wiping his face with his hands, and sat on the arm of the couch next to Morgan. "Jessie. We... please remember, people come to us. You've heard some of this before. Crazy theories. Unjustified thoughts. And our answer to them is that it's none of their business. That they should take any concern they might have and take it to you, and use it to serve you, and Paul, in your time of grieving. I know you're both grieving deeply."

"Are you sure?" I said, still with an edge. "I mean, I'm not just *over* my husband dying? Paul hasn't just blown right past losing his wife?"

"Jessie..." he started again, but Morgan cut him off. "Jessie, you can see how people might question the timing, just the... rapidness?"

"Sure. I can see how they might. I probably would have in their shoes. But I am in *my shoes*. And if anyone bothers to ask,

I will tell them how uncomfortable those shoes are. They don't even match. One is still married to a man I've lost after loving him for 35 years and mourning him and trying to figure out how life *should* look now. And one is enjoying every moment with another man whom I have known and cherished for a long time, and slowly concluding that that is *okay*. I'm not breaking any rules here. My husband *died*. Leah *died*. No one's judgments can make this situation any harder for us, so maybe they don't need to bother trying."

I almost smiled, because in the back of my head, Paul was beaming at me. Maybe I was finally getting it.

"Jessie," Carter said again.

"Yes, Carter?" I still sounded a little bitey, and I didn't even want to.

"Can you write that down, so when people do ask us, we can give them the full text?"

He smiled then, and I broke into a slightly embarrassed laugh. These were my friends. *My friends.*

Please God, just let me keep some sanity and stability through all of this.

"I'm sorry, Jessie," Morgan said. "We should have called you sooner. I should have just... asked you."

"You should have just knocked on the door," I said. "You've always been welcome in my home. You always will be. So many things are changing; I would rather those simple facts did not."

"We wanted to respect your space and your privacy," Carter added.

"I appreciate that," I said, honestly. "Let's... just move on. I don't... I don't know if I'm ready to come to church and sit next to Paul, but we are not a secret. You don't have to cover for me. If anyone asks how *I* am doing, or what I'm doing, you can tell them I'm processing. And if they ask you how they can help, tell them I like Dunkin' Donuts coffee before 2 P.M., and Moscato after..."

"Fair enough," Carter said, as Morgan reached over and hugged me fiercely.

We chatted for another hour, about every little thing. We made plans for dinner, the three of us for now, the following week. I drove home without any anger, but also feeling completely drained. Would even happy moments always be so complicated from here on out? And if it was this hard with people who "approved" of us, how crazy was it going to get with anyone who didn't?

Chapter Sixteen

It had *only* been months before, after his very high-school-esque year at our local tech college, that we finally sent David off to college at USC, less than three hours away in Columbia. But it had been momentous, and Randall and I shared much of Labor Day weekend with Paul and Leah, attending a Journey tribute concert at the House of Blues Friday night, doing a 5K with some other friends from church on Saturday, and then actually hanging out at the beach for much of Sunday afternoon before heading to the Marshwalk for a perfectly beachy dinner.

"Here's to the empty nest," Leah had cheered, raising her glass and laughing. She had told me that time would start passing at light speed, but that she had absolutely loved the past six years or so of having all the kids grown, even with the setbacks that were usually brought on by Katy (hotheaded unicorn!). "There's one in every family," I'd murmured, knowing I had been the one in mine (teenage, unwed mother!) and David was likely to be the one in ours (unfocused baby of four!).

"What's next, then?" Paul asked boisterously, as though we'd never talked about it before. Everyone at the table already knew that *Deep as the C* – our curriculum balancing act of creativity and Christian worldviews in literature, history, education, and even parenting – was winding down, and probably knew that I personally had no clue what I would do after.

"Hopefully more grandkids and some annual passes to Disney World," Randall said, giving my knee a squeeze. I smiled grandly at him. Disney was just the top of a long list of travel plans we'd been making.

"Yeah. I'm going to try to get hired to play the Fairy Godmother at Cinderella's Castle," I quipped. "And I'm totally hoping there's a baby in the family soon. I bet you can't wait until Danielle's is born!"

We sailed off into easy chatter, babies, kids, travel. The guys started talking about football season and which of our friends would be allowed to come over for the Carolina/Clemson game. But quite unusually, the conversation circled back to me.

"Jesse won't spend *all* her time with grandkids," Paul said, peering at me. "You'll keep writing, won't you?"

"Geez Paul, you're not her guidance counselor," Leah told him. "Maybe she's going to collect seashells and read in her hammock. Leave her alone."

Leah herself had given up her real estate license a few years ago and was focusing on property management (a duty Paul shared) and home staging, meeting her sisters on the regular at a timeshare in Hilton Head, and occasionally, getting Paul to go shagging. She also loved taking little Christian to the children's art museum and out for crepes. She did freezer cooking with Danielle, and she road-tripped up to Katy's with Julie or by herself every few weeks. No one was telling Leah how to live her "second act" or third act or whatever it was supposed to be. She was having fun figuring every bit of it out herself. It was one of the things I admired about her.

"You're going to keep writing, right babe?" Randall said. Like most writers, I had a thousand ideas for essays, a children's story, a how-to, perhaps even a tome. I'd never had time to explore any of them, but I was also afraid to proclaim myself a free-lancer.

"Sure," I said with a shrug. "I don't know what, or how much, or if it will be just for fun. I don't know."

"You could teach writing, you know," Paul said.

"I've told her that," Randall added. "But—"

"I don't enjoy kids," I said. "This is not news." We all snickered. I mean, of course I loved kids, but I was done teaching them, for sure.

"You could teach adults," Paul continued. Leah widened her eyes at me across the table before she swatted his shoulder.

"Stop it, Paul. She doesn't want to teach. For the love...!" Randall was laughing, but Paul didn't smile. Leah didn't seem to notice, but something felt off to me. Almost tense.

"Truth is," I said, swirling the orange around my sangria glass, "I don't know. And I know that I need to know, because if I'm unfocused I will end up eating all the Oreos and starting a scrapbook I'll never finish and cooking too much soup and writing two ill-fated chapters on why the 90210 reboot never really worked... I gotta have a plan." David's ADHD had come to him honestly. When I wasn't under a deadline, I was often under six million other things. I looked across at Paul, who gave me a small smile then. "But truth is, we are still months away from being finished, so I don't need to have one yet. Plus, Mikayla *is* going to be pregnant any day now and *that* will give me a focal point for sure!"

"Allow me to toast this time," Randall said. I scrunched my nose up at him and raised my glass. "To whatever Jessie rocks next!" He leaned over and kissed my cheek. "I can't wait to watch."

Later that night, at we often did, Randall and I rehashed the evening. He didn't seem to notice anything worthy of note about the conversation or the mood that surrounded it. I had been mildly annoyed – less so than Leah, for sure – about being put on the spot over big life decisions I had no intentions of making yet. Every cent of writing royalties I'd made had been put away as my contribution to our retirement fund, and Randall still made enough to support us comfortably and pay David's room and board. If this *was* my retirement, so be it.

The only thing looming about the end of our publication contract was that it was the end of *our* publication contract. I'd never had a job in which I worked with the same person for 15 years, and I never would again. Paul and I hadn't talked about it, but I wondered if he was feeling weird about it. Nothing else made sense about his unusually pointed questioning during a night of casual fun.

"I'm sure Leah will be glad to share more of the property duties with Paul," Randall observed, clad in his boxer briefs and looking out our window. "Maybe you could get into that business with them. No one knows this side of the beach like you..."

I returned his smile and patted his pillow. Of all the things I didn't know, I knew for sure that I did not want to be a property manager in any capacity. "Eh..." I answered.

"You really could do nothing for a while, too," he said, arranging the covers. "I'm still working because I want to be, but you can relax. In fact, I'd love for you to relax..."

"Mmmm." I returned his kiss and laid my head on him. "We are miles and months away from me having to figure it out. Plenty of time."

#

Now it was Labor Day weekend's springtime cousin, Memorial Day, and Paul and I were embarking on our first getaway together. Our digital library was done, at least our part of it. He was declared free of all walking apparatuses. And after spending the whole month navigating our own emotions and those of seven grown children, we both just wanted it to be quiet.

David had come home from USC, and he promised to take good care of Cash while we hightailed it to Cherokee, where we'd stay in a cabin, read, take some walks, maybe fish, maybe ride horses, maybe nothing. With two duffels of clothes and two sacks of groceries in the back of Paul's silver Jeep, and a specially-curated playlist on my phone, we made great time on the 350-mile trek. I sang along with equal passion to Chicago and Billy Ocean, Guns 'n Roses and Dolly and Kenny, but Paul absolutely drew the line twice: switching off Stone Temple Pilots right in the middle of "Flies in the Vaseline" and Four Non-Blondes just as I was waking in the morning and stepping outside.

"Grunge is the dumbest music ever," he insisted.

"Maybe you would appreciate them if you had four non-blonde children!" I protested zealously.

"Dumb. And Brittney is blonde."

I laughed. "You think that's real? How long have you been around?"

He shrugged. "I make it a point to pretend not to notice those things. And let's not go down the road to Tori Amos and Alanis Morissette."

I gasped. "Blasphemy! Those are the female voices *of my time!*" I scrolled through my list and proceeded to sing him every word of "Hand in my Pocket." He shook his head and was rewarded afterwards with Aerosmith and the bag of peanut M&Ms I had stashed for him.

The road trip was without event, and when we arrived at our cabin (after stopping at a tiny local market for eggs, cream, and steaks), we unpacked our bags in fairly quiet unison, and Paul followed my lead, to the hot tub.

(Because *nothing* says quaint, simple, mountain cabin like an outdoor Jacuzzi with a view. In the literary archive of my mind, my superhero Claire Fraser was judging me).

We were now on a self-declared (and lack-of-internet-induced) technology break, but Paul had found a radio in the linen closet that ran on batteries and changed stations with a dial. There was some static cutting into the oldies station; they were playing real oldies, not *the music of my childhood*, for crying out loud, but The Temptations and The Four Seasons and The Beatles and The friggen Monkees.

"Oh, I love this one," I said, as "Cry to Me," aka, the *Dirty Dancing* sexy-time song, came on. "Turn it up!"

Paul smiled and shook his head, leaning over to the shelf and adjusting the volume. When he settled back in, his legs stretched out and intertwined with mine. "How do you even know these songs? None of these people ever wore flannel shirts or ironic combat boots."

"Hush," I said. "My mom had music playing all the time. All the good stuff from the '60s and '70s. And this song, darling, was the one to which Baby and Johnny consummated their star-crossed and very unseemly relationship."

"Sometimes I feel like you'd be happier hanging out with Katy than with me," he chided.

"What times are those?" I asked, sliding across the water to him.

He brushed a piece of hair from my face. "The times when I don't know what the hell you're talking about. Like whether Baby and Johnny are actual people."

I chuckled, and he stifled me with his kiss.

"I can't believe you don't know them," I said, a little breathlessly.

"You can tell me all about them," he said. "Later."

And then we proceeded to use the song in much the way that fictional 17-year-old and her older guy did. It was only our second time being intimate. After the first, I'd still felt shy and regressively cautious. And then, time just was what it was. It was easier and much more comfortable to fall exhaustedly into bed each night after a chaste kiss, and the mere act of sleeping next to each other was still crackling with intimacy.

This time, everything was slower and brighter and eyes-opened-wider. He buried his face in my hair and breathed, murmuring to me that it was like his favorite hiding place. He kept his legs wrapped around me as we explored each other. I paid attention to details I had missed before and let him linger in places even when I felt self-conscious.

And I thought I just about felt myself having a holy exhale.

#

When our steak dinner was cleared away and the remnants of raspberry pie scraped clean from our dishes, Paul lit the fireplace and we sat in its dim light. The radio batteries were already drained, and we had no intentions of going anywhere that night. Though there was a DVD player and a stack of movies present, we left the TV off and sat on opposite ends of the couch, legs stretched toward each other, comfortably silent.

"Remember Labor Day weekend?" Paul said, his voice low, so as to pierce the quiet but not shatter it.

"Hmmm. Of course. It was busy. And fun. And a million years ago."

"Seems like it," he agreed. "Remember talking about this, right now? Being done working together?"

"We aren't *done*, done. We still have that God-forsaken planner to finish."

"Um, you do," he said. "And you have access to every usable note I've ever written. I don't need to be anywhere near that."

"Grrrr." I knew he was right. I just wished I was done, too. "Anyway, yes. And I'd venture to say I am even less inspired or sure about what I am doing after than I was in September."

"Are you worried?"

Again with the pointedness. "Not per se," I started, slowly, because I was figuring it out as I spoke. "I'm not worried financially. I think CPA Tracy has me all figured out. I mean, if I want a yearlong European sabbatical, I might need to work part time at one of the beach stores. I don't know which is better though. Wings, Eagles..."

"That would be a sight," he laughed. "I bet you get a great discount on hermit crabs and shell necklaces."

"Haha. Yeah. So I don't know. I'm sure Rachel could connect me to some fitting opportunities. I still just don't know what I want to do. The house is paid off, but the insurance is on the expensive side and the upkeep is a little high maintenance for me."

Paul suddenly sat up straighter. "You're thinking about selling? You *love* your house."

I smiled at him, feeling warm adoration wash over me, for him and the house. "Well, I do. But it's a lot of house and a lot of management, and maybe something simpler would be a better fit for me. I would also make a profit to put away. As long as I could stay close to the water and avoid HOAs, then, I don't know." I shrugged, like I was talking about replacing my computer or a pair of jeans. "We'll see."

Paul stared into the fire for a minute, his whole countenance suddenly quieter.

"What is it?" I finally asked. "Are you thinking about what *you're* going to do?"

He shook his head, a small, forced smile creeping over his lips. "All the time. Yeah, all the time. But for work? Nah. Not really. Property management is about to get real during the summer. I'm just realizing how much Leah did to keep everything occupied and maintained and turning a profit. When my teaching pension kicks in, it can go straight to savings if things stay like they are now."

I nodded. This was good for him; it would keep him busy. But I knew we were dancing lightly around a subject that loomed.

"Are any of your properties, um, livable for you?" I asked, cool, casual. "Or are you planning to stay put?" Paul and Leah's house was almost massive compared to ours: four bedrooms including two master suites, formal dining, formal office, "Carolina" room, gourmet kitchen, plus the finished office in the garage, the small saltwater pool, and tiny guest room separated off the back, which, far as I knew, rarely if ever got used.

He looked at me, a bit startled. "I'm not sure any of our rentals would be livable for me. They're all in pretty high-touristy areas. There's one that's possible, maybe... But on that subject, if anything, the main house, *our* house, would make a great annual rental. I could probably list the she-shed or whatever it is separately if I really wanted to."

I giggled at his use of *she-shed*, picturing Leah out there with a bottle of wine and a stack of back issues of *Real Simple*. That's precisely how she utilized the space the first weekend after they'd finished it. And then...

The silence was awkward. I was getting more used to that between us. It was, I suppose, an expected byproduct of our context changing. I looked down at my lap. Paul's feet were right next to it. I caressed his ankles absentmindedly, soothing him, soothing myself.

He sighed with pleasure and relaxed his head against the armrest. His next words didn't come until I reached the soles of his feet.

"Stop it," he said. "No tickling."

"Didn't mean to," I said. My eyes were closed too. I moved my massage to his insteps but found myself getting sleepy.

"Maybe we should go to bed," he suggested.

"It's like, 8:30."

"So? Are there rules?"

I opened my eyes, perhaps searching for a sign or wonder, but I didn't see one. "If there are, I am pretty sure we've already broken them anyway."

He looked at me more intently then, and I looked back. In that particular moment, I searched but could not find a difference in the way he looked at me here, with the two of us almost naked and tangled together in front of a cozy fire-for-two, and the way he'd been looking at me for years.

I was comforted and unnerved, assured and confused. It should have bothered me, but I was always at odds with myself anyway.

"You have always loved me well," I said, tears automatically springing to my eyes.

He couldn't really reach me without finagling quite a bit, so he patted my feet, his own eyes verging on shiny. "I *have* always loved you, Jess." There was an honesty in it that hurt my heart, and I couldn't begin to know why.

I went ahead and finagled, moving quite clumsily to the floor, kneeling in front of him, our eyes locked in unasked questions.

"I... I was never unfaithful," he said.

I shook my head. I knew that.

"But you... having you around... well, Jess, it didn't take long for you to become the *easiest* person to be around. My favorite, sometimes. It never occurred to me that we would be here, ever. Not even... not *ever*."

The correction was too obvious to ignore. I would not and did not. "Not even *when*, Paul? Not even what?"

He looked away. I would wait.

He didn't look back at me when he spoke. "Leah and I were not exactly living... *intimately*. I hadn't slept in our bedroom since Katy moved out. We were... *together*... We ran the business. We ran the house. We ran the family. But we were not *Together*. Not like you and me right now, and maybe not even like you and me *before*."

I felt a pang tear at me. What he was saying was not exactly earth-shattering. Randall and I had observed and discussed our friends as a couple through the years, how Paul and Leah were different than we were. They didn't hold hands. They didn't compare their daily plans to ensure a sync-up. They didn't go away on trips, just the two of them. Sometimes, quite honestly, they didn't seem to necessarily regard or enjoy each other very much. It worried me sometimes; it worried *us*. It didn't seem to have a bearing on my partnership with Paul, the time we spent together. But I also never asked Leah about it. She would mention Paul, of course: *Did Paul mention blah-blah-blah? Did you hear Paul and Randall are golfing Saturday... you want to get brunch?* I always assumed that to a sentimental empath like me, Leah was just casual. She didn't have family pictures as the wallpaper on her phone. She didn't tear up at sappy songs or celebrate Facebook Friendiversaries. She didn't end calls with "I love you." But she loved Paul. *Of course* she did.

Still, other images flashed from my memories: Paul's vulnerability the day his mother died. Paul good-naturedly coaching me during my first weeks of empty nest syndrome. Paul faithfully acknowledging the anniversary of Jamie's birth and death, though I didn't even know him when we'd lost Jamie. His raw sense of betrayal on display when Katy left town in his stolen Mustang. Our shared exhaustion during deadlines. Our inside jokes. How easy it was to hug him. How much I wanted to talk to him the days after the funerals. How I pretended to be aggravated the first night he came over, but how glad I actually was. How he melted me and kind of always had.

I never used the label on us, but it was clear Paul and I had an intimacy before Randall and Leah died. At that time, it didn't compete with the intimacy I had with Randall, but it was still there. Now he'd just said there was a lack of intimacy between him and Leah. Did that mean ours had been something other than friendship? Did it change anything at all?

I exhaled what felt like all the oxygen in my body. I sank so that I was sitting on my feet. I'd always felt protective of Paul. I equated it to a sisterly love. Was it something else? Did I do something wrong? Did we?

"That's a giant can of worms we busted," he said quietly. "And you're trying to chase 'em all right now, aren't you?"

"Of course I am," I said evenly. "And you know that because you always know. You always know me better than I know myself."

He nodded.

"Did we do something wrong?" I asked, and my heart was racing.

Paul pulled at my hands until I gathered myself up next to him. He held them as I faced him, squeezing them tight.

"No, Jess. I was never unfaithful. You were never unfaithful. And I never, ever thought we would be here."

"But... did you want to be? Did you think about it?"

He shook his head. "Not really. No. I'm only saying... loving you is easy for me. This doesn't rattle me because..." He shrugged. "It's just not that big of a jump."

I squeezed his hands back. His words didn't really settle me. I wanted a definitive answer. I guess I wanted Jesus to manifest as a sparkling, somewhat sassy African American sister (my Maggie, but kinder) or maybe just a handsome thirtysomething carpenter, and tell me in plain speak that Paul and I were not wrong, had not been wrong, and that not only were our belated spouses sitting in Heaven all happy for us, but everyone on the face of the earth was celebrating too.

"You are too used to being the teacher's pet," he added, a small grin in place. "Just because some people will think we are wrong doesn't mean we actually are."

"You *promise* we aren't?" I asked, a hint of whining in my voice.

"Would you have left Randall for me?"

"Paul! No..."

"Did I ever, in all these years, make you wonder if I would leave Leah for you?"

Boiled down, Paul-style, to simplicity, the answers were clear. "*No.*"

"People love whom they love. I loved you then, and I love you now. Maybe it's not totally different. Maybe it's just... more. Can you deal with that?"

Could I? My heart was racing as though I was taking a test, or being watched. I wasn't nervous about Paul himself anymore, but why couldn't I shake the nagging feeling of being disapproved of, talked about, or simply wrong?

I closed my eyes and exhaled in an attempt to still myself. "I love that you love me." I said.

Mimicking my whine, he squeezed my hands again. "Can we go to sleep *now?*"

#

I was up for hours before Paul in the morning. There was a chill in the mountain air, and I was absolutely blissful on the porch with a blanket, a carafe of coffee, and a library book I'd been on the waitlist for since the beginning of the year that now seemed ridiculous. Star-crossed love was so simple and easy for thin and successful heroines in their 30s, living and shopping and juggling handsome though flawed executives in New York.

Ah, but... the truth in my own love story, though it was almost impossible for me to get there, was that while it was not simple in its background, it should be nothing but easy in execution. I was not looking for a prince, a father to my children, or a rescuer. I just wanted to love Paul and receive his love in return. Without guilt, if that was at all possible.

I am 56 years old. My story isn't over...

That phrase, those three dots, had taken on new meaning for me, approximately 21 years ago. Who was I kidding? It had been 21 years ago on February 26, the day that I gave birth to our son Jamie, who had already died.

He had been a surprise. Randall had adopted Sam the year after we were married; seven years later we had Mikayla and Brittney in pretty quick succession (14 months apart, to be exact). For a while we'd been concerned that we *couldn't* have children together, and then, after the girls came, we were fine being "done."

Another seven years later, Randall was staring down 50 and we were glancing toward the future, what we might do with ourselves when kids didn't need us all the time. Then, during a bizarre, South Carolina, four-day ice storm that November, I realized I hadn't had my period since before Halloween. Randall was out of town but made amused and knowing noises to me over the phone. As soon as the roads were cleared, I drove to the Dollar General and bought five pregnancy tests. Each one was an immediate double line.

We welcomed the news of "Baby J" (James, after Randall's dad, or Joy, after my grandma) with an overflowing bag of mixed emotions, but it only took about a day for celebration and excitement to rise to the top. A surprise baby after all this time was surely meant to be. We recalibrated all of our plans. I recalibrated my entire self. I went to a pregnancy group run by a midwife, determined to try for a VBAC (Brittney had been a footling breech, requiring delivery by Caesarean). I prepared my excited little girls and their reservedly-pleased big brother to make room in their lives for another sibling. And when we went for the gender reveal ultrasound, we took both Mikayla and Brittney with us, with plans to shop afterwards for whoever was *in there.*

The details are always unbearable in their relaying, from the look on the technician's face as she moved her wand over my abdomen, to the look on Randall's face as he held our sobbing daughters, staring at me with tears coursing down his own cheeks, from the moment I acquiesced to another C-section, to the moment we had to let Jamie go after holding his lifeless but otherwise perfect form for four and a half hours.

We left the hospital the next day, carrying a teddy bear and a few arrangements of white flowers. Randall tucked me in, bear and all, and blacked out his travel schedule for a month; Morgan had come over and taken the girls to the park, Sam brought me a milkshake and a stack of magazines and watched three episodes of *Dr. Quinn* with me before returning to campus. Maggie brought whiskey and laid right in the bed with me until the sun went down and it was Randall's turn. My fog was broken up by bursts of weepy reality, hollowed-out-center-of-being reality, needing-to-cough-and-oh-Jesus-that-hurts-my-insides reality. Recalibrating had to occur again, but we couldn't go backwards to life before Jamie. He had been there, and he was gone, and we were changed.

Two weekends after we lost him, Brittney had a birthday party to attend. The atmosphere in our home was so fragile and heavy that I was happy for her to have a pre-determined retreat. I was helping her to place whatever little trinket, I think it was a jewelry-making kit, into a gift bag and write out a card. Her seven-year-old self-spoke the words as she wrote them,

"Happy Birthday Mia.

Love, dot-dot-dot,

Brittney."

And then she told me, "See, Mama? I put three dots, so she'd know it isn't over."

In the mystic, tried and true vein of "a child shall lead them," my then-baby put a little something in perspective for me. Jamie would always be a part of us. His story wasn't over. Neither was mine. Neither was *ours*.

With that, my seven-year-old, who'd been ecstatic about becoming a big sister, gave me the strength to express my wishes to Randall. I didn't know how he would feel about my wanting to try again, but...

"I know it, too," he had said. "Jamie was supposed to be here. And I don't know why we didn't get to keep him, but I believe him being here got us ready for whoever's next."

My accountant husband, though a stalwart Christian, didn't talk in the mystic and spiritual very much. His choice of words showed his whole heart to me. We didn't know if another pregnancy was possible, but four months later, we were listening to David's heartbeat. And the story went on...

"Room for one more?" Paul's husky-morning voice broke into my thoughts. He kissed my cheek and settled in the rocking chair next to me.

"Need some blanket?" I answered. He was wearing a gray sweatshirt, zipped to the top, but was also barefoot and in shorts. He smiled and pulled the tartan-esque covering over his lap.

"Having a good read or a good think?"

I beamed at him. It seemed almost ridiculous to be known so well by another person.

"A fine read," I said. "It's as predictable as I am, it seems, because I am, in fact, thinking *all the thoughts*."

He unceremoniously lifted my coffee to his lips and sipped. "You figure it all out?"

I sighed. "Hmm. A little bit. Thief."

"There's another pot brewing," he replied, only making me love him more.

"I guess I understand now," I started, "Why you'd rather sleep at my house than yours. You didn't want to explain about using the guest bedroom."

He shrugged.

"It's weird to me," I said. "And I don't mean *you* are weird. It's just weird to me that you're more comfortable sleeping in a bed that I was just sleeping in with my husband than sleeping with me in a bed you slept in by yourself."

"Jess-"

"No, wait." He hadn't rolled his eyes or sighed, but I knew I only had a small bit of leeway before he did. "Just... take that as an example. I can't control these thoughts, Paul. I mean, once I have them, I can choose to hold them at bay. And I mostly am. But they keep coming. Like an attack of killer bees."

"You don't catch killer bees and contemplate their effect on you. At the very least, you run from those em-effers. At most, you kill them before they kill you."

"I don't think either of those methods is necessary here," I said. "Plus, they can chase you for almost a mile, and I don't see either of us running very fast for that long at this stage..."

"Jess."

"Paul. Okay." I emptied the last ounce from the carafe into my mug, and as a sign of goodwill, passed it to him. "I'm trying to let go of my fears. And I *know* most of my questions are mostly pointless. But please respect that you are the only person I can talk to about the whole of it, and sometimes I just need to hash things out."

"I completely understand that. And I always respect you."

I thought there was going to be more, but he swallowed the lukewarm dregs and rose to fetch our refill. I waited with a stupid smile on my face and was already feeling warmer before he handed a fresh, full cup to me and relaxed back into his chair.

"Your house is like you," Paul said. "It's open and warm and familiar. I love my house; don't get me wrong. Leah and I worked hard and *long* to make it exactly what we wanted. But it's *our* stamp on it. I don't feel like it's *mine*. I'm positive I won't stay there; I just don't have a plan yet. So I don't feel a pull to make memories there with you or fight any mental or perceived hurdles to get comfortable with you there. But your house is different. I can't be there without feeling relaxed and at home. I'm sorry if that's been bothering you, that we spend most of our time there. But I hope you understand and consider it a compliment."

"Pau-aul..." I said his name like he was a little boy being commended for tying his shoes or keeping his pants dry. I recognized the tone and giggled. His way of saying the perfect thing was just so worthy of celebrating.

He smiled, slowly, but fully.

"So, are you planning to list it?" I asked.

He nodded. "Probably soon. I know it will be hard for the girls, but I don't think it will surprise them. Anyway, Leah has completely redecorated almost everything since they were living at home. Hopefully the nostalgia factor won't be too difficult to navigate."

Knowing my own daughters, and knowing his a bit, and knowing Julie's take on us, I thought he was being overly optimistic with that. I didn't argue, though. The idea of selling my house wasn't totally out of the question, and it was a house that I loved and of which I'd curated every inch.

But when the picture of the future changes so suddenly, it's not impossible to imagine that it could change even more completely.

"And... where are you thinking of going?" I asked as tentatively as I could, with a neon-flashing prayer (*don't go far!*) and a silent but growing wish (*stay with me!*) ruminating in my head.

"We should talk about that," he said. Steady as a beating drum.

I waited, needing him to lead.

"So the one place I mentioned, it's on your side of the beach. Half of a duplex on an annual lease, but the tenants want out early. It's pretty small and not really what I would pick out, but it would still be plenty of space for me, and I'd be closer to you while we figure things out."

It wasn't necessarily what I wanted him to say, but I didn't know what I expected.

He continued without a response from me. "Jessie. I don't... I don't have any delusions about what has occurred the past few months. We've taken the time to consider and we've been straight with each other. So this isn't a big revelation. I love you. I have no desire to hide that, to fix it, or to change it. I believe you love me and you're pretty close to being mostly okay with that, too." I sighed. He made me want to be okay, so, so much...

Then he continued in earnest, "And it's getting harder to leave you at the end of the day. And when I wake up in the morning alone, I don't even understand the point. Everything can change tomorrow. It can change this afternoon. We saw that. And I was standing next to you when I saw it. And I don't want to go anywhere else in the time I have before it all changes again."

"So." I couldn't finish all fluidly like he did. My insides were trembling. I remembered back to a different time, when I was holding the hand of my eighteen-month-old little boy and Randall was kneeling in front of me, asking *us* to marry him. Forever with him had been a long time: a *beautiful*, long time. But it hadn't been long enough. It hadn't been as long as *my* forever. And I did want a new one. I did want one with Paul. "You want to move in?"

He nodded, not quite containing the vastness of his smile. "I do."

We sat there smiling like a pair of teenage morons for a minute. And then I said, "But it's a sin." And I both giggled and meant it.

"Not if we get married." He didn't miss a beat.

I had *not* quite expected that response, and I wasn't sure he was serious. But who was I kidding? We were a little old-school, after all, and we were church people, and in spite of all the crap we'd both lived through, making things official seemed appropriate and reasonable, save for the hit on my forthcoming social security benefits.

I felt shy as I looked at him. "I want to be with you for *as long as we both shall live.* I know that. But we don't have to decide on a hashtag yet."

He nodded. It was not a rejection, just the propriety called for in the moment.

"Plus," I said pointedly, "You can't really shop for rings when you're still wearing one."

Paul smiled sadly, looking somewhere I couldn't see. He'd stopped wearing his ring right after we told all of our kids about us. I never asked him about his rationale, but I'd endlessly weighed my own reasons and timing.

"What do you do with a ring for a life you don't have anymore?" I asked aloud.

"You know I can't tell you that." We weren't touching at that moment, but I felt him stiffen, as if suddenly, he couldn't get too close to Randall's wife.

I shook my head. "No, no. I'm not asking *you*. I'm asking the collective. God. The universe. Randall. *What do I do?*"

"Jessie. What do you *want* to do?"

Most of the time, I wanted to rewind to March 12 and have it be a completely different day. I wanted Randall to have not ignored any symptoms and gone to the hospital instead of picking up Leah. I wanted him to be on medication or maybe even be recovering from surgery, and maybe all four of us would be here in Cherokee right now, celebrating health and blessings and a new lease on life with our friends.

Since the night of Randall's birthday, my heart had shifted. I wanted to calm down. I wanted my emotions to settle. I wanted not to feel all the things all the time. I wanted to be certain that I was not committing a crime by having a new relationship. I wanted to be free to be as happy and excited in our new relationship as I naturally felt.

I wanted my kids to be magically okay, which, other than changing history, was the biggest fantasy of all. Their father was gone. He was going to miss all or most of their adult milestones. They would have children he would never meet. They had no warning and no goodbye. If I waited another year to have a new relationship, or another five, none of that would change.

"I know what I want," I said, so quietly I almost couldn't hear myself. There was not pain nor anxiety as I slipped off my 36-year-old platinum band with the marquee-cut diamond and placed it on my right ring finger until I had somewhere safe and sacred to keep it. I looked at Paul, really looked at him, and knew that I could trust him completely. "I'm scared, but I *know*."

He allowed himself to reach over and take my hand then, fingering the stone that his friend had first placed, on a much younger woman who was even more unsure of herself. I wonder what would have happened if we had known each other then, before Randall and Leah. I wonder what would have happened if we had met after becoming widowed. When Paul was close to me, and all the distractions and questions were outside our bubble, it was hard to imagine never loving him.

"So tomorrow, we go home," I said, surprised how steady I sounded. "We make it our home."

He stood and moved in front of my chair, bending over to kiss me deeply. He broke off and held my face against his, and I could feel the emotion quaking at the surface of his voice as he repeated one word. "Home."

Chapter Seventeen

Clinical strength deodorant was no match for July in the south. I was showering at least twice a day. Cash pretty much raised his eyebrows at me and asked "Seriously?" whenever I made him go out in the afternoon. And Paul wouldn't be caught dead, with a cane, or otherwise at the beach. In fact, he liked the AC at an unprecedented 68 degrees. I usually tried to avoid the thought, because it was morbid and also inapplicable in cases of cremation, but more than almost anything that had transpired since March, I felt like the setting on my thermostat would have fiscally conservative Randall rolling in his grave.

But Paul, ever the outdoorsman, didn't want to marinate in his sweat while watching his sports documentaries, or God help me, golf tournaments, on TV. So, 68 it was, whenever he was there. And *whenever* had pretty much turned to *always* since May.

In fact, Paul spent most of June purging, then packing; his house sold *three weeks* after we returned from Cherokee, pretty much before it was even officially on the market.

Without much ado (except in my inner life, because my nerves practically gave me morning sickness), we had spread the word amongst the kids that we were moving *forward*. Not on, not away from, just forward. I am not sure any of them appreciated the nuanced difference I intended with my word choice. Their reception, on average, was quiet. I found that unsettling, but understandable. Brittney shrugged, which was her code for "I don't really get this, but it's your life." Sam and Mikayla both kind of nodded bravely, asking questions about Randall's personal things, and of course, looking out for David. David himself shrugged with a whole different kind of tone. He wasn't going to be home for long in the summer, as he had travel plans with friends, things to keep him busy near campus, and much like last summer, plenty of places to crash. He did mention to me, without looking at me, that Julie was devastated and angry, and that they had agreed not to talk about it. I didn't express my doubts on that strategy, just told him I hoped things would settle down soon.

I mean, really, what else could I say? What does anyone say? I went and read a few blogs by other women who had been in situations like mine. New Life Widow. Widow Abundantly. Widows Gone Wild, for the love of God. They all gave me permission through their life experiences and witticisms to do what I was doing... to empty the closet of Randall's affects, divide the special things amongst the kids, keep some treasures for myself, and donate the rest to make room for Paul and of course, the ever-evolving new normal. They encouraged me to let Paul see me cry and include my children in my grieving process as well as my "rebuilding." They offered downloads of pretty, bulleted printables that coached me in how to honor old traditions while building new ones, and how to practice "self-care" during one of my life's biggest, wait for it... transitions.

Bless it. I created this kind of crap for a living, just in a different realm. I coached women how to tutor their children. These women were coaching me how to simultaneously be a widow and a girlfriend. Meanwhile, I had Morgan sending me careful, supportive texts a few times a week and Maggie practically chanting "Fight the Patriarchy" at me, as though the Founding Fathers and possibly Donald Trump were responsible for any opposition that existed to my new life. Of course, she wasn't as tough as she liked to come off and went home one afternoon with mascara tracks, Randall's awful orange Crocs, and a framed picture of him with her girls and mine.

There were too many voices around me, and whether they were bellowing support or restraining their disapproval, they drowned out any peace I hoped to claim. I savored early mornings and could barely wait until the early evenings, when my new life created space for just Paul and me, not working, not explaining ourselves, just together.

Oh. And trying to figure out where to fit two lives that would still sort of be two but also be joined: clothes, curated memories, completely different hobbies, and a few businesses. It was like playing Tetris. Should I use some of the almost-abandoned closet in David's room? Do I keep all the same pictures on the walls? How often does Paul like the sheets changed? Does he vacuum? Where should his office space be?

Finally, for a few hours, I was alone this day, the third of July. I wasn't clearing my head so much as taking a few things out to make space for more: I had just finished a "stuff I forgot" grocery list for the family gathering we were attempting to have for the holiday; grilled ribs and veggie kabobs were on the menu, as well as homemade hummus and pita chips, spicy cole slaw, and red, white, & blueberry trifle.

All of our kids – *all of them* – were supposed to be coming, so I felt like dessert might also include a healthy portion of shit hitting the fan. Though the collective had mostly calmed themselves over the past month, Julie's version of passive aggressive was *almost* laughably antagonistic, and I couldn't help but sense that there was more, I don't know, *feedback* simmering beneath the surface.

I scribbled "more wine" on the bottom of my list. I wasn't sure there could possibly be enough. Jello-o shots, perhaps. Usually, the Fourth of July at the beach was as festive as Christmas. It was summer Christmas, without the pressure of gifts. Even real clothes were optional. I hoped we could be afforded just a little of that feeling.

I sat back down at the computer to resume some work on the planner. It was pretty much the easiest project we could have possibly been given for our last, but my motivation to complete it was an all-time low. Paul was a heavy sleeper and I was not, so I'd been spending most of my days reorganizing the house, and my late nights slogging through work until the wee hours.

With a sigh, I opened my master file and went back to February, (thankfully, it started with August, so I was on the second half), thinking about historical and scriptural applications for Valentine's Day, President's Day, Black History Month, and the blahs of winter.

But I didn't get far. Summertime, even in the *old* normal, occasionally made me feel like all my kids were living in the house again, and here came Brittney, crashing through the door quite inexplicably for a Tuesday afternoon.

"Maaaaaaaahm! Mamaaaaaa!"

"Good grief. I'm right here." I stood from my desk, partially relieved to put off George Washington trivia for a few more minutes. "What's up?"

"Have you talked to *your SON* today?" she bellowed, throwing her bag on the counter (one of my pet peeves. *Sweet Lord, hang that thing on a chair or a doorknob or the flippin' coat rack, would you?*) and taking a dramatic swallow from her bottled Frappuccino.

"Um, I talked to Sam this morning..." I talked to Sam every morning, but she either knew that already or didn't need to.

"Of course, you did." Eye roll. She knew. "I mean your *baby boy*. I could hit him with my car!"

Sigh. "What did he do, Brit?" I figured it was somewhere between hacking her Facebook and hacking her Amazon Prime account.

"He's *moving!*" She was at a full-on yell. I couldn't help it. I stifled a giggle and handed her a snickerdoodle from the batch Summer and I had made the day before.

"Honey? Really? Why are you mad about that? I figured he would. He hasn't even been sleeping here. He's been sleeping over the surf shop at Ben's place." I was having a hard time keeping track of who knew about whose logistics these days. Maybe we *should* have a group text. In fact, I was suddenly surprised that we didn't.

"The first summer Dad is gone he can't even stay here? He's such a punk..."

"Okay, so Brit. Here..." I brought her bottle to the table, gesturing that she should sit. "Does it really surprise you that your brother doesn't want to live here once Paul moves in?"

"Yeah, well. I can't believe you're not more upset about this," she mumbled.

"Upset? No. I mean, we had actually talked about him renting a studio Paul has over by the library, but it didn't work out. The tenant who was supposed to be leaving had a big life change instead. She's pregnant with twins, her boyfriend proposed, but he lost his job and is working double shifts at the wax museum to make up his wage..."

"This woman tells her property manager more than I tell my gynecologist."

"*Anyway*," I continued, noting that she was right and this whole exchange was ridiculous. "He felt bad. He extended the lease after all."

"That explains *some* of it, I guess."

I wordlessly handed her another cookie. I had no shame in my palette-pleasing, angst-distracting tactics. "I'm lost, honey. Do you feel like this conversation is going to require wine?"

She actually looked thoughtful, then shrugged. "Yes. But happy hour would be even better."

"It's 3 o'clock. Once you tell me whatever it is you're going to tell me, we'll leave..."

I had a sinking feeling. But I was only partially right.

"He's moving in with Julie," she started. I nodded slowly. She wasn't done. "And they're moving to Arizona."

Arizona.

Across the country.

My baby boy and his girlfriend, who hates me.

My son, who is only halfway done with college, and the daughter of my boyfriend, who had mentioned marriage again just a few days before.

"Arizona?!" *There is no Arizona*, I wanted to say. Stephen King and country music had a line for everything.

"Just outside of Phoenix," she said. "The *birth industry* is booming out there."

"And he's dropping out of school?" I already knew the answer.

"Transferring, supposedly. He seems to think he can get employed as a health care analyst as long as he's working on his degree." She scoffed. "But Julie has him interested in, get this, being a *midwife*. And the two of them opening their own birth center. Like they're on a Shonda Rhimes show or something. It's--"

"Ridiculous," I finished. I snapped my laptop shut. George Washington's lack of cherry-tree-demolishing had nothing on this.

"What are you going to do?" she asked.

I was rummaging in the pantry for my canvas totes and a granola bar. "I still have to get a few groceries. And then we'll meet Aunt Maggie at Wahoo's. And when I'm high on Bohemian Rolls and strawberry-lemon drops, I might call your brother."

"Hmm. Sushi and confrontation? I'm in." she said.

"Come on..."

Paul called when we were halfway through Food Lion. Katy had just come in for the holiday and told him everything. His voice went from careful to seething. I shrugged and told him to meet us at Wahoo's.

It was a bizarre combination. Daughters, best friend, and us, the couple. It felt like seating arrangements took an hour and a half, all of us standing there smiling awkwardly, until Maggie sat down in the middle and pulled Brittney next to her. Katy sat across, I sat on Maggie's other side, and Paul was across from me, flashing me a secret little grin and a small eye roll as he distributed the menus.

By the time drinks were consumed and abundant platters of sushi set down, we'd settled into a much easier rapport. Paul was so used to being surrounded by females, he murmured random observations and details from his day to me one moment and then traded barbs with Maggie the next. Katy and Brittney remained fairly occupied at their end, eliciting a bigger eye roll from Paul when their second (maybe third?) round of cocktails arrived.

And that was how long it took for the subject of Julie and David to fully get discussed, and what we knew was:

1.   Julie had already put her notice in at the hospital (she worked at one a bit south of us, in Georgetown).

2.   David had already withdrawn from USC.

3.   They already had a lease.

4.   They had definitely already told Katy and Brittney, the siblings most likely to be cool. But neither was.

5.   They were planning to announce to the rest of us tomorrow at our 4th of July bash.

I did most of the question asking, while Brittney and Katy did the answering and Maggie, a bit more demure than usual with Paul in our midst, reserved commentary only for the most outrageous parts of the revelation, namely: the speed with which this was all to take place.

Paul only interjected occasionally, encouraging good sense and manners, for the most part. I watched his face as carefully as I could in the urgent, borderline obnoxious environment created by each of our unicorn daughters talking at once, mustering all the energy, passion, and moxie they had as well as all the fire, pessimism, and erraticism. They played off each other, worked each other up, paused for sidebars and fill-ups, and looked more radiant the more revved up they got.

"I say we let them get as far as, *We have something to tell you*," Katy said, "And then we all yell something in unison."

"Like what?" Maggie asked, with me giving her a firm *Don't feed the animals* look.

"'HELL NO!'" Brittney suggested. "Gets right to the point. Or, we could just stage a walk-out."

"And leave all Daddy's ribs? No to *that*." Katy said. "Wait until you taste them."

I turned away, trying to suppress my own bewildered smile. My insides were twisted with every thought of David, but they were a different kind of something over my daughter and Paul's, who, yes, had been casual friends for years, but were now talking to each other in a whole different way, comparing Paul's dry rubbed ribs to the saucy ones Randall preferred, reminiscing about the Fourth of July when Leah made an extraordinary version of a Paula Deen pound cake (dripping with caramel sauce), and pondering whether to lace Julie and David's dessert with laxatives or Prozac (only a little funny).

Paul remained mostly silent, and as we waited for the check, he reached across the remnants of our sushi platter (pause to praise Jesus for the south and fried chicken rolls...) and took my hand. It was not a big deal, except it was. I saw Brittney stiffen the tiniest bit, heard Katy pause in the slightest before continuing a story about a 12-year-old boy named Ryne who wanted to learn to play the sitar, and sheepishly returned Maggie's beam. He only held on for a moment before letting go and taking out his wallet. Happy Hour was on him, but as I looked over into his eyes, they seemed to be guarded to everyone but me, signaling that the heaviness of what tomorrow would bring was indeed on *us*.

#

Paul and I returned to my house alone. Brittney and Katy decided to stay and hear some bands on the Marshwalk, a charming restaurant district along the inlet's boardwalk. Maggie, who was leaving early in the morning to visit her daughters for a long weekend, also knew enough to know we probably needed some time to... whatever you do when you find out your and your lover's kids are moving out west to shack up...

"With any luck, y'all won't become the plot of a Danielle Steel novel," she whispered to me as we hugged goodbye.

So here we were again, in the kitchen. I was waiting for my toasted sesame seeds to cool, Paul was sitting at the table, pretending to focus on QuickBooks. The "Yacht Rock" station was streaming in the background, providing us endless classics like

"The Dock of the Bay" and "Kokomo." I was pounding water (pre-toxing, Maggie called it), but my head was pounding, too.

"Let me get this straight," Paul finally said, closing his laptop. I braced for something profound and maybe angry. "You *make* the tahini that goes into the hummus... that you *make*."

"Mm-hm," I said, smiling with relief and drizzling oil into my food processor.

"You know you can buy a vat of it in three different flavors at Costco for like six bucks?"

"*You* buy hummus? At Costco?"

"I hear endless discussions about it from Danielle and Leah."

We took the requisite pause, the one in which we both silently acknowledged that Leah was no longer here, that life was sad and crazy, that we honored her memory and Randall's even as we planned to sleep in the same bed in a little while, and that the past tense was always implied even if we didn't say it because it was all so damn weird.

After the appropriate allotted time, he asked, "Are you going to be okay?"

I just nodded, scraping my bowl and slightly swaying as "The Boys of Summer" cued up.

"Jess? You don't really seem okay?"

"My head hurts," I muttered.

"Then stop *cooking*," he pleaded, suddenly at my side, his hands on my hips.

I dropped my spatula and let myself lean into him. There was a tiny, timid inner voice that asked me if this was safe, if it was okay to weather the storm of David's decisions with the father of the eye of said storm. The freedom was still new, still raw, still confusing, still... made my heart beat really kind of fast.

"I know. But this is really easy," I said, hearing the sleepiness in my voice. "I just want to have it done, so I won't have to do it in the morning. Everything else is simple. This just takes a lot of dishes, and I can run the dishwasher tonight. And it will taste *so good* tomorrow. You will be very pleased with me."

I thought I heard him sigh, possibly with a bit of an impatient overtone. He pulled me uncharacteristically tightly into him and held me there. "I'm gonna walk Cash," he said, his words vibrating off my hair. "Hurry up."

I smiled as he stepped away with my dog, motivated to get done quickly.

#

I took three ibuprofen and a shower, Paul leaning against the bathroom counter as we talked more directly and in unnecessarily quiet voices about David and Julie's big move. Paul's main focus was dissipating drama; he did not want the siblings, especially Katy, stirring up any more tension than what was natural and inevitable. Julie would only grow more resolved in anger, he said. My main focus was trying to stop the whole thing, get David to see reason: not that he and Julie should break-up (although that was my unspoken and probably obvious ultimate goal), but that Arizona wasn't going anywhere, and finishing his degree at USC would make much more sense than time off and transferring. I was probably going to have to get him alone to accomplish the communication of this perspective, or possibly convince Sam to do it, which kind of conflicted with Paul's no-sibling-drama policy.

I fell in to bed next to Paul with a level of anxiety that was only surpassed by my exhaustion. I didn't want him to see, either, how upset I actually was at the prospect of my youngest moving across the country with his daughter, whom I viewed as kind of a man-eating dragon, or the level of fatigue I was fighting through in order to throw a proper post-Randall holiday for my family, with the added pressure of *Paul's* family. The whole thing was a ridiculous idea, and nothing out of *Food and Wine* was going to make it less awkward and more *The Brady Bunch*.

"How goes the planner?" he asked, hitting play on "The One in Massapequa."

I yawned my response. "It's fine."

He lay flat on his back, focused on the ceiling. "Forty years in education, and you'd never know I ever cared a lick. I'm so sick of it."

"Yep," I echoed. "So done. Who cares about the parts of a sentence? Everyone just communicates by abbreviation anyway. On pictures of parking spaces and unicorn hats. In Snap Chat."

He reached for my hand. "It's almost over," and I knew he was talking about more than the planner. "Try to sleep tonight, okay?"

I snuggled closer to him, determined.

Seven hours later, I was slightly less tired and kabobbing onions, bell peppers, and zucchini while Paul emptied the dishwasher. We were joking about how he'd spent more time in the kitchen in the past two months than he had in the past twenty years. He made us eggs-in-the-hole, and we ate breakfast on the porch. For the first time since David was a toddler, I was not looking forward to a big family holiday. I was actually daydreaming about our cabin in Cherokee with no working internet.

"Jess, whatever happens today, let's just, be steady," he said somberly. "I don't want a big battle. Take David aside, tell him how you feel. Know that I feel the same."

"Are you... have you heard anything from Julie?" I knew he had texted her from the restaurant last night, asking her to call him.

"Just that she would see me today," he sighed. "I can't believe she thinks Katy wouldn't have told me. I don't understand how people who are going on 30 years old don't understand relationships."

"David isn't even close to 30," I grumbled. "Boys don't figure it out until they're like... I dunno. Sixty-five?"

He shrugged. "At least Randall got there."

"Yeah..." I said, letting myself smile. How would Randall be handling this situation? Would it even exist if he were still here? Should I put a little sidebar somewhere in the damn planner about the butterfly effect, because thoughts of it were ruling my mental state and possibly ruining my mental health?

"Jessie?" I turned my head to face him completely. He was clearly trying to muster up whatever it was he needed to say next. I bit my tongue against the goading and wisecracks and even the pep talk that could naturally pour out of me. I waited for him to say it.

"Just know that... I'm with you. I don't know what today will look like, but I know that."

"I'm trying to be hopeful," I replied, offering a grateful smile, "But I think it's likely going to be a shitshow."

"That's what I'm afraid of. But then again, with this many people, even if there weren't a couple of salacious affairs going on, wouldn't it be one anyway?"

#

At 1:03 P.M., Abby, Brittney, and I were sitting in the ocean with Summer and Jacob and approximately 15 million (or at least a couple thousand) half-drunk, half-naked tourists, watching a military flyover that was one of the highlights of our day every year. Travis was skim-boarding with a few of his friends and Sam and Paul were at the house, babysitting the ribs, while we remained somewhat cool in our traditional viewing place for the Salute from Our Shores. Jacob was radically waving a 3x5 American flag, and Summer was flipping cartwheels in her new red suit, pausing long enough to wave to each plane while doing the splits. I applauded and smiled and chatted with them all, attempting to ignore the tightening of my stomach muscles and a constant nagging wonder as to whether *they* had arrived at the house yet.

Brittney didn't bring it up, so I also wondered whether Abby knew. I felt like a ginormous elephant was standing on the shore near us, ready to stampede the whole celebratory lineup into a bloody mess. I eased that notion away as I smiled at Jacob's suggestion that we "Go back to your house, Mimi, for some of that yummy dip," and held his hand as we trekked gingerly amongst the blankets and coolers and bocce ball setups to home.

We walked up the driveway to find Sam and Paul chatting it up near the grill, joined now by Katy, and Matt and Christian, who was *stoked* about all the planes he just saw, and Mikayla, who was already heading upstairs to join Danielle and the baby. Altan wouldn't make an appearance until closer to dusk, when he could close the marina on one of its busiest days of the year.

I greeted everyone, promising to send down a platter of hors d'oeuvres ASAP. Paul asked if I could also "send one of the kids down with the veggies," and gave an almost imperceptible shake of his head to my unasked question. I led Abby and Brittney upstairs, planning to pour myself some wine before I sent anything anywhere.

Danielle was nursing in the third bedroom, so I sent Mikayla in there with a tray of snacks for the two of them (*Mamas*, I thought happily, because nothing could put a damper on my daughter's pregnancy), sent Summer downstairs with popsicles for her and the boys, and sent Brittney down with all the other stuff.

Where was David? What was he planning to do? Announce his big move over watermelon? Spell it out in fireworks? Could I talk to Abby about this? Was it okay for her to know? Did she already?

"You want the coleslaw out now?" she asked. All I could see was her messy bun as she poked through the fridge. "Sam said they should be done with everything in about 20 minutes."

"Sure," I said. Then, I added as casually as I could, "I guess David didn't feel like coming in time to help. Good thing I had Brittney bring some drinks, too."

"Mom —"

"Yep? You want a glass?" I plopped a strawberry into my glass of Moscato. Festive.

"I do," she said emphatically. "Um, so... David..."

"You know, don't you?" I took a large swallow.

"*You* know?"

I shook my head. Ridiculous. "Brittney told me. And Katy knows, and Paul. So who doesn't know? Was I supposed to be the only fool it got *announced* to today?"

"Brit should have let him tell you," Abby said. I felt my knots tighten a bit. This did not seem a likely opening to her declaring herself my ally.

"I guess she thought the one writing his tuition checks might appreciate a clue."

She took a drink before answering. "Is that really what bothers you?"

"You know it isn't, Abby."

"I don't know why he hasn't told you," she sighed. "And for what it's worth, when he came to tell Sam – not us, Sam. I'm just included by default – Brittney was there. He really...he really wanted to make it a big, happy thing today. So you need to act surprised."

I felt like I'd taken a sharp turn into bizarro world. "Surprised?" I echoed. "Abby, I'd like to have him drug tested. He cannot be serious about pulling this stunt, much less making a grand announcement like it's some amazing thing."

She looked nearly as perplexed as I felt. "But Mom... he is, wow... He's *really* excited. They've looked into lot of details and... He thinks you'll be proud. That it's an adventure."

"White water rafting is an adventure," I said. "Auditioning for *Survivor*, maybe. This is ridiculousness. This is a huge, disastrous mistake."

"It's not... the most conventional thing," she admitted. "But none of us have gone that route, really. And we all have a pretty good outcome. Maybe he's inspired."

"Maybe he's reacting emotionally. You know, out of grief," I snapped.

There was a foreign, awkward silence between us for which I immediately felt guilty and responsible.

"I'm sorry," I murmured. "I just... I'm blown away by this. Do you... Can you ask Sam to come up? I think I just... I'd rather have someone stand beside me in this when I speak to David. Sam's approval still means everything to David, and his wise, brotherly counsel in this particular instance would mean the world to me..."

The tension falling over Abby only heightened. "Then I worry you're going to be disappointed. But you're right... you really need to have this conversation with Sam. I'll be right back."

Sam walked in with an empty pan and a few dirty utensils. He smiled as he passed me to dump things in the sink, and I already knew how this was going to go. I knew that forced smile as well as I knew my own. He'd already made up his mind, and that meant there was no changing David's.

"So Abby says you already know?"

That was just the trigger, the fire was lit that sent my blood boiling. "I'm amazed that this is suddenly a crime. For the mom to know what the kid is doing when the kid is moving across the country with his new girlfriend. Who hates his mom."

"She doesn't hate you—" Sam started.

"This is really how this is going to go? With you defending Julie?"

"Mama—"

"Sam."

"I'm just saying... David needs you to hear him. I know it's impulsive, but he isn't going out there to live in a tent and sell churros at a strip mall. And part of the reason the mid-wifery thing is appealing to him is *because* of you. Because of how much you wanted a natural birth with Jamie and with him, and how disappointed you've always been that you couldn't get one."

Randall had this great trick where he could raise one eyebrow. With one raised eyebrow, he could say, "Baby, take me to the bed," or "Son, that's the dumbest thing you've ever said," *or,* "Kids, pack your overnight bags. It's been a long time since we made a trip to Carowinds." I could see his trademark brow as clearly as I could see Sam's muted hopefulness mingled with apprehension, right there in front of me. I longed for him in that moment. Even the notion that Paul was outside grilling stuff and playing host to our families didn't help. I wanted Randall. I wanted something to make sense. And I really wanted to be able to raise one eyebrow at my eldest son.

"Sam. I am willing to listen. But can you at least admit that's a stretch? Your brother. As a *midwife.* And inspired in part by my birthing problems 20 years ago? Come on."

Sam shrugged. I might have seen an eye roll. He was better at hiding them than his younger siblings, a sure sign of his age. "Whatever the case, Mom, he's decided, and I've decided I want to help him."

"Of course you will," I said, trying to soften. "Are you... I mean, are you driving out there with them? He doesn't really have that much stuff to move. Are they both taking their cars? Are they getting a truck?"

Sam exhaled deeply. "Mama, I really wish we could just wait and have this conversation when he's here."

"What is the deal, Sam? He *isn't* here. He hasn't said a word to me about any of it, even when he *was* over here two days ago doing his laundry. He wants to talk to me about this in front of everyone? Is that it? To ensure I *won't* get mad or protest?"

"That's probably part of it."

"Fine. I'll wait. But you tell me what *you* mean. About helping him."

Sam looked at his shoes. For a moment, he was about nine-years-old again, faced with the prospect of no longer being my only child, our only child, and therefore prince of the world. He had wanted a little brother, and news that a baby sister named Mikayla would be joining him instead did not make him any more excited about sharing his throne. He didn't remember the days of it being just the two of us, when he was my lifeline and purpose in the tiny body of a baby. He only remembered lighting up the world of both his mom and his dad, one who'd *chosen* him (a truth we disclosed when he was five and we first started trying to have another). I had loved nine-year-old Sam with a veraciousness that I didn't feel again until David was born. There is something about sons, about future men needing their mamas, about the drive to mold them to be wise and brave in a way that, in spite of modern inclinations, seems very specific to males. Sam had been a sweet and easy little boy, and he had grown into a Good Man, and I still needed to be careful not to squash the nobility of his intentions with my angry reaction.

"I'm giving him money," he said, without looking up. He

didn't have to say more. I knew. He knew I knew. But I said it anyway.

"Your money from Dad?"

"Not all of it." He raised his head only then. "I'm not touching what he left for the kids. And we already significantly paid down the principle on the house. The rest can sit in savings, or it can help David start a new life..."

"Sam, Dad left him the same thing he left you..."

"But he can't touch it until he's 25."

"And there's a reason for that." Now I was talking to him as though he *was*, in fact, nine-years-old. "To reduce the probability of him throwing away thousands of dollars on a whim..."

"Mom—"

"He's not *you*, Sam!"

"No. He's not me. By the time I was his age, I had married my pregnant girlfriend."

Zing! Damn if I didn't teach my offspring the power of a trump card. Sam had played his.

"Sam, I hear you. Like it or not though, David is made of different stuff. His whole experience as a young adult to this point is so different from yours. He's the baby, and we have treated him like The Baby. He's been carefree and cheerful and coasting, and up until now, has never had a real trial. He's still immature, and Julie is very much not that way. And I'm just afraid that Julie is responding to his inner joy and his energy because she's sad. What's going to happen when the season changes and nothing looks the same?"

Sam looked steadily at my shoes this time, and barely loudly enough for me to hear, said, "And that is exactly what we're all afraid of for you and Paul."

That was more than a *Zing!* It felt a little like a bullet. But this wasn't the time or place to bleed. "I see," I said, as stoically as I could. I put on my fake smile, knowing Sam knew, but it had to be good enough anyway. "Well, let's get your 20-year-old brother settled, shall we? And then we can dissect everything *I'm* doing wrong."

I turned from him, back to the platter of cucumbers and pita bread and the damn hummus. I was sure at some point in my life I had felt as idiotic as I did in that moment, but I couldn't remember when.

He started to stammer, then felt better of it and retreated back down the stairs. A minute later, Mikayla and Danielle emerged from the bedroom, and I traded them jars of strawberry lemonade for a sleeping Vivi. I held her there alone in the kitchen, where I could hear the sounds of banter and celebration wafting upward, wondering if everyone was really okay spending the day together or if it was all an illusion, carefully crafted and agreed-upon to humor ol' Mom until she came to her senses and put on end to her tryst with Uncle Paul.

It was Paul who broke my sort-of-solitude first, carrying a huge tray of ribs and wearing a rueful smile as he announced, "Look who I found!"

David trailed in behind him, carrying a case of soda in each hand and sporting a smile that colored outside the lines of his face. "Hey Mom!" He called. "Sorry we're late! Julie wanted to check on her *Yankee Doodle Babies*. There were *three* different women who gave birth right after midnight!"

Bless it. That was pretty cute. I waited until he set down his load and accepted his bear hug. "Thanks for bringing drinks," I said. David didn't know me the way Sam did, so I hoped the pleasant formality in my voice hid everything else, at least for the time being.

Sam walked in with the kabobs, followed by Travis with the hot dogs, and the kitchen was soon filled with every last one of us. As I arranged our meal on the counter, as I listened to the sound of conversation and ice cubes and hand washing, for a moment, I believed this could be it. The remaining Oakleys and Jamesons, holidays together.

When I scanned the room, Julie and David were side-by-side, his arm around her, both their faces bringing to mind cats who got canaries. She was in animated conversation with Danielle, and he was still talking to Paul. I wanted to feel what they were feeling, the anticipation and adrenaline and grab-life-by-the-balls-dom, but I couldn't. All I could do was give a stiff smile to Mikayla and ask if she'd heard from Altan, if we should wait for him.

"He won't be here until at least six," she said. "We'll save him a plate. It's all good." She reached over and grasped me by the elbow. "Mama. Look at me. It's *all good.*"

So she knew, too. So maybe the whole announcement thing was a ruse anyway. Maybe David just wanted to tell me when he had all his older siblings there to protect him. They already were. Would Brittney do the same? I had no foundation for an argument, not a fair one, even if I had what I thought was an overwhelmingly reasonable one.

I supervised the plate-filling and the "sit wherever you're

comfortable" announcing, and when I filled my own dish at last, I sat at the bar between Jacob and Summer, just as we did every Tuesday with our tacos. Summer asked if I wanted to come watch her at dance camp the next week and if her friend Emmy could come over with her on the next Tuesday. And then, simultaneously gnawing on a rib bone, Jacob asked me if we could go have tacos in Arizona with Uncle David.

I dropped my fork. It wasn't subtle. It bounced off my plate and landed on the floor. I stooped to pick it up, and when I attempted to straighten, I banged my head off the granite counter. By banged, I mean concussed. Saw stars. Almost swayed for a second. Jacob looked at me with wide eyes and Summer called, "Maaaaah-meeeeee," as if everyone hadn't heard the thunk. I gave her what I hoped was a reassuring smile and headed down the hall to my room.

I closed the door most of the way and leaned against the wall behind it. The top of my head was throbbing and stinging, and when I checked, there was some blood, though not an alarming amount. In the bathroom, I reached a little blindly for a washcloth and made the water ice cold, closing my eyes and trying not to think about the enthusiastic little voice that had said, "Uncle David says they have even better tacos in Arizona. Can we go some time, Mimi?" Of course, it was the only thing I could think of.

When I looked, David was standing right behind me. His reflection in the mirror was a cross between concern, amusement, and resolve.

"Oh my God, Mama, are you okay? Are you bleeding?"

"Just a little," I said. If this was my chance, so be it. "My head is not as hard as some others in this family."

"Mom—"

"David, how could you? How can your six-year-old nephew know about this ginormous life change you're making, and you haven't seen fit to tell *me*? How long have you been planning this? Did you ask anyone for any guidance, or did you just run it by people you knew would cheer for you no matter what?"

The kinda-hurt-feelings expression took over his face. "Aren't *you* going to cheer for me no matter what?"

"That's not fair, nor is it the point," I said. "I want you to succeed, David, and of *course*, I want you to be happy. But that doesn't mean I'm going to pretend I think this is the pathway to either. And I'm frankly really, really pissed that you've hidden it from me."

"I knew you would be upset, and I wanted Sam—"

"What? To stand in front of you? To tell me *for* you? How can you make grown up decisions if you can't even communicate them to your own mom?"

"So this is fair?" he asked, the heat raising in his voice. "You think maybe I didn't want to tell you because I knew you'd be like this? Calling me immature and incapable of making my own choices?"

"Well, think about it, David." Damn. My head was *throbbing*. "How would you not telling me change anything about this conversation, much less make it better?"

"David?"

There was a voice outside the bedroom door. How long had she been there?"

"I'm in here, Jules. You can come in."

I shook my head, which hurt. I took the compress off of it, steeling myself for the next play.

"Are you alright, Ms. Jessie? Want me to take a look?"

I honestly had no idea if she was being condescending or actually nice. For the hundredth time that afternoon, I forced a smile. "I think I'm fine. Hard counter, hard head, so..."

She smiled back. Yep. Hers was fake, too.

"So, David, are you on the same page? Fill your mom in on all the details?"

Bloody hell. *Fill me in.* Did this chick have any idea what she was getting herself into? David didn't share details. David had to be reminded to wear shoes half the time.

"We... um... we were just getting to a few things."

"Oh, Ms. Jessie, we were really lucky to find a lease that started mid-month. Really, the timing couldn't be more perfect."

"Mid-month?" I asked. "You mean—"

"Yeah, um, Mom," I had to sit on the bed. It was awkward, but between the sledgehammer seemingly embedded in my skull and the one about to be plunged into my heart, I could not trust my legs to hold me. "We're leaving next week. Julie found a great place near the birthing center that hired her, and it's already available, so we'll have a few weeks to get it together before she starts work."

"And where will you be working?" My attempt to keep my voice steady was an abject failure.

"It's called, get this, the Babymoon B&B!" Julie was suddenly emoting as though we were old buds. I tried to remember that she was a twenty-something, that she had just lost her mama, that the whole world was ahead of her, that my son loved - or at least was crushing hard - on her. I also tried to keep in mind that she was Paul's daughter, but even that didn't keep me from wanting to throat-punch her in that moment. David might have had a mind of his own, but there was no way he'd have come up with this idea. He was along for the ride.

"That sounds... interesting. Will you be a nurse there?"

"For now," she said. "In about two years, I'll be a Certified Nurse Midwife. My program starts in September, so I'll spend this summer getting doula certification, and then I can be kind of a floater on their team. Hopefully I'll be over patient care by the end of the year. That's my goal, anyway. It's such a great opportunity."

"Sounds like it," I murmured. "It's too bad Myrtle Beach doesn't offer any options like that."

"Well, we are a little behind the times here," and I had to give her that. "Maybe someday we can come back and start our own center. But for now, the timing is so perfect. I even talked to Dad about sub-leasing my apartment if he needs to. We sure never expected our house to sell so quickly."

I was currently sitting in a master bedroom that had half of its ocean-view windows covered by cardboard boxes and Rubbermaid totes, all filled with her Dad's possessions. She seemed to be towing a line between crazy with denial and blinded with resentment.

"I'm pretty sure your Dad already has a plan," I said. I met her gaze this time. She didn't blink. Was this part of her strategy?

"Well, it's always good to leave options open. The whole month is already paid for."

At that moment, David walked to her side, and, praise baby Jesus, Paul walked in the room. I wasn't sure if I felt dizzy from the blow to the head or from the alternate reality that seemed to be unfolding between my eyes.

Last year – just last year, when the Jamesons had gone to meet Leah's sisters in Dahlonega— Randall had planned our "just us" Fourth of July menu: dozens of all-beef hot dogs. A toppings bar with selections ranging from chili and onions to bacon and BBQ corn nuts and even, gag, peanut butter chips. It was surprising and obnoxious and totally fun. We made s'mores on the grill and ate them while Randall and Altan set off some fireworks in the street, then we toted a sleepy Jacob and went to the beach to watch the magnificent amateur display there that went on for hours. Sam made fun of us because we could have just as easily watched from our front porch. Brittney brought her then-kinda-boyfriend Dan and he got obnoxiously drunk. Randall called him an Uber and told Brittney to start looking for dates somewhere besides the Beaver Bar. She, Travis, and Summer spent the night, and David still lived at home. Randall had the whole week off, and the next morning, we piled in the golf cart to have bagels at our favorite little bakery by the pier.

Would I have done it any differently if I had known? If I could have foretold the future, that Randall would be gone, that Mikayla would have miscarried, that David was moving away, that everything would be upside down a year later, would I have insisted on a grander plan or a better meal or more photos? Should I be insisting on a different path *now*?

Paul's mouth was set in a grim line, but he looked at me with concern. "Are you okay?"

I nodded gingerly, afraid to say any more words.

"Give us a minute, guys," he said. "Everyone is cleaning up in there..."

They exited with pod-people expressions on their faces and without another word. I collapsed back on my mountain of pillows.

Paul sat on the edge of the bed and looked me over, his eyes resting on the compress in my hand. "You still bleeding?"

I shrugged. "I'm fine."

"Why don't we have you looked at, just in case? That sounded like you cracked the counter in half."

"Paul, I'm fine. We aren't going anywhere. Everyone is here."

He put his hands on my shoulders and spoke to me in what I imagined was his Principal Paul voice. "Understand me. If you need to be seen by a doctor, I don't give a rat's ass if Queen Elizabeth is out there. Or Eddie Vedder. Or the entire cast of *The Golden Girls* singing Cher-a-oke."

"Paul." I tried not to laugh because it hurt. "I really think it's okay. I don't want to go to that hospital again. Ever."

"We can go to a different one."

I glowered at him.

"Fine. But I think we should call it a day."

"Because I bonked my head?"

"No. Because I heard Julie tell you about the sub-lease idea, and I'm a little concerned her head is next."

I glared at Julie now, even if she couldn't see me.

"I don't know what to say. Or do."

He nodded. "I'm not changing my mind and taking her apartment. Let's start there."

I stiffened. I wanted him to be mad at her, and I didn't want her idiocy to change things between us. But I also kind of wanted him to stop the whole thing, and he couldn't exactly give a 27-year-old a time out.

"Good... I didn't think you were."

"But they seem set on going," he continued. "And almost all the siblings seem to be rallying around them a bit."

"*That* is really blowing my mind!" I said, a little too emphatically; though the stinging had stopped, the throbbing was still present. "Sam wants to give him money! Inheritance money! Abby is all tra-la-la about it. And where are Brit and Katy with their indignation and darts of truth?" Traitors.

"Right now they are loading the dishwasher and doing Lady Gaga no justice." The look on his face made me laugh. I felt a little better.

"Let's have us some ibuprofen and rejoin the party," I said, thinking, *Come what may* and trying to believe I meant it.

#

It's easy to get distracted in the mixed company of 15 people of various ages and volumes. Gingerly, I spent a while with the mommy crowd, talking co-sleeping and pre-natal yoga with Danielle and Mikayla, gripping myself internally for Julie to join the conversation, though she never did. By the time Brittney and Katy (*traitors*) joined us and a bottle of wine was consumed, my headache was also gone, and I joined in a game of cornhole on the beach. After the first round, I took Vivi from Danielle and walked with Summer to the pier and back, Summer talking the *entire time* about everything, from what we were going to have for dessert to dance camp to the teacher she was going to have for fourth grade ("Mrs. Hirschman! She JUST got married LAST MONTH! Her name used to be PRATT! Don't you think Pratt is better? It's easier to spell. Although, it does rhyme with *fat* and *splat*, and those are kind of yucky words. Boys will tease her, I bet. When I get married, I am keeping my name. Summer Olivia Oakley gives me the best initials *ever*! SOO many puns! Get it, Mimi?!")

When we rejoined the others, Abby and Mikayla had gone to the house to get dessert ready, and Paul was looking at me as if to say, "Let them do it. Unclench." So I did. Setting fruit salad and cake on the kitchen counter didn't need to be a big production. I let him briefly put his arm around my waist and lean in close to me, nodding when he asked if I felt okay. Groups and pairs trailed back to the house, chatter and laughter rising, Christian playing "1-2-3" while holding Julie and David's hands.

It should have warmed me. All these people were spending the first summer, the first major holiday, really, without one of their most important people, and yet were finding joy and fun and making new memories. What was wrong with me that I couldn't focus on the positive?

But I'm not wrong. The thought resounded in my head, as I held Jacob's hand to cross the street, as I promised him there were brownies *and* ice cream waiting, and even as Danielle accosted me in my own kitchen with a hug of thanks for taking Vivi for the walk. It resounded as I hung back and watched plates filled again with *soo* much dessert, when I saw Summer spill ice cream off her plate on to the floor and Sam attempt to wipe it up with a used napkin, when Matt sat Vivi on top of Cash long enough for half the phones in the room to get whipped out for photos. I scanned the faces in the room. They looked amused and comfortable, maybe even content. But Paul's expression was drawn, and his smiles were forced. My heart was thumping in my ears.

It just didn't feel right.

So when Julie took her first sip of coffee - the good stuff that I'd been rationing, because Morgan and Carter had brought it from Hawaii and given it to us at Christmas - and wrinkled her nose and said to David, "I'm so spoiled by that organic Yukon we've been drinking," I lost it. I just did. I lost every fake smile and controlled answer and good manner I had used all day. Because I was about to lose David to this girl who was set on letting me know she was against me, and it felt like too much.

"Julie," I said too loudly, "That might be something to think about. College students who work part time giving surfing lessons usually aren't drinking organic anything. It's dollar and quarter beers over at The Sundown. That is, if they're actually over 21."

David was gaping at me. I'm sure if I looked around, everyone else would be as well. But Julie didn't gape. She had been waiting, and she was ready for me.

"It's ok, Ms. Jessie," she said, all syrupy. "I can afford the coffee I prefer. David is moving in with me because I want him to, not because I need him to."

Zing!

And as it turned out, I wasn't ready for Julie. All my hand-wringing and brow-raising and plans for rabble-rousing were drained from me. This 27-year-old who had convinced my son that love conquers all - *for them* - was also perfectly poised to prove that it did not conquer anything for me, not with *her* dad. And I felt absolutely no strength to fight her.

"Julie—" It was Katy's voice that broke the tension, because most of the room, save for a few kids and moms, had fallen quiet at the impending showdown. "C'mon. We're having a nice day. Everyone is down with the *live and let live*. Can't you just be, too?"

"Last year we ran a 5K with Mom on Fourth of July morning," Julie started. "We kayaked with Dad in the afternoon. And then we sat on the deck of that winery and watched the fireworks. And no one was moving, and no one was pretending. We were still a family. We were still us. How can you all just forget about that? Or pretend to forget about that?"

"We're not..." Danielle said.

"We are still *us*," Katy added.

"How can you say that? Look around! I don't even recognize *us*." Julie actually had tears in her eyes.

"This is not the time for this conversation," Paul said quietly.

Mikayla, who had just heated up a plate for Altan, looked at me a little mournfully, and Brittney was ushering the kids down the hall. David looked at the floor.

"Why not?" Julie asked. "You gathered all of us here together today like some big happy family. Why can't we talk about this stuff? It is suddenly too personal? I mean, you have your underwear and Mom's pottery packed in boxes just down the hall. How much more personal can it get?"

"That's really enough, Julie." Paul's voice was firmer this time. It didn't appear to phase her.

But they were not my focus. I was staring at David, waiting

for any sign of conflict or gumption or emotion from him. He continued to look at the floor.

"I understand that you and Ms. Jessie aren't happy about our decision," she said, and this time, her voice was also void of any emotion but steel resolve. "But *no one*, not one of us, is happy about your moving in together. David, let's just go."

David looked up then, to Julie, to Sam, but not to me. Everyone around us started bustling, throwing paper plates away, gathering their affects. We hadn't gone to see any fireworks yet, but it was clear the night was over, and everyone had had enough.

I walked the five feet to David and said, "Son. Can we please talk more about this?"

"Mama..." He managed to look at me. "All you want to do is change my mind. And all I want to do is change yours. So what is left to say?"

"It's not just about you going," I said. "I want you to be okay, and I want you to be okay with what you're leaving."

"I would have stayed," he said, "But you're taken care of. So we can just live our lives. Everything will be fine. I can be happy for you if you can be happy for me."

I looked over my youngest. He was my third baby born by C-section, long after Brit, shortly after Jamie had been born with no life. They were doing "gentle" Caesarians by then, and they placed David in my arms for the duration of surgery, even while my fallopian tubes got the old cut/tie/burn. Randall watched and made small talk with the staff while I stayed in a glazed-over bubble with my baby boy, watching in wonder as he rooted for the early, golden milk and trying to drink in every part of him. How is a fifth child such a wonder? He was. He still was.

Now, Katy stood between us and Julie, and they were having their own conversation. Even so, Julie was staying in earshot to hear how this ended.

"David, I'm not saying don't ever go. But you'll be done with school in two years. Can you not wait awhile? You're still so young..."

He would not meet my eyes, but his voice held more resolve than I had ever heard.

"You and Dad didn't have his 70th birthday. You didn't have his retirement cruise on the Mediterranean. You didn't have Mikayla's baby. You didn't have Brittney's kids or mine. Mama? I... don't *have* two years. None of us does."

That was his version of reality, and how could I refute it?

Meanwhile, my reality was all of theirs – alongside the blow Julie has just delivered, the disapproval bomb that I had been afraid of for weeks had detonated. I really didn't know if what she said was true, but it wouldn't surprise me. Had I not been expecting that everyone was resentful or at least uncomfortable about Paul and me? Had any one of them argued with her? The room felt increasingly uneven and uneasy.

I finally caught the blue eyes of my youngest - my rainbow baby, a constant source of humor and cheer for me, and the only child that Randall and I weren't quite done raising. I had failed him. Failed Randall. It was clear to me now that my concern for my own loneliness, my own heart, had driven David away, and if I wasn't careful, would drive the others away as well.

I met the cautious hope and restrained disappointment I saw

there with all the jubilance I could muster. It was not much. It might not have been convincing. But I demurely kissed my son's cheek and said, "David, I'm happy if you're happy. I'm sorry if I caused you to doubt that. I just wanted... I just want you to be sure."

"I am," he said, immediately beaming.

"And I pray every blessing on your next chapter..." That was unconditional. That would be true no matter what, even though everything felt different now.

I could deal with my kids not being happy for me, but them not being happy *with* me gave me a sensation much like choking. I let David turn his attention to Sam, and I sat at the kitchen table, allowing the bustle to happen without me. Altan was still eating, and he told me a little about the busyness of his day, how much he looked forward to having the next morning off, how much he enjoyed the hummus, and even how much he thought summer agreed with me, teasing that I was almost as brown as he was. When he stood up to clear his place, he bent beside my chair and said, "I'm happy *you're* happy, *Anne.*" The Turkish word for "mama" was his reserved nickname for me. I reached for his hand and he hugged me, and I almost cried, but the last thing any one of us needed was another start to another scene.

They left like they came, in residential clusters, carrying empty canvas bags and Tupperware bowls, damp beach towels and sleepy little boys. None of them said goodbye any differently than any other time: Sam, Abby, Mikayla, Altan, and the younger kids were affectionate, Brittney and Travis were breezy, David was oblivious, and Paul's family members were each polite and sincere. Other than to say, "Good night," Julie did not speak to me, and why should she? She had all she needed from me.

I looked at the remnants of the day, random bowls and cups, scattered watermelon seeds and ice cream drops, a phone charger here and hat there, even one of Christian's *Paw Patrol* Crocs. The house was disheveled and messy and exactly how I felt.

Paul walked back in from the outside, his face red. He did not waste time or mince words.

"I told her not to come back around either of us until she could speak like a respectful human being." He sat on the bench across from me, jiggling his leg.

"It's not like she'll have much opportunity," I said. "They leave in six days, Paul."

"I don't know what to say, Jess. I know... I really do know how hard this is."

I thought of unicorn Katy's California adventure... and believed him.

"Do you really think they're all... unhappy with us?"

His eyes turned immediately and immensely sad, and I realized how much Julie's resembled his in color and expression. "Aw, Jess. I hate all this he said, she said, no one saying what they mean, utter bullshit. I don't think she flat-out lied about it. But I also know she's not dealing in nuances when it comes to us. I'm certain none of them are entirely comfortable with me moving in right now, much less *happy*, but I don't think there are parent traps or voodoo dolls involved either."

"But maybe there's been a sushi happy hour here and there, discussing how ridiculous and selfish *we* are?"

He laced his fingers through mine as he nodded and suppressed a grin. "That's pretty much your worst nightmare, isn't it?"

I smiled in spite of myself. "Yep. I'm going to have to reread *The Emotionally Healthy Woman*. Again."

"Is there a passage in there about *grace and freedom* in leaving the kitchen a big damn mess and going to bed?"

"Yeah," I said, getting up. "She wrote it in the third edition. Apparently, it's easier to quit your pastor-husband's church than it is to leave dishes in the sink overnight."

"I believe it," he said, reaching over and squeezing my behind. I smiled and kept walking, ignoring all the normal rituals of nighttime and embracing my bed - our bed - like a lifeboat.

Chapter Eighteen

July 5th came in polar opposition to the day before. The house was thankfully quiet, but unfortunately, still a bit sticky and sandy. Paul was sleeping like a rock, and I woke stealthily to take care of Cash and start reestablishing order. It was well past nine, and I'd been texting Maggie the high-level summation of events when Paul padded into the kitchen. I expected him to be restored, hungry, ready for conversation, maybe a bit indignant. Instead, there was a shadow beneath his eyes unaccounted for by the rest he'd just gotten. He wordlessly took the mug of coffee I handed him and slumped on a stool.

I couldn't do the give-him-a-minute thing. I knew he preferred it, or at least was used to it, but I just could not. "What in the *world*?" I said, studying his face.

He took a long sip and then did the fingers-through-his-hair thing. When he finally spoke, he didn't look at me, but past me.

"Charlie's dead."

Honestly, it took me a moment to register about whom he was talking. We'd basically had a crash course in each other's supporting casts of characters over the past few months. Leah had a niece named Charlotte, and I think maybe he had a colleague from somewhere named Charles, but Charlie? Oh, my God! *Charlie!*

"Charlie! Paul! What happened?"

"I – he died." Paul shrugged, seemingly as dumbfounded as I was. "His stepson... He emailed my old AOL account. Princi*Paul*777, if you can believe that. Eight days ago." Now he looked at me, an expression of incredulousness across his face. "Eight days. I only check the thing every few months, probably. Sometimes my old students email me there. I just... He's dead." He threw his hand in the air, shaking his head.

Silence filled the space. I had no idea where Charlie lived, who his family was, and certainly not what, if anything, Paul would need or want to do. I stayed on the other side of the counter, keeping restraints on my physical urge to hold him, actually biting my tongue against the instinctive soothing words and rapid-fire questions in my head. My hands wrapped around my mug. I might have been rocking back and forth slightly, like a harried mother of an infant (or a lunatic). My insides were shaking at the heaviness in the room. Seeing him in pain made me feel like the air was crushing me. I wanted to wave a wand and rescue him, but I still wasn't confident of my role in his space, and there certainly wasn't anything I could do to fix it.

Maybe a minute passed by, maybe five or maybe not even thirty seconds, before I heard him exhale.

"You can come here."

I took my own deep breath as I crossed to him, my heart racing as I gathered him, as he very naturally and a bit urgently buried his head against my shoulder and melted against me. I could feel his heart racing, too.

It felt fitting to bear his weight. In the moment it was like another unexpected gift between us, that what I was aching to give him was something he could accept. "What happens now?" I murmured after a beat. "What do you need?" He didn't answer right away, so I just kept holding him, tightly. I would not let go before he did.

When he did, his cheeks were wet, and the usual sparkle of his eyes was eclipsed by weariness. "There's nothing," he said quietly. "There's nothing that happens. Let's take a walk before it gets any hotter and find some breakfast, okay? I'll help you clean up when we get back."

I watched him walk down the hall to ready himself. Suddenly yesterday didn't bother me so much. How could our group of offspring disapprove of us like we were having a wild party without their permission or something? What Paul and I were building might have been mysterious or questionable or just plain weird, but that didn't mean it was wrong.

#

Like the day we met, we settled ourselves over fluffy pancakes and too much coffee, though this time, we sat near the windows at the Pier Café (non-vacationers do not eat outside during daylight in the summer), both of us occasionally looking out at the swarms of people on the beach. I was surprised we could get a table at all, and we'd maybe have an hour until the holiday crowd would come charging back in, ravenous for lunch. I was determined not to waste any time with my own questions, though I had many when it came to Paul's family of origin.

Clearly, he was ready to talk. He recounted the bits I already knew: unspecified abuse from an alcoholic father, lack of protection from an acquiescent - and perhaps also abused - mother, and the failed attempt of two underage brothers to run away together, which resulted with Charlie's removal from their home and Paul being left there to deal with the aftermath alone.

"Charlie had to get away from the beach when he left the group home. Daddy was... Charlie was an adult, and even though he was mad, and he was tough, and he vowed all the kinds of revenge a young guy will vow, he knew Daddy would beat him to a pulp if he came around me or Mama. So he got out of here, and I never blamed him for that. The only thing I blame him for is that he didn't go far enough.

"He set himself up in Lisle." Ugh. Lisle, North Carolina was a few hours away and basically known for meth labs in outdoor sheds and way too many deals-gone-wrong headlines for a small town. "He got on a construction crew right after high school, and he did really well for himself for a while. He roomed with some guys. He went to church on Sundays. He bought a nice car. But he drank on the weekends, and he liked to get stoned every night after work. It's just what they did. I mean, when he would talk to me, he didn't *tell* me that's what he was doing. He just mentioned those things like he'd mention, *Hey. You think Mama would come here for Thanksgiving without Daddy?* or *Did you see that hot little chick just pull up in that stupid yellow Geo Tracker?* He didn't see the danger of messing with the same crap our dad messed with."

That I could get. Charlie was a kid. In spite of years of my warnings about being a teenager and single and pregnant and without a plan (to which he had rolled his eyes, and who could blame him, really?), Sam came home one night during his third year of college and began sobbing as he told Randall - not me; he would not even look at me - that Abby was pregnant.

I remember wondering how in the hell he couldn't remember me talking about the stigma and the fear of being young, expecting, and unmarried. Had it not been for the miracle of Randall coming into our lives the very year Sam was born, I have no idea where life would have taken my firstborn and me.

At age 20, Sam's know-it-all-guard was suddenly down, as Randall kept an arm around his shoulder, and my son begged for *my* forgiveness, as though it was mine to give. The next night was even more emotional, when Abby came alongside him, telling us how angry her own mom and dad were, and Sam not asking permission, but letting us know, that he was going to marry her. They had applied for family housing at Coastal that day, and he was working early shifts at Bojangles and late shifts as a custodian in the university's science labs. At first, Abby said she was prepared to put school on hold and find a work-at-home opportunity. I felt a million things rising up in me, the disappointment and heartache and also the utter weariness. I was home myself with a two-year-old, homeschooling our two nearly-adolescent daughters. But Sam was mine, and Abby already felt a little like mine too, and I didn't want them to lose all their dreams before they even got started.

I didn't even look at Randall before I said, "Nonsense. You're not dropping out, Abby. We'll - I'm home. I'll help with the baby." She started crying. I felt like it. The mere fact that we were able to have a serious discussion with the two of them for more than five minutes felt like a small miracle in our chaotic household, and I was inviting another tiny, helpless person to join the fray. When I finally caught Randall's eye, he nodded in his own grim acceptance. There was never a question we would help. But it would come with a sacrifice.

Sam and Abby were worth it. They stayed in school. They loved Travis like he hung the moon. They were never anything less than grateful for the hours and days I kept him, trading off with Abby's mother Whitney, who had just become an empty nester but committed herself to part-time nanny in order to help her youngest make her life work.

When they graduated, Sam was hired for a coveted spot on the marine biology team at the aquarium, and Abby got an entry level position at one of the legacy advertising agencies in town. They put two-and-a-half-year-old Travis in daycare around the time I put my three kids in school. We were in parenting trenches together.

Kids just can't take our word for some things. They have to get it themselves, and usually, it changes their lives forever.

Sam got it, but Charlie never did. Paul described how he eventually left Lisle, wandered the Carolinas for awhile, tried living in Chicago, then Indianapolis, and then followed a woman out to Colorado.

"He would fall in love with these amazing women," Paul recounted with a slight smile. "I mean, not just looks, but the whole package. Executive types. Scientists. People who had it all together *and* who would actually love him back. And then he would bolt. Time after time. I think he had a running account at the jeweler. He was always engaged and never married. And then he met Jenna. She was the change. He mellowed out. He quit getting high. And he married her."

The waitress came and filled our cups. Paul excused himself while I ticked off a dozen more questions his story had raised and told myself to save them for later.

When he returned, Paul went on to talk about Jenna's two middle-school-aged sons, how excited Charlie had been to be a parent to a version of himself and Paul. The recurring theme, though, of kids not being easy, of teens not listening, of raising them being a strain on a marriage, hit all the right chinks in Charlie's armor.

"I think she stayed with him long after she should have, or past what most people would. Maybe she struggled with the same stuff. I never really knew her. I never really knew Charlie much after he went away, you know?"

I did. I thought of Tony and our utter lack of a relationship since he and Maggie divorced. And I wondered if Paul had ever had anyone the way I had Maggie. He didn't seem to hang out with anyone on a regular basis, except his golf buddies, and I didn't even know their last names. He'd had Randall and me, but was it the same?

"I'm sure Charlie had seen things at home that I didn't, or at least remembered things that I didn't. I'm not making excuses for how he was; I'm just saying I don't know what it was like for him, so it was hard to stay distant, but it was easy to give him grace."

I smiled, reminded in the statement what a Good Man Paul was.

Without vocalizing our plan, we paid the bill and started

walking home, all while Paul kept telling his story. He'd gotten to the last time he saw Charlie, twelve years prior, after their mom had died. There had been a small funeral with their aunts and uncles and some extended family, well-wishers from the church, old neighbors and friends that neither of Mrs. Jameson's sons remembered. Paul went to his Aunt Sue's house to accept condolences, but Charlie didn't come. After visitors cleared, Paul went to the only bar in town and found him.

"I tried to talk to him. He didn't act angry like Daddy, but he was abrasive and obnoxious. Everything was a joke. Jenna wasn't with him and trying to find out where she was or their status was impossible. He didn't ask about Leah or the girls. And when I asked if he wanted to come visit for a few days before going home, he called me a rich, know-it-all cocksucker. Then he pretended he was joking.

"We both knew he wasn't. Compared to him, I was rich. Compared to him, I had everything together and was looking down on him. So I decided to just own that identity. I gave him five hundred dollars and my number. He bought the house a round and said to put it on his tab. It was gin, what our Daddy always drank. The smell of it made me want to vomit. But I knew I was probably never going to see Charlie again, so I drank it, I kissed his cheek, and then I left."

I squeezed his hand as we crossed the street to the house. I thought he was done, but something lingered. We walked up to the porch and he collapsed on one of the chairs. The ceiling fans barely registered on my sweat-soaked form, but I didn't want to cut him off by moving us inside.

Finally, he looked intently at me and said, "It was always

a conflict for me, how not to be like them and still... I don't know..."

"Love them?" I suggested, tentatively.

He shrugged. "Yeah. That's part of it. It's not all. It's hard to explain."

I nodded, trying to give him space to finish and permission not to. "You know, Paul, you're... you're what Mags and I always call *A Good Man*, capital letters. Maybe, you can just have faith that some of that lived in Charlie, in your parents. You'll never understand it all, but you can believe that you honor all of them just by how you live."

There was another shrug. He smiled at me then, lips tight, and scooted to the edge of the chair, ramrod straight. "If I'd hired a therapist years ago, maybe I wouldn't be throwing up all over you today. So let me tell you one more thing about me. I succeeded in not being like them, but it did come close. Once."

Suddenly, his narrative felt less like it was about characters I didn't know and more like a deeply important insight into the person I was about to spend what was left of forever with. I was dying to get us some water, but I didn't want to interrupt him for anything, so I just leaned in.

"It was 17, 18 years ago... I was drinking," he started. "A lot. My desk... you know, in *the principal's office*, was never without a little velvet bag of Crown stashed behind some files. And that was back in the day. I would give kids rides home from school, buzzed. A few times, absolutely bombed.

"One day I had to bring the girls home with me. Leah had just started working, and she had a showing, a big house up in Grand Dunes. And I'd had a swallow or two, and was just... a little dazed, too sleepy. I swerved once and almost ran off the road. Katy screamed, and Julie yelled at her. They both ended up crying, but Danielle just stared at me from the passenger seat. I knew she knew. She was maybe 10, 11? She knew. It was horrible.

"So I told Leah everything that night. I'll never forget her face. It was like one of those digital picture frames, or a screen-saver, the way it changed. She wanted to hit me. She wanted to scream at me. She wanted to cry. She wanted to kick me out. But when I was all done talking, she sat there with her stiff upper-lip and said she would help me. She would help me get sober, she believed in my ability to be better than I was. She said I was not my brother, I was not going to carry on my father's legacy, I had already risen above and would rise higher. She believed it.

"But she also said, if I ever drove our children, or anyone's children, or at all, after drinking again, I would never see our girls again. And I believed that, too."

He smiled. My instincts wondered how a person could smile while remembering such a dark moment, but I also knew that kind of defining moment in a marriage: the gritty, unpretty, life-defining muck you have to slog through in order to make a right turn away from divorce court.

"She was fierce," he continued. "She came and checked my desk, every day for the first few weeks. And honest to God, Jess, I didn't buy a thing from that day. It all scared the hell out of me... losing her, my kids, my job, and maybe the most important, my right to say that I was not Walter Jameson, that I was not any-thing like him."

I reached for his hand again, no longer able or perhaps just unwilling to keep myself from touching him, with hopes to reassure not just the man standing in front of me, but the one gaining his sobriety all those years before.

He stared down at our hands, there above the rough wood of the porch. Then he stood and pulled me to my feet, and it was only then, for the first time that day, tears reached his eyes. I looked at him questioningly.

"Just one more thing, because I'm sick of my own voice," he said. "And I need you to really... *get* this. I haven't told you because... you struggle so much with the guilt and the doubt of *us*. Yesterday didn't help, I know. But you need to know: Leah and I were not like *this*. This emoting, this hashing out, this... what is this you do to me? Comfort? Coddling? We didn't. We were partners. We shared necessary information. We supported each other. And we loved each other. But we weren't like *this*."

I nodded, resetting my hands at my sides. I didn't know what to say. I knew Leah. I knew she wasn't like me in how she related to people. I wasn't sure what it meant for her and Paul, or for me and Paul.

"We didn't touch like this. We weren't open like this. It's not just that you are a different kind of person; it's that you bring out something different in me. You've always been this way, loving people with this ease, like you're wrapping them in a blanket on the beach. I watched you when we were first working together, at church, with your family, with *my* family, with random people who always seemed to open up to you. With me. And I think *that* is what unsettles Julie, maybe all my daughters. You put *me* at a level of ease I haven't lived in, in... maybe ever."

I was pretty sure he blushed, but I did, too. It wasn't like I tried to keep my intense affection for my people a secret, but his description was another reminder of how much had changed, how quickly, how intensely. It made me feel responsible. And scared.

He likely knew that. "Yeah. This level of *you*, Jess, where we are... you're giving me something I've never had. You're touching wounds I... tried to forget. And you're redeeming things I thought I'd laid to rest. Maybe a 63-year-old man shouldn't need that, and definitely shouldn't want it, but now that I have it, I can't imagine letting go."

Sigh. "That's pretty much one of the sweetest things anyone has ever said. In the history of the world." My face was hot. "Other than, *We just made a fresh pot*, and *Your ass looks great in those jeans.*"

"Hey..." He reached for me again. "Don't do that. Don't shrink away from who you are."

"I don't," I said, eyes wide.

It really was useless arguing with him, because of course I did and of course he knew that. After the depth of everything he'd just shared with me, it felt superfluous to disclose my own fear, that once he looked at me closely as more than a friend, he would ultimately be disappointed in what he saw. My kids sure were.

And whether he needed my big, quilty comfort or not, it sounded more and more like I presented a big change from the wife and life he was used to. It stirred the same knots in my stomach that had been tightened by yesterday's revelations.

We went inside and ignored our plans to clean; we chugged water and made love and then took a nap, in the darkened bedroom with the air conditioning blasting, the hard-sleeping kind you take in the late afternoon when you're on vacation at the beach and on the verge of heat stroke. Paul had nothing on but his shorts, and I had nothing on but a tank top, and we tangled together in quasi-comas. I woke around dinnertime to the sight of him returning to the bedroom, toting two glasses of tea and the big bowl of leftover watermelon. I stretched and sat up next to him, flipping the TV to a *M*A*S*H* marathon and opening up in time to accept the first sweet, chilled bite he popped into my mouth.

At first, I tuned out the show, bored by a typical hi-jinks plot about a makeshift bowling team. But a rare somber scene between Hawkeye and Winchester caught my attention; Hawkeye was worried about his father having surgery back in the states and recounted how his mother died when he was a boy.

The theme for the day just wouldn't leave us. Paul glanced back at my questioning gaze and rolled his eyes. "I've spent enough time talking about them today."

I shook my head. "It just happened. It's okay..."

He took me at my word, launching into another recollection. "Our father died first..."

Since we'd established my role as a human quilt earlier that day, I skipped pretense and patted the pillow next to me as he began. He obligingly laid his head there, stretched sideways on the bed and looking up, at me, past me, while I caressed his temples, his neck, his shoulders, in an attempt to soothe his soul.

"Of course, Charlie and I talked about it," he continued. "We thought maybe things would change with Mama, that she would want to try to reconcile. But she didn't. She said all the right things and gave us both some money, and then she headed to Pennsylvania, because her sisters lived there, she said. She never let us know when she was sick, and it was cancer. It was less than a year later. It took her fast.

"My aunt called and told me she died. And I just..." His voice didn't follow his thoughts.

"I remember," I said softly.

He peered up at me, looking confused.

"That day..." I led. "I was with you... when your aunt called? I didn't know *who* called. You just... You just told me what happened, and I waited with you..."

Paul nodded, seeing it.

"Yeah... now I remember." He had my hand pressed to his face and the words vibrated off my skin.

Sometimes I had to remind myself that, sensitive and reflective though our men might be, they are still men. They don't have the same bookmarks we do, most of the time.

"I'll never forget it," I said simply. Even more so with him close to me, I could still feel the poignancy of that moment, the first glimpse of my work-friend as a real person. "I wanted so much to comfort you, and I felt so helpless."

He nodded deliberately. "You helped me."

I smirked, eyebrows raised. "How can you say that when you didn't even remember?"

"I didn't, but I *do*. I do remember," he explained. "Not so much what you said, or what happened in the moment. I remember being validated." He broke off, paused, nodded, looking somewhere else again.

"Good..." I answered, wondering if there was more to be said. "You rarely *ever* strike me as who *needs* validation, for anything."

He sat up, shaking his head. "That's because you're you, Jess.

You ask for it often and rarely need it. I don't... I didn't... ask for it. But when it came to all of that, my parents, the past... I did." He shrugged. "I needed it."

"For what, though?" I asked. "You were a kid. You didn't... none of it was your fault." It was the lame protest of someone who grew up in a safe home with two loving parents.

But he just smiled, sadly. "Sure. Of course, it wasn't. But by the time Mom died, I'd lived a long, stable life, made a family, overcame my demons, established myself as Better Than My Father. And my mother. When she died, it meant I'd have to face Charlie, and Charlie's reality, which, like I said, was basically the opposite of mine." He swallowed. I didn't want to press, but I wanted him to feel safe telling me all he wanted to say.

"Why would you need permission for that?"

He squeezed my hand, sighing. "I spent so much energy distancing myself from them. And as much as I needed to, I still felt guilty. I wasn't sure I was allowed to... mourn them."

With that, fresh tears sprang from his eyes, and he used my hand to wipe them away. One of the graces of aging, I suppose, is the ability to temper our sadness. I know his heart was broken for his brother, and now for the reliving of other losses, yet he was not overwhelmed by grief. He was filled with a quieter kind.

I felt it, too... for a man I'd never meet, for two little boys who'd tried to navigate an impossible situation with no voices and no advocates, for two brothers who loved each other but couldn't journey onward together, for Paul, so sure of himself in a million ways and yet looking for peace in a situation that wouldn't let him go... and that led me to mourning the distance between me and my own brother, the absence of my parents, the fact that Randall's family was probably lost to me as well.

I scooted closer still to him and wrapped myself around him, thinking about all the lack of peace in my own heart. It felt selfish to pray we could find it together, but as we exhaled and melted back into each other, I prayed it anyway.

Chapter Nineteen

Paul quietly closed on the sale of his house on July 9th. Everything he was going to move in was in by then, so with no ado, he came home from his attorney's office, and we resumed our activities of work/unpack/organize/sit down and look at each other in bewilderment.

Then that evening, Katy and Brittney came over with takeout meat-and-three and helped us break down some boxes and generally clean up. There hadn't been another mention of our arrangement since the Fourth, so their gesture was a sweet and strange surprise. Before the night was over, Brittney sat with me on the porch swing and lay her head on my shoulder, and we both cried. A few minutes later, Katy emerged from the house red-eyed and holding Paul's hand. He looked at me thoughtfully, started to say something, and then sighed, putting his arm around Katy.

So unsettling, for word people, not to have words. Our daughters gathered themselves, and before they left, Katy hugged me, which wasn't anything unusual. But Brittney walked to Paul, looked him in the eye, and said, "I'm glad it's you," and then she hugged him goodbye. She didn't say another word before walking away. Paul looked at me, shrugged almost shyly, and dropped wearily next to me on the swing. I put *my* head on *his* shoulder and didn't even try to say anything.

Though we had been staying together for weeks at that point, everything felt awkward again for the next few days. Sam didn't call me for two mornings. I had an internal debate over going to the bathroom with the door open (which I'd always done, and you can't see anything from outside of the bathroom anyway). Paul checked in with me over *every single* place he went, even if he spontaneously decided to pick up Dunkin' iced coffees on his way home from his mailbox. Even Cash was confused and took to sleeping back in the guest room for those first nights.

It was all weird.

Finally, by our third evening, the restlessness that pervaded the house overflowed. Paul came in the door from his accountant's office with a bouquet of colored daisies and a sheepish grin. I looked up from my desk and beamed at him, knowing he knew.

"Wanna go out? Or... eat peanut butter and go to bed early?" he offered, taking a seat at the kitchen table and handing me the flowers.

I gave him my biggest and most heartfelt smile. I smelled the flowers, set them down, and then shook my head.

"The kids leave tomorrow..." I reminded him.

"Oh, crap..." he said. "Jess. I'm so tired. Do we have to?"

We had to. We were not foolish enough to attempt another big family gathering. The Oakley crew was meeting for pizza, and the Jamesons were having dinner separately, and then whoever wanted was meeting up for ice cream.

"Why all the eating events?" he continued. "Why don't we all weigh 400 pounds? Why does this have to be a *thing?*"

I let him whine, feeling much the same. I didn't want an event for this in any way, but I was definitely afraid that if I didn't attend a gathering, I would not get a real goodbye with David. I had only seen him once since the Fourth, and Travis had been with him, and it had been very careful and polite. I had already lost him in many ways; this I knew. But I wanted a goodbye.

"I think Julie would be really hurt if you didn't go," I said, trying to stay reserved.

"Of course, I'll go," he sighed. "But ice cream? I don't know. It feels like we're forcing it."

"I know, but it wasn't our idea," I said. "It was David's, so..."

"*I* know," he said. "I'm gonna go get ready." He kissed me quickly before walking down the hall. I watched him, marveling at how good it felt that he was home there. It still felt strange, but the goodness outweighed the strange. And I needed it to outweigh the sadness, too. David was *leaving*.

Paul left a half hour before I did, as his crew was gathering at their favorite BBQ place in Pawleys Island. Mine was gathering down the street for Old Chicago pizza. I was the last one to arrive, wearing a black sundress - instead of the USC Mom shirt I'd tempted myself with - and a pasted-on smile.

"Saved you a seat, Mom," Sam said, getting up to pull out the chair between him and David. They had already ordered a big antipasto salad and enough thin-crust, sausage pizza to feed a small tribe, or our whole family.

But our family wasn't whole.

I took a deep swallow of whatever beer had been poured in front of me, trying to pretend like my heartbeat hadn't increased, with manic thoughts of David and Randall and Paul and Julie flashing, no – searing, through my head. This all felt wrong. David's father should be here. Randall and David and I still should have had time together.

"You okay?" Sam murmured to me.

I looked at him and didn't bother to paste the smile. I just shook my head slightly.

"I know this is hard, Mama," he said, reassuringly.

"I want him to be happy," I said, turning to watch him trade barbs with Brittney. "I just wish it could be *here*."

"We all wish that, wish a lot of things," Sam said. I gave his knee a squeeze and turned to David, pretending to admonish him for whatever ridiculous thing he was teasing his sister about.

Dinner was so uneventful that I might have been bored if I hadn't been heartbroken. Altan said his goodbyes to David in the parking lot; he'd had another long day and would have another early morning. I had to turn away.

The rest of us caravanned to Painters, stood in line for 20 minutes for pricey scoops of delectable, made-on-site ice cream in red velvet and Butterfinger and banana pudding. The Jamesons had already been through the line and were waiting for us on a few of the painted picnic tables outside.

Paul was standing behind his girls, in conversation with Matt. He looked up at me and winked, reserving both his smile and the cynicism in his eyes. I felt slightly strengthened by his presence, as long as I didn't think about wanting Randall to be there. It went against my polite instincts to wish for one over the other. And it went against my intellect to feel that way. It's not like I was wishing Paul was dead and Randall was not. And if I wished none of it had ever happened, then I was wishing away what Paul and I had made. So I was left with a sense of mania. David appeared at my side and slung a casual arm around my shoulder. I swallowed and smiled and began my greetings.

We were an ode to putting on happy faces. Julie was holding Vivi the whole time, clearly in love with her baby niece. (God bless babies for being a perfect distraction.) Danielle shared a dozen anecdotes; Matt, Paul, and David played catch with Christian, who laughed hysterically as they tossed his gangly 4-year-old body between them, Jacob waiting patiently for his own turn. It was only my sweet Summer who showed her real feelings. She sat between her mama and me and cried into her ginormous, chocolate-dipped waffle cone.

It was actually Julie who tried to pep-talk her, "When you come visit, Summer, there is a ranch that takes people on sunset horseback rides in the mountains. It's so beautiful! And we aren't far from the Grand Canyon either..."

Summer sniffled and let out a very grown-up-sounding sigh. "Can we FaceTime on Tuesdays? Uncle David always used to have tacos with us before this year."

As Julie and Abby both assured her they could, I suddenly felt myself washed with exhaustion. I was so blessed with the fullness in my life. There were always people around me, love around me. But more than ever, this year, this season, someone was always sad. Someone was always missing. And I could not fix any of it, not with tacos or ice cream or hugs or words. I tried not to be mad at David or at Randall, but in that moment, I felt completely betrayed and more than a little useless.

Sam was standing with the guys, silent. Travis and David were messing, really more like brothers than Sam and David were. Sam was more to David. Sam could almost be David's dad, and certainly, his father figure for this time. I wondered if Sam was as sad as I was.

I couldn't help but be quieter than usual. Julie was doing a good job of steering the conversation around the tables. It was her moment, and I was relieved to be part of the background. Before long, the uneaten treats were melting, the mosquitos got worse, and David reminded her that they were planning an early start in the morning.

The goodbyes started.

I relegated myself to the back, trying not to watch. Travis wiped at his eyes. Summer's shoulders shook. Brittney looked sullen, but both Mikayla and Katy let their tears flow.

Paul and I, on opposite sides of the crowd, were saved for last. David went to him, and when Paul extended his hand, David hugged him. He looked very grown up in the moment. To any random observer, he looked like a young man hugging his dad or his uncle. To me, the moment was layered with a thousand complicated emotions.

David, you're my baby. My baby. Like flashing, neon words: *My baby.* I wanted him to have his dad. I wanted him to stay. And I wanted Julie to live happily ever after, just with someone else.

As Paul said something that was likely perfect to David, Julie appeared at my side. We stood facing the men together, and she murmured, "Goodbye Ms. Jessie." I turned to look at the side of her face, a blend of Leah and Paul, a blend of confident woman and morose girl, and allowed myself to forget for one moment that she was the one escorting my "baby" on this foolhardy mission, and also the one making our tentative new life more emotionally taxing for the man I loved. I tried to think of the young woman who had been running races with her mama since her teen years, who had perfected her Sangria recipe, who cooked and manned phones for Leah when she was worried sick about Katy leaving town, who took care of her dad when he couldn't walk, who maybe, oh Jesus, who just maybe, really cared about my son and wanted to help him find some direction in life.

So I took the only liberty I could think of and brushed my lips against her cheek. She looked startled, but she turned to me and offered a half-smile. "Be careful," I murmured. She nodded and walked to Paul.

I accepted David's embrace. I fiercely held him back with no words to say. He pep-talked me instead, just as I had done for him countless times in the last two decades. He would be alright. He would make me proud. He knew Paul and I would take good care of each other, just as he and Julie would. He couldn't wait for us to come and visit.

He said every sweet, reassuring thing. So I waited. I waited until Paul and I were in the Jeep, the radio kind of loud, the windows up, the air blasting, heading toward home. And then I let everything go, weeping quietly, but with abandon I had not allowed myself since Randall's birthday. I had my face turned out toward the street and my hands in my lap. Paul put a hand on my knee and stayed silent.

By the time he trailed me up the stairs, I was merely sniffling.

I waited while he unlocked the door, the door to *our* home. Once inside, I stalled in the entryway, noting the teakwood sign above the door that simply read, "HOME," the hand-painted little table that always displayed a child's recent drawing and held a basket for everyone's keys, a teal and red braided rug that should have been replaced long ago, but I never could find one I liked as much. I recalled and marveled that it had only been three months since Paul had stood there like an awkward acquaintance, jangling his keys and not knowing what to say. Now, it was his home, too. I wondered how he felt, if he had the same whiplash I sometimes did.

I turned to face him and silently wrapped my arms and my whole self around him. More so than the bouquet of flowers or the empathetic smile from just a few hours ago, his steadiness made me feel safe. He held me tightly and made soothing sounds, a subtle catch in his own breath that echoed my own sadness. I tried to relax into the notion that, sometimes, there simply would not be any words.

Chapter Twenty

Without anything to anchor the transition, summer still felt like summer in late-August, because it was still 90 degrees and 200 percent humidity or more on any given day, traffic was still everywhere, and I had no one going back to school. I did take Summer and Jacob shopping for new backpacks, and I finished draft one of that damn planner with a flourish, ready to be done thinking about school for the foreseeable future.

Paul and I had settled into some kind of *new normal*. He stayed busier than he liked with property management and was mulling over either a partner (and no, it would not be me) or a paring down. We started going to church together, at first sitting on either side of Danielle and her family, per my neurotic insistence, and finally mellowing into restrained coupledom.

Evie and a few of her specific brand of contemporaries chose to pretend as though we weren't there at all, which was fine, as I had never in my life been quite so peopled-out. Small crowds felt safe, and it was nice to open my little circle up to include Carter and Morgan again. So one day after church, we dared to join them for lunch (truly, they dared to join us), believing we would not cause the world to spin off its axis. We sat, somewhat trying to be incognito, near the window in the corner at the back of Cracker Barrel, almost relaxed into comfort food and laughter.

"Hey everyone!"

We looked up. The fake smile of anticipation was pretty much always pasted on my face out in public, so it wasn't a stretch to keep it there for Darla Roberts, a random church lady who filled her social media with passive aggressive, bumper sticker platitudes mistakenly attributed to God and thought that Leonard Cohen's "Hallelujah" was suitable church music.

Paul squeezed my knee, and her eyes immediately traveled downward.

Morgan and Carter greeted her as pastors do, politely, pleasantly, formally. People like Darla would not read the room, even if they could. She didn't care that we all felt a little awkward, maybe even protective of our foursome, that we were possibly having a private or solemn conversation (yes to the former, no the latter), or that we simply didn't want our sourdough French toast or chicken 'n' dumplins to get cold. She made all kinds of small talk, then she launched.

"Aw, Jessie. How are you?" She didn't wait for a response. "Last time I saw you here, it was with Randall and the grandkids. Come to think of it, that wasn't so long ago."

My fake smile stiffened. I kept looking at my coffee mug and started adding unnecessary creamers. I remembered filling those tiny cups for Jake and Summer the last time Randall and I brought them here. I remembered Darla stopping by our table, much like this, showing me the heart-shaped cast iron skillet she'd just bought and delighting in the fact that she'd gotten the 40% off pre-Valentine's sale price on it. And I bought one. And I made Randall a jumbo heart-shaped cinnamon roll the Saturday after Valentine's Day, and a heart-shaped pizza one Sunday night. *Not long ago.*

"The older we get, the more time seems to fly," Morgan responded.

"Yes. Something like that," Darla relied. "Paul, don't you love that chicken salad? That was Leah's favorite too, wasn't it?"

Paul squeezed me again. "She pretended to love the salad, but pretty much just ate all the chicken. I just don't remember Leah eating here with you, Darla."

Now I was trying not to laugh. I still could not look at her.

"Well, you know. Bible study and things..."

The waitress, lovely, saving-the-day Erica, returned with coffee at that moment. We all turned our attention to her, leaving Darla standing there in what would have been awkward silence for anyone else. But she kept up.

"Carol said you'd moved, Paul. I hope your new place is as beautiful as yours and Leah's house has always been."

Now Paul was not typically at a loss for smooth responses, but he gaped at her. He knew Darla even less than I did. And I didn't know who the hell Carol was.

"Darla, how is Carol managing after Tim's surgery?" Morgan asked. Now *she* was smooth. Preacher-Wife Superpowers.

Darla rattled off something while the rest of us schmoozed with Erica and gratefully accepted refills. I thought we were done.

"I just want to tell you, Jessie, that I understand." She actually tilted her damn head. "My sister lived with someone from her gym after her husband left. It didn't last long, but it helped her get through some of the hard parts of being alone."

"If she's anything like you, I'm sure being alone worked out best for everyone."

Now Morgan and I gaped at Paul, who rarely used his verbal powers for evil. Darla actually uttered a TV-movie-esque, "Humph," before nodding to the Duffields and sauntering away.

Paul tucked back into his salad, and I took a swallow of coffee, accepting Morgan's sympathetic smile. The men went back to discussing a golf course down the way being converted to yet another planned community, and I tried to turn my thoughts from that heart-shaped skillet and the southern 50-something version of Mean Girls.

#

Darla was just a piece of the puzzle of "new normal" on social media, which was becoming even more like a minefield than usual. I was posting nothing but the occasional beach shot or plate of food, the kind of fodder that fit my typical Jessie-"brand" without giving away any of the personal narrative that I used to share naturally. I said nothing about David having moved away with Julie. I said even less about Paul moving in with me. But word was clearly out. I was texted or Facebook-messaged by no less than a dozen acquaintances from church or around the beach, "checking on me," prying. Even an innocent quote I shared – *from a homeschool article* – caused a small shitstorm of comments like "I don't know how you do it," "I'm sure Randall would want you to be happy," and my favorite, "Even grown kids benefit from having a father in their lives." That comment as well as the old pal from the PTA got deleted.

Meanwhile, my fatherless David texted me every few days with updates: photos from the apartment (the only sign of his touch appeared to be his surfboard mounted decoratively over the couch), a link to Isabella's Kitchen, a restaurant in Scottsdale that he knew I would love, and his *part*-time schedule at Capella University, where he'd decided he was going to work on a certificate in health care analytics before deciding on an actual degree program.

That was not my favorite bit of news, but also zero surprise. When I told Paul, he set his mouth in a straight line and shook his head, but he refused to join me in any outrage or scrutiny. He was determined to let the Adventures of Julie and David play out on their terms.

It drove me a little crazy, but I tried not to press him into a conversation and kept my venting to Maggie.

Rachel came to town right before Labor Day and asked Paul and me to meet her for lunch. But he had been working overtime fixing a fence at the duplex and his ankle was giving him a new round of trouble, so I sentenced him to the recliner and an ice pack and met her myself at the tea room down the street. He would have hated it anyway.

I hadn't seen her in person since The Accident; she was based in California and there was really nothing we couldn't accomplish from a distance. We typically met up at an occasional convention, but we had become friends through the years. She hugged me and gave me plenty of head-tilted, empathy-brimming, yet actually sincere questions as we analyzed the exhaustive tea menu. By the time our pots of white ambrosia and chocolate rose appeared, she could no longer stop herself from the inevitable subject.

"So I've been thinking about you and Paul," she started, and I had to make a real effort to keep myself from spitting out my delicious, perfectly-balanced-with-cream-and-honey first taste. Outside of church, the last month had been uneventful, and I was hoping Paul and I would become a piece of non-news for a minute.

"You're in good company," I answered, switching from Friend to Author & Personality. "In fact, we've had so many inquiries, I'm considering starting a housewarming registry on Amazon. And probably at Kirkland's."

Rachel tilted her head back and laughed, a little too hard. "That is *exactly* what I want to talk about, Jessie! You and Paul... you have a *story!*"

In that moment, I was very thankful for my California editor of seven-plus years and a friend who was far enough removed from the emotions of it all that I didn't have to care about editing my actual life for her. "Rachel, what are you talking about? Unless there's a classroom-based audience for post-widowhood romance, we are not textbook fodder. Not by a long shot."

"Oh honey," she said, with a wave of her hand. "We haven't talked in a while. My contract with Castle & Rapp is up in a month. I'm moving on, too. And I'm already talking to some more mainstream houses, including McMillan Media - which I think has a great niche for the kind of story you have to tell."

"Well," I said, taking a prolonged sip and mulling over my response. "First of all, congratulations. I personally relate to the wonders of being free from educational press. I mean, it's wonderful and altruistic and should have a limited life span for all of us. That said, I cannot fathom what story I really have to tell at this point that anyone would pay actual money for."

"I actually think you have *many* stories to tell, Jess!"

"About what? People become widows every day. You mean I'm the only one who shacked up with a friend a month later?" Yuck. I hated putting it into such inelegant terms, but the truth was the truth, and that was the popular version anyway.

"Oh Jessie. Do *not* shortchange yourself. There is a whole lot of material in these five-and-a-half decades of yours. Teen mom. Stillbirth. Second act career. Now this. Drama for days. You could do fiction *or* non-fiction. Paul could co-write with you. You already have a notable social media following. We could get you on the morning talk show circuit. IGTV. Together. It could be a *thing*."

In the moment, other than a call from David saying Julie was pregnant, I couldn't think of a *thing* I wanted less than *inviting* people to weigh in on my post-Randall romance. When I had ventured out and posted a simple photo of Paul and Cash on my Instagram (which was followed more by strangers than real-life friends), I had to block a handful of people for their snarky comments. (They were always, always a version of *Wow. Thought your husband just died.* As if I didn't know that!)

But after smiling as the server set down our quiches, I gave Rachel my most benevolent beam and said, "Tell you what, Rach. Get settled somewhere, and then talk to me. It sounds... interesting... but I don't think Paul wants to write at all, and I'm not sure how our... well... how the families would feel about us sharing everything so publicly. So... we'll see. 'K?"

"*Okay*, Jess," she said, winking. I'm sure in her mind there couldn't possibly be a reason why anyone would pass up on a possible book contract, especially for something as simple as telling her own story. Maybe I should be more like her and cash in on all my craziness.

When I got home, Paul was still reclined and texting furiously. He looked up at me with a grim smile.

"Oh my. What? And you want new ice?"

"Nah." As if to prove himself, he made his way to his feet and tossed his phone where he'd been sitting before doing the stressed-out-hands-through-hair-thing.

"What in the world?"

"Well, Grayson just called, and the damn fence isn't holding. And you probably missed it during your meeting, but there's a hurricane forming that's already getting things mobilized."

"Oh crap. A real one?"

"Metaphorical, Jess."

"I'm serious, Paul. Who? What? Where? When? I don't have to ask why at this point because we are surely the reason."

He shook his head, almost laughing. "No, for real. Hurricane 'Gabe' is in the Caribbean, about eight days out, and two of the models show it landing right here. At least a Cat 3."

I muttered an expletive. I hated hurricane watches almost as much as hurricanes themselves.

"But to answer your questions, Julie is actually the one who alerted me to it, and she thought if we have to evacuate, that it might be a great opportunity for us to come visit."

Mmm-hmm. I was sure she wanted *us* to visit. "Evacuate? Are they already talking that route?"

"I mean, my messages to Ed Piotrowski have not yet been answered..."

The sarcasm was strong with him that afternoon. "Never mind. I'm already texting Maggie," I said. "She's been his banker for a hundred years." Ed was our local celebrity meteorologist, and I had no doubt Maggie would actually check with him if I alerted her.

Paul did laugh briefly before getting really serious. "I'm going to have to hire someone else to do that fence. I'm at the end of my abilities, and it needs to be done right before the weather comes."

"And you may also need to call your PT," I said, "Before you change your mind and start rebuilding the friggin' thing."

He limped past me into the kitchen, not answering me, pouring himself tea.

"I don't really want to go to Arizona," I added.

"I don't want to go anywhere!" he replied.

"Hmm. Well, welcome to coastal living," I said. "You're second row now, bub. If it comes in as anything stronger than a tropical storm, we're outta here..."

"Hmph."

"Maybe we can go somewhere fun..."

Paul was not ready for a lighter mood. "I gotta go chase down a fence company," he said. Without a glance, he shuffled past me, down the hall to his makeshift workspace in David's old room.

I slumped into my own desk chair, ready to call up my list of hurricane-readiness tasks. Before I got there, my phone dinged:

Maggie: *Ed says this one is more likely to hit than any he has seen in the last few years. But you didn't hear it here. Wanna go to Vegas?*

Me: *Send him a kiss emoji for me, just for answering. Dreading hurricane. Speaking of, Julie already invited "us" to Arizona. My Aunt Fanny. I'll check with P about Vegas, baby!*

Maggie: *He don't own you. Tell his scrawny ass he needs a cheap steak and a few wins at the craps table.*

Me: *He's really crabby.*

Maggie: *You're probably overdue for your first fight.*

The thought had already occurred to me. And then I looked down.

Paul: *Come talk to me about Rachel. And maybe yes to AZ? :shrug emoji:*

I sighed. *A world of no* was my answer, but I'd listen to him, *after* I checked my list and the hotel prices in Vegas.

#

I stood in the doorway of my youngest son's former room. Paul was leaning forward in his chair, squinting at the monitor... and muttering an expletive under his breath.

The first fight might as well come with a flourish.

"The smallest hint of hurricane weather can undo the most stable person," I began.

He was not amused. "I'm not undone."

"You're stable, though?"

"Jessie..." I hated being the object of his impatience, so I sat on the end of the bed and tried to be a good listener. "I just booked a fence guy with an opening here at the end of his day. I need to get back over there. You know, because the Graysons have a dog, and this is affecting their *standard of living...*"

"Paul—" Crap. I was already failing.

He swiveled to face me but held up a hand. "I know. I know. It's utter bullshit. But they pay their rent on time so I need to take care of them. Have I mentioned that I hate being a property manager?"

I didn't attempt to answer that time. So he continued –

"I mean, I have no idea how Leah did this. There is no evidence anywhere that hints at a process. Her contacts must have all been on her cell phone." Ouch. It had been smashed to smithereens in the accident. "Of all the things I didn't picture, I definitely didn't think I'd spend my early-retirement years pounding on fence posts to no avail or trying to replace a stove with something that fell off a truck in order to save a few dollars."

I didn't plead *Then do something else.* I just looked at him in a way that suggested those words.

"I don't know what else to do," he sighed.

"Well," I started carefully. Then I launched into a quick summary of Rachel's book ideas.

"I think that's great." But his voice was low, and he wasn't looking directly at me. "You should do it."

"I mean..." Everything I had said included *us.* Something *we* could do. He cut me off, but he was still reading my thoughts.

"Creative writing just isn't my forte." That was a crock, and we both knew it, but his voice dropped in a way that let me know he was done. I recognized it. He used it to deflect, and there'd been more of that than I was used to with him lately.

You never lived with him before, dunderhead. Sometimes the voice in my head sounded just like Maggie.

I shook it off. "It's not the worst idea," I stated. "I just worry about, you know, reception here. The family. The... community..." I wasn't used to Paul not feeling like a safe place for my doubts, but every word I said suddenly felt silly.

"Oh, for fuck's sake." He stood up and pushed the chair, slammed it really, into the desk.

"What?"

"Jessie, if you don't get over this, no one ever will. I'm sorry, but I don't care what random churchgoers or your Planet Fitness crew from 10 years ago think about your life, and I don't know why you do. And the kids have their own crap to deal with. Do what *you* want to do, Jess! Go on TV. Tell the story. Our spouses were in a freak accident together and here we are. We should get something out of it besides our chops busted every other day."

He wasn't yelling at me, but he wasn't creating a warm fuzzy in the room either. He turned back toward the computer, still standing. I sighed and stammered like a teenager getting in trouble with her parents.

"I just—I guess I don't know what I want to do either," I managed. "But we kind of have to figure out what a hurricane will look like for us first."

There was a loud, pointed exhale. He sat back down in the chair, crossed his right foot over his left knee, clasped his ankle quite gingerly, and dared me to say anything else.

"I took some Advil. I made three appointments with her for next week. I *don't* want to fuss about it."

Then fuss about it when you're in a cast, man. I was almost biting my tongue. He was all the way being a stubborn ass.

"Okay. Then maybe we should just talk about the weather."

I'd been hoping for a smile, but there was just another sigh. I stared behind him, to the picture on his desk. It was two adolescent boys, one with guarded green eyes and a charming smirk. The other was taller, broodier, and had a protective hand on the younger's shoulder. They were standing in front of an open garage door, several of the tokens of small-town life visible behind them: lawn mower, gas can, a few rickety lawn chairs, a turned over bike. They were both wearing t-shirts with the arms cut off to the shoulders, the taller one with sunglasses on his head, the younger with a visor. I could almost smell the marshy grass and feel the soupy, humid air. It made me want a popsicle and a John Mellencamp song. It made me sad all over again for little Charlie and Paul. But I couldn't say a word about it, because Paul had gently but firmly silenced every mention of his brother since the day news of his death had arrived. It was as if he'd used up all the words he had for Charlie, or worse, regretted sharing his stories with me.

"I know you have to go... I just... Paul, I really don't want to go to Arizona yet."

My voice was so quiet that I barely heard me, and I wondered what had happened in the span of the afternoon that turned me back into my own teenage self, embarrassed, self-conscious, worried that Paul was displeased with me. This was *Paul*. Ever since our partnership developed into a friendship, long before we were widowed and dating, he'd had a knack for making me feel safe. He used ridiculous superlatives like *amazing* and *magical* to describe my graphics and layouts, he always took my side in the meaningless squabbles I shared with him, and his ability to seemingly read my thoughts and respond in perfect affirmation was not new. I counted on it. I counted on the knowledge that I could lean on him with the silly or the heavy and he would be a solid rock. I guess I even counted on our sappy mutual admiration to last through this twisted Brady Bunch scenario we were living in.

I shook my head, trying to clear it. Of course, he could not live up to the expectations I had of him. *But please, Paul,* I silently pleaded, *don't freeze up on me.*

Even as I pleaded, he was looking through me, and I shivered. But then I launched.

"You know, my brother Tony lives out there." I took a deep breath. I abhorred feeling weak, and family drama made me feel weak and foolish. "I don't expect you to remember, but he left Maggie high and dry. Left Chicago, went to Charlotte, barely saw their girls. We convinced Maggie to live by us, and Tony was only three hours away, and still didn't make the effort. I know I took sides against him, but it wasn't the first time lines were drawn. He gave me holy hell for choosing to raise Sam without a father and not giving him up for adoption, and then he abandoned his own kids. It took a long time to get over that, you know? And then he didn't even come here when Mom died, said what did it matter since they were both gone at that point? Obviously, he didn't see fit to be around for anyone when Randall died. But he's been trying to reconnect with David. Freaking Facebook hero. It's convenient to have a relationship when there isn't one fucking drop of effort involved."

"We don't have to see him," Paul said. It wasn't the answer I wanted, but he was softer. Closer.

I held up my hand, to stop whatever over-compensating motivational tidal wave might be coming. "Paul, I'm going to be painfully honest with you right now. We are barely set up here, in our own new life. Everything, ev-er-y-thing, has changed in the last six months. We're finally steadying out some. I'm finally not waking up every morning thinking first thing about David and how I have failed Randall. I don't want to go out there right now and worry about our roof blowing off while also wondering in what ways Julie is judging me for being with her dad or having to see my supposed only sibling after two decades of nothing. My heart needs a break, Paul. It just does."

He nodded slowly. I was certain then that he was understanding me, that he was about to make a glorious, bring-it-home speech. I could hear the opening measures of Bonnie Tyler "Holding Out for a Hero."

"And my head just needs a break, Jessie. If we have to get out of here, I'd just as soon buy a ticket and crash on a couch instead of trying to figure something out, plan a trip, try to mash our people together in one place. I don't really see how your brother is much of a consideration. We can ignore him. But I do see that you and Julie are going to have to get over this some time..."

I gaped at him. But I was trying so hard not to argue the points. Another deep breath. Pretty soon I was going to have to strike a Cat-Cow just to keep myself grounded.

"Okay. Well... Maggie mentioned Vegas," I said carefully. "Spirit has cheap flights—"

"Vegas is not much fun when you're not drinking," he said. I winced. I did tend to drink a lot more when I was there, and I also didn't often consider that Paul was a recovered alcoholic. It was still new information.

"I appreciate that," I said. "We could just drive over to Atlanta for some city life, or hit those peaceful mountains again..."

He said nothing. His mouth was set in a straight line, and he looked at his phone instead of me, a practice he both disliked and hid behind.

"What, Paul?"

He tossed the phone again, this time onto the bed. When he looked back at me, his eyes blazed in a way I had seen before, though never directed at me.

"Jessie, I don't know right now, okay? I don't know. If we have to go, we'll go. If I go to Arizona and you don't want to, it will be okay. Okay? I have to go meet this fence guy in 20 minutes. Can we hash it out later? Or better yet, not hash it out later? Just do what you want."

I was taken aback. "What? What is that supposed to mean?"

"I told you. I'm just tired. I don't feel like talking about all this. It doesn't matter right now."

"It might not even matter this week. There might not be a hurricane here at all. But I guess these are decisions I assumed we would make together. And I suppose I also assumed that in cases of natural disaster, we would actually be together. That's kind of the point."

"I know you're used to handling things a certain way. I just need some head space."

"Uh-huh. That's not really an answer, Paul."

"You didn't ask an actual question, Jessie."

He had stood, and I knew he was about to walk out of the room. I wanted more words. I wanted resolution. I wanted a bigger fight, really. So I followed him out and down the hall.

"Why are you giving me semantics? Why won't you have this discussion with me?"

"I have to go," he muttered.

"I can come with you... maybe I can help. And we can—"

"Jessie!" He stopped right in front of the door, keys jangling. "I have to go."

He left. He walked out the door and closed it and left.

\#

Maggie randomly stopped by after work. I hadn't asked her to, and it was something she used to do all the time *before*, so I was grateful for the timing. She found me sitting by the window in the bedroom, attempting to read from an inspirational book called *When Grace Walks In*, kind of praying that it would, and there she was.

"What the hell is up?" She bounced onto the other chair, dropped her bag on the ground, and looked at me with intense scrutiny.

"What?" I closed the book and let it drop to my side, knowing that much as it was with Paul, there would be no hiding anything from her.

"You're mad. And sad. And something else. Hurricane Stress? Because it's a little early. Aw, but it's your first one after Randall..."

I actually cackled a little. "That whole idea has become such a misnomer. Am I even allowed to have *after-Randall* things? Thoughts? Because I have Paul, so everything keeps going on exactly the same, right?"

"Jessie." She sounded on the verge of a sermon. "I repeat, what in the *hail* is up?"

"I think Paul wants to go to Arizona."

"To live?!"

"No." I laughed some more. "If we have to evacuate. Julie is the one that had been watching the trackers and told him there was a storm system, and she told him he should use the time to come visit."

"Just him?"

"Well, apparently, she wouldn't turn me away or anything, but the invite was to *him*."

"And he wants to go?"

I mulled over my answer. A simple "yes" wasn't really a fair characterization.

"He's thinking about it. I think. He was already pissy when I got home, and I—"

"You pushed the man, didn't you?" Like Randall, she had the one-eyebrow thing going for her.

"I just wanted to figure out—"

"Jessie Rose. He is not Randall. You know that. You gotta give him time."

"I know he's not Randall. But reasonable adults have conversations about important things. And not just when *he* feels like it, but sometimes when he doesn't."

"But did it have to be right now? They ain't even talking bread and milk yet."

"It's just the *point*!" I insisted. "I drop everything when he needs to work something out. Why can't I expect the same?"

"Because he isn't you. And you both are coming out of a way of doing things that lasted for decades. *Decades*, man. You gotta cool your jets now that you're living together. This isn't dating or courting or working a dream job together. It's *life*. Good, bad, ugly. And he's not—"

"I know he isn't Randall!" I hissed. "Can you please stop saying that? I know. I'm not asking him to be Randall."

"But you're expecting him to respond to you like Randall did."

I stopped. I knew she was right. And furthermore, I wanted Paul to be mad at Julie.

"I didn't just lose a husband," I said, more carefully. "My kids lost their dad. And David losing his dad, in particular, is sometimes even harder. And it's also hard to separate sometimes. And maybe part of the reason I'm so angry about David and Julie is because it means Paul can't ever be... another... *dad* to him." I nearly choked on the word, and I looked down, a bit disgusted with myself.

"I think," Maggie said, with a softer tone, "That you are getting the cart waaaaay before the horse. First of all, you are the last person who should make that assumption. Look at the relationship you have with Abby. And with Altan. You think you're not a mama to them? Paul can be a dad to your kids. He probably will want to be *even if*. But honey, really, the odds of our baby boy and Ms. Julie staying together are... sliiiiiim to nill. At best."

Was she right? In my head, I had them married inside of six months, David working two jobs because he wouldn't ever finish school or be an actual midwife, and Julie would run his life, and he would never really make any choices because his growth was stunted. He would be a Peter Pan getting nit-picked and nannyhenned for the rest of his life until it all ended in a blaze of glory and—

Sigh. It was possible I was getting way ahead of myself.

No wonder. The world had spun far away from my control, again.

Maybe I was trying to make Paul my axis, my anchor, and I had to remember he was working through his own changes and fears and family responses. Was I being completely unfair to him?

"You wanna go grab a drink?" Maggie asked.

I snapped out of my own thoughts. "Hmm. Yes. But no. Thank you. I think I'm going to go for a walk and then... actually start prepping a little, in case Gabe turns into something."

"Tell you what," she said. "Let's hit the Half-Shell for one." (The Half-Shell House was right on the beach, totally mediocre, and walking distance from my house). "Then you can go walk and I can go pack for Greenville."

"You're leaving already?"

"Moni has a conference there for a few days. I was planning anyway, to crash her hotel room Thursday night. So maybe I'll just follow her back to Charlotte if I have to."

We started talking logistics, and I grabbed my bag, because obviously, I was going with her.

#

One hour of happy with Mags and one hour of my own thoughts and prayers (the non-ironic kind) settled me immensely. When Paul answered "Yes" to my "Will you be home for dinner?" I strode back to the Half-Shell and picked up a grouper basket and a crab cake platter to go. I was drenched by the time I walked in the front door, and I was greeted by a freshly-showered Paul, turning to me from the stove, where he was stirring something that smelled tomato-y and garlicky and heavenly.

His smile was wide and welcoming.

"You cooked," I said. Duh. And I was smiling too.

"You ordered," he said, walking toward me and taking the bag. "It's like we switched places."

"Indeed," I said, murmuring while he planted his parted lips on my sweaty neck. I waited until the bag was out of his hands before I pulled him into my arms, wanting to hold him tighter, afraid of my own need.

"I'm sorry," he said. "Also, I'm gonna sit down now."

"Paul..."

"I'm okay, Jess. Honestly." I watched him stretch his legs out, feet propped onto a chair. He drank heartily from a jar of tea. I peered at the stovetop and saw meatballs in sauce and a pot set to boil for spaghetti. I went to the freezer and wordlessly handed him an ice pack. And I marveled at how I could know a person so well, and also not at all.

"Thank you," he murmured.

"You gotta—" I stopped myself. "I wish you would take better care of yourself."

"I overdid. I know." He set the ice on his ankle and reached for my hand. "But I hired the fence guy. I see the Witch Doctor in the morning. And then we can hang plywood and close shutters and pack."

"Yeah? Where we going?"

"I honestly don't care," he sighed. "But Piotrowski is already doing a Facebook live in 20 minutes, so we're probably going somewhere."

"Paul." I slowed my talking, but my heart was racing. I wanted to say it right. "I'm sorry. I'm trying. I'll try harder."

He pulled me right onto his lap. "Maybe we don't have to work so hard at it. Maybe we just need to keep giving ourselves time."

"You're the one who keeps reminding me that we don't know how much time we have." I didn't want to argue, but dang...

He acquiesced. "It's a conundrum, isn't it? I just think... we're good. There will be bumps. There will be adjustments. But we both want the same things. We'll be okay. We *are* okay."

"I worry about... I don't want to smother you."

"You don't," he said. I moved over to a chair and stole a sip of his tea. "But you're used to taking care of everyone. And I am not used to being on the receiving end of that. We... Leah and I and frankly, the girls, operated pretty independently. I'm not saying that's better or worse. Jess, I *like* partnering with you. Obviously. I just need time and space to adjust, and sometimes just to mull. And maybe even to brood. But I know when I come out of it, I want you there. I have zero doubts about that."

I nodded and smiled, refusing to analyze any further and choosing to be satisfied. "How do you feel about fish and spaghetti? Because my Nonni Romano would be *proud*."

"I'm ravenous," he said. Then he sniffed intentionally in my direction. "Why don't you um, freshen up, and then we can eat to the weather report?"

Our pre-storm was weathered. It was all pretty minor for a first fight.

Chapter Twenty-One

There was no hurricane, that round. Gabe started breaking up over the Caribbean, and all we received were some heavy rains and steady winds. It was enough to keep Paul busy, mostly hiring out for tree-trimming and roof repairs. He stuck to sealing windows and checking some plumbing, but the whole thing made him miserable. I smiled to myself during a Sunday dinner when Altan offered to give him some assistance. Marina business slowed down considerably after Labor Day, and Altan was not only much younger and free of chronic injuries, but handy, teachable, and available for the extra work.

I took on the new writing project with Rachel, who had landed at a Christian publishing house. She tapped me immediately for a devotional for moms. The market was flooded, and I didn't really understand why she thought I was a good fit, but the short bursts of encouraging Biblical application were good for my widow's-brain-induced attention span and for my agitated soul.

Tentatively, Paul and I booked airfare for a long weekend in Phoenix in late September, when hopefully the degrees would be in the two-digit range. We also reserved a little casita about 10 miles away from David and Julie's apartment. He was looking forward to some time away. I was... trying to keep an open mind, and very excited about the casita.

David texted every few days, but phone calls were definitely sparse. His excitement from the first week or so they'd been in town had definitely waned, but to hear Paul tell it (not that he said much), Julie was very much taking to life out west. She had, in fact, become the supervisor of patient care at the birthing center in the span of a month. David was working at a Panera Bread. Tra-la-la.

So on a slightly breezy mid-September evening, as Paul and I tucked in over an actual "fall dinner," I wasn't hugely surprised at the cryptic texts I received from the other males in my family: Travis, Sam, and Altan, letting me know that they'd talked to David and he could probably use a pep talk from me. On top of that, I had one from Mikayla asking me if I'd talked to him, and I also observed a ridiculously dramatic "vaguebook" update from Brittney about people reaping the consequences of their stupid choices.

My mouth was full of meatloaf when the phone actually rang, and a picture of Randall and David on his high school graduation day flashed across my screen. "David," I sputtered, and Paul nodded distractedly (he had his own thing going on with a contracted painter) as I got up from the table and went out to the porch.

Sometimes, the setting is so contradictory to the moment. Example: the day in March, seven months and a lifetime before, when I got the call about Randall, could not have been a more perfect predecessor to spring. Literally, the sun was shining, and the birds were singing, and a perfect breeze was blowing. This evening, with my youngest on the line from three time zones away, was much the same, except the sun was already beginning to sink itself into a sea of red and purple and gold, and the ambient sounds were provided by the ocean and some bamboo wind chimes that had once belonged to Leah.

"Hey, Mama."

"Hey, love! How's it going?" I heard the fake in my voice, so I was certain he did as well.

"Well. It's okay. Um..." He took a deep breath. My stomach was immediately filled with butterflies. David didn't get nervous about bad grades or on-the-job snafus. Something bigger was wrong.

"What's up, honey?"

"I... well, I hate to ask you this, but do you think I could use my old room for a while?"

"Oh David..." I didn't try to act surprised. I would not tell him I had been counting the days, and it had taken exactly 64 for this to happen.

He went on to tell me that he just couldn't get with the vibe there, that Capella couldn't be more different from USC (*come ON, son*), that he missed the ocean, and finally, that Julie had fallen in love with a pediatrician she had met at church.

"You can always come home, David," I said, mustering all the restraint I could. There was still anger and probably disappointment in my voice, but he wouldn't know the fullness of it. Not yet, anyway.

"But you and Paul—"

"We will figure it out, son. This is your home, and it will be fine. Just... when do you think you're going to leave?"

"I'll pack tomorrow morning and leave in the afternoon," he said. "I don't have many ends to tie up here."

Two months of his life, lost. It wasn't a tragedy at age 20, but it could have been avoided. I swallowed every version of *I told you so* screaming its way toward my mouth, told him I loved him, to be careful, to call me once he was on the road.

Then I hung up the phone and closed my eyes. I hated the defeat I had heard in David's voice. I hated how conflicted I felt walking back into the kitchen.

Paul was standing over the sink, scrubbing mashed potatoes from a mixing bowl and singing "All the Gold in California" with total abandon. I wanted to wrap my arms around his waist and lean into him and pretend like I hadn't just had the conversation I had. I should have.

He sensed me behind him before I could think of how to start. "How's David?" he asked, without missing a beat.

"Mmmm. Well..."

I watched him carefully turn off the water, dry his hands, fold the dish towel, before he turned to face me. I thought again about how much I loved knowing him so well. It felt so magically soon, and yet so deeply engrained. But right now, it also felt scary, because I was predicting his nobility and calm, which was almost the opposite of what I was feeling.

"What is it?"

"Julie broke up with David, and he's coming home." I tried to say it evenly, but there was simply no hiding myself from Paul.

He didn't say anything. His mouth was set in a straight line.

He shoved his hands in his pockets. My stomach sank when I re-alized.

"You knew," I murmured.

"Julie called this morning."

I nodded slowly, counting in my head, shrugging, though ap-athy was the antithesis of what was simmering inside me. Then I shook my head and held up my hands. "I don't know what to say."

"I knew you would be upset," he said, as even as I was.

"And yet."

"Jess." I stiffened at the prospect of him gearing up a defense. "They're adults. It's complicated. We knew something like this could happen... probably *would* happen."

I nodded again. I could almost feel my brain sloshing around in my head. "Yes. And I guess if it had been *David* leaving *her* for some girl he just met, you would be this calm and reasonable about it. I guess if *she* was 20 years old, and David had given her three weeks to take over the rent or find a different place to live, we would shut our mouths and let her figure it out herself. I guess if Leah and Randall were still here, the four of us would just laugh it off over crab legs. Nice and benign."

His eyes narrowed by the end of my rant. I could almost see his blood pressure rise, which is kind of what I wanted.

"Are you always going to bring them into it? What do they have to do with anything?"

I shrugged again. "It just seems, in hindsight, that the whole foundation of our friendship is based on very controlled emo-tions, all very polite and sweet and mutually-admiring. But we – you and I – can't afford to do *this* life like that. There are a lot of people and circumstances and feelings involved, and it goes deep, and *I* go deep. I cannot be Switzerland when my son has been screwed over by someone, whether that someone is a stranger or your daughter."

I was seething, but he remained controlled. "And if I choose to remain neutral, even though you aren't? Then what?"

"Then I'm not sure I'm comfortable with some of your relationship philosophies..."

His head snapped backwards like I'd slapped or cursed him. "Relationship philosophies?! Jessie, our kids are grown. Why do we continually have to get involved in their drama?"

"Quitting school and moving cross country isn't *drama!*" I retorted.

"Okay. You're right. It's a stupid, immature, big life decision that involves risks and consequences."

"Indeed. Consequences that an almost-30-year-old professional with a new doctor on her arm is much more equipped to deal with than a 20-year-old college dropout!"

"Okay. Fine, Jess. Julie has behaved despicably. She should have been the wiser and more mature one here, and instead she acted carelessly. And now she's being inconsiderate and petty. What would you like me to do about it? Ground her? Suspend her allowance until she apologizes? *Tell her who to love?*"

I would not be thwarted by his insinuations of hypocrisy. "Well, what did you say to her?"

His brows furrowed, and he raised his voice. "I *told* her she was being inconsiderate and petty. And irresponsible. I told her she was making a mess. I told her to be careful."

"Careful? Does she even feel an ounce of remorse?"

"She is sorry she's hurting David." He'd switched to a mutter.

"Great." I turned from him and picked up the tea kettle, trying to focus on something, anything. The water running. My hands shaking. My heartbeat rapid and angry in my ears.

"I understand why you're upset."

"Gee. Thanks." I stared at the stovetop.

There was loaded silence for a minute, and I couldn't stand it.

"It's going to be super awkward when David moves back," I finally said.

"We'll figure it out..." he said, not convincingly.

I flipped the burner off, changing my mind. "I'm going to go for a walk."

He gave me a small, very guarded smile and nodded. "Be careful."

I nodded. His hand reached out and squeezed my arm as I passed him. My instincts to melt into him and flee from him were in such direct conflict that I almost froze. But my mind's eye flashed a glimpse of my boy, David crying at his daddy's casket, David vacuuming the interior of my car, David waving excitedly the night we said goodbye at Painter's. And suddenly the real conflict was my previous life versus *this* life, this right-now life with Paul that had gone to an explosive level of intensity and maybe taken over every vision and action of mine in the blink of an eye.

It was too late to be careful.

When I returned, just forty-five minutes later, the Jeep was gone, the note on the counter saying Paul had gone to the driving range. By the time I showered, he still wasn't back, and though I planned to wait up, I woke up at 2 a.m. with my Kindle on my chest and no one beside me.

I tiptoed hastily to the living room to behold Paul's sleeping form on the couch. He was in his jeans and t-shirt, his feet bare, and an old quilt he'd brought from his house thrown haphazardly over him. It was one of the few housewares he'd kept here, most of the rest put into storage until we "figured it out." It didn't look much like the décor of his and Leah's. It was goldenrod and sage and white, some of the patches bearing ducks, some suns, some sunflowers. I wondered if it had been from his childhood, or if his mom had made it.

There were countless untold things between us. In spite of all the talking, in spite of the somehow both gradual and instant intimacy between us, I didn't know *so much* about him. And here I was so surprised that he didn't have David's back, even though of course, he needed to have Julie's.

Part of me wanted to lie right there with him on the couch and will things into being okay or talk and talk and talk until we put all the pieces together.

But he'd chosen to sleep there for a reason, another thing that was a mystery to me. So I turned back to my own bed and spent the rest of the night alone.

#

From the house noise, I could tell that Paul's morning had started just as early as mine (around five) and that he was just as confounded about what to do. I heard the shuffle of coffee fixings and the din of the morning news. He was using the guest bathroom when I finally brought Cash outside, and when we came back in, he was sitting on the sofa, the sight familiar as he held a mug and smoothed his hair. His voice, though, that was different, and his eyes were as guarded as I had ever seen.

"It was a rough night," he began, diplomatically.

Normally, I would feign a laugh to set myself and the atmosphere at ease. There was no ease.

"It was," I agreed.

"I did a lot of thinking, not just about the situation and Julie and David, but specifically what you said about relationship philosophies."

"You thought that was stupid," I said.

"Not stupid, just... not the kind of thing that I, as a 63-year-old widower, am interested in tweaking right now."

I started to feel a little panicky and a lot confused. "What?"

He leaned forward and set his mug on the coffee table.

I knew this posture.

"Jessie." Suddenly, for the first time, I hated his voice saying my name. If he noticed, he didn't miss a beat. He had prepared a speech, Paul of the Perfect Words, and I hated them, too. "This thing we've been doing isn't real. It's all blankets and candles and cooking and... sweet music and sweet coffee and sweet...ness. All the time. It's like being inside a Christmas snow globe. It couldn't last. We should have known. You *did* know. You're the one who called it, and I refused to see it. It was too soon; it was too much. And now here we are."

Here we are. "Which is... nowhere," I concluded. What a speech. A perfect Paul speech. He reduced everything to its lowest common denominator. He reduced me and the life I thought we were making to a piece of shmaltzy home décor. And he left no room for me to edit any of it.

"Not nowhere, just..."

"Paul." I didn't like his name on my lips any better. "If it's time to move on, then we move *on*. There's nowhere left for us to go."

His expression told me he knew; he knew not to utter the word "friends."

The silence dragged, and it wasn't awkward, nor did I feel compelled to fill it. We both looked around and back at each other several times, and then he finally flinched, wearily rinsing his mug and putting it in the dishwasher, exhaling deeply, and finishing.

"I'll get my stuff out... I guess... today. The freedom of retirement being such a gift..."

I forced a wan smile. "Yeah. Um... might as well, I guess. I'm going to run some errands and have lunch with Maggie, so just..." I shrugged and exhaled just as deeply. "I'll stay gone until tonight. Take your time. Leave your key... I guess on the porch somewhere. Or leave it with Danielle and she can give it to Mikayla. No... You can honestly just throw it away. Whatever..." I started walking to the bedroom.

"Jessie..."

I looked back at him, my eyes already glistening and threatening to overflow. "Nope. Paul, I can't. I'm not going to stand here and try to conclude it, and I don't want to be bitchy, but I think that's what I'd be right now. So do what you need to do, but please try to finish it all today. Because you're right. We should have known."

I turned away quickly. I didn't want to know if he was teary too, or if he held a blank expression, and I didn't want to see him turn away. I walked briskly to my room, grabbed my purse while shoving my feet into flip flops, and looked at Cash. "Come on, buddy," I said, deciding Paul wasn't getting my dog for the day. Maggie was not expecting us, but she would welcome us.

#

"Where is he going to go?"

I shrugged. Like any proper best friend, Maggie had taken a PTO day, and now, we sat in her twin recliners, which faced her fireplace and were peppered with super soft throws, also something like the inside of a damn snow globe. It would have been a cozy spot to process the near tangible breaking of my heart, except our mid-September was still as hot as a freshly-glazed Krispy Kreme, and Cash lying across my lap felt as suffocating as it did mystically precious.

"I have no idea. He owns all those properties. Maybe one of those. I didn't ask. And I cannot care."

"Except you do."

"Of course, I do," I muttered. "But I don't want to."

"Jess." Her tone was a little too reminiscent of Paul's from just a few hours ago. It already felt like days. My mind went into electromagnetic shock every few minutes, when it instinctively planned tonight's dinner or the trip to Arizona, or that Paul was going to take my car for an oil change the next day...

"How the hell did we build a life together so fast? I have one million things to reconfigure now. Again!"

"Jess. I gotta tell you..." Her tone did not signal anything I was going to like. "It's a million and *one*."

"What? What else? Is someone else pregnant, or moving to Alaska? Nora? You?" I actually laughed. It was absurd and impossible, but so were the last six months of my life.

"I hate the timing," she said, "but you have to admit, I am overdue for this one."

"What are you talking about? *Are* you pregnant?"

She giggled. "Twenty years ago, that might have been nice. No. I'm not. But I am... well, I *am* moving. I'm also getting married."

"WHAT? When? Where? WHO?"

She laughed and held up her phone. "Soon. To Greenville. His name is, ahem, Sheldon."

In two seconds flat, we both yelled, "Ride me, big SHELDON!" and laughed a hearty laugh. Thank you, Nora Ephron and Billy Crystal.

"Well, for Heaven's sake. What is he like? When did you meet him? And when do *I* meet him?"

Turned out while I was living my best version of a Lifetime movie, Maggie had met Sheldon during Spring Bike Week, when he had traveled to the beach with his other biker/attorney friends. It had been, of course, not long after The Deaths, but also not long before Paul moved in with me, and, having had a few of her own intense, ill-fated romances through the years, she had become pretty guarded about bringing anyone around. She also figured I had enough to think about.

I flipped through Sheldon's profile pictures on her phone. "Learning of your fine brown-attorney-biker-lover would have been a most welcome distraction, Mags. Maybe it would have inspired me to get out of my own backyard and be more adventurous."

She shook her head so emphatically that her red and orange scarf came loose. Fixing it, she insisted, "No regrets, Jessie! If we lived that way, we'd never do anything. If we lived that way, I'd have given up after The Puerto Rican Sailor Incident of 2005."

I tried not to laugh, because it had been awful when it happened. For a few weeks, Maggie had gotten totally taken by a supposed tourist who turned out to be married, dishonorably discharged from the Navy, 12 years her junior, and virtually homeless. He had also been, however, absolutely gorgeous, and thankfully, she hadn't given him too much money.

"Oh Adrian," I said. "Thanks for the memories."

Maggie gave me one murderous glance before continuing her rally speech. "I watched you and Paul from that first awkward morning y'all were cat-nappin' together. That was real. He couldn't keep his eyes or his hands off you, and ever since, you've been acting like Mary Bailey letting George yell at her that he never wants to be married. Old-fashioned, lovesick, putty. No sense in pretending it wasn't good while it lasted. It won't make your heart un-break any faster."

"I don't know what's worse," I admitted. "Losing him, losing him so soon after losing Randall, or feeling like the biggest fool who ever lived."

"It's all bad," she said, reaching over to stroke Cash's head. "Take your time and go through it, though. It's life. And we already know, it won't always be this way."

I looked at my sister-in-law, the one who had magically become my sister after my own brother left her devastated. She was the strongest woman I knew. Maybe I could believe her.

#

I finally pulled into my driveway a little after 11, queasy. Paul was gone, of course. He really didn't have *that* much to move out, and I was sure he'd called someone to help.

Of course, I'd been silently hoping he was waiting inside with a thousand yellow daisies or something. So I sat in the car looking up at the porch, listening to my "Angsty" playlist. Jon Bon Jovi sang sadly to me, as there was an ideal Bon Jovi song for every chapter of life. I had no idea what the next one was going to be. Maybe I'd just be the old, *solitary*, bohemian grandma. I'd let my hair go totally gray. I'd stop pretending I wanted to wear anything that wasn't black. I'd be me and my dog and the beach.

I went through my nightly routine, the old one, the one that existed for three weeks between Randall dying and Paul basically beginning a six-month sleepover. Maybe it wasn't so bad if I did think of it that way. We weren't really trying to build a life. We were just on an extended playdate, sharing the pain and delaying the loneliness.

I walked Cash. I made my tea and drank half. I showered and slathered my nondescript coconut-with-lavender-oil mix on my face and neck and legs. I braided my hair and grabbed my Kindle. I went to plug in my phone but tapped my mail icon one last time for the day. And I saw his name.

Paul Jameson.

}

}

}

He'd entered the brackets on the first three lines so there was no preview. I could choose to read it or not. His knowing me so well used to be disarming, and charming, and now it just felt like a giant shaker of salt over a gaping wound.

I didn't have to read it, but, of course, I would.

Jessie,

I put the key under the citronella candle on the porch. It's not original, but I am not thinking very creatively today.

Neither of us was fit for conversation over the last 24 hours. I try hard to live with no new regrets, so I must take a small space to tell you what I'll always want to say.

You helped me to BREATHE. Not just in these last months, but ever since I met you. You have always seen and brought out the best in me. I hope, to any degree, you see that I tried to do the same for you.

...though it is easy to see the best in you. Your devotion and affection are stalwart and priceless. You're smart and funny and imaginative and empathetic. You have amazing hair and hilarious taste in music and know the perfect beverage and snack for every mood and situation.

I will miss all these things. It's unfathomable to me that my daily life in all capacities will be without them, without you.

I can't completely comprehend or explain what is happening right now, why we are at another major transition in such a short period of time, and one that feels so final. I hope somehow, we can find a way to fit back into each other's lives, at some point, when the dust on these two old souls has settled some.

That was too poetic, and I fear if I keep writing, I will stop writing, and come back to you begging.

I love you, Jess. I wish it was enough.

- Paul

We had exchanged thousands of emails through the years. This was the longest, the most expressive, the best, the worst.

I hit reply, ready to start typing long and fast and furious. I kept erasing everything and then finally settled on,

"I've got the key. I wish there was more, but I have run out of words.

I do hope you know that I was in this for real... and in love with you."

Nope. Still too much. I erased the entire second line, hit send, flung my phone to the floor, and punched up *Gilmore Girls* on Netflix, ready to be lost in someone else's ridiculous relationship woes.

#

In the morning, I texted the kids that Paul had moved out, that I was fine, and that I needed a few days to reset. They responded with their varying levels of worry and affirmation and then mostly left me alone.

But David called, from the road trip back, every bit a hot mess, taking all the brunt and blame, for wasting "Dad's money" on two cross-country moves, for how behind he would be in school, for looking like a fool and changing his goals to follow Julie's, and for ruining everything with Paul and me. I assured him that all his situation did was expose the cracks we had between us, and that at my age, I felt much more like a fool than he should.

I'm not sure it helped him. It didn't help me. I tried not to worry about him driving across the country alone. He decided to stop in Tennessee to visit Randall's family, and I was pretty sure, to check out UT and see if that wasn't an option for him. I didn't want him to be in Chattanooga much more than I wanted him to be in Arizona or on Mars, but maybe a change for him would be good. I hoped we could both be brave, but I was more confident in his chances than my own.

I cleaned out my desk. I finally sold the golf cart that Randall had always used much more often than I did. After carefully backing up photos, I deactivated all of my social media profiles. I somewhat mournfully threw out all the booze in the house, and with equal parts dread and anticipation, re-upped my Beachbody On Demand account. I did cardio every morning, yoga or weights every night, plus my regular walks with Cash. I tried to exhaust myself so I could sleep. It took me an extravagant new quilt (purchased from a local artisan with about a third of the golf cart proceeds) and six nights before I slept in my bed for more than an hour at a time.

Early on a Tuesday morning, I texted the whole family again... even Maggie, who was in Greenville furnishing her and Sheldon's new apartment.

It was Sam who came. He had a dentist appointment scheduled and had already planned to go in to work late. Instead, he found his recently-widowed, recently-dumped mama sitting on the recliner in the yoga pants and tank top I had worked out in the night before, a heating pad stuck behind my lower back, and my sweet Cash lying in front of the bookcases, where I had found him when I woke up without him.

"I'm sorry," I started. "I wanted to bring him downstairs myself, but my back went out last night and I couldn't—" My voice caught in my throat. I stopped, took a breath, and tried to start over. "He never comes out here in the morning without me. He didn't make a sound last night. He must have known. He must have come out here so he wouldn't be on the bed. And I— I can't lift him! I—"

And that was it. The sob sputtered out and opened a dam. I sat in the perfect recliner in my black uniform, feeling helpless, ridiculous, old, and alone. And I couldn't stop crying. My son looked at Cash mournfully, and then looked at me with such compassion that I only cried harder.

He waited, God bless him. Sam knew me just about better than anyone, Paul and maybe even Randall included. And besides Maggie, he was the person in my life who'd known me the longest. He knew I was embarrassed to need his help.

Only when I was able to calm myself did he come and sit on the arm of the recliner. He handed me the entire tissue box, causing me to smile a bit. Then he put his arm around me and said, "I'm sorry, Mama. He was the best dog we ever had."

I nodded, leaning into him a little. Cash was never really Sam's dog, but he belonged to everyone, the whole family. And just like that, just like Randall, he was gone without any warning, and in this moment, I couldn't believe either of them was really gone forever, and I felt like my life was out of control, off the rails, and maybe just getting stupid.

"I'll take him to the vet," he continued. "But what about you? What's up with your back?"

"Too many *surrenders*," I muttered.

"What?"

I gestured toward the counter, my little red and green containers still sitting out from last night's carbless, butterless dinner. "Working out... I'm on a 21 Day Fix..."

Sam actually laughed at that. "Didn't we just eat steak Alfredo and chocolate pie on Sunday?"

Sunday had been forever ago. "Yes," I said. "And I will continue making steak Alfredo and chocolate pie, but I will be fitting mine into those little containers and eating spaghetti squash and grilled chicken the rest of the week."

Sam rolled his eyes and took back his arm. "Why?"

"Trying to lose all my baby weight," I sighed, and we both managed a giggle.

"I just... need a reset," I explained. "Everything has been a whirlwind since March, and I haven't paused to... assess." Another eye-roll. I couldn't blame him. "I want to lose anything I don't need anymore, and these twenty pounds weigh me down, kid. Don't worry. I'll never give up cheese and wine. I just need to consume less of them."

"You're fine. You're healthy," he insisted.

"This isn't a big deal, Sam."

"I've watched you diet most of my life," he said. "I thought you were over it. You've been... well, since David went away to school, you've just been freer and more active and... well, with Paul around..."

I had been like chilled champagne on the patio, in the spring, in a fragile glass on a rickety table, ready to be merry and light but in danger of being knocked over and cracked, maybe shattered. And now I was, and I was trying desperately not to regret the champagne, nor the grapes it came from. But I didn't want Sam to see.

"Yeah. Well. Times change, honey." I threw off the heating

pad and attempted a stretch. The heat always helped, but more slowly than when I was, sigh, younger...

"Have you guys talked?"

"Nope." I tried to be abrupt, but my voice just wouldn't do that. "He has one of Leah's nieces working for him part-time, office stuff. We don't have much business at this point, but for any that we do, I contact her."

"Wow." Sam got up and faced me. "So, that's it? Like, really it?"

"Really it, Sam."

"But... I mean... he isn't just some guy you started dating. He's been, like one of your best, like our... he's family, Mom."

Really? Now he's family? Why wasn't he family on the Fourth of July? Oh God, I was so petty. "Did you have this talk with your baby brother?" I asked, instead. "Because I'm not the only one who blurred the lines and messed it up. I'm sorry, Sam. You can have any kind of relationship with Paul you want to have. Play golf. Have dinner. It's fine. But I can't... I can't just go back to being friends with him. Not now."

Sam had walked to the kitchen and returned with two cups of coffee. I held mine without sipping. It seemed a little irreverent with Cash in the room.

"If you get him in the car, I'd like to go with. To the vet."

Sam nodded, swallowing. "Of course, Mama."

The "Mamas" were doled out more rarely than they used to be. Tears refilled my eyes, and I swallowed just to distract myself.

"You're not alone," he said simply.

I knew that. But it was different, and he didn't understand, and I hoped he never would.

#

By the time Sam bought me *grilled* Chick-Fil-A, sans bun, superfoods side salad, and dropped me back off, I was walking more normally, and there was nowhere to go. My buddy and I walked all times of day. Now there was just his *stuff* to take care of. The bed he occasionally used, the brush, the balls, the huge box of treats I'd just gotten at Costco, the Tennessee Vols Smokey doll Randall had bought him. Well... I would keep that. The rest had to go.

And that's when I decided it *all* had to go. No more half-crazed, Nora-Walker-inspired nostalgia. No more hoarding memories or fantasies about being an old woman on the beach. I needed order. I poured myself some cucumber water and reluctantly reactivated my Facebook. There were a thousand realtors in Surfside. Surely, I was friends with one of them.

Chapter Twenty-Two

Resolved and exhausted, I pretty much stayed in my bed for three days. Without Cash needing to go outside, I found no reason to leave. I pretended I was reclaiming the early, single, childless adulthood I'd never had, filling the hole in my heart with Special K Protein and frozen EVOL burritos while rewatching familiar, mindless movies and ignoring my phone.

Maggie was the only one who dared stop by, and it wasn't until night two. "I come bearing refills," she called from the hallway. I listened to her tinkering in the kitchen with half a smile on my face and nodded my approval as she set a tray of very much *not-21-day-fix-approved* Moscato and Havarti on the bed before sliding in next to me. We watched the *Sex and the City* movie, getting mad at stupid Mr. Big all over again, and misting up over the simple wedding/pancake breakfast at the end.

"So, on to sunny Mexico?" she finally asked as the credits rolled.

I shook my head. "Nah. I have a different plan. It doesn't involve travel, although I will probably need a vacation when I'm done."

"Jess—"

"Just listen." I swallowed the last of my drink. "It's not that big of a deal. But I think I'm going to sell."

Her eyes narrowed. "Cars? Real estate? Yourself on the board-walk?"

I rolled my eyes in response. "The house. I think... I think I just need to rip every Band-Aid off and really start over."

"Jessie, that is not ripping off a Band-Aid. That is a hysterec-tomy with insufficient anesthesia. Why in the world would you want to sell the house? This house? Your Barbie dream house?"

I shrugged. It was the first time I'd said it out loud, of course, and it didn't sting or shock me.

"I love the house," I acquiesced. "But it was my house with Randall. And I thought maybe it could be my house with Paul. But it's going to be just me for the foreseeable future. And I need the *home* for just me. Maybe smaller. Maybe a condo on the water. Or maybe something completely different. I don't know, Mags. I've belonged to someone else since I was practically a kid, since before I was David's ridiculously young and stupid age. So I love this house, but maybe I need to take a breath and figure out what I actually love for and as just *me*."

I stopped, surprised by the passion I was able to muster, and then added in a sheepish mumble, "That might have been part of the problem with Paul."

She nodded, which embarrassed me some. "Did you all really think I was nuts?" I asked.

"Jessie. Girl. It was not so much a question of anyone being crazy or being wrong. It was just a matter of it being fast. And maybe even of it being *too* right."

"Whatever, man. How can something be too *right*?"

"If you made a list of things you want in a man for your... latter years, a second husband, a third act, whatever you want to call it, what would have been on there?" She didn't pause for me to answer for myself. "Someone stalwart and steady. Someone healthy. Someone pleasant and easy to love. Someone who knows you and adores you. Someone your kids would like. Someone safe. And all of that equals a four-letter word."

"Well. Shit." I said.

"Paul," she said, through a giggle. "The word is *Paul. Paul* is perfect. You were perfect together. You were these cute, cuddly buddies who landed together from a terrible fall. And I think maybe... you convinced yourself that was enough."

"Shouldn't it have been? It's more than what most people start with."

"No. Because you didn't really know his whole story, and he didn't know yours. You thought because you weren't trying to save for a house and raise babies that it would be easy. You thought because you knew each other's birthdays and favorite sandwiches that it would be simple. And you both were married so long you forgot that there is a big ol' gully between making someone dinner and cleaning up after them. And it's flooded with kids and memories and scars and tics, and this drama with David and Julie brought every single one of those to the surface. For *you*."

She didn't sound accusatory, but there was definitely an insinuation of blame. I had heard it in her voice before.

"I let my feelings about David and Julie spoil everything. Is that what you're saying?" I wasn't even sure I was mad about it.

"Honestly, Jessie? Pretty much. I mean, if Julie had been some random girl David met on campus or the beach, you would not have ranted and raved to her parents the way you did to Paul."

"I didn't *blame* him," I said, aware of the pout in my voice and not sure how to conceal it.

"Then why isn't he here?" She gestured to my room in a 360, like it was the Capitol rotunda. "You said it yourself; you built a whole life together."

I had said that, but had it been true? How many times had Paul had to assure me, to tread carefully, to placate my neuroses, to listen to my ruminations on the same theme? And how many times had I found myself editing what I wanted to say or do to make sure we stayed comfortable.? Is that really a *whole* life? And does a *whole* life fall apart like a house of cards, like ours did, based on one phone call... one situation that in most ways wasn't even *our* situation?

"He called it an extended play date," I finally said. I had been too ashamed to repeat that one out loud before.

"That's pretty harsh." She waited for a beat that held more consideration than what she usually exhibited. "So, you held him responsible for his grown daughter's behavior, and when faced with that conflict, he degraded the whole thing?"

"Can we talk about something else now? Like your wedding? Otherwise," I gestured with my chin toward the Hulu still of the *Sex and the City* gals, "I'm going to make you watch the sequel."

"Anything but that," she said, slouching into my pillows. "By the way, it's in four weeks."

#

The Myrtle Beach Train Depot held about 75 of Maggie

Dunn's closest friends and cohorts from her nearly-20 years as a resident of the coastal town. She wore a Kelly-green maxi dress and gold strappy sandals, her black locks piled on top of her head and the biggest and most open smile on her face that I had ever seen. Moni and Nora were her attendants, and their delight for their long-single mom to be getting remarried (and subsequently moving much closer to them) was palpable.

Sheldon, (who actually went by Don to everyone but Maggie, it seemed) was tall, dark, and handsome, a little on the quiet side, enchanted by my best friend, and equally jubilant. His son Eddie, his daughter Maya, and her son Quinn stood next to him during the ceremony, and Carter prayed something beautiful over the whole of them at the conclusion, right before "Lean on Me" started playing and the new couple, who didn't have an aisle to march, started the dancing right then and there.

Maggie was radiant, and it was all perfect, even if it meant she was going away.

Though I'd helped her decide on decorations (Mason jars, because shut up; it's the south, filled with sand, shells, tealights, gold-whatevers) and a menu (fried chicken, grilled shrimp, and a mashed potato bar), I had not dared ask if Paul would be at the wedding. I assumed she wanted to invite him but either had a diplomatic conversation with him about his exclusion *or* he had nobly decided not to come. Either way, he wasn't there.

Around the time the piña colada cake and strawberry wine were being distributed, I noticed a frazzled looking Katy Jameson make her way around the room, stopping to drop something off at the gift table before accepting a hug from Brittany. They talked in frantic animation for several minutes, and I tried to focus on Abby's recollection of her agency's attempt to film a commercial for a local magic shop. She was just getting to the part about the co-owner/illusionist using his *mind* to bend a fork into a raised middle finger when Katy headed straight for our table.

Sam and Altan stood up like perfect southern gentlemen to greet her. Cheek-kisses and greetings were exchanged. Abby looked at me with a pointed smile before she excused herself to the bar, leaving the chair next to me open. Katy sat without ado, but she spoke to me with such uncharacteristic trepidation that I had a hard time hearing her.

"Hi, Aunt Jessie."

"Hey, Unicorn," I said. I felt sincerely happy to see her, and I wanted her to know that, but I also did not want to talk, even a little.

She did.

"I wasn't going to come," she said. "Maggie invited Daddy, and he said I could come in his place. He's still pretty much completely off his feet, and he didn't think this was a great idea anyway..."

"Wait." So Maggie had invited him. Probably hoping for a *When Harry Met Sally*-esque final scene. "What? Why is he off his feet?"

Katy rolled her eyes. "He finally agreed to that operation. Ligament reconstruction? Two weeks in a cast. I've been rooming with him at one of the condos for a month now. He's a total pain in the ass."

"I can't believe he agreed to surgery," I muttered, trying to be cool, trying not to care.

"He sprained himself like 2 or 3 times in a row after..." She broke off awkwardly. "Dad's pretty stubborn, especially with no one keeping him in check. No offense. I mean, not that he's your responsibility."

"Nooo..." I said, slowly. I was torn between wanting to ask more questions and not wanting to talk about him at all. "But he's doing... okay?"

She looked at me so intently that I honestly couldn't tell how much was put on and how much was real. "Not entirely. I mean, he's medically right on schedule. Two more weeks in the cast. He's very methodical and by-the-book, you know? But he's grumpy and quiet and... I don't know. He's not himself? Or maybe he is himself. Maybe this is him without a woman around or without enough to do. He's already read all the *Longmire* books and binge-watched the series, and I think he's moving on to Dan Brown, and no one wants him critiquing those plot holes."

I snickered in spite of myself. Paul was quite a snob when it came to popular fiction, and Dan Brown's conspiracy theories would certainly not have a positive effect on a bad mood.

"Well, I'm sorry he needed the procedure, but I'm glad it's over. And going well. And how are you? How are you managing teaching in Wilmington and being here?" I needed the subject to change, but it was hard to steer away when all our common branches were entangled.

"I'm commuting. I mean, I kind of owe Dad at least that much. But also, my cousin Maureen is helping with stuff. I mean, all his property things and like, logistics. Driving. Danielle makes sure he eats. I'm sort of like watchdog, and um, a little shower help in the mornings. He hates it."

My memory was tossed back to that first morning Paul and I

shared, many moons ago. I had no doubt he vehemently loathed needing so much help.

Brittany had returned and was standing between our chairs. Assuming they'd want to catch up, I said, "Well, send my best. It's so good to see you, Katy."

Maggie was sparkling next to a few of her work friends. I anchored myself next to her until Sheldon collected her for another dance. It was my chance to escape. Her happily ever after meant the world to me, and it also made the loss of my own sharp as a blade.

Chapter Twenty-Three

My old neighbor Roger, from way back in our HOA-hey-day, was the realtor I inevitably chose. He had my house staged into something out of a Cape Cod beach read, and I had two offers in the first three days. They were both below my asking price, so I decided to keep packing and turn them down. I wasn't in a hurry, and I didn't feel like negotiating. Though I was initially a little leery of making him work harder, Roger seemed to enjoy the challenge.

Besides, I had no flipping clue where I was going to go.

Morgan came over one morning with contraband bagels and a clear desire to help fill my Maggie-gap. I gratefully ate and lost myself in her deliberations: another wedding to plan, another PET scan passed (thank you, Father-Son-Holy-Ghost), and more church drama than any human alive should ever have to deal with. I got up from the table long enough to find her a dog-eared copy of my favorite emotional health book with its original title, *I Quit.*

"You and Carter should take a sabbatical. Or something."

She sighed and smiled. "It's really okay. I mean, I do wish retirement was a little closer, or that Carter would decide to roll the dice and buy some ice dispensaries. Those have to bring in some money, right? It just wears me out to see how often so many people focus on the wrong stuff."

I nodded, pushing away the second half of toasted, Asiago amazingness and refilling Morgan's cup from my French press.

"We mortals get very protective of our comfort, I guess."

"We do. And it's understandable, unless it involves trying to tell other people what should be comfortable for them." There was an apology on her face and in her voice.

Now I shook my head. "Morgan, I know I'm a bit of a mess right now, but I do think everything this year has helped me conquer one thing: I don't care what people think. Finally. Fifty-six years, and two giant heartbreaks, later. I mean, my whole circle thinks I'm crazy for selling this house. But it's what's true and right for me. And I would *love* for people to support me or even understand me, but I'm exhausted from asking them to validate me."

She nodded solemnly, taking a sip and then smiling. "And I am exhausted from debating tattoos, the repetitiveness of worship songs, and whether Carter should have to perform the wedding ceremony of every small group leader's grandchild. So, you're not alone."

People kept saying that to me. Maybe I wasn't. But maybe I was and just shouldn't mind anymore.

#

Roger brought in the perfect buyers. They had cash, they were not in a hurry, and they would pay for as much of the furniture as I was willing to part with, especially the dining table. They were a couple retiring from and relocating from Pittsburgh, but because the husband was a high school principal (ouch), they wouldn't be moving in until June.

However, there was a bonus involved if I was out in time for them to spend Christmas break there. My head spun from it all. I brought Sam with me to my attorney and signed, signed, signed. Then I started purging and driving to Goodwill once a day and collecting boxes and packing. The only time I really stopped to think was when the kids asked me what the hell I was doing.

"Mimi, can you move into the house next door? That man who smells like sushi all the time is going to Texas." (Jacob)

"Hey Mimi, it's cool and all if you move away from the beach, but please don't move anywhere with grass. Dad says I'll have to cut it." (Travis)

"Mimi, are you moving because Cash and Mr. Paul don't live here anymore?" (Summer. *Ouch*).

"Mama, what if David decides to live with you?" (Mikayla, and he was still in Tennessee, so whatever, David).

"Mom, where are you going to go? You're not moving in with Maggie, are you?" (Brittney).

"Move. Here. Now." (Maggie).

"Mom, um, you know you're always welcome, but... Abby and I are a little tapped on space..." (Sam. And *as if*).

I had answers for them in the moment. But the truth was, even though it was somewhat impulsive and definitely huge, I just wanted to start over. Everything I said to Maggie about my reasons was true, weeks and declined offers and lots of healthy, grown-up decisions later.

I was making hard choices daily. Veggies over nachos. Books

over Facebook. Ignoring the two emails I got from Paul instead of answering them with every color heart emoji and the lyrics of Damn Yankees, "High Enough."

He was brilliant. He also knew me too well. He didn't persist. He spaced things out. He didn't try to call. The next communiqué I got was in the mail. It was one of those beautiful, trifolded greeting cards that I used to want to spend hours reading in Kmart when I was a kid. I even wrote my own versions of them and wondered how I could get a job creating them for Hallmark someday. I'm pretty sure he knew that. There had to be a reason he spent 5.99 on a card that I might throw away, unread.

I didn't. I shoved it in a moving box, unread.

But I read the text he sent. He tricked me and sent it from his business cell.

I really want to see you. I hope enough time has passed that we can just talk. Please? I miss my... friend. I know you'll hate that simplified term, but... P

I could picture him typing it, not pausing to edit because when he was passionate about something, he expressed himself perfectly. So unlike me, choked to either silence or incohesive monosyllables by my emotions.

What did he want?

How would that go?

What else could be said? He dumped me.

I thought about all the not-subtle ways Maggie had let me know it was fixable. She had done it again the night before she moved, when we sat on my porch and attempted to tie every loose string in the world before suddenly living four hours apart. I talked her out of the notion that she needed to have her own bedroom. We decided Moni needed to dump the guy she was with and pondered whether Brittney would find more possibilities for career and romance in Greenville. We planned my first weekend there, and how it should be around my birthday. And then she asked me, one more time, if I really believed Paul and I couldn't be reconciled.

So again, I'd summarized the argument we had, only this time, I kept in the part that had (inexplicably, to me), seemed to irk him the most: my comment about his relationship philosophies.

"You said that to him?" she said, and I already knew where she was going to take it.

"Well, yeah. I don't subscribe to the hands-off approach. Maybe it worked for him and Leah, if you consider basically living separate lives in the same house *working*, but I can't do it."

"Well, they did do it. For like 40 years. And that man, whatever his flaws are, had no role models to speak of, but he was a damn decent husband, and those girls adore him."

"I know that, I just—"

"Jessie. Stand up."

"What?" I glared at her, not sure if it was Palmetto Distillery's finest or genuine indignation that had her going.

"Just stand up."

I did.

"Now do 10 burpees."

"Maggie, seriously."

"Just do them!"

"No!"

"Fine. Sit down." She took a big sip. "Now tell me, why didn't you do them?"

I rolled my eyes. "Well, partly because I'm concerned my knees would dislocate. But mostly because it's 10 o'clock at night, I'm buzzed, I'm in the AARP, and I don't flippin' *want* to."

"Boom!" I was glaring at her at this point. "He don't want to get into his kids' relationship drama, Jessie. He had relationship drama when his daddy was locking him out of the house or putting his brother's head through the storm door. His philosophy was *surviving*. And then it became loving and protecting his people. That's the whole of it, ma'am."

She was right. I told her as much, fully ashamed of myself. And sitting on my porch again, reading his text, I wondered why exactly Paul and I had let that conflict, those words, be the end of all things. Could it be fixed?

But that wasn't the only question. The other question was, should it be fixed? Was it worth my constant sense of anxiety, the unease of our kids, the judgment of others?

I looked at the empty chair next to me. Randall had not been much of a porch-sitter. If he was outside, he was tinkering with something or shooting hoops with David and Travis. Paul, at least my version of Paul, was a stiller sort. We'd had more conversations in these chairs over the last four months than Randall and I had ever had in them.

I hadn't been filling Randall's spot with Paul. I had been adding to my life.

But I did it wrong.

And I still had no answers.

So, not wanting to ignore him again, not wanting to end

everything we'd shared in 15 years and four months on a completely icy note, I texted back the non-committal, *Okay. I'm around. Just let me know. :smiley face emoji:*

Not the blushing smiley face, the generic one that looked like an old-fashioned sticker. I didn't want to go too soft.

#

He didn't text back. He'd hit that stupid thumbs-up response. So I was not prepared the next afternoon, when I turned around and Paul was standing there, just like that first night he had come to my house so unexpectedly, unceremoniously. Back then I might have cared that I was drenched in sweat, that the floor was littered with half packed boxes and random bits of bubble wrap, that the soundtrack to Stephen Sondheim's eyebrow-raising *Assassins* was randomly blaring from my speakers. This time, I only cared that I put my guard up as soon as possible.

"Hi," he offered, as though he was just coming in from the store. "I knocked, but I don't think you could hear me over this magnificent canticle." I swallowed hard. The familiarity of our brief time was still lingering in this place.

"...it's why I have to leave," I said out loud.

He cocked his head, his gaze too intense. I stooped down, gathering mess, shrugging. "It feels so right... you standing in the middle of my chaos." Let him fill in the blanks. I didn't have the energy to explain, and he would know what I meant anyway.

"I really wanted to check in with you. Wow, Jess..."

His voice and my name were among the most painful combinations I had endured of late. I looked down at myself, knowing what he meant, and shrugged.

"Turns out the 20 pounds I've been wanting to lose... only

needed to be 12. I mean, it only needed to be 12 to make my pants fall down at the beach."

"No!"

"Yep," I said, inwardly groaning at the memory and easing myself off from the humored and casual feeling I was starting to feel. "Anyway, eating a little more simply is good. I feel good."

"Good." Oh boy. Back to our monosyllables. Why was he here? He was staring at me. I didn't want to let him off the hook, but the silence was maddening.

"Katy told me about your surgery. You... I mean, that was a big deal for you. Wow, indeed."

Now he shrugged. We were such troopers, weren't we? "It was much easier than I expected. I dreaded it to the point of getting ill, but I dreaded that damn cane more."

"You seem to have recovered really quickly."

"First week without the boot. Not golfing yet. But walking. And swimming at the Surf Master. I got used to ownership privileges when I was staying there."

So he'd been recovering approximately 200 yards from me. That was a sure hallmark of little tourist town; small as it was, the grocery stores intermingled with Dollar Generals on every other block meant you could avoid familiar faces among the throngs of vacationers and snowbirds. I didn't know if I was grateful or sad, and I didn't ask any follow up questions. He took my silence as an invitation to keep talking anyway.

"I just decided, I guess, that temporary pain was better than a lifetime being afraid of it."

Zing! Paul, telling me mountains in a speech the size of a molehill.

He was amazing.

This had to move along.

"So, why... what can I do for you, Paul?"

"I heard... I mean, I heard a lot of news."

"Yeah," I said, half trying to figure out why the box in front of me had both extension cords and hand towels in it. "Well, I guess that's always going to happen. At least some of our kids are still speaking."

"Maggie and I... we still talk some," he answered.

"Oh."

"A biker-slash-malpractice lawyer," he chided. "Leave it to her."

I rather resented his familiarity toward *my* best friend, and I would be having some intense fellowship with her for being all *in touch* with him. Traitor. I stood up and braced myself for what I knew was coming.

"I'm sorry you don't have her here," he said carefully. "And I'm really, really sorry about Cash."

I definitely couldn't look at him after that. I walked directly to the kitchen and guzzled from my water bottle. His intrusion into my house and my heart was not fair.

Paul didn't stop, though. His eyes were still piercing as he continued. "She wants me to talk you out of selling this place. That is, unless you're willing to move to Greenville."

I shook my head. "There's already a contract on it. And it's not like I didn't consider this carefully. It's just a house."

"You love this house," he retorted.

"I did. But it's just a house."

He sighed deeply. I remembered a Bible study I was in once,

when the notion of sighing was defined according to its Greek meaning. It was used to describe a feeling of repugnance that defied words, an inward groan. I was watching the definition, and it made me angry.

"Okay," he finally said, nodding his head. "So your best friend moved away. Your dog died. And you're selling your home on the beach with your teal sparkles and rustic damn starfish everywhere, *that you love*, because now it's just a house. Got it. Who's writing the country song?"

"You forgot," I said, slamming my bottle on the counter. "My husband died and then my new-lover-slash-old friend-slash-kinda-fiancé walked out on me. Those are pretty much the best parts."

"You're being absolutely asinine," he said.

"You don't get to tell me that," I said, my voice shaking. I hoped he couldn't tell, as I was also barely speaking above a whisper. "You gave up on me."

"Is that what you think?"

"It's all I see."

The CD skipped then. Stupid old technology. I could not bear the quiet, and I filled it, my voice rising.

"You walked out. So you don't get to call me names, or feel sad about *my* dog, or walk into any place I live without *knocking first*. OKAY?!"

Now I was so close to screaming, to picking up that aluminum bottle and hurling it at his careworn face. I fixed the disc instead.

"Where are you going to live?" he continued, in a softer but very even tone. "Maggie said you didn't know."

His tenacity was astounding. "I don't," I answered, still trying unsuccessfully to be curt. "I'll just rent for a while until I figure it out. Maybe I'll live in a hotel until spring, like some Real House-widow of the Grand Strand. Why? You have any properties open?"

He was gaping at me now, and I couldn't fully blame him. I was in full-on attack mode, one I had never, ever shown him, much less pointed toward him, before. I turned away, walking past him back into the living room, so I wouldn't have to look at his face.

I went back to packing books. They were modular and simple, and I could focus enough to let myself breathe in and out and try to pretend like he wasn't there.

He just stood there, staring at me, all Hugh Jackman-as-Wolverine pining after that conniving heifer Jean Grey.

"What?" I snapped. "*Why* are you *here*?"

"I wanted to see how you were doing," he said, still quiet, still matter-of-fact. "And I wanted to tell you, because I think you're the only person in the world who would understand, that Jenna came to see me. Charlie's wife. Not his ex-wife. His widow. She never left him, even when he left her over and over again."

The topic of Charlie, being sacred, chipped solidly at my veneer. I gave Paul my attention. "That's incredible," I said. "Why hadn't she ever reached out to you before?"

He shrugged. I fixed my eyes momentarily on how his black mechanic shirt sat on his shoulders, hugged the outline of his slim chest, accented the tan he must have worked on in the swimming pool. Then I tore my gaze back to his green eyes, no less distracting.

"Same reason I never tried harder to reach her. All the complications, and mostly the fact that Charlie had distanced himself from both of us. I was as much an urban legend to her as she's been to me."

"I love this for you," I said quietly. "I love that she came here to see you."

His sad smile nearly knocked me down. *Be. Strong. Jessie,* I willed. Nothing had changed. I was happy for him because he deserved that closure and peace. But nothing had changed for us.

"She got me thinking about all the ways I failed."

My muscle memory took over, and I was momentarily Paul's constant and partner again. "Come *on*, Paul. You didn't fail him. You just didn't *find* him. You never stopped caring. You would have done anything—"

"I mean you, Jess. I failed *you*."

I will not hope. I will not listen to this. Nothing has changed.

"She loved him through addiction, dishonesty, abandonment. He left her in a hundred different ways, and she always waited for him to come around, to come back. You knew me and loved me unlike anyone, ever, and I walked out over one impasse. I should have done better."

I shook my head. It was not one impasse. It was our whole way of looking at family. Wasn't it?

My doubts were too much. I doubted his apology. I doubted my own reasons for doubting him.

"I can't do this, Paul. Not... now..."

"Jessie. Please." His voice didn't break. But his eyes glistened, which was worse. I wanted to go to him. I would not let myself.

Instead, I turned slightly away from him and resumed my

packing. Another box and "I am going to the Lordy" later, he was still standing there, staring at me.

Good God.

"Anyway, since you asked," he finally continued, "Yes, I do have a place. I think it might be perfect for you after a few modifications. So why don't you think about it and call me if you want to see it?"

It took me a long time to figure out how to answer. He stood completely still and waited, looking right at me. His endurance was maddening.

"If it's perfect, why don't you live in it?" I said, trying to sound less mean but not nice all at once.

"Jessie, just come see it if you want. I'm temporarily staying at Danielle's. There's a play date just about every day around 10. Sometimes those mamas drink coffee and I think sometimes wine, but either way, I'm bound to be out somewhere – *anywhere* – while that specific brand of crazy is occurring. So late mornings are good. If you want to see it."

Now I sighed. Why hadn't he gotten a place to live? How was he not going insane shoved into a tiny guest room? Is this really the life he had chosen over spending it with me?

Finally, with at least a fake steely resolve, I looked at him. "I'll think about it," I said. "I just... I don't have a plan, and maybe that's okay right now. Plans don't seem to be working so well for me."

"It's almost your birthday."

I let the awkward pause stay there, because I wanted to ignore my birthday, but Maggie wanted me to spa with her in her new hometown, and clearly, he was trying to get at something that I didn't feel like seeing.

"Think I'll skip this one," I said. "A well-meaning friend told me I can handle these milestones however it's best for me."

He actually winced at that. "Maybe this wasn't... a good plan either."

I had no less than a half dozen smart-ass responses, but I remained silent. I didn't want to maim him. Hurting him this much was hard enough.

"I get where you're coming from," I finally said. "I trust your good intentions. I just don't have anything to give you right now. This mess –" I picked up a handful of brown wrapping paper and more bubble wrap – "This mess is me. It's all going to get organized and packed neatly away. But it's a process. And it is messy until the very last minute."

I managed not to waiver as I said those things, but he did not. The expression on his face was so wrought with ache that I wanted to physically melt into him. I hardened myself. *He left you*, my inner voice reminded me for the zillionth time.

"Jess." Another sigh. The always stalwart shoulders slumped. He looked at his shoes. "That was my whole point, you know. We skipped some of the mess. I had to deal with mine."

I nodded, glaring. "And now you have?"

"I think so," he said simply.

"But you don't think I'm doing the right thing?" I prodded.

"I think," he broke off, considering. "I think you're doing what you think is right, in a chasm all alone. It genuinely surprises me that you would ever not want to live here, but I certainly understand how things change."

I taped my next box. I had no reply for him.

"I know you don't want to hear it from me. I just want you to be happy."

It might have been fine until that last part. I couldn't. Paul and me and the notion of happy in one room were officially too much.

"Please leave," I said. The tears were spilling, and I didn't want him to see.

"Jessie, let me—"

"Please," I said. There was no way he didn't hear my voice break, and I was so afraid he was going to move toward me instead of away.

But he surprised me and stood still for a moment. I had my face in my hands. My sobs were shaking me but at least they were quiet.

I will control myself until he leaves. Please, please, please go.

It would never change, I supposed, how he reacted to me as though he'd heard my thoughts. I heard his footsteps and the click of the door. And I felt my heart break all over again.

In my bed that night, sprawled in the middle, I stared at a collection of totes where I'd managed to neatly collect the entire contents of my closet, save for six shirts, one pair each of jeans/shorts/leggings, my black wrap dress, my sneakers, and my flip flops: a late-middle-aged-boho-widow's capsule wardrobe. Why was I packing so furiously when I had no idea where I was going? Why did I think for a moment that it wasn't obvious, how I was just running away from everything?

I reached for my phone on the nightstand. I had to scroll to find his number, because I had deleted all our texts.

Me: I'll look at the place you suggested. Tomorrow at 10? Just let me know the address.

Paul (immediately): *231 Sparrow. See you then. Sleep well.*

I could read the good-natured concern, the sweetness, the sincerity coming from his simple message. I hugged my pillow to my side and tried not to dwell on it. It was an unbelievable miracle that I had found love twice in my lifetime. To have lost them both so close together seemed just as unfathomable.

#

There wasn't much sleep for me again that night. I gave up some time before dawn and moved to the couch. I was restless without Cash to walk. My stomach was too nervous for coffee. At sunrise I combed the beach. I got home around 7:30 and checked my phone, wondering if Paul would change his mind, or if I should. I drank my shake. I read *Grand Strand Magazine*. I spent a half hour deciding between two black tank tops. I wore a Cubs hat and lip-gloss. I wanted to look pretty enough that he would regret leaving me, but not like I was trying hard to make him notice me.

I felt 16 and ancient all at once.

When I pulled up to 231 Sparrow (honestly, it was so close, I could have walked), I sighed. There was a turquoise front door and a matching mailbox. It didn't face the ocean, but it was three blocks away and had a lovely front yard with a full-grown magnolia tree. It looked a little big and certainly "sparkly," and probably expensive. Maybe Paul thought I would want to buy it and rent it out, or I had somehow misled him on what I could afford.

He was waiting on the porch swing, phone in hand, feet crossed, sunglasses perched on his head. I could anticipate the smell of him freshly showered, maybe with just a hint of bacon or if he'd been hurrying, Fruity Pebbles. I also anticipated the way he would look up and cock his head before smiling at me. He did.

"Sleep well?" he greeted.

"Not really," I said bluntly. "Paul, this place has a lot of curb appeal, but it looks like a bit much. Are you trying to go month-to-month with it until you sell? I mean, it's a new one for you, right?"

"It is," he answered. "Why don't you just come in and look?"

He stretched and rose and opened the door for me, making a tiny, gentlemanly gesture to direct me across the threshold. I stepped inside onto weathered, beach wood floors. I looked up at a ceiling that matched the color, beams running the opposite direction. The old paneled walls were stained seashell white with a wainscot accent a few shades darker. The trim and much of the fixtures gleamed the same shade of white, with accents of teal, lime green, and oyster gray. It was furnished like a *Coastal Living* editor climbed out of the magazine and touched it with a magic wand, from the throw pillows on the worn, light gray sofa to the beaded vase on the white wicker and glass coffee table. Paul didn't say a word as I made my way through it, two large bedrooms, a bath and a half, all within the same color scheme, with pops of red and coral. Standard issue beachy with touches of whimsical: a built-in desk in the kitchen with a chalkboard top, an old-fashioned cast iron stove acting as a fireplace in the living room, braided rugs in the bathrooms, but my favorite of all was a hidden bonus room in the center of the house. It held a little cove encasing a set of bunk beds, with a curtain around them that practically screamed "Cousin Sleepovers," another built-in desk with a flat-screen TV above it, and a three-step staircase leading up.

Somewhat slack-jawed, I stepped up and saw a lengthy hall-way with two doors. The first I opened was a standard linen closet. The second was the master bedroom. It was decked out in white and bright red, a deeper aqua blue, and bursts of amber sunshine. There was a canvas above the bed that didn't really match anything. But I recognized it immediately. It was from a photo Paul had taken when we were in Cherokee, of the golden sunrise over the mountains.

I stared at it, willing my eyes to suck the tears right back in. I didn't have to consider or wonder long. *I think it might be perfect for you after a few modifications,* he had said.

But the house itself didn't need a single change. It was me. *I* did. *I* had an internal list of DIY projects. Quit worrying so much about my grown kids. Quit trying to control the narrative of a story that had spun off on its own. Quit trying to fit Paul to a label that didn't suit him or cram us into a mold we didn't fit.

Quit feeling so damn guilty for loving him so fully, for feel-ing, so soon, happier than I'd ever imagined being again. I pic-tured the beaded vase downstairs on the table. It was covered with shining synthetic gems of every shade of red and blue and green. It wasn't pristine or collectible; there were random stones missing. But it was just jovial and pretty and perfect for holding the silk dogwood blooms that stemmed from it.

It was like me. It was like *us.*

"I love it," I said, knowing that he was behind me now.

"I hoped you would," he answered, just as evenly as last night, but with a cautious note of confidence in his voice.

I turned around and took him in. Nothing obvious had changed since he *handled* his stuff. His gray shorts still hung a little loose. His black golf shirt was untucked but fitted and wrinkle free. His ankles, the right one bearing its new scar, were whiter than the rest of his legs, even though he always wore those little no-show socks with his black sneakers. His green eyes were intense, but the corners of his mouth were slightly pointed upward, charming, charmed. He ran his hands through his hair and knocked his sunglasses clear off. Maybe he *was* a little nervous. I definitely was.

But I walked to him anyway, just a few feet to cross a chasm. My arms flew around his neck for just a moment before his were around my waist. There were no tremors or tears or even words, and for once, that didn't scare me. I just held tight and welcomed our familiar melting together. There was nothing else in the moment but the two of us, our room, our home. And our story, the one that was not a continuation of a different tale, but one we'd write together, was just beginning.

Epilogue

The tiny, perfect head of Josephine Malina Remzi, named for her maternal grandfather and her paternal grandmother, was cradled against my shoulder. Altan was sitting in a chair beside the bed, he and Mikayla groggily lost in their burrito bowls. I was lost in the scent and feel of my new granddaughter.

Brittney was there too, having arrived with a Dunkin' Box of Joe and a baby-sized Tennessee Titans *quilt*, which elicited squeals from Mikayla and me; Brit had been working on it secretly all year. Sam and Abby and the kids were waiting until the next day to visit. Mikayla's labor had lasted a *meager* 10 hours, overnight, and the new parents were holding onto a thread of hope for some sleep before leaving the hospital.

Ocean's Edge Hospital. I was back again, but no one in our family was there having the worst day of his or her life, or in a triage room deciding whether tripping in a hole or the awkwardness of dating at 60 was more painful. Today was the day of pure joy we'd all prayed it would be, the one we all needed.

"Mama, you're going to chafe her sweet little head," Brittney laughed. I couldn't stop kissing our Josie. She was fast asleep and oblivious to my lips, the scent of DD Original Blend, the din of *Younger* playing on a TV Land marathon in the background, the smiles we could not contain.

"David called," Mikayla said wearily, her cardboard container scraped clean. "He thought it was a good day to tell us that Tennessee is going to transfer his general credits. He starts in January, as a mid-year sophomore, nursing major."

My smile got bigger. David had decided to stay with his Aunt Chrissy and Uncle Joel indefinitely, working on the custodial crew at the university like his brother had once done. He was going to spend the month of December home with us. I couldn't wait to have some time with him and reconnect with my baby boy, as an adult.

Julie was still in Arizona. She was planning to come visit for Thanksgiving, and she'd be staying with Danielle (though, God bless, Katy had requested that the two of them stay in the magical bunk bed cubby. Predictably and much to my relief, her twin had denied her).

The day after Paul had given me a new ring - white gold, bearing a modestly-sized but bluest-ever sapphire (God, I loved it...), she emailed me. The summary of it was, "Any fool can see how happy my Daddy is with you. I hope we all can move past some of the awkward and unfortunate experiences this past year has brought."

Okay. Maybe I had it memorized.

I wrote back that I was committed to Paul and his happiness, and I believed we could all be supportive toward each other. I also let her know that David was going to be fine and I hoped "we all" had learned from the unfortunate experiences. I hoped a lot of things when it came to Julie and David and Paul and me and our families meshing. Because we *were* going to mesh.

The lessons I had learned showed up all over the place. My holiday philosophy, for example, had undergone a big tweak. I was not going to try to make the most wonderful time of the year feel as close to possible as it used to be. Our family was different and growing, and it seemed a perfect time to figure out new traditions, or lack thereof.

Therefore, Paul and I were hosting a Thanksgiving brunch and volunteering at the community kitchen dinner that evening. Whosoever wanted to come was invited to whatsoever interested them. The only permission I asked was from Summer and Jacob, and they were cool as long as brunch included chicken tenders and Mickey waffles.

On Black Friday, we were foregoing shopping and doing a 5K together, raising money for Big Brothers, Big Sisters of America. Paul had just taken over as their local fundraising director. He was ridiculously overqualified, paid next to nothing, and 100 times more fulfilled than he had been managing properties (He was still in the process of selling or transitioning management on most of those).

Meanwhile, I was doing a little contract work, writing website copy for the advertising firm where Abby worked, while finishing my devotional for Rachel (*Grace in the Transitions*), and writing a proposal for my next book: tentatively titled, *Grace in the New Normal*. (Shut up, everyone.)

Paul had actually been reading through my draft all day and was picking me up at the hospital. Shortly after Brittney left and

Altan went home for a shower, I texted him the room number and *Please come meet her.*

We had already talked about it - succinctly, directly - and he agreed that whatever Mikayla wanted his role to be was fine with him. When I tried to ask if he needed to check with Danielle on the whole title/role thing, to make sure it wouldn't infringe on her territory with her children, he simply reiterated, "Whatever Mikayla wants is fine with me." I stopped asking.

Since Summer and Jacob has taken to referring to Paul as "Poppy Paul," and just "Poppy" when they got lazy, Mikayla quietly told me the night after her shower that he would be "Poppy" to her baby as well.

"He won't be Daddy. He won't be Grampy. But he's here with you and here for us," she said, with a tiny tremble in her chin, causing a few big tears to escape down my cheeks.

When Poppy Paul entered the room, Mikayla and her daughter - her daughter! - were both asleep. Josie was nestled in the mystically, perfectly carved crater between my chest and my neck, making me sweat with her radiating warmth, smelling like comfort and promises.

Paul squatted right in front of us and admired her. "She's perfect," he murmured, placing one hand on my knee and the other across her back. "And smart."

"How can you tell already?" I asked with a smile. My hand could not resist reaching out, brushing the side of his face.

His smile grew wider as he leaned into my touch. "Easy," he said. "She's nestled in my favorite place to be."

Acknowledgments

I began writing this in my head on a road trip from Chicago, Illinois to Myrtle Beach, South Carolina in July, 2016. I was driving my mom, who was coming to help us move, along with my kids who were then ages nine, eight, and one. The roads were never ending, but Jessie and Paul and the beach house *we* were about to move into in real life (along with the one on Sparrow Drive that got away!) kept my thoughts occupied. At the time, I was overcoming postpartum depression after a traumatic miscarriage, though I didn't know it. Along with my steadfast husband and friends, Jessie and her story helped me to heal and move forward.

I finished writing a little more than a year later, while we were hunkered down during a hurricane. Completing this task during this season of life is one of my proudest achievements and also proof that "it" does indeed take a village! So with many, many thanks to:

My children, Josh and Paige, who made me a parent and let me grow up with you, and Miranda, Kaity, and Jack, who call me

Mama and still teach me every day. I love that we keep pursuing our dreams together: happy, brave, and free.

Jerry and Rose Capriotti, my Mom and Dad, who have remained stalwart and proud even when you thought I was crazy. Thank you for giving me the best of you.

Shannon, Terrie, Maureen, and Jen, the sisters who showed up when I least expected and most needed.

Tracy, Deanna, Martha, April, Kirsten, Paige again, Morgan, Whitney, Aleisha, Liz, Renee, Christina, Paula, Becky, Judi, The GSU Crew, Ashley, Shawn, Talli, Obea, Amy, and anyone I inevitably forgot - whether near or far, every day or once in awhile, at home or on the road, I am beyond blessed to have you.

Tom Wallace, the brother and pastor who has always seen me and taught me how to see me, too. Because of you, I have Magic Beans.

Luis, Rick, Brandon, Jimmy, Jamie, Tim, Doug, David, Mike, and other brothers who graced my adult life and reminded me there are Good Men!

Mike Hopkins, for reading this twice and being an absolutely stellar fellow writer-runner-rider, an encouraging realist, a generous and hilarious editor, and one pleasant surprise of a friend. Watch for his upcoming novels... they'll be adapted by Netflix any day!

Lady Jane, who works very hard to keep starving artists fed and grounded, and to Mort Castle, who teaches them. Mort still remembers Jake the Blind Knight. I remember every word you've ever told me, and I am forever your kid.

The Capriotti-Buxton clan, especially Jer and Gina, for making me want a big family.

Wayne and Wanda Deering, for making us family.

Team Black Dog - all you amazing runners, but especially our little core fam of Daniel, Dawn, Akemi, Bill, Diane, and (& Hoka!), fellow Mother Runner Lacey, my role models Tucker, George, Slim Jim, and Nancy, and so many more buddies. You are magical and you changed my life. I'm a sap for you!

Junie, Crista, my Dad again, Judi, Bev, Fran, Sue, Carol, Julie, and every widowed person who shared his or her heart with me. I honor your journeys.

Sabra and Cali, for loving Jack when we both needed it!

Bette Vallone, who taught me journalism and specifically, modular layout, thus setting me up for life.

My communities, especially at Journeychurch and Silver Lining. Being in "this" together is everything.

Heidi Faith, the founder of Still Birthday, Dr. Lisa Masselli, my midwife Maureen, and every woman who ever shared the story of baby loss with me. Your story isn't over...

For Andrew, my first blonde boy, and our amazing Super-Nora.

To Geri Scazzero, for writing *I Quit/The Emotionally Healthy Woman*!

To all my daughters' friends who make me feel like a rock star. If you're feeling low, make friends with teenage artists. Their support is unmatched!

The town of Surfside Beach, its roads and trees and beaches and whimsical houses that turn my runs into fictional settings and great escapes.

And of course, to my online friends, who are awesome and diverse and listened to me blather on about this for over three years until they could actually see it was real. I hope you find something here to make you feel and to make you smile.

Rod, you are the love of my life and best friend, the co-author of my best stories, and my favorite finish line. Our cheesy romance is my favorite.

A native of South Chicago Heights, Illinois, Kelly Capriotti Burton is a professional running enthusiast, online church producer, marathoner, and licensed minister who resides in Surfside Beach, South Carolina. She does life with her husband Rod, their five kids, granddaughter, parents, two dogs, a Harley, and lots of gathered family. It is the perfect setting to explore for her writing mantra: happily-ever-afters for complicated relationships.

Kelly loves to connect via her social media at:
kellofastory.com
facebook.com/kellofastory
instagram.com/kellofastory

Made in the USA
Middletown, DE
01 October 2021

49043204R00192